LIARS & THIEVES

SCOTT CULLEN BOOK 6

ED JAMES

To Rhona - sincere thanks for being both a brutal editor and a friend.

OTHER BOOKS BY ED JAMES

SCOTT CULLEN MYSTERIES SERIES

1. GHOST IN THE MACHINE
2. DEVIL IN THE DETAIL
3. FIRE IN THE BLOOD
4. STAB IN THE DARK
5. COPS & ROBBERS
6. LIARS & THIEVES
7. COWBOYS & INDIANS
8. HEROES & VILLAINS

CULLEN & BAIN NOVELLAS

1. CITY OF THE DEAD (Coming March 2020)

CRAIG HUNTER SERIES

1. MISSING
2. HUNTED
3. THE BLACK ISLE

DS VICKY DODDS

1. TOOTH & CLAW

DI SIMON FENCHURCH SERIES

1. THE HOPE THAT KILLS
2. WORTH KILLING FOR
3. WHAT DOESN'T KILL YOU
4. IN FOR THE KILL
5. KILL WITH KINDNESS
6. KILL THE MESSENGER

PART I

CHRISTMAS STEPS

DAY 1

Monday
23rd December

1

He tried to keep in the shadows as Steven opened the front door. Blinking, he stepped back as the taxi swept past the house before it trundled up the hill, headlights illuminating the wet street. He waited for it to pass and the dim glow of the street lights to return. 'Can you not hurry up?'

A man passed them on the opposite side of the street, coat tucked tight against the rain, looking overweight. Had he seen them? His breath quickened.

'Got it.' Steven fumbled with the front door, finally nudging it open. 'Sorry about that. Too much to drink, obviously. Come on in.'

'Thought you'd never ask.'

Steven looked down at the cream carpet in the long hall. 'Can you at least take off your shoes?'

'No.' He smiled before walking through to the living room, flicking on the mother and child light by the sofa, but remained standing. 'I'm fine as I am.'

Still standing in the hall, Steven reached down to untie his own laces. 'Can I get you a drink?'

'Now that would be good.'

Steven marched across the wide room, switching a side light on. He paused in front of an oak cabinet behind a leather recliner, like he was going to say something, before pulling down the horizontal cabinet door, revealing a sizeable collection of spirits bottles. His hand hovered over them before settling on a whisky, black label embossed with silver. He sniffed it then poured healthy measures into a pair of glasses. 'Here you go. Hope it's still to your taste.'

'Dunpender, right?'

Steven took a sip and nodded, eyes staring into space. 'Right.'

He took the glass and wandered over to stand just to the left of the window, before sniffing the drink. Pure darkness. 'Still think it's the best whisky in Scotland, Steven?'

'I like it. Get through a bottle every month.'

'That's a lot of drinking.'

'Helps with the stress. You know how it is.'

'Don't I just.' He finished the whisky in one, the liquid burning his tongue and throat. Sucking in a mouthful of air, letting it dampen the heat. Bliss. He held the glass up to the light and inspected the lines of the crystal.

Steven finished his dram and put his own glass down, hand shaking. 'What is it you want?'

'A chat. One that can't wait. It's important.'

'Why?'

'It just is.'

'Come on. You dragged me from the pub to hear whatever it is.'

'You'll want another drink.'

'Do I?'

'Aye, I think so.'

'I've had a skinful already.' Steven turned his back and poured out another measure of Dunpender, his head bowed. 'Fine.'

He spotted a crystal quaich, *Dunpender 100* etched into it, next to another tall bottle matching the design but gold replacing silver. 'Nice little trinket you've got there.'

Steven ran a finger over it and nodded. 'Cost me a pretty penny.'

'Disappointed you're not opening that one for me.'

Steven sighed as he looked down at his glass. 'Like I've got anything to celebrate.'

'Quite.' Taking a deep breath, he set the empty glass down on the dark brown window sill. He lashed out, connecting the base of his hand with the back of Steven's neck, forcing him against the cabinet, fingers clutching at the glass doors. Steven fell forwards, grasping for the hinge as he sprawled across the machined wood flooring, the bottle of Dunpender tumbling and smashing, a pool of gold liquid forming around his prone body.

Stepping forward, he followed through with kicks to Steven's stomach, head, balls. He kicked the head again. And again.

He knelt down, breathing heavily, fingers crawling up Steven's throat, clasping the pulse point. His heartbeat was faint.

Still alive. Good.

~

HE DROPPED the toolbox in the middle of the living room, the trail of oil muddying the bleached wood of the floor, before sifting through the tools inside.

Pliers. Excellent.

Hammers. Two of them. Which one? The ball-peen for definite, its small head giving precision. The claw hammer was all about brute force. Maybe he'd need both.

He rummaged through the second layer of tools, finding a long cord, the sort used on a drying green. That's the ticket.

He got to his feet and untied the kitchen cloths on Steven's wrists, replacing them with the cord, the solid knot at the back of the chair just out of reach.

Breathe. Slowly, deeply. Take your time.

He picked up the glass of water from the coffee table and tipped it over Steven's head. He didn't wake up.

He raised the hammer, bringing it down on Steven's middle finger.

Steven's eyes shot open. He screamed, a primal roar from the pit of his gut, his gaze darting around the room.

The noise curdled his own stomach. He swallowed, his throat constricted. 'So you're awake then?'

'What are you doing?'

'Come on, Steven, you know what I'm doing and why.'

'I can pay you.'

'Can you really?'

'Please, how much do you want?'

'This isn't about money. At least not to me. No, it's about the betrayal of trust.' He reached for the pliers, gripping the fingernail on Steven's left thumb and yanked. The scream turned his stomach anew.

∼

ONE, two, three...

Two minutes — one hundred and twenty — that's all he'd allow himself to enjoy his work.

He stayed in the shadows, watching the yellow flickering in the living room and kitchen windows at the back. The briefest smell of charcoal and petrol.

Glancing around the street, he couldn't see anyone.

One nineteen, one twenty. Time up.

A cough. Somewhere to the left.

He looked around. There — a fat man stood a few doors down, focused on his phone as a small dog ratted around the bushes of the compact front garden, cocking its leg as it sniffed the air. It was the man who'd almost spotted him as Steven made a hash of getting in.

The dog sensed him, its brown eyes locking on, its mouth curling.

He stepped back into the shade. The dog's bark rattled around the small space.

'Benji, will you bloody quit it?'

One, two, three...

After sixty he peered out, the phone's backlight illuminating the man's face, thumbs working at the screen, the dog pulling the lead tight.

He clenched the claw hammer, hoping he wouldn't have to resort to another murder just to get away.

'Come on, Benji.' The man tugged at the dog and led him inside.

He let out a breath, watching it mist in the cold air, before walking off. He headed for home, his work complete.

He allowed himself another glance at the house, the flames now visible and obvious to anyone who cared to look.

2

'Secret Santa's another thing I hate about Christmas.' Detective Constable Scott Cullen put the bondage ball gag to his mouth, biting on the red sphere and tugging the black dog collar but not tying it. He took it out and chucked it on the table, before looking around at the other four officers. 'There's not a bigger waste of ten quid in the western world.'

'Maybe someone's trying to tell you something, mate.' Acting DC Simon Buxton took a sip of red wine, chasing it down with lager. He ran a hand through his hair, long on top and flicked, but shaved at the side. He was tall, athletic and looked older than his twenty-five years.

'What's that supposed to mean?'

'Well, you're always whingeing on about how nobody wants to promote you. You chomping on a ball gag is probably the only way you'll stop.'

Cullen scowled at him as he sunk more wine. 'Was it you?'

'No, mate. I got Methven a change jar.'

'Priceless.' DS Sharon McNeill doubled over with laughter, her dark ponytail dancing a jig. She sat up again and folded her thin arms. 'Was it made of crystal?'

Buxton raised an eyebrow. 'For a tenner?'

'Christmas is bullshit.' Cullen finished his pint and moved onto the next one, the glass still cool. 'The only good thing,' he stabbed a finger in the air, 'the only good thing is I'm not working this year. I just want to spend a day not dealing with scumbags killing each other. It's always the same every year, dickheads slotting other dickheads on Christmas Eve. Just absolute bollocks.'

'Bloody hell, Cullen.' DC Chantal Jain shook her head, her dark hair fanning out. 'You're a bloody nightmare. I'm not exactly the most Christian of people but I *love* Christmas.'

'That's because you've usually got about three men chasing after you, throwing flowers and bottles of perfume at you.'

Jain scowled at him. 'I think you've had enough to drink, don't you?'

'Bugger off. I took tomorrow off so I don't have to worry about how much I get through tonight.'

Jain smirked. 'Never usually stops you.'

'Look, the hard-core alcoholics wouldn't even bother to turn up to this sort of thing in case they showed themselves up.'

'So, why are you here?'

'Charming.' Cullen looked across the upper floor of Tigerlily, the wide room split into sections, each decorated with flowery tablecloths, dark green table lights, red roses. 'See next year, can we not just go to a proper pub for our Christmas night out? We always end up in places like this.'

'I organised tonight.' Jain folded her arms. 'You'd much rather end up in the Elm, right?'

'Even the Elm beats here.' Cullen took another drink, now well below halfway. 'Anyone fancy going to a proper pub?'

'No chance.' Jain scowled at him as she tossed a handful of club tickets into the middle of the circular table, just missing the light. 'We've got free entry to the club downstairs.'

~

'COME ON, SCOTT!' Sharon tugged his hands. 'Why don't you want to dance?'

Cullen leaned back against the bar, stumbling a few steps. He steadied himself against the wood, snatching a few seconds to take in the club area, music thumping and dry ice burning his nostrils. 'Give me a minute.'

'Come on, I'm in the mood for dancing.'

'I'm not stopping you. Chantal's over there.' Cullen waved across the dance floor. 'Is that Turnbull she's with?'

'Aye. He's hammered.' She raised an eyebrow at him. 'No more than you, mind.'

'I'm okay.'

She prodded him in the chest. 'Five minutes and I want you doing your best John Travolta.'

'You've seen my worst.'

'Five minutes.' She turned and sashayed across the dance floor.

Cullen turned to raise his empty glass at the barman, who immediately started pouring another lager. He handed over a tenner, getting a lot less change than he reckoned on.

Sipping his pint, he watched Sharon on the dance floor with Chantal Jain as they pranced around doing fifties moves. He looked around the room, watching the idiots in the team making bigger idiots of themselves.

'Evening, Constable.'

Cullen spun round.

DI Colin Methven handed an empty glass to the barman. A baggy Christmas jumper, mostly red with a green reindeer, hung off his athletic frame, his pink work shirt just about breaking cover at the neck.

Cullen raised his glass. 'Evening, sir.'

Methven leaned in close. 'Can I get you anything?'

Cullen inspected his pint glass, already halfway down. 'Aye, get us a whisky.'

Methven arched his bushy eyebrows. 'Will Dunpender do?'

'Aye, go on. Cheers.' Cullen took another gulp, the bitter tang of the Spanish lager hitting his tongue.

Methven raised a finger to attract the barman's attention. 'Can I have a Dunpender, please.' He nodded and Methven turned back to Cullen, giving him the up-and-down. 'Any plans for Christmas Day?'

Nosy bastard. Cullen shrugged. 'Just going to spend the day in front of the telly with DS McNeill.' He tapped his nose. 'Got her a box set for Christmas. Shhh.'

'I see.' Methven handed him the whisky, his heavy eyebrows almost lowered over his eyes. 'There you go.'

'Cheers, sir.' Cullen swirled it around the glass before throwing it down his throat in one go. Heaven. 'What about you, sir? Any plans?'

Methven's eyes remained locked on the empty glass. 'Got some family commitments. My mother and father are coming over.'

'Sounds like fun. I'm glad to be avoiding mine.'

'You should come into the station.' Methven paid for the drinks. 'Double time on Christmas Day.'

'I'd much rather not do anything, if it's all the same.'

Methven flared his nostrils as he pocketed his change, fingers jangling it around. 'Very well.'

Cullen finished his pint. 'Back in a second.' He staggered to the toilet, his shoulder brushing off the patterned wallpaper. Bloody symbols — which was the gents? He pushed open a door and had a look around. Empty.

He tried the cubicles, all locked. No urinals. Strange. He took a deep breath and considered his options.

Sod it, it'll have to be the sink.

'Scott, what the hell are you doing in here?' Sharon grabbed his shoulder, the door swinging shut behind her. 'This is the ladies!'

'Is it?' Cullen frowned as he tucked himself back in. 'Shite.'

'Were you pissing in the sink?'

Cullen looked away, shame burning his neck. 'The cubicles are all full.'

She let out a deep breath. 'Come on, we're getting you home. Now.'

DAY 2

Christmas Eve

Tuesday
24th December

3

Harsh winter sunlight made Cullen blink as he waited, icy wind cutting straight through him as it tore downhill from the Royal Mile to the Scottish Parliament. His head was thudding, his mouth full of the bitter taste of hangover, his mind reaching for whatever he'd done to get into that state.

Drinking. So much drinking. George Street. Pissing in a sink.

Not again...

He leaned back against the glass front of the World's End pub and loosened his tie, his body wanting to sweat out the booze even in the crisp air. He hauled out his phone, watching the tribes of tourists as they milled about, laden with shopping bags and coffee mugs. He texted Buxton. *'Where are you?'*

Just as he pocketed it, the phone rang. What now? He held it up, trying to focus on the display. Sharon. 'Hey.'

'Where are you?'

'I'm waiting on Budgie.' Cullen looked around, a young couple pointing in a jeweller's window a few units up. 'I'm supposed to be off today. Bloody Crystal. I should go to the Police Federation about this.'

'Right. That's not the sort of attitude an officer chasing a promotion should display...'

'You've maybe got a point.'

'The reason I'm calling is I'm just out of my sergeant's meeting — Methven's spitting teeth about the state you were in last night.'

'What state?'

'Don't muck about, Scott. You pissed in a *sink*.' A pause he wasn't going to fill. 'Look, I've stopped Crystal going to Turnbull and Cargill about it.'

'Cheers.' Cullen tugged his hair with his free hand. Couldn't remember much past unwrapping the ball gag. Where had he left it? 'Is this why I've got to come in on my day off?'

'A suspicious fire goes right to the top of the pile. Crystal's already short-handed with all these secondments at the moment. He's got people helping uniform out for tonight and he's lost Chantal to Davenport's case. Pissing him off today isn't the wisest move.'

Cullen sighed as he took a few steps away, looking down the street for Buxton in the pool car. 'I get it, I'm Satan.'

'It's not just that. He's complaining about you not having an appraisal with him for six months.'

Cullen closed his eyes and bit his lip. What a wanker. 'Right, I'd better do something about that.'

'I'm really worried about you and your drinking, you know?' A long pause. 'We'll have words later.'

Sounded ominous. 'I'll see you after work.' Cullen left a gap but she didn't fill it. 'Love you.'

'Bye.'

Cullen ended the call, spotting a text from Buxton. *'Five minutes.'*

He put the phone away again and tugged his scarf tighter. Did he have time to grab a coffee?

~

'COME ON, MATE.' Cullen rubbed his forehead, damp with sweat, before crumpling his coffee cup. 'What else are they saying about last night?'

Buxton turned off the City Bypass before turning right to head under the dual carriageway. He took the last exit from a round-about and stopped at the lights. 'Chantal Jain overheard you and Sharon talking about something in the ladies' toilet.'

'That's all?'

'That's all I've heard.'

Cullen let out the deep breath he'd been keeping sucked in and loosened off the scarf. The heater was all the way to the red. 'Honestly?'

'Yeah.' Buxton sniffed as he glanced over. 'Go on, what did you do?'

Cullen undid a few buttons. 'I pissed in the sink.'

'Classic.' Buxton tilted his head back as he laughed. 'That's not so bad, though, is it?'

'Not sure Sharon sees it that way.' Cullen reached over to turn the heater down. 'Just glad nobody came out of the cubicle while I had the old fella whipped out.'

Buxton smirked, the corners of his lips turning up. 'They'd have to see both inches first.'

Cullen shook his head as he laughed. 'Piss off.'

Buxton waved his hand, gesturing across the road. 'Isn't that Phonebox Jimmy?'

Cullen frowned as he clocked a figure trudging along Lanark Road, clad in a parka and several layers of fleece. 'That name sounds funny coming from your lips.'

'Suppose it does. I've seen him a few times. Just goes through every phone box in Edinburgh, looking for uncollected change.'

'Surprised he's still with us.' Cullen shrugged as they passed him. 'Everyone's got mobile phones these days. Nobody uses phone boxes.'

'He still seems to manage, though.'

'True.' Cullen sniffed as he looked at the houses around them. 'Bit far off his usual patch this. Poor guy will no doubt be having a shite Christmas.'

'Yeah, can't be any life, can it?' Buxton laughed. 'Bet he didn't get a bondage gag in a Secret Santa, though.'

Cullen felt the jolt of booze recollection. 'What happened to that?'

'Just left it on the table when we went downstairs.'

'Thank God.' Cullen tugged at his coat, separating his shirt from his back, now sodden with sweat. 'What time were you out till?'

'Late.' Buxton turned right onto the main road before clearing his throat. 'And I didn't wake up in my own bed last night.'

Cullen felt his stomach lurch as they descended to the Water of Leith, his mind filling with an image of Buxton on the dance floor. 'You were dancing with someone in Lamb's team, right?'

Buxton tightened his grip on the steering wheel. 'Geraldine. Can't remember her surname.'

'Classy. How old is she?'

'Forty.'

'Another cougar?'

'That's not a very nice term, you wanker.'

'So you'll be seeing her again, right?'

'Not if I can avoid it.' Buxton turned down Woodhall Millbrae and parked behind a pair of fire engines blocking the road, the firefighters now packing away their equipment. On the other side was a row of police vehicles — SOCO van, patrol cars, the forensic pathologist's Lexus. 'Looks like the gang's all here.'

'So it does.' Cullen stared past them at the house, mostly intact apart from one corner still smoking. Like the rest of the street, it was yet another turn-of-the-millennium new-build, stark cream stucco inset with huge chunks of stone, dormer windows dotting the third floor. 'No prizes for guessing which house we're looking for.'

'Yeah.' Buxton took his coffee cup from the side and drank it down in one go. 'It's bloody lukewarm.' Scowling, he craned his neck forward, looking around. 'Can't see Crystal, though.'

'Shame.' Cullen got out of the car and stretched out.

The place stank of the fire, the deep stench of burnt wood. It was freezing, the bitter wind swooping down towards the river just behind the houses, making him shiver from cold rather than the alcohol for once. He wrapped his winter coat tight around him and waited for Buxton to get out. He took in the street, the City Bypass rumbling above them. In the distance, a man in a salmon polo shirt walked a small terrier along the street, apparently oblivious to the temperature, staring at his phone.

'That's like you and me, right?' Buxton slammed his door, nodding at the house they'd parked beside, encased in a mesh of scaffolding and looking like it wasn't far off being finished, the gang of workers with half an eye on the crime scene. 'Those boys are milking the Christmas overtime before heading to the pub, I expect.'

'Remind me, again, what's this overtime of which you speak?' Cullen ground his teeth. 'Besides, I'm supposed to be off today.'

'So you keep saying. All the way out here.' Buxton chuckled as he took in the area. 'It's bloody expensive out here, isn't it?'

'It is, aye. Sharon'd kill to live in Juniper Green.'

'Not you?'

'Maybe a bit of assault and battery but not killing.' Cullen set off towards the hubbub, a wave of dread hitting his stomach as he thought of the words they'd have later. 'Come on.'

A uniformed officer was manning the crime scene outside the house's front gate. He held out a clipboard as they approached. 'Need to get you to sign in.'

'Right.' Cullen filled in both of their names. 'Is DI Methven here?'

'Aye.' The uniform rolled his eyes. 'He's inside the house now.'

'Cheers.' Cullen led over to the building, noting DS Catriona Rarity running the inner locus, the interior. She stood in the front doorway, the door open wide; inside, the cream walls were soot damaged higher up, the expensive wood-flooring covered in mud and sailing with water.

A figure in a SOCO suit stormed out — tall, athletic and male — before tugging at his mask and goggles and letting the whole thing rest behind him. DI Colin Methven.

Another figure followed him, a similar motion revealing Jimmy Deeley, the city's chief pathologist. He led two assistants as they took great care to roll a gurney into the back of a van, a black body bag lying on the top.

Methven trotted up the path towards Cullen and Buxton and watched the pathology team load up the van. 'Morning, Constables.'

'Morning, sir.' Cullen did up another button on his coat, the sweat now turning to a sheet of ice. 'What's made you drag me in today?'

Methven scowled at him before nodding over to the van. 'The fire service got the call late last night. It's taken them until this morning to stabilise the building and do a proper search. That's when they found the body.'

'How bad is it?'

'Not that bad. My understanding is they got here in sufficient time to prevent the blaze getting out of control. Our victim is reasonably well preserved.'

'Victim?'

'Indeed. I'll come on to that. The body found was not a blackened lump, put it that way.'

'I see.' Cullen folded his arms, the cold now biting into him. 'Any idea who it is?'

'Steven McCoull.'

'How do they know it's him?'

'He had a distinguishing feature, Constable.' Methven leaned down and ran his hand up and down his leg below the knee, the suit crumpling with the motion. 'Deeley managed to get hold of his GP. Reckons Mr McCoull had a metal pin inserted in his leg as a result of a cycling accident in his teens. Knocked off in front of a bus on Lothian Road. Needless to say, they've found it.'

'Okay. So, you said he was a victim?'

'Which is the reason we're here, gentlemen. This is bloody suspicious.' Methven clapped his hands together and turned his back on Deeley's crew, closing his eyes as he spoke. 'All of his teeth and fingernails were removed and his arms were broken.'

'So he wasn't that badly burnt?'

'Quite. I've seen the corpse and I'm thinking the cause of death was smoke inhalation rather than fire.' Methven finally reopened his eyes, little slits beneath his thick eyebrows, little strands escaping up. 'We found what looks very much like a toolbox in the living room. The metal's charred rather than melted.'

'So, you're saying it looks like he was tortured before he died?'

'That's my working hypothesis, Constable.' Methven smoothed down his eyebrows, a couple of strands still escaping. 'People in Juniper Green don't tend to pull out their teeth before setting fire to their own house.'

'You live here, don't you, sir?'

'Currie.'

'Right.' Cullen waved around, his arms taking in the entirety of the house. 'What else's been happening here?'

'We've now got street teams going door-to-door around the neighbours under Catriona Rarity's command.'

Bollocks. Cullen winced. 'And you want us on that?'

'I do.' Methven focused on Cullen as he thumbed behind them. 'Make yourselves useful and go and speak to an Alistair Walker. Lives two doors down in number fourteen. He called the fire in last night.' He sighed. 'Too late, obviously.'

4

Cullen stopped outside the house — more a set of garages with attached living quarters than the other way round — to look back at Methven and scowl. 'Still can't believe they made that wanker a DI.'

Buxton shook his head as he pressed the buzzer. 'You're *still* going on about that nine months on?'

'Maybe it's because they busted me back to a DC at the same time.'

'At least you're a full DC, mate.' Buxton took a step back and peered in the living room window. 'I'm still acting. Been going on too long.'

'Aye, sorry.' Cullen nodded. 'If I had my way, that'd be sorted out long ago.'

'Cheers.' Buxton brushed his hair back. 'You know he hated you calling him Acting DI all the time, right?'

'I like to find an angle.' Cullen shrugged as he rested against the frozen garden gate, feeling the burn in his fingers. 'He shouldn't have been such a pompous git about it.'

'Speak for yourself. Always moaning about how you're not a sergeant.'

Moaning? Bloody hell. Cullen stepped forward and stabbed his finger against the buzzer, holding it for a few seconds. 'It's reporting to Rarity that's a bloody nightmare.'

'And Methven would be better?'

'Maybe.'

The door opened. The man Cullen had seen earlier stood there, the collar of his polo shirt now turned up, a large Nokia in his piggy fingers. 'Can I help you?'

Cullen flashed his warrant card. 'Police Scotland. We're looking to speak to Alistair Walker.'

'That's me.' Walker frowned. 'Is this about the fire?'

'It is.' Cullen cleared his throat. 'We need to ask you a few questions.'

'Sure.' Walker led them inside, his shoulders hunched and arms wagging at his sides. He led them into a sitting room, the din of small children coming from down the hall, accompanied by the acrid smell of fried food — pancakes done with too much oil. 'Sorry about the noise, officers. Kids are off school for Christmas. Can't get a moment's peace.'

'No problem.' Cullen sat on an armchair before getting out his notebook and clicking his pen. 'We understand you called to report the fire at Mr McCoull's house last night?'

'Aye, that's true.' Walker clicked his fingers and a white Scotty dog raced across the room. It sat on its hind legs in front of him, ears pricked up and left paw raised. 'I took Benji here out for his constitutional last thing. Be about half eleven. I smelt smoke. It clearly wasn't Eric next door doing some winter barbecuing, didn't smell anything like that.'

'Winter barbecuing?'

'Aye.' Walker chuckled. 'He likes to cook steaks on his gas barbecue.'

'Even in winter?'

'Aye. And at half eleven sometimes.' Walker reached down to stroke the dog's fur, smoothing out some dirt. 'It's been known to happen. Big Australian thing he's got. Picked it up from a garden centre sale.'

'But you didn't think it was him cooking steaks?'

'As I say, the smell was different. It wasn't meat. It was like a fire, you know, in a blazer or something.'

'So you went over to inspect?'

'I did, aye. I put Benji inside and hurried over. There were flames leaping out of one of the windows that had burst open. I could feel the heat on my skin, you know?' Walker held up his phone. 'So I dialled 999.'

'And what did you do after you phoned us?'

'I made sure Benji was in his bed and told the wife. We both went back over. There were a few people out by then. The fire had really taken off. There were flames in the windows and stuff.'

'Did you recognise these people?'

'Aye. Most of the neighbours.'

'Did you see anyone you didn't recognise?'

Walker sat forward, clasping his fingers and staring into space for a few seconds. 'Not that I can think of, no.'

Cullen noted it down. Something to check with Rarity later.

Walker frowned, though he avoided eye contact. 'Listen, what's this about? Are you investigating it as an insurance job?'

'What makes you think that?'

'Two detectives pitching up at my door asking questions about a house fire, seems a bit strange to me.'

'It wouldn't be a Major Investigation Team working an insurance fraud case, Mr Walker.' Cullen clicked his pen shut. 'Mr McCoull's body was found inside the building.'

Walker swallowed before blinking a few times. 'Steven's dead?'

'He is.'

'And you think he was murdered?'

'It's a possibility.'

Walker frowned. 'Could it've been a chip pan fire?'

'We don't believe so.' Cullen noted it as something to check in the fire service report. 'Do you know if Mr McCoull was partial to late night chips?'

'No idea, really. Just knew the boy to speak to, in all honesty. At barbecues, in the street and that. He doesn't have kids so I've never had the opportunity to get to know the punter, you know?'

'Were you in all night?'

'No, I was at the pub.'

'Locally?'

'No, in town. I work at Alba Bank. Few of us finished up for the break at three o'clock yesterday so we went for a few pints. Finished up about eight and got the bus home.' Walker frowned, the lines on his forehead deepening. 'When I got back last night, just as I was coming down the hill there, I saw a taxi come out of our lane.'

Cullen clicked his pen again and made a note. 'What kind of taxi was it?'

'Just a standard black cab.'

'And what time was this?'

'Be about eight forty, something like that?' Walker stretched out, putting his hands behind his head, staring out of the window. 'There was something else. It's probably nothing…'

'What was it?'

Walker focused on Cullen. 'Just when I got back in Sheila — my wife — was moaning at me to take Benji out to the toilet. I'm not a hundred per cent sure on this, but I think I saw Steven outside his house.'

'Was he alone?'

'See, that's the thing. He might not've been.'

Cullen sat forward on his seat. 'Can you describe who he was with?'

'I didn't quite see.' Walker locked eyes with his dog, his forehead creased. 'It was really dark and the streetlights aren't the best round here.'

Cullen held up a hand. 'Please, take your time.'

'Sorry.' Walker shook his head. 'I think they went inside with Steven but that's it.'

'Male or female?'

'Male, I think, but it was dark, as I say.'

'What were they wearing?'

'A jacket.'

'Heavy? Light?'

'No idea. Light, maybe.'

'Okay. What style of hair?'

'Didn't see, sorry.'

'What time was this?'

'Be about quarter to nine, I think.'

'Thanks.' Cullen made a few notes. Be lucky to get anything out of that. 'Did you see anyone leave the house later on?'

'Afraid not. Sorry.' Walker rubbed his hand across his nose. 'When I got in, I read a story to my girls then came down to watch the second half of *Die Hard* on the telly.'

'What about when you were on the street last night after the fire engine arrived?'

'Nothing, sorry.'

'You didn't see this person?'

'Don't think so.' Walker massaged his temples for a few seconds. 'Sorry, I just can't think.'

'That's okay.' Cullen got to his feet before handing him a business card. 'Give me a call if you think of anything that might help us, okay?'

~

'SODDING HELL.' Methven gave an almighty sigh before shaking his head. 'And this neighbour has no idea who McCoull entered the house with last night?'

'Afraid not, sir.' Buxton shrugged, eyes avoiding Cullen and Methven. 'Plus, he never saw him leave either.'

Cullen looked back down the street at Walker's house, his frazzled brain thinking things through. 'Was there another body in the house?'

'We've been over this already, Constable. It was Steven McCoull.'

'That's not what I mean.' Cullen snorted, trying to kick his brain into gear. 'We know McCoull wasn't alone last night. Could this other person have died inside?'

'I see what you're getting at now.' Methven clicked his fingers, distracting a firefighter. 'Mr Simpson, can we have a word?'

He put down the hose he was in the middle of coiling and walked over. 'Aye, what is it?'

'We have a report of a figure entering the house at about quarter to nine last night.' Methven crossed his arms, the fingers of one hand stroking his chin. 'Is it possible there are two bodies?'

'No way.' Simpson shook his head before clearing his throat. 'We've had a fair amount of time to scour that place. Your SOCOs have been in there, too. We found only one body, the one we called you lot out for. We got here before the fire was too far gone. You can see for yourself, the house isn't too badly burnt. It's not like it had a chance to devour another body.'

'Absolutely none?'

'None. At. All.'

Methven narrowed his eyes. 'So there's no way this additional body could've been hidden with what was used to start the fire?'

Simpson scowled at Methven for a few seconds. 'There was an accelerant used. However, we'd still have traces of a body if it was near the accelerant. No matter how hot a house fire gets, it's nothing like cremating someone.'

Methven nodded. 'Okay.'

Simpson smiled, the top half of his face not moving. 'Now, do you mind if I get back to packing this stuff away? Got a big night of chip pan fires ahead of us.'

Chip pan fires. Cullen frowned. 'Do you know what caused this?'

Simpson turned to face him. 'I said there was an accelerant used. If you're thinking there's a chip pan involved here, think again. There wasn't one. Could even dust the thing off and use it.'

'Okay, thanks for your help.' Methven avoided eye contact with him.

'Cheers.' Simpson trudged back over the road, shaking his head as he went.

Methven let his arms go, one hand going for the pocket with its familiar keys and change. 'Nobody else in the sodding street team has mentioned a sighting yet.'

'Maybe we lucked out, sir.' Cullen looked down the long street, spotting a couple of paired officers heading away from them on either side. 'Have they turned anything up yet?'

'No. Nobody's seen or heard anything.'

Cullen scowled. 'So you're telling me McCoull had his teeth pulled out and arms broken and nobody heard him screaming?'

'It would appear that way.'

'This bloody city.' Cullen gave a bitter laugh. 'So, basically, someone went inside with McCoull. A man, but not definitely. And the next thing we know, the house is on fire. And we don't have anyone leaving?'

'That's correct.'

'Well, we've got our arsonist then.'

'Or rather we don't, Constable. We need to find him. Or her.' Methven made a note in his notebook. 'I'll get Catriona's team onto it.'

Cullen stared back at Walker's house. He'd better come up with a proper description soon.

'Oh my God!'

Cullen spun around in the direction of the shout.

A tall woman with blonde hair and red lipstick wrestled with the uniform guarding access to the McCoull house. 'You need to let me in there!'

Cullen followed Methven and Buxton as they jogged over.

Methven managed to separate her from the uniform. 'I'm asking you to get back, madam!'

'Get away from me!' She lashed out with a hand, catching Methven on the cheek and clawing out a chunk of skin.

'You sodding witch!' Methven slammed her against a police car. He reached into his suit jacket and retrieved his cuffs, slapping them on her. He dabbed his cheek, blood already weeping down to his shirt collar. He spun her around. 'Tell us your name!'

'I'm not giving you it!'

The uniform raised a hand. 'Sir?'

Methven glared at him. 'What is it?'

'She gave me her name.' The PC held up the clipboard. 'It's Evelyn McCoull.'

'Sodding hell. Is she his wife?'

'No idea, sir.'

'In that case, Constable, I want you to read her sodding rights, chuck her in a car and take her to Leith Walk station for me.'

The uniform nodded and led her over to another car.

Watching them, Methven reached into his pocket for a white handkerchief before glaring at Cullen. 'Can you get down to the station and interview her?'

'You think she's a suspect?'

'I want you to find out whether she is or not.'

'Walker could've seen Evelyn entering the house with McCoull.'

'It was dark, Constable. He could've seen anything.'

'Right. We'll see what she's got to say.'

Methven held the tissue out for a few seconds before dabbing his cheek. 'She's sodding paying for this, though.'

'I'll pass that on to her.'

'Good.' Methven got out his Blackberry, his wrinkled thumbs

tapping the buttons. 'Right, well, I've got to go to the post mortem now. After I've had this sodding cut tidied up.'

'Sure.' Cullen ground his teeth as he watched his superior retreat down the road towards his car, phone clasped to his ear. 'What a wanker.'

'You love him, really.'

'That's eighteen months I've been working for him.'

Buxton laughed. 'Better or worse than the last one?'

'Don't even start.' Cullen led off in the opposite direction towards the waiting patrol car. 'Come on, let's get her down to the station.'

The uniformed officer was now in the driver's seat. He was fiddling with his phone, a high-end Samsung. He took his time finishing whatever he was doing before tossing the phone to the passenger seat. Took even longer getting out. He leaned against the side of the car and sighed, arms crossed. 'What?'

'You arrested her yet?'

'Aye. Doing her with assault. That said, the boy with the eyebrows had it coming to him.'

Cullen checked he was out of earshot before grinning. 'Been lording it over you, has he?'

'And then some.' The PC shook his head. 'Where do you want her?'

'Leith Walk. Get the desk sergeant to process her. We'll be down shortly. Make sure she's got a lawyer by the time we're there.'

5

B uxton stood in the corridor, arms folded. 'Think she might have done it?'

'Either that or she knows something.' Cullen checked his watch. Still no sign of the lawyer. 'I know a few women who'd happily tear their ex-husband's teeth out with a pair of pliers.'

A middle-aged man appeared, clutching more folders than seemed possible. Dark brown hair, black-framed glasses, pinstripe suit and shoes you could see your face in. Tall but slouching. 'Scott Cullen?'

Cullen flashed his warrant card, vaguely recognising him. 'That's me.'

'Michael Nelson of Nelson and Parker. Evelyn's lawyer.' He dropped a couple of files and knelt down to pick them up. 'Oh, shuffle.'

Cullen nodded to the door, trying to avoid laughing. 'We'll just be in the room.'

Nelson smiled as he got to his feet, getting in Cullen's way. 'I know you, don't I?'

'Don't think so?'

'Yes, I've seen you in court a few times. Kenny Falconer case a couple of years back.'

'Thanks for reminding me.' Cullen felt a vein in his temple throb.

Nelson looked him up and down. 'So they're letting you play grown-up these days?'

'I've had my stabilisers off for weeks.' Cullen took a step back, recoiling at the coffee breath. 'Do you need a few minutes with your client?'

'No, I should be fine. Thanks for the offer, though.' Nelson shook his head before creasing his brow. 'This is just due process at the moment, isn't it?'

'Hardly. She scratched my DI's face.'

'Ah.'

'Aye, she'll be getting done with that.'

'But she's not under any suspicion over her husband's murder?'

'No comment.'

'Well, thank you for waiting for me.' Nelson pushed his glasses up his nose. 'This way you'll get a solid conviction if she did do it. I gather from my colleagues you're not exactly one for going by the book.'

'That's a slight exaggeration.' Cullen narrowed his eyes at him. 'We'll be a few seconds.'

Nelson nodded before entering the room, leaving the door open. He sat down next to his client. Evelyn McCoull tossed her hair from side to side. Looked like she was mid-forties but dressed late twenties.

Cullen glanced at Buxton, hungover brain working out cougar jibes but coming up short.

Buxton rubbed his hands before leaning in to whisper. 'That bloke's a clown. Didn't check his shoes — they weren't two foot long, were they?'

'Don't be fooled by the bumbling Clark Kent act. Never dealt with him directly, but Sharon has. He's a total arsehole.' Cullen scowled at the door. 'Right. I'll lead here.' He entered the room and sat opposite Nelson.

He started the digital recorder. 'Interview commenced at twelve thirty-two. Present are myself, Detective Constable Scott Cullen, Acting Detective Constable Simon Buxton, Michael Nelson and his client, Evelyn McCoull.'

He licked his lips, trying to get some moisture in his mouth. 'Mrs McCoull, we're investigating the death of your ex-husband, Mr Steven McCoull. The circumstances surrounding his death appear to be suspicious.' He left a pause, just enough to make Evelyn think he was expecting her to speak, before continuing. 'Can you confirm your relationship with the deceased?'

'Yes. We were married. We divorced three years ago now.'

'So what were you doing at his house this morning?'

'I got a call from his next-door neighbour. Eric. *Our* old neighbour.' Evelyn sniffled, the lines around her eyes crinkling. 'He called me and told me what happened. The fire. He told me Steven was dead.'

'This was the first you'd heard?'

Nelson smiled at him. 'Constable, are you implying something?'

'Just trying to establish a concrete timeline. It'll help you as much as us.'

'Very well.' Nelson sat back in his seat, leaning one arm on the back. 'If that's the case, I'd appreciate a bit more directness with the questions. I don't want you playing games with my client.'

Cullen ignored him. 'Mrs McCoull, was this the first you'd heard?'

'It was, yes. Eric said some officers had been round asking about Steven. He called me when they left.'

'Any reason why Eric would let you know?'

Evelyn played with her necklace. 'Just that I used to be married to Steven?'

'Constable...' Nelson adjusted his glasses. 'Can you please quit with the innuendo?'

'I wasn't aware I was using innuendo.'

'You are.' Nelson peered over the frames of his glasses. 'Please keep your questions informational.'

'Okay.' Cullen glared at him.

Nelson lifted up a sheet of paper and read it. 'I'd appreciate some facts to be presented in support of such an accusation.'

Buxton looked up from his notebook. 'Do you and Mr McCoull have any children?'

'We don't have children.' Evelyn twisted her mouth into a smile, eyes remaining frosty. 'My husband wanted kids, but I didn't.'

Cullen exhaled through his nostrils as he focused on Evelyn. 'Please tell us about your divorce.'

'We split up three years ago.'

'So you said.' Cullen folded his arms. 'Who divorced who?'

Evelyn looked away. 'He divorced me.'

'But you kept his name?'

'I still loved him.'

Cullen frowned. 'Then why the divorce?'

Nelson tugged his glasses off his face. 'Is this strictly necessary?'

'This is a murder inquiry, Mr Nelson. Your client may have had motive to kill the victim.'

Evelyn swallowed hard, her eyes bulging. 'You think someone's killed Steven?'

'We believe that may be the case, yes.'

'Jesus.'

'Did you kill your husband?'

'No!' Evelyn blinked back tears. 'No way did I kill him. How could I?'

Cullen gave her a few seconds. 'What did your husband do for a living, Mrs McCoull?'

'He ran a company. JG Markets & Investments. Managed assets and so on. Gave advice on how to invest. It was something to do with stocks and shares. Dealing them, that sort of thing. I don't know the ins and outs of it.'

'We'll need to speak to his colleagues.'

'You'll need to find that information yourself, I'm afraid.' Nelson put his glasses back on, fingers resting on the legs for a few seconds. 'My client has been divorced from Mr McCoull for quite some time and has no active role in his affairs.'

'Very well.' Cullen turned his focus back to Evelyn, her eyes twitching. 'Do you know if Mr McCoull was involved with anyone since your divorce?'

'Believe me, I'm the last person who'd know.'

'Any family you can think of?'

'Steven was an only child and his parents are both dead. I think he had a couple of cousins in Canada and one down south. St Albans maybe.'

'So nobody local?'

'No.'

'And nobody with any antagonism towards him?'

'Not that I know.' Evelyn shrugged. 'It might've changed.'

Cullen thought it through for a few seconds. 'Mrs McCoull, why did you and Mr McCoull divorce if you still loved him?'

Evelyn tugged at her necklace, the metal links tautening. 'Because I had an affair.'

'And your husband found out?'

'He did.'

'Any idea how?'

'He received a note one day.'

'A note?' Cullen clasped his hands behind his head. 'What sort of note?'

'I never saw it. It was hand delivered, I think.'

'Who by?'

'I suspect it was from Eric.'

'Your neighbour?'

'Aye. Eric Young.' Evelyn closed her eyes and gave a slight nod. 'The man I had the affair with.'

Christ on a bike. Cullen scribbled it down. 'Why would Mr Young have done that?'

Evelyn shrugged. 'Guilt?'

'Are you still with Mr Young?'

'No.' Evelyn rubbed a hand across her shoulder. 'We didn't last that long. Just long enough for Steven to find out, really.'

Buxton cleared his throat. 'Could this fella have killed your ex-husband?'

'Eric?' Evelyn checked her fingernails. 'They're still good friends.'

'They're still mates even after your affair?'

'Indeed.' Evelyn looked away. 'Steven chose his friend over me. He forgave Eric but he never forgave me.'

'Any idea why?'

'Steven could be like that.' Evelyn stretched out her hands, the fingers pushed as far apart as they'd go. 'Eric's in Steven's rugby club. They were thick as thieves, that lot.'

'Which club's this?'

'Juniper Green RFC.'

'Did either of them still play?'

'No. Steven just wanted to help young kids out, really. He was the treasurer of the club. Last I heard, Eric was the president. Might've been the other way round.'

Cullen made a note. Eric Young was worthy of more detailed attention than the cursory checks of the street team. 'Anyone else at this rugby club?'

Evelyn stared into space for a few seconds. 'There's Donald Ingram, I suppose. He was president or something a few years ago.' She rummaged in her purse, getting out her phone. 'Here are their numbers.'

Cullen noted them both down. 'That's all you can think of?'

'Listen, I suggest you speak to Eric.'

'Fine.' Cullen glanced at Nelson, now lost in the contents of a document.

Evelyn picked at her sleeve. 'Steven and Eric weren't just rugby club mates. They ran a business together.'

Cullen rolled his eyes. What the hell? 'Why didn't tell us that earlier?'

'I'm not thinking straight. Steven's dead!'

'How long have they been in business?'

'Five years, I think. At least.'

'So before your divorce?'

'Aye.'

'Is it possible Mr Young could've killed Steven?'

Evelyn twisted her head to the side, her eyebrows raised. 'I don't see why he would.'

Cullen took a deep breath. Why indeed. 'Okay. That's all for now.'

'I can go?'

'Not yet. DI Methven will want someone else to speak to you about the attack on him.'

6

'Give me a call. Thanks.' Cullen pocketed his phone. 'No answer from Ingram.'

Buxton collected their coffees and led away from the counter, handing one to Cullen, before making for the stairwell. 'You think she's involved in this?'

'Evelyn? Doubt it.' Cullen started down the stairs, careful not to spill the coffee. 'I doubt she'd be capable of tearing out the guy's fingernails. Might chip her own.'

'Good point.' Buxton took a sip through the lid. 'Why does Methven need another update from us? We just saw him out in Juniper Green.'

'You know what Crystal's like, right? Micromanagement to the nth degree.'

'Don't I just.'

'Let's get this update done before we head out to speak to this Young boy, okay?'

Buxton nodded. 'How's the hangover?'

'Fucking shite.'

'Watch it with the swearing, Sundance.'

'Stop it, *Budgie*.'

'Yeah, sorry.'

'Just a shame I can't call you Britpop since you lost the Weller coconut.' Cullen waited inside the door at the bottom of the stairs.

He reached over and ruffled Buxton's hair, rock hard from the tub or so of gel he'd used to cement the side parting.

Buxton dodged away from his hands, putting a few paces between them. 'Get off!'

Cullen tried to rub the gel off his fingers. Failed. 'That's a Hitler hairdo.' He put his finger to his top lip. 'You just need a toothbrush moustache and you'd look like Hitler.'

'Shit. The barber called it a 'disconnected pompadour'.' Buxton messed up the side parting, the long hair falling down the front, almost touching his eyebrows. 'Bloody hell. I'll need to get a bloody haircut after work. Go back to the skinhead.'

'You'll be lucky — it's Christmas Eve.'

'Yeah, right. It'll have to be a set of clippers out of Argos.' Buxton opened the door to their floor and walked through the open plan area.

As they approached, Cullen spotted Methven in the glass-fronted meeting room. Buxton entered first, leaving the door for Cullen.

Methven stood at the whiteboard, DS Rarity and DC Angela Caldwell were sitting at the meeting room table. The place reeked of marker pen and the heating was at full volume.

Cullen sat next to Angela, smiling at her before looking at Methven. 'Thought you were at the post mortem, sir?'

'It's not started yet. Means I've had time to get this applied.' Methven patted the large pack of white gauze taped to his cheek as he jangled change in his pocket. 'I'm throwing the sodding book at her for this. I doubt she'll get a custodial sentence but a healthy fine would be ideal.' He sat at the head of the table and handed out some photographs of Steven McCoull. 'These are from the street team, should come in handy. Now, what happened in the interview?'

Cullen got out his notebook, shoving a couple of photos in the flap at the back. 'Got a couple of leads for you, sir. First, they were divorced and it looks like it was her fault. Had an affair with his mate from the rugby, who also happens to be their next-door neighbour. Guy called Eric Young.'

Methven stared at Rarity. 'Has the street team been in with him?'

Rarity nodded slowly. 'They have.'

Cullen smiled. 'And did he say anything to them?'

'Nothing of note.' Rarity went through a set of papers, a skinny hand brushing back her mousy brown hair to reveal grey roots. 'Said they were friends. Didn't see anything last night. Nothing about sleeping with his wife.'

Methven flicked up his eyebrows at Rarity. 'What else did you get, Cullen?'

'They're both equity partners in a business called JG Markets & Investments. JG as in Juniper Green, apparently.'

'So Evelyn slept with his business partner?'

'Seems like it.'

Methven glowered at Cullen. 'Anything else?'

Cullen flipped the page in his notebook. 'They were both members of a rugby club. Juniper Green RFC.'

'They're small beer that lot.' Methven shot a withering look at Cullen. 'Is that it?'

'It's some people to speak to.' Cullen shrugged. 'Thought you liked doing things properly, sir?'

Methven bristled. 'So, should Mrs McCoull be on our list of suspects?'

'Not really, sir. I think she's just in shock.'

'More's the pity.' Methven focused on Angela Caldwell. 'Can you do a few background checks on her?'

Angela patted her swollen belly. 'About all I'm good for, sir. I'll do some digging.'

'Thanks.' Methven held her gaze for a few seconds. 'Could you also get a background check done on Mr McCoull?'

Angela sighed. 'Already doing that, sir. Taking some time, I'm afraid.'

'Can you look into his business as well?'

'JG Investments, right?'

'Aye.' Cullen checked through his notebook. 'Stocks and shares company.'

'That's all you got?'

'Sorry. His ex had very little idea what the business actually does.'

Angela stabbed a pen on her notepad. 'I'll see what I can dig up.'

Buxton coughed. 'She did mention a Donald Ingram.'

Methven steepled his fingers in front of him. 'In what context?'

'Used to be the rugby club president. McCoull was the treasurer.'

'I tried calling after we spoke to her.' Cullen shut his notebook. 'Left a voicemail with him.'

Methven nodded. 'Okay. Anything else?'

'No family, I'm afraid. Well, there are, but she thinks they're highly unlikely. Shall I pass them to Angela?'

'Please do.' Methven rubbed his fingers together slowly. 'This neighbour, then. Eric Young. You said he had an affair with McCoull's wife, correct?'

'So she says.'

'Can you go and speak to him and the other members of the rugby club as well?'

'We'll have our work cut out for us, sir.' Cullen shut his eyes. 'It's Christmas Eve. They'll all be down petrol stations buying last minute presents for their wives.'

Methven let out a deep breath. 'Always time for a sodding joke with you, isn't there?'

Cullen closed his notebook. Always time for sodding pomposity. 'Sorry, sir.'

'I want you straight back here when you finish. No messing about. Am I clear?'

Cullen pocketed his stationery as he stood up. Don't say crystal. 'Absolutely, sir.'

Methven got to his feet. 'I need hourly updates from you.'

7

'I could've done with a nice simple stabbing. Something open and shut.' Cullen tried Young's door, the last of the crime scene tape from next door attaching to the shared metal fence. He turned to take in the BMW 5 Series shining in the sunlight. He could smell frying meat and onions from somewhere.

The front door opened a touch. A man peered his head round. 'Yes?'

'Police Scotland.' Cullen showed his warrant card. 'We're looking for Eric Young?'

'Yes, that's me.' Young opened the door to its full width. His solid torso covered in a pink shirt underneath a grey apron with *'DAD'S COOKING!'* emblazoned in orange. His red face extended up to his bald head. 'Is this about Steven?'

'It is.'

'Well, I'm afraid the police have already been here.'

'We need to ask some supplementary questions, sir, if that's okay.'

'Look, I'm cooking steaks for my family. It's Christmas Eve.'

'This is important, sir.'

'Well, I certainly hope it is.' Young took a step to the side. 'You'd better come in, then.' He led them down a long cream hallway, the nutty brown carpet dotted with kids' toys — trucks, dolls, cars, teddy bears — opening a door at the end. 'If you could just wait in here. I need to sort the food out and inform my family.'

'That's fine.' Cullen entered the room, finding a plush office filled with modern equipment. Two white leather office chairs sat in front of two desks. He slumped down in one before checking his tie was done up, keeping an eye on the window in case Young made a dash for it. 'This room's bigger than our flat.'

'Don't know why you live there, mate.'

'It's handy for work.'

'Really? Get your arse down to Stockbridge is all I can say. Much handier for work and it's in a nice part of town.'

'Need to earn proper money to buy down there, mate.'

'Now.' Young returned to the room, carrying another chair, his apron removed and his shirt sleeves rolled up to reveal hairy arms. 'What do you want to know?'

Cullen got out his notebook. 'We're interested in your relationship with Mr McCoull.'

'I went over this with your colleagues earlier.'

'We'd appreciate if you went into some further detail, sir.'

'Fine.' Young took a deep breath. 'Steven and I played rugby together since university. About 1995, I think. We're both members of Juniper Green RFC.'

'You're on the board there, right?'

'We are.' Young pointed to the only photo hanging on the wall, a shot of twenty or so well-built men of varying ages, Young standing in the middle in a tight suit, arms outstretched. 'He's treasurer whereas I'm the president.'

'And you just played rugby with him?'

'No, we're neighbours, of course.' Young smiled. 'And Steven was my business partner in JG Markets & Investments.' A sigh. 'I'll need to get the whole arrangement unpicked and settle his estate. Believe me, his death will be an incredible encumbrance.'

'Mr Young, we believe Mr McCoull's death was suspicious. We're looking for people with axes to grind with him.'

Young swallowed. 'I didn't kill him, if that's what you're getting at.'

'How's business been?'

'Booming. We've grown the company to a staff of six. We make a very solid profit.'

'Would any clients or competitors have a grudge against your-self or Mr McCoull?'

'Not that I can think of. We're a very professional organisation.'

'You don't seem particularly upset by his death, I might say.'

Young stared at Cullen for a few seconds, as he swallowed. 'I've never been one to let grief get in my way. I lost my mother as a boy and my father when I was sixteen.'

Cullen didn't quite buy it. 'So let me get this straight. You stayed in business with Mr McCoull, even though you slept with his wife?'

'You know about that then?' Young rolled his eyes. 'Steven and I managed to sort out our differences. Evelyn was another matter. I think he was looking for any excuse to get out of their marriage. She gave him an easy out.'

'Any idea why?'

'Just the way he was.' Young rubbed his trouser legs, the khaki cargo pants rolling up to reveal his ankles. 'Steven was very loyal to his friends. Didn't really have the best of marriages, shall we say.'

'And yet you're still married?'

'I am. Took a long time to regain my wife's trust.'

'You still keep in touch with Mrs McCoull?'

'From time to time.' Young raised a finger. 'There's nothing going on any more, though. My wife threatened my testicles.'

'Do you know if Mr McCoull was seeing anyone recently?'

'No. He swore off women after his divorce.'

Cullen frowned. Swore off women? He was last seen entering his house with a man. 'What about men?'

'Steven? Gay?' Young laughed. 'No chance.'

Cullen made a note of it. Not quite buying it either.

Buxton leaned forward in his chair, flicking through his note-book. 'What about Donald Ingram?'

'Ah, Donald.' Young sucked his teeth. 'Mr Ingram was the pres-ident before me. I was company sec at the time. He sold up here and shipped out to Nerja couple of years back. Me and a couple of boys at the club were going to head out there, but we've never got round to it.'

'Was Mr McCoull one of them?'

'He was, aye.' Young shook his head, his face softening as his eyes flickered. 'I can't believe Steven's dead. I just can't.'

'The body has been confirmed as that of Mr McCoull. There was a metal pin in his leg.'

'I only spoke to him yesterday. He dropped off presents for my boys.'

'When was this?'

'About five. Stopped in for a wee dram.' Young rubbed his eye. 'He was going out drinking in town with some lads from the club afterwards.'

'Did Mr McCoull like a drink?'

'And then some. If Steven had a pint, he'd be out till after midnight.'

Cullen frowned. Yet more leads coming out of nowhere. 'Can I have any names?'

Young shrugged. 'Steven just mentioned Robert. That'd be Robert Heald. He's the rugby club captain.'

'Do you know where were they going?'

'I don't, I'm afraid. George Street, presumably.'

'And you weren't with them?'

'No, I wasn't. Chance would be a fine thing these days.'

'Where were you?'

'I swear, I didn't murder Steven.'

'All the same.'

'Myself and my family were with friends in Linlithgow. We left here just after Steven was in.'

'We'll need their names, sir.'

'Of course.' Young scowled as he picked up a phone from the desk nearest him. He wrote a phone number on a Post-It note. 'This is their number. Catherine and Brian Hudson. Do you need credit card receipts from the petrol station, too?'

'This'll do for now.' Cullen pocketed the note.

Young got to his feet. 'Now, is there anything else?'

'No, I think we're good.'

∾

ROBERT HEALD LIVED at the top of the hill in Juniper Green overlooking Woodhall Millbrae.

Cullen pressed the bell and turned around to look south across the rooftops, including McCoull's partially blackened slates and the scaffolding further down the street. To his left was the drone of the City Bypass, the stench of car fumes heightened by the dry winter air.

He chuckled. 'It's like the Billy Goats Gruff down there.'

Buxton looked up from his phone. 'What are you talking about?'

'The troll lived under a bridge, right?' Cullen waved his hand at the dual carriageway as it sprawled across the valley over the river. 'Just like that one.'

The door opened. A bald man with a protruding belly stood there, arms folded. Combat trousers, rugby shirt, pink slippers. 'Yes?'

'Robert Heald?'

'That's me.'

'DCs Cullen and Buxton of Police Scotland.' Cullen showed his ID, struggling to keep his eyes off the slippers.

Heald inspected the card before handing it back. 'How can I help?'

'Need to ask you a few questions about a Steven McCoull?'

Heald smirked, his whole face lightening up. 'What's Steve done now?'

'Mr McCoull died last night.'

'Shit.' Heald swallowed. 'Right, you'd better come in then.' He opened the door wide then led them into a sitting room, the wall-mounted TV paused in the middle of a rugby match. 'Have a seat, lads.'

Cullen perched on the edge of a sofa, the leather cold. 'We understand you're acquainted with Mr McCoull?'

'Pretty well, aye.' Heald rubbed his eyebrows. 'How did he die?'

'There was a house fire.'

'I saw the fire engines. That was Steve? Bloody hell.' Heald gritted his teeth.

'How did you know Mr McCoull?'

'From the rugby club. Juniper Green. I'm the captain. Steve's the treasurer.'

'We understand you were with him last night?'

'Aye, that's correct. We were out in town for a few beers.'

'Whereabouts?'

'The Living Room on George Street. You know it?'

'I do. Were you there all night?'

'We were. Had a table reserved.' Heald frowned as he crossed his legs, a pink slipper dangling off the toes of his right foot. 'Actually, now you mentioned it, Steve wasn't there all night.'

'What happened?'

'He just upped and left at the back of eight, I think.'

'Suddenly?'

'Aye. Left half a pint, as well. That's not like him.'

'Did anyone leave with him?'

'None of our lot, that's for sure.'

'Who else was there with you?'

'Roger and Tim.'

'Can we get names and numbers?'

'Sure.' Heald got up and walked over to a hi-fi unit at the back of the room. He scribbled something on a blank sheet of paper and returned. 'Here you go.'

'Thanks.' Cullen pocketed it. 'Do you have any idea why he left?'

'None at all. Sorry.' Heald shook his head as he hissed out breath. 'It's a real shame. Steve was a great guy. Real solid guy. Loved his rugby. Loved coaching it.'

'He was involved in coaching youths?'

'He was, aye.'

'Could any of the players' parents have taken against him?'

'Don't think so. He was loved by the players, like an uncle. The lads in the club loved him too. Nobody was ever kicked out by him, even some of the spikier little shits. He worked with them to calm their anger and focus their attitude, you know. There'd even been offers from the SRU. Sorry, the Scottish Rugby Union.'

'I know what SRU stands for. What sort of offers are you talking?'

'They wanted Steve to oversee junior level rugby in Edinburgh, but he didn't want to give up his business.'

'Do you know much about the business?'

'Not really, sorry. I'm a teacher myself. Business isn't something I'm particularly interested in. Just give me the money and let me get on with my rugby. Watching, playing or talking about it, I don't care.'

'Was there anyone in the club who'd taken a dislike to Mr McCoull?'

'No. Steve was well liked across the board.'

'So nobody?'

'Not Steve, no.'

'What about friends in the club, then?'

'If you're meaning anyone he was close to then there's only really Eric Young and me. Roger and Tim, maybe.'

'I see.' Cullen got to his feet and handed him a card. 'If you think of anything else, don't hesitate to call us, okay?'

'Will do. I just...' Heald sucked in a deep breath, nostrils flaring as he clenched his fists. 'Give me a minute or two in a room with whoever did this.'

'There's already a long queue forming.'

'I bet there is.' Heald led them outside, a bitter smile on his face. He waved the card. 'I'll call if anything else comes to mind, okay?'

'Thanks.' Cullen watched the door shut then started off down the path towards the pool car. 'Not sure that got us anywhere.'

'Yeah, me neither.' Buxton unlocked the car. 'This is weirdsville, mate. And I don't just mean his slippers.'

'Welcome to Edinburgh. Old school tie and all that. It'll only get worse if we vote for independence.'

'You reckon?'

'Ach, that's probably my hangover talking.'

Buxton laughed as they got in the car. 'What do you reckon's going on here?'

'I've absolutely no idea, but I don't like that guy.'

'Worse than Young?'

'Maybe. I can't stand rugger buggers.'

'So, back to Methven then?'

'Guess so. Much as I'd like to go off on one of my wanders, I don't see where else we can go.'

Buxton tapped the steering wheel. 'What about going to the Living Room to check the story out?' A shrug. 'It's on the way.'

'Aye, sod it.' Cullen grinned as he tugged the seatbelt on. 'You're starting to sound like me.'

'Shit.'

8

Cullen stood staring at the Living Room, a chunk of George Street townhouse given over to style bar boozing. Don't think about last night. A modern extension jutted out from the old stone, the row of windows reminding him of an American diner. 'I hate this place.'

Buxton frowned. 'Quite like it.'

'Not my sort of bar.'

'What about Tigerlily?'

'That's definitely the last time Chantal Jain books the Christmas do. Cops shouldn't be drinking somewhere like that.'

'Wonder if they've cleaned the sink yet.'

'Drop it.'

Smirking, Buxton flashed his warrant card at the bouncers on the door before entering the bar, shaking his head as they crossed the floor. 'Can't believe they've got bouncers on already.'

'They'll need them tonight.' Cullen looked around the room, the place staffed by a gang of waiters dressed in black uniforms paired with long white aprons. He made for the bar. One of the staff raised an eyebrow and cupped his ear. Cullen flashed his warrant card. 'Can we speak to the manager?'

'I'll just get him.' He wandered to the back, tapping a burly man on the shoulder and speaking in his ear.

Buxton looked Cullen up and down. 'Not getting any flash-backs, are you?'

'Trying to avoid thinking, full stop.'

The bar manager came over, dressed in black. His eyebrows were pockmarked by piercings but he'd left the rings out. 'Paul Gellatly. Can I help?'

'We need to speak to you about some people who were drinking in here last night.'

'What sort of people?'

'It's relating to a murder inquiry, sir.'

'Of course. I see.' Gellatly took a deep breath before smiling. 'Just follow me.' He led them through the bar into the extension, finding a free table in the window. 'Please, have a seat.'

Cullen sat on a long bench and got out his notebook. 'We're looking to identify a group of men who were in here last night.'

Gellatly sat opposite them on an armchair, fingers rubbing his palms. 'Got anything that'll help narrow that down?'

Cullen grinned. 'They were from Juniper Green rugby club.'

'Oh. Them.' Gellatly rolled his eyes. 'Aye, they were in. Had a table booking.'

'Do you know who seated them?'

'I do, aye. Me. We were short-staffed last night so I had to earn my corn on the floor.'

'Can you describe them?'

'They were pretty rowdy.' Gellatly tapped the table. 'Sat right here, in fact.'

'How many people are we talking?'

'I think there were seven of them, maybe eight? I can check the till roll if that would help?'

'It would.' Cullen made a note, the ink in his pen starting to dry up. 'What time did they get here?'

'Booking was for five, I think. We kicked them out at eleven.'

'You mean you set the bouncers on them?'

'No, it was closing time.' Gellatly laughed. 'Looked like they were heading to a club or a lappy. There were a few times I almost set the bouncers on them but they were big lads, you know? To be fair, they weren't causing much mischief. They were just being loud and obnoxious. I wish they'd keep that for the rugby club. They can be worse than squaddies.'

Cullen reached into his pocket to retrieve a photo of McCoull, handing it to Gellatly. 'Did you see this man?'

Gellatly took one look at it and nodded. 'Aye. I recognise the boy all right.'

Cullen retrieved the photo. 'So he was with them?'

'Definitely.'

'Did you see him leave?'

Gellatly frowned. 'Not sure.'

'Was it with the others?'

'Can't remember. They left after about the fifteenth rendition of the dirty version of *Alouette*.' Gellatly laughed. '*The bigger the cu* — Sorry.'

Cullen showed the photo again. 'This man definitely left with the others?'

'Think so, aye.'

'Well, this is Steven McCoull. He was found dead later on last night.'

Gellatly swallowed. 'I see.'

'We have statements placing him in Juniper Green at somewhere between eight and nine.'

Gellatly snatched the photo back. 'Now you mention it... It was pretty weird.'

'What was?'

'Well, I was collecting glasses from this table and taking an order. They were being a right bloody nightmare.' Gellatly shook his head. 'Anyway, your boy there must've seen something cos he just got up and left.'

'How do you mean?'

'He chucked a twenty on the table and just walked out of the bar.'

'Any idea why?'

'None, sorry. His mates thought he was off to the gents' but they didn't notice he'd taken his coat with him.' Gellatly let out a breath before rubbing his thinning hair and staring out of the window on the darkening George Street. 'Actually, the boy had been looking out of the window for a bit.'

'At what?'

'Don't know. Seemed distracted by something.'

'Any idea what?'

'No, sorry.'

'Girls walking past on the street?'

'Don't think so. It's like that thousand yard stare, you know? Like he was thinking hard about something.'

'Right. Was he singing *Alouette* with the others?'

'Up to a point, aye. Then he just didn't. I remember it now. When I took their previous order, he was staring out the window. When I came back twenty minutes later for the next one, he was still at it.'

'What time was this?'

'Be about ten past, quarter past eight, maybe?' Gellatly shrugged. 'Could've been earlier, I suppose.'

'Did you see what he did on the street?'

'Not really. Well, he might've got in a taxi, I suppose. I went back through to the bar, saw one sweeping past not long after he left and I don't recall seeing him out on the street.'

'Do you have CCTV recording here?'

'Like you wouldn't believe.' Gellatly grinned. 'I'll get them sent down to you. Where you pair based?'

'Leith Walk station. Cheers.' Cullen got to his feet, business card out. 'Call me if anything comes up, okay?'

9

Methven stood at the whiteboard, arms folded and eyes shut, scowling as Cullen and Buxton sat. 'Thanks for joining us.'

Cullen shrugged. 'Sorry, sir.'

Methven snorted. 'First things first. The post mortem was par for the course — other than the suspicious items which resulted in us being called out in the first place, there was nothing else to report.'

Buxton frowned. 'Did they confirm identity?'

'Mrs McCoull provided that.' Methven raised a hand to his cheek, patting down the gauze. 'Due to the presence of carbon particles in Mr McCoull's lungs, Deeley is adamant he was alive during the early stages of the fire. Additionally, there's a high level of carbon monoxide in his blood, pointing to the fact he died as a result of the smoke rather than as a direct result of the injuries. That said, he did confirm the wounds Mr McCoull sustained peri-mortem would have otherwise been fatal.'

'Was petrol poured on him?' Buxton rocked back in his chair.

'No accelerant was found on the body, Constable.' Methven rubbed a line out on the whiteboard pointing to *Forensics*. 'The only useful information Mr Anderson and his team have put forward is confirming the fire wasn't a result of a chip pan or anything so ordinary.'

'So what did cause it?' Rarity tilted her head to the side.

'The fire service detected signs of an accelerant being used in different locations in the house, both upstairs and downstairs. Four on each floor. Eight in total.'

'What was the accelerant, sir?'

'Looks like petrol, though more tests are underway as we speak. Fortunately, the swift actions of the fire service prevented the fire getting out of control and preserved much of the crime scene.'

'That's a positive result.' Rarity ran her hand through her hair.

'Quite.' Methven narrowed his eyes at Cullen. 'How have you two fared?'

'Not bad.' Cullen flicked open his notebook with a flourish. 'We spoke to Eric Young. He reckons it's going to be a bit of a nightmare sorting out the company ownership now McCoull's dead.'

'In what way?'

'His shares will go to his estate, I'd imagine.'

Methven jotted on the whiteboard — *Estate??*. 'Do you think Young is a suspect?'

'Possibly.' Cullen raised his hands in the air. 'Young did sleep with McCoull's wife.'

'I think you're reaching here, Constable.' Methven switched his gaze to Angela. 'What have you found on the business?'

'Nothing yet. Companies House not getting back to me is the main reason. Well, the only reason.'

'I see.' Methven jangled change in his pocket. 'Did you do any further digging on Mr McCoull?'

Angela got out another sheet of paper. 'Still waiting on some reports back from HMRC and Companies House again. I've made myself pretty unpopular on Christmas Eve. Shouldn't be too much longer, mind. I've been chasing them every fifteen minutes.'

'Do you expect it back today?'

'I hope so.' Angela nodded. 'Didn't sound like they had much else on so they were happy to help, just not particularly quick.'

'You've earned a good couple of days off.' Methven beamed at her. 'Leave it with DC Cullen when it turns up.'

'Thanks, sir.' Angela rolled her eyes, just enough for Cullen to notice.

Cullen turned to Rarity. 'Have the door-to-doors turned anything up?'

'Just salacious gossip, really.' A shrug. 'Nothing we don't already know.'

'Did anyone else confirm the story from the neighbour who reported it? A Mr Walker, wasn't it?'

'What, about him seeing Mr McCoull with someone?' Rarity tapped her pen on the tabletop. 'Nothing concrete, I'm afraid. A curtain twitcher across the road saw someone with him, but she's not given us anything like a concrete description.'

'So we still don't have an ID of his companion?'

'No.'

'Okay.' Cullen looked at Methven. 'Could it be Young?'

Methven frowned. 'Doesn't he have an alibi?'

'He does.' Cullen raised his shoulders. 'He could be lying, though. It's been known to happen.'

'What is the alibi?'

'Says he was visiting friends in Linlithgow.'

Rarity got out another sheet of paper. 'I think we had a statement saying the Young family left home about six o'clock last night.'

'That tallies with his story. Said McCoull dropped some Christmas presents off for his kids.'

Rarity scowled at her own notebook. 'I don't have that.'

'Interesting.' Cullen checked over the page. 'What about coming back from Linlithgow?'

'Their car turned up later on, as per the other statements.'

'Okay.' Methven added another box to the board, *Young alibi?*. 'Let's check it out. Catriona, can you get some of the street team reallocated to checking the CCTV?'

'Will do.'

Buxton exhaled. 'Thank God it's not me.'

'It might be.' Rarity winked at him. 'Let's just say it's in your best interests to get down to the CCTV suite after this.'

'Bloody hell.' Buxton stabbed his pen against his notebook. 'Sure thing, sarge. I was already heading down there anyway.'

Methven jotted an action on the board then stared at Cullen. 'What else did you two do? You've been gone a while.'

'We spoke to one of the guys McCoull was out drinking with

last night. Bloke called Robert Heald. We backed up his statement with a visit to the Living Room afterwards to validate.'

Methven scowled. 'You mean you went to the pub?'

'We didn't drink anything, sir.' Cullen ground his teeth. Cheeky bastard. 'Anyway, he left halfway through the evening, quite suddenly according to the guy serving them. He reckons McCoull might've seen something out of the window. We need to speak to the other people he was with.'

Buxton raised a hand. 'I'll do it.'

'Thanks, Simon.' Methven drew a box and labelled it *Leaving Bar*. 'So he just upped and left last night?'

'That's the exact phrase they used.'

'That certainly sounds odd.' Methven made another note. *Trigger for leaving?* 'So he could've met a random guy in the street and invited him home?'

Cullen frowned. 'Are you suggesting this is a gay thing?'

'I wasn't, no.' Methven smoothed down his eyebrows for a few seconds. 'I was thinking it was maybe one of his friends he'd just bumped into?'

'Not that we know.' Buxton flipped forward a few pages. 'Yeah, found it. He reckons he left on his own.'

'He could've seen someone he knew in the street and invited them back for a few nips of whisky.'

Cullen scowled at him. 'Why would anyone do that?'

'Used to happen a lot, Constable.'

Cullen shrugged. 'Must be a generational thing.'

Methven gave him a withering look. 'Yes, we all know you're usually not particularly *compos mentis* by the time you're instructed to head home.'

Cullen clenched his fists under the table. 'Look, the guy in the bar said he didn't leave with anyone.'

'I still think it's a possibility he met someone on his way back to Juniper Green.' Methven faced the board again, drawing new connections between the boxes. 'We know he left the Living Room on his own at the back of eight but was spotted outside his house with someone at quarter to nine.'

'Hang on.' Cullen rifled through his notebook. 'Alistair Walker said he saw a taxi coming down the hill when he got back around that time.'

'So the taxi driver could've seen whoever he was with?'

Cullen folded his arms. 'Maybe.'

'So what do we know about this companion, Constable?'

'Nothing, sir. That's where the barman's statement runs out. It's possible McCoull got a cab home but we've got nothing confirmed by any means. He could've picked this person up on George Street, somewhere on the way home or met him in Juniper Green.'

'Buggering hell.' Methven slapped the cap of the pen back on. 'We need to find the taxi driver and we're not going to get anything out of them today of all days.'

'I'll get someone onto it.' Rarity made a note in her pad. 'See if we can get *something*.'

'Thanks, Catriona.' Methven tossed the pen onto the meeting room table. 'The sodding press release isn't going out till Friday given the holidays. I'll need to speak to Jim Turnbull about this, see if we can expedite matters.'

'Best of luck with that.' Cullen shut his notebook, hoping the meeting was over.

Methven looked at the board for a few seconds. 'So, given what we have here, what do we reckon?'

Cullen thought it through for a few seconds. 'I'm thinking it could be Eric Young. He had an affair with McCoull's wife. He'll be able to buy out the other half of the business now, I'd imagine.'

Methven tapped on *McCoull* on the whiteboard. 'Do we know who stands to inherit Mr McCoull's estate?'

Cullen shook his head. 'Not to my knowledge, sir.'

'Can you look into it?'

'Will do.' Cullen leaned back in his chair, tensing himself to stand up. 'I take it Evelyn McCoull is still downstairs?'

'She's not been charged with this yet to the best of my knowledge.' Methven patted his gauze. 'Why do you ask?'

'She's not in the clear for her husband's murder.'

'I know that. She's not exactly in the frame, either.' Methven fiddled with the tape securing his bandage. 'Catriona, can you arrange for someone to interview her again?'

'I'll see what I can do, sir.'

Methven frowned at Angela. 'While we're on the subject, how's your investigation into Mrs McCoull going?'

Angela picked up another sheet of paper. 'Nothing on house ownership, nothing on the life insurance.'

Methven clapped his hands together. 'Oh well. Thanks for trying, Constable.'

'Anything else you need from us, sir?' Cullen got to his feet, his dry mouth needing at least a litre of water. 'We're supposed to be in the pub.'

Methven looked past him. 'ADC Buxton, I want you to head downstairs to the CCTV suite.' He switched to Angela. 'You can go once the report from HMRC turns up.' Then Rarity. 'Catriona, I'll let you decide when you want to leave.' Finally, Cullen. 'I want a private word with you.'

'What about?'

Methven looked at the other officers before scowling at Cullen. 'Regarding your appraisal, Constable.'

10

Cullen sat in Bollocking Corner, looking across the canteen at the darkness outside, white and red lights stationary on Leith Walk. Someone had burnt a pot of filter coffee again. He checked his watch — just after four. Roll on summer or at least a hot island in January.

'Here we go.' Methven sat next to him, accidentally jostling his knee as he pushed a coffee across the table to Cullen. 'You look like you could do with one.'

'Cheers.' Cullen lifted off the lid to let it cool. He tried to be subtle as he took a sniff; this wasn't part of the burnt lot.

'We've needed to do a one-to-one for a while now, Constable.'

'I don't see why I can't just do it with DS Rarity.'

'You're fully cognisant of Superintendent Turnbull asking me to make sure your career development sits with me and not Catriona.' Methven took a sip of scalding coffee, gasping as he set the cup back down. 'Do I need to go and inform him of the fact we haven't had a single one yet?'

'No, that's fine.' Cullen blew on his coffee but didn't take a sip. What a twat. This was as much about Methven's development. 'Can we get on with it?'

'Very well. I appreciate we're in the middle of a case, but I'm not aware of any pressing activities currently requiring your attention, so it's important to round off this year ensuring the paper-work is in order.'

'Shouldn't we be doing this in an office, sir?'

'If there was one free, Constable, yes.'

'Okay.'

'Excellent. We'll get to the formalities soon, but I want to have a word with you first, if that's okay?'

'As if I've got a choice.'

Methven's eyebrows sunk down to almost cover his eyes. 'Cullen, we took a huge gamble giving you Acting DS duties late last year.'

'And then you busted me back to DC. No need to rub my face in it.'

'What's this about?'

Cullen folded his arms. 'You know I should be a full DS by now.'

'We've been over this. It's up to you to show you're capable of doing it again.'

'You know full well I *can* do it again. Give me it now and I'll prove it.'

'I remain to be convinced.'

'Why?'

'Well, while you've got a very strong arrest record, you don't seem to be much of a team player, shall we say.'

'Maybe I need a better team, sir.'

'That's something DCI Cargill and I are actively working on with Jim Turnbull. The calibre of officer we inherited left a lot to be desired.' Methven took another sip of coffee. 'What I mean, Constable, is I need you to show a lot more maturity on duty.'

'In what way, sir?'

'For starters, at official functions.'

'I don't recall having been invited to any official functions. I'm just a lowly constable, as you keep reminding me.'

'Sodding hell.' Methven put both hands around his coffee cup. 'You made a bit of a tit of yourself at the Christmas party last night, didn't you?'

'That was nothing.' Cullen focused on the swirling steam coming from the pitch black surface of his coffee. 'Superintendent Turnbull was as bad as I was.'

'Superintendent Turnbull didn't do what you did.'

Cullen tugged at his hair. 'Excuse me?'

'You know full well what you did, Cullen. It's completely unacceptable behaviour.'

'I'm not sure what you're talking about.'

'You're not sure?' Methven glowered at him. 'The state you were in, I'm not surprised. I saw you entering the ladies' toilet.'

Cullen nodded slowly, his heart pounding. What was Methven after? How much did he see? 'I was drunk, sir. You're right, it shouldn't have happened.'

'You're bloody right it shouldn't.' Methven took an experimental sip of coffee before wiping his lips with his hands. 'I've heard rumours you urinated in a sink.'

'Those rumours would be incorrect, sir. I got confused by those symbols on the toilet doors down there, I can't tell them apart.'

Methven put the lid back on his cup, eyes locked on Cullen. 'I'm afraid you'll need to come in tomorrow to progress this case.'

'Are you kidding me?' Cullen raised his eyes to the ceiling. 'First, you drag me in on a day of confirmed annual leave and now this?'

'Constable, I'm afraid I've got an unavoidable family commitment.'

'How do you know I don't have one?'

'I know you don't, Cullen, because you sodding told me just before you entered the ladies' toilet!' Methven pushed his coffee cup away, eyes narrowed at Cullen. 'You were just planning on spending the whole day drinking, weren't you?'

'I was going to spend it with DS McNeill, sir.'

Methven shut his eyes for a few seconds. 'You and I have had conversations about your drinking before, haven't we?'

Cullen sighed. 'We have, yes.'

'Well, I don't appreciate cheeky little jokes at briefings about you wanting to head to the pub. You're a police officer. You cannot let alcohol take over your life.'

'I know, sir.' Cullen nodded with a little more vigour than intended. 'Look, I'm not an alcoholic. I'm a social drinker, that's it.'

'I'm not convinced. Look at the state of you.'

'We've been over this, sir. I took today off so it wouldn't impact my performance in here. It was your decision to bring me in under duress.'

'I acknowledge that.' Methven put a hand to his coffee then took a sip. 'I want to know why you're behaving like this. If you're a senior officer, you'll have impressionable young officers looking at your behaviour. I need to know this is going to stop.'

'Okay. I get it.' Cullen put his head in his hands. 'You know I've had a few things going on in my private life over the last few months, right?'

'We all do, Constable.'

'Do you?'

'Of course. I know what happened with yourself and DS McNeill. It's... unfortunate.'

Cullen struggled to swallow back a tear in case a torrent burst forth. Put his teeth together. Tongue to the roof of his mouth. 'It's been a bit difficult to process, sir.'

'We've all got this sort of thing going on in our private lives, Constable. I need to see you rise above it, okay?'

'Will do.'

'There are opportunities forming here. If you want to grasp them, you need to demonstrate you've grown up a bit.'

'You know I'm better than most of the sergeants you've got.'

'I don't doubt you are. The good thing with Catriona Rarity or Brian McMann is they don't show themselves up to be complete idiots every so often. Do you understand what I'm saying?'

Cullen nodded, his teeth clamped together. 'I understand where you're coming from, sir.'

'And especially not on police nights out.' Methven downed the rest of his coffee then crumpled the cup, pushing it to the side. 'I'm not in tomorrow and Catriona will have her hands full with the street team so I'm leaving you in charge.'

'Oh, come on...'

'Listen, Constable, I'm fed up to the back teeth with you complaining about lack of opportunities. Here's one. Take it. Demonstrate you're not all mouth and no trousers, okay?'

Cullen looked around the room. Hoist by my own petard. He nodded at Methven. 'Fine.'

'Make sure your little friend Buxton comes in as well. Show me you can lead an investigation.'

Cullen felt his guts churn. Happiness or excitement, maybe. Or coffee. 'Thanks, sir. Will do.'

Methven tugged his chair closer to the table. 'Now, have you brought your appraisal form?'

~

'THERE WE GO.' Methven pushed the form back across the table. 'Let's have another one of these in three months, okay? I'm not best pleased with having to do this at half past seven on Christmas Eve, but you've left me no choice.'

'Okay.' Cullen leaned back in his chair and folded his arms. 'You know I've tried to get time in your diary.'

'Drop it, Constable.'

'Fine. Are we done here?'

Methven got to his feet. 'Yes.'

'Happy Christmas, sir.'

'You too.'

Cullen watched Methven race across the canteen, hand in pocket. He let out a sigh. Glad that's finally over. Two hours he won't get back. He headed to the fridge, looking for a sandwich. Nothing much tempted him. He looked at the counter.

Barbara stood there, fingers dancing across a calculator. She glanced at Cullen. 'I've got some bacon in if you don't mind waiting?'

'You're a lifesaver.' Cullen grinned as he walked over, reaching into his pocket for his wallet. 'Surprised you're in today.'

'Got to provide Christmas cover, don't we? Mind you, there are still rumours about shutting this place down.'

'That'd be a disaster.'

'Tell me about it.' She glanced to Cullen's right. 'I'll just make your roll. Got to cook the bacon from scratch.'

'Long as you don't have to kill the pig as well.'

'You're one of my favourites.' She smiled before wandering off into the kitchen.

'That your next conquest, Sundance?'

Cullen swung round.

DI Brian Bain stood there, arms folded, leaning against the counter. He sniffed, his top lip still bereft of his moustache.

Cullen tightened his grip on his wallet. 'What the hell are you doing here?'

'Charming.' Bain dumped a sandwich on the counter and crossed his arms. 'First day back.'

'On Christmas Eve?'

'My choice.' Bain shrugged. 'They're desperate for cover tomorrow and Boxing Day, so I thought fuck it.'

'Tell me you're not based through here again?'

'Aye. I am.'

'Shite.'

Bain laughed. 'Should see your face, Sundance.'

'You aren't, though, are you?'

Bain looked away. 'Bloody DCS Soutar made me come through here to apologise to that fat bastard.'

'Who?'

'Don't fuckin' play that game with me, Sundance.' Bain ran a hand across his scalp, the salt and pepper stubble now more white than black. 'Jim fuckin' Turnbull. Should've seen the state of him — looked like he'd been going pint for pint with you. Prick was acting like I'm five years of age.'

'Right. Well, you were kind of out of order in March.'

'No, I fuckin' wasn't. I was cleared of any wrongdoing and you know it.'

Cullen nibbled at his bottom lip. 'I wish I'd told them the truth about what you were doing.'

Bain got in his face. 'I was just taking a leaf out of your book, Sundance. Your nice wee cowboy streak always gets results, or so you keep telling people.'

'Don't start.'

Bain nodded over to Bollocking Corner. 'That what Crystal Methven was speaking at you for?'

'You saw that?'

'Been here a while. Found your wee boyfriend downstairs watching home movies, asked him where you were. Told me you'd be up here.'

Cullen took a step back, Bain's acrid breath getting too much. 'You glad to be back?'

'Beats lying in a fuckin' hospital bed, Sundance.' Bain laughed.

'Anyway, got out of the whole thing alive. Can't really complain, can I?'

'You still a DI?'

'Mind your own fuckin' business.'

'Right.' Cullen stepped away from him, craning his neck to see where Barbara had got to with his roll. He could smell the bacon frying.

Bain nudged his shoulder. 'You not going to thank me, then?'

Cullen frowned at him. 'What for?'

'For saving your fuckin' life, Sundance!'

'That.' Cullen sighed. 'Cheers.'

'I was in a fuckin' coma for three days cos of that and I've been signed off for over eight months! If that's all the thanks I get, I might as well have not bothered.'

'Right. Aye. Cheers.'

Bain shook his head. 'You're something else, Sundance. You really are.'

'Look, I appreciate it, don't get me wrong. It's just...' Cullen shrugged. 'I don't know. It's good to see you. I'm glad you pulled through.'

'At least somebody is.'

'There you go, precious.' Barbara tossed Cullen's roll on the counter, her eyes bulging as she spotted Bain. 'I thought I'd banned you from here?'

'Aye, well you're welcome to try chucking me out.' Bain handed her exact change for his sandwich before patting Cullen on the arm. 'I need to get back through to civilisation, all right? Keep in touch, you grumpy sod.'

'Will do.' Cullen watched him retreat to the exit, a ghost from his past he didn't need to see again.

11

'Here you are.' Cullen stood in the doorway to the CCTV suite. 'It stinks of Pot Noodle in here.'

'Yeah, I got hungry.' Buxton paused the tape. 'Found a chicken and mushroom one in the corner. Only a month out of date.'

'You're a brave man.' Cullen sat next to him, the chair crunching with effort. 'What have you been up to?'

'Been through the CCTV from the Living Room and I checked it out with these Roger and Tim geezers. The story stacks up — McCoull did just hurry out of the place. Neither of them know why.'

'Seems really strange. Did you see a taxi?'

'Sort of.' Buxton held up a still, a grainy shot of the bar's front door as a couple in their forties entered the building, a black blur in the background moving off. 'You can just make out a taxi.'

'Bugger. What about the person he was with?'

'Nope. Nothing outside the bar.'

'Can you get onto—'

'Already have, mate. Phoned the CCTV numpties on the Royal Mile just now. No ETA.'

'You say numpty like a true native.' Cullen picked up the still and examined it. Nothing conclusive, certainly nothing that tightened the timeline around McCoull. He set it down again and sniffed. 'The bar manager said there were seven in the group, right?'

'Yeah. Got names of the other three and passed them to Rarity.'

'Good.' Cullen slumped down in a chair. 'What else have you been doing?'

'Watch this.' Buxton pressed play on the video app on the screen. 'This is footage I did get from the CCTV control team on the Royal Mile. The numpties can do something.'

Cullen frowned at the monitor — a series of shots cut across various stretches of motorway, the same BMW in each. 'This is Young's car, right?'

'Yeah. Joined the A720 at Juniper Green then onto the M8 at Hermiston Gait as you'd expect. Off the M9 at Linlithgow.'

'This is just snapshots, though. How do we know he was in it all the way?'

'The timing for one. It tallies with how long it takes to get up there. While I don't absolutely know he was in the car on the way there, it's pretty tight. Geezer drives slow.'

Cullen grinned. 'Have you been onto his phone company?'

'I haven't yet. Want me to give Tommy Smith a call?'

'Aye.'

'Will do.' Buxton made a note.

'What about on the way back?'

'We've got this.' Buxton opened another video file and hit play.

The screen filled with a petrol forecourt, the BP logo visible. A couple of hatchbacks jerked across the tarmac, pulling up by the pumps, drivers getting out to fill up, one of them struggling as he pulled the nozzle over his Audi's roof to reach the fuel cap.

Buxton tapped the screen. 'The automatic number plate stuff said he came off the M9 at Newbridge on the way back and took the A8 to the airport where he doubled back so he could stop at the BP.' He raised a hand. 'Before you ask, I checked with them. He bought just over sixty quid's worth of diesel, two litres of milk and a bag of biltong.'

'What the hell's biltong?'

'Dried beef. Spicy. It's South African, I think. Like beef jerky.'

'Whatever.' Cullen burped, his bacon roll already starting to repeat on him. 'So this shows Young wasn't in Juniper Green when the blaze started, right?'

'The call was made at ten p.m. This was half past. I followed his movements at that petrol station, he just goes in and out. No swapping cars, nothing like that. The car didn't leave the motorway till Newbridge, so it doesn't look like he swapped beforehand either.'

'So it's him, right?'

'Yeah. I'll get the mobile records to back it up.'

'Fine.' Cullen got to his feet. 'Come on, let's go tell Crystal.'

'Been looking forward to that. Not.' Buxton led out, locking the door behind them before setting off for the stairs. 'Where have you been anyway?'

'Crystal toasted my nuts at my appraisal.' Cullen rubbed the back of his neck. 'Then I bumped into someone.'

'Bain, right?'

'Aye.'

'Right. He popped into the CCTV room. Gave me the fright of my life, mate. I heard he died.'

'Rumours of his death were greatly exaggerated, sadly.'

Buxton shook his head as they walked. 'What did he want?'

'The usual.' Cullen started up the stairs. 'Saving my life, all that shit.'

'You shouldn't be too much of a wanker about that. My jaw still clicks when I eat after that guy tonked me one.'

'Maybe you're right.' Cullen opened the meeting room door.

Methven was putting his coat on, phone to ear, scowling as he waved to them. 'Bye, dear. Yes, I'll see what I can get at this hour.' He glowered at them. 'What?'

'Simon's closed off Young's alibi.'

Methven flared his nostrils. 'I'm very pleased for you.'

'So, do you mind if we leave?'

'I don't particularly care. I'm heading home after I speak to Jim Turnbull. I'll see you both on Boxing Day.' Methven dashed off, leaving the door stuck open.

'Thank God for that.' Cullen slumped against the table, watching the DI jog across the office. 'Right, then, where we headed?'

'Doubt Tigerlily will let you back in.'

'No.' Cullen clenched his jaw. 'The Elm?'

'It's pretty much the only boozer that'll not be really busy tonight.'

'Good. I'll text Sharon.'

～

CULLEN SAT at the window table, watching the pedestrians battle against the wind and the rain, just as they'd done. He took a gulp of lager and gasped. 'Oh God, that feels better.'

'I'll pass on the kind offer, if it's all the same.' Buxton sat next to him, clenching a bottle of Peroni. 'Glad to be out of there for a few days.'

'That's what you think.'

'What?'

'Methven's dragging us both in tomorrow.'

'Oh for Christ's sake.' Buxton grimaced as he took a pull on his lager, the fizz rising up in the bottle. 'My mate's invited me round to his place tomorrow. His bird's cooking for all their friends. I'll be popular.'

'Look, we're going to have to play it by ear. He's put me in charge so I ca—'

'He's put you in charge?' Buxton laughed, the bottle poised in front of his lips. 'Seriously?'

'Aye. So I can make sure we get out sharpish.'

'That's cool, I suppose.' Buxton took another drink of lager.

'He's got me with the carrot and the stick this time.' Cullen took a sip, eyes tracking a ned as he staggered up the Walk, hoodie pulled up. He sighed, watching a black cab pull up outside the pub, wipers on full, a crowd of tarted-up young men getting out. 'I just have to keep him sweet.'

'Tell me you weren't going on about getting a DS gig then?'

Cullen nodded. 'That's the carrot he's got me with.'

'Anything specific?'

'Never is with him.'

Buxton finished his bottle. 'Reckon Sharon'll be pissed off at you being in?'

'Maybe. We were just having Christmas to ourselves. She'll be wanting to watch *The Wire* box set I'm giving her.'

'Buying a copper a police TV series. Classy.'

'She loves it.' Cullen shrugged and took another drink, almost down to the bottom. 'My folks are with Michelle and Sharon's are with her sister in East Linton. It was going to be absolute bliss.' He tapped Buxton's bottle. 'Another?'

'Aye.'

Cullen walked over to the bar and dumped the empties on the counter.

The barman looked up from his newspaper. 'Same again?'

'Aye.' He spotted a few familiar faces playing pool in the back room. Best avoid them. He checked his phone, still no reply from Sharon.

The front door opened, a gust of wind sucking the heat out of the pub. He paid for the drinks and took them back to the table. 'Here you go.'

'Cheers.' Buxton took a slug of beer. 'You definitely coming to my birthday next month, Scott?'

That was when he and Sharon... Last year. Becky. Cullen swallowed hard. 'When is it again?'

'My birthday's the thirtieth of January, but we're going down on the first. That's a Saturday. Will get pretty messy.'

'It's just a pub night, right?'

'Come on, mate. It's down in Newcastle. My mate's wangled tickets for the Tyne-Wear derby, man.'

'I forgot.'

'Listen, I need to pay the accommodation or cancel it. You said you were definitely coming.'

'Aye, I'll be there.'

'Not Sharon?'

'Doubt she'll come to a boys' weekend at the football.' Cullen took a drink.

Buxton finished his bottle and set it down. 'I need to move onto pints. You want a top up?'

'No, I'm good.'

'Back in a sec.' Buxton went over to the bar.

Cullen watched the stream of traffic heading up and down Leith Walk, letting it blur as his eyes lost focus. He took another sip, starting to feel woozy. Pissing in a sink in the ladies. A new low for him. Why was he doing it?

Oh, he knew all right.

Buxton set a pint down on the table and chucked a bag of Kettle Chips across to Cullen. 'There's your bird.'

Cullen focused on the front door, seeing Sharon shaking off her umbrella. She gave the universal signal for 'pint'. He held up his full pint and shook his head.

Angela waddled over, settling on the seat next to Buxton. 'Evening, gents. Sharon caught me in the meeting room. Don't mind if I crash your party?'

Cullen smiled. 'By all means. Thought you'd have been away back to your love nest in Garleton ahead of a busy Christmas.'

'I wish.' Angela gripped the edge of the table. 'Bill's stuck in a meeting with Turnbull and Cargill. He's going to pick me up when he's finished. Didn't fancy getting the train home and Stuart Murray's already left, so I thought I'd come for a Coke with you lot.'

'It's good to catch up without Crystal listening in to everything.' Buxton took a gulp of his pint.

'He's doing my head in.' Angela scowled back over the road, the police station just visible.

Cullen nodded at her. 'Did you finish your homework for Crystal?'

'Aye.' Angela lifted up a thick financial report and dropped it to the table. 'Their company accounts for the last year on record. 2011/12. Didn't want to leave it lying around.'

'Great, now I've got to do something with it.' Cullen flicked through, heading straight for the director's remuneration section. 'Have you read it?'

'Aye. They show a decent profit. Looks like they took well over a hundred grand out of the company in dividends and salary, plus they each made massive pension contributions.'

Cullen took a sip of lager as he scanned down the page. Young took ninety thousand in dividends, McCoull seventy-eight. 'Hang on. Says here they're not taking the same amount out of the business.'

Angela grabbed the report back. 'There's other dividends of twelve grand.'

'That doesn't make sense, though.' Cullen took a sip. 'Neither of them could've taken that without disclosing it.'

'You're saying there's a third shareholder?' Buxton was frowning.

'I think so. Hang on.' Cullen got out his phone and went into the calculator app, battering the screen. 'The way that stacks up, there's a fifty per cent ownership to Young and only forty to McCoull.'

'What about the other ten?'

'I don't know.'

Angela frowned. 'You only have to disclose shareholders above twenty-five per cent, I think.'

Cullen focused on Buxton. 'I've got a shitty feeling Evelyn McCoull is the other shareholder.'

12

'T hanks for doing this. I appreciate it.' Cullen ended the call and crunched on the mint, savouring the burn. He breathed into his hand and smelled it for alcohol. Clear. 'Give us that Lynx, would you?'

'Sure.' Buxton tossed the can over.

Cullen caught it and sprayed himself, twice round for good measure. 'That was the woman from Companies House Angela's been dealing with. Evelyn does own ten per cent.'

Buxton stared down the corridor. 'Why the hell didn't she mention this before?'

'Let's find out. I just need to catch Crystal again.'

'Want me to start the interview?'

'Please.' Cullen dialled Methven's number again as he watched Buxton enter the room. Nelson and Evelyn sat in conference on the opposite side of the table, the lawyer doing most of the talking.

The call rang through to voicemail. Cullen turned away as he started speaking. 'Sir, it's Cullen. We've got a lead on the McCoull case. Give me a call back, please.' He pocketed the phone, popped another mint in his mouth and entered the room, sitting next to Buxton, gesturing for him to lead.

Buxton nodded. 'Mrs McCoull, we've discov—'

'Why is my client still here?' Nelson pushed his glasses back up his face.

Cullen tapped at his watch. 'Mr Nelson, we've got until ten o'clock until we have to release your client from detention.'

'She's not done anything.'

'Scratching a police officer's face isn't nothing.'

'It was under duress. We've been over this with the officers who were in here for over an hour.' Nelson tapped his fingers on the desktop. 'Need I remind you, her husband has just died.'

'Ex-husband, but I'm sure that'll be taken into account.' Cullen leaned back in his seat. More pissed than he should've been on two pints. 'We're just playing by the rules here. I'm sure you can understand that?'

Nelson twitched his nostrils before tapping his watch. 'Well, you've got another eighty minutes with her.'

'We'll see.' Cullen turned his gaze to Evelyn, shifting uneasily on the seat, her make-up now smudged or worn off. 'We understand you own ten per cent of JG Investments.'

Evelyn's eyes bulged. She blinked a few times. 'Excuse me?'

'I just got off the phone to Companies House. They reckon you're a shareholder of the company.'

Evelyn looked over at Nelson, who shrugged. 'It's part of the divorce settlement. Steven couldn't afford to buy me out of the house completely. The deal we came to was he gave me ten per cent of the business.'

'Nice of you to mention this earlier.'

Evelyn squirmed in her seat. 'I'm sorry.'

'Mrs McCoull, do you know who will inherit your husband's estate?'

'I don't. We've been divorced for three years remember?'

'It wouldn't be you, would it?'

'I'd be very surprised.'

Cullen scribbled on his notebook. 'What were your whereabouts last night, Mrs McCoull?'

'I was at home.'

'Falcon Road, correct?'

'It is.'

'Were you alone?'

'I was.'

Nelson leaned over to Evelyn and whispered in her ear.

She shook her head. 'No.'

Cullen arched his eyebrows. 'What was that?'

'Nothing.' Evelyn sucked in breath. 'I was watching a DVD. I got it from that Lovefilm thing.'

'What was the DVD?'

'*Before Midnight.*'

Cullen wrote it down. Sat through it with Sharon at the Filmhouse. 'Do you still have the disc?'

'I sent it back this morning, I think. Before Eric called me.' Evelyn raised a finger. 'It'll be on my account. You can check.'

'That will show us you've received it, maybe. It won't show us you've watched it.'

'I swear, it's the truth.' Evelyn nibbled at her bottom lip. 'Look, I was on the phone to my sister, if that would help?'

Would it? Cullen tried to think through the lager — if she was on the phone, it might pin her location down. He glanced over at Buxton. 'We'll look into that.'

Buxton made a note, a scowl on his face.

'Is that all from you?' Nelson took off his glasses and blew on the lenses, misting them up. He rubbed them on his shirt before replacing them. 'She would like to spend Christmas in her own home.'

Cullen leaned forward. 'Interview terminated at eight twenty-one.' He smiled at Nelson. 'Mrs McCoull's release is not up to us, I'm afraid. We're just mere constables.'

'I see.'

Cullen nodded at the PCSO before leaving the room. He checked his phone for messages. Nothing from Methven. 'Reckon Crystal's in his den?'

'Bloody hope so, mate. I'm starting to get a hangover here.'

Cullen trotted up the stairs, losing breath with each step. 'The sooner we find him the quicker we get back over the road.' He led down the corridor to the meeting room. 'Don't want our pints getting warm now.'

Methven and Detective Superintendent Jim Turnbull were scowling at the whiteboard. Methven pointed at them. 'Here they are now, sir.'

'My rising stars.' Turnbull shook their hands, his meaty fists hairier by the day. 'Have you solved this case then, lads?'

'Not quite, sir.' Cullen glanced at the whiteboard, barely any of the background free of Methven's scribbles. 'We're getting there.'

'Well, I'll let you gentlemen round-table this.' Turnbull patted Methven on the shoulder. 'See you around, Colin.'

Methven waited for the door to shut. 'Well?'

'We've just been in wi—'

'I know that, Constable. I've listened to all five voicemails. A text will suffice in future.' Methven tugged the collar of his coat. 'I want to know what you've got out of her.'

'We've confirmed she's a minority shareholder in the business.'

'Sodding hell.'

'That's good for us, isn't it?'

'Possibly.' Methven added *Shareholding* to the board. 'Have you got anywhere with the inheritance?'

'Not yet, sir.'

'So what conclusions does it lead you to?'

'Assuming Evelyn's going to inherit McCoull's forty per cent shareholding...' Cullen thought it through for a few seconds. 'I'm thinking her or Eric Young did it. Maybe both. If she inherits the shares, they both own the business. Not the most original of motives but a good one.'

Methven added her name to a list marked *Suspects*. 'And if it's Mr Young?'

'Well, if it's him, I assume he knows how McCoull's estate is going to be divvied up.'

'Explain.'

Cullen put another mint in his mouth and crunched, buying time as he thought. 'McCoull had no kids, he was divorced and both parents are dead. It's either going to go to a distant uncle or to the Crown. If it's the Crown, Young will be able to come to an arrangement.'

'I see.' Methven tapped on the board. 'Find out.'

'Will do, sir.'

Methven sniffed the air. 'Is that you two?'

'What?'

'The deodorant? You smell like a pair of Tesco delivery drivers.' Methven glanced at his watch. 'Sodding buggeration, is that the time?' He left the room, his trench coat swinging after him.

Buxton slumped back against the wall. 'Nice to see Turnbull entertaining us peasants.'

'Called you a rising star.'

'Rising star, my English arsehole.'

13

'Because Scrooge is a wanker!' Angela shook her head before taking a drink of Coke. 'Why can't you see that?'

Cullen sat back in his chair and shrugged. 'Scrooge didn't have to put up with getting a bondage ball gag in the Secret Santa.'

'That was funny.'

'It was you, wasn't it?'

Angela looked away. 'Might've been.'

'I knew it.'

Sharon sat down. 'Why are you lot talking about Scrooge?'

'Scott had a visit from Bain earlier.'

She raised an eyebrow. 'Bain?'

Cullen nodded. 'I said he feels like the ghost of Christmas past.'

Sharon slapped Buxton on the shoulder. 'Unlike the ghost of Christmas present here.'

'Piss off.'

Cullen's phone rang. He didn't recognise the number so got to his feet. 'Better take this.'

Angela raised her eyebrows at Sharon and Buxton. 'Another of his little errands, right?'

Buxton grinned. 'He's supposed to have stopped all that stuff.'

'Never.' Cullen left them and headed out into the cold to stand with the smokers, regretting not taking his jacket. He answered the call and walked up the street, the smoke already snaking its way towards him. 'Cullen.'

'Hello there. It's Donald Ingram.'

Donald Ingram? Cullen frowned as he waded through the four pints on top of last night's excess. Donald Ingram? Nope, no idea. 'Thanks for calling, sir.'

'Is this about Steve McCoull?'

Got you now. Cullen patted his trouser legs, searching for his notebook and pen. Both inside. Bugger. 'Yes, it is.'

'Aye, I just heard now. Robert Heald called me. Terrible news. Got a couple of Edinburgh boys over for Christmas so we were out in the town. That's why I missed your call earlier.'

Cullen started to walk in a tight circle, his full bladder adding to the misery of the cold. 'How well did you know Mr McCoull?'

'We were pretty good mates. We played rugby for a bit back in the day, before I had to retire. I supported him as he rose up through the club. He was a good lad. Solid.'

'When was the last time you heard from him?'

'Not recently.' Ingram cleared his throat. 'I've been out here for the last two years. Got fed up of the old country. The weather mainly. Even the golf's not bad out here.'

Cullen gripped his phone tighter. Get to the point. 'So, when exactly did you last hear from him?'

Ingram sighed. 'Got a few messages from him about six months back through that Schoolbook thing. Other than that, nothing.'

'Was there anything suspicious in the messages?'

Ingram paused for a few seconds. 'Not really. He was chatting about a few old pals. Sounded like things were going well with him and Eric. You know, their business.'

Was there anything else? Cullen shivered, the biting cold and the stink of cigarette smoke making him want to head back inside. 'Give me a call back if you think of something, okay?'

'Aye, will do.'

Cullen returned to the warmth of the Elm, pocketing his phone as he sat. He rubbed his hands. 'Bloody freezing out there.'

Buxton nodded. 'Who was that?'

'Donald Ingram returning my call. Doesn't know anything.'

Cullen looked around. 'I'm just off for a slash, anyone want anything?'

Sharon took a drink of red wine, peering over the rim of the glass. 'I just want you to remember which one's the gents.'

~

ANGELA SMILED. 'You're both in tomorrow?'

Cullen avoided Sharon's glare. 'We are.'

Angela folded her arms. 'You don't need anything from me?'

'We'll be fine.' Buxton nodded. 'So long as Crystal's not in, it'll be okay. Be like the last day of school.' He nudged Cullen. 'Can we bring games in?'

'I've still got a Subbuteo set somewhere.' Cullen finished a long sip of lager, already starting to look over to the bar, wondering whose round it was next.

Angela glanced at Sharon. 'I thought Chantal would be coming out tonight?'

Sharon smirked. 'Simon's scared her off.'

Buxton frowned. 'Have I?'

'Put it this way, you've entered the friend zone, I'm afraid. Just stop trying it on with her.'

'Wish she'd stop flirting with me, that's all.' Buxton focused on Angela instead. 'So how far along are you now?'

'Seven and a half months. Not long to go.'

'You didn't exactly waste any time after...' Buxton creased his brow. 'Sorry, I can't remember your boy's name.'

'You're worse than Scott.' Angela scowled at him, eyes like tiny slits. 'His name's Jamie.'

'Right.' Buxton winked. 'Didn't exactly waste any time, did you?'

'Wasn't planned.' Angela shrugged. 'We're going to need a castle at this rate, not Bill's flat in Garleton.'

'You still planning on getting married?'

'Next summer.'

Buxton smirked. 'Unless you're knocked up again?'

'This is the last one, believe me.' Angela swirled the ice cubes around in her glass before patting her belly. 'I told Bill he's getting a vasectomy after this one. It's that or I'm smashing his balls between two bricks.'

'Classic.' Buxton snorted beer up his nose.

Cullen finished his pint and got to his feet. 'Anyone else want anything?'

Buxton held up his glass. 'Another Peroni, cheers.'

Angela squinted over at the bar. 'Get me a bag of those pickle-flavoured Mini Cheddars, would you? I've got a monster craving for them.'

Sharon got to her feet. 'Come on, Scott, time to get home.'

'Okay.' Cullen frowned. What's got into her? 'You two be okay without us?'

Angela held up her phone. 'Bill's just texted me to say he's on his way.'

Buxton finished his pint. 'I think I saw Wilkinson and a few others through the back.'

Cullen wagged a finger at him. 'Eight o'clock tomorrow, all right?'

Buxton gave a salute. 'Sure thing, boss.'

Cullen tugged his suit jacket over his shoulders, struggling with the left arm. Sharon had already made it to the front door.

Angela creased her forehead. 'Was it something I said?'

'Maybe.' Cullen waved at Angela and Buxton before he jogged out of the pub, heading up the frosty street to catch up with her. 'What's up?'

Sharon stopped, hands on hips. 'You didn't tell me you were working tomorrow.'

'Didn't I?'

'No. You didn't.'

'Sorry.' Cullen stared at the ground, nostrils twitching at the cigarette smoke. 'I should've told you when Crystal dropped the bombshell, shouldn't I?'

'Aye.' Sharon set off up the hill, arms crossed, her breath clouding the air.

'Are you okay?'

'We had plans, Scott. I need a proper Christmas. This year of all years.'

'Do you want to go to Deborah's? I can come over when we've finished.'

Sharon stopped at the London Road crossing, prodding him in the chest. 'The last thing I want is a *family* Christmas, people fawning over *children*. I want to spend time with *you*.'

'Right.' Cullen shut his eyes. Now he got it. 'This is about the baby.'

'Of course it's about the bloody baby. You saw Angela in there, didn't you?' A tear slicked down her face, leaving a trail behind it. 'Sitting there, patting her belly. She *knows* what happened. If it hadn't, we'd be having our own family Christmas.'

'I know.' Cullen swallowed, the fug of booze slowing his brain. 'Do you want to talk about it?'

'No, I don't. I just want something to take my mind off it.' She crossed the road, powering up Leith Street past the cinema complex. 'As it is, I've got nothing to do other than lie in bed drinking a bottle of Baileys.'

'Just the one?'

'Scott, I'm not in the mood.'

'Sorry.' Cullen walked alongside her in silence, crossing side streets and passing smokers outside the pubs and gay bars, the cigarette smoke hanging in the cold air. 'Are we going to have those words?'

Sharon glanced over at him. 'I'm not in the mood for that either.'

'Okay.' So what was she in the mood for? 'Look, I'm sorry about pissing in the sink.'

'You should be.'

They waited for the lights to let them across Waterloo Place, the street empty and dark, wind from the west blasting them. They passed Phonebox Jimmy as he sneaked down the old bridge, heading away from town.

Sharon watched him retreat. 'Poor guy.'

'These must be the last ones left in the city centre.' Cullen tapped the first of a row of phone boxes, Waverley station below and the crags just about visible in the east. 'I've no idea how he copes.'

'You know a lot about it, do you?'

Cullen shrugged. 'Me and Budgie saw him earlier. We had a bit of a discussion about it. Poor bastard.'

'Maybe he's the ghost of Christmas future?'

'What, because I'm a hard-core drinker?'

'Maybe.'

'That's what I hate about all this Christmas shite. It's all about the haves. Bugger the have-nots. That poor guy will have a miserable time.'

~

CULLEN TOOK three goes to hang his suit jacket on the coat rack in the hall. 'I'm off for a slash.'

'Charming.'

He went into the bathroom, lifting the lid and catching sight of himself in the mirror as he started to piss. Lines around his face, eyes struggling to focus. Rough as hell.

He stared down at the toilet pan, the water barely discoloured by his urine and shook himself off. He put the lid down before flushing, not wanting another bollocking.

As he turned to open the door, he spotted a trail of yellow in the bath. Fluffy. He shook his head before he went through to the living room.

Sharon sat on the sofa, the cat snuggling into her, his yellow eyes glaring at Cullen. She lifted a bottle of wine and poured him a glass. 'It's one of those cheap ones from Aldi. Needs a bit of breathing but it's not too bad.'

'Excellent.' Cullen sat down with a groan before taking a big slurp of wine. 'Your lover there has pissed in the bath.'

'What is it about the men in my life urinating against enamel?'

Cullen blushed. 'Right. So I take it you're in the mood to talk about it now?'

'I am.' Sharon ran a hand across her forehead. 'You've got to watch what you're doing, Scott. People still think you're a wild man.'

'I'm not that bad.'

'You heard what Angela said. You go off on your little cowboy trips and then you piss in the sink. In the *ladies'*.'

'I get res—'

'Stop it. I know.' She took a drink and slammed the glass down on the coffee table, a bead of wine dribbling down the side. 'Scott, with your record, you should've been a DS by now. Six months acting isn't making it.'

'This is what Methven was going on about earlier at my appraisal.' Cullen took a sniff of wine, his nose way past functioning. 'You wouldn't happen to know anything about it, would you?'

Sharon looked down at the cat, rubbing his chin as he leaned against her, his paws resting on her breast. 'We had a sergeants' meeting today. I shouldn't be telling you this, obviously, but Lamb reckons you should be getting the next Acting DS role.'

'Just acting?'

'Scott, drop it. Methven wants it on rotation across you, Chantal and Stuart Murray to build up the team.'

'So you're telling me I should go and work for Bill?'

'That's not exactly going to help, is it?'

'How?'

'It's Methven you need to impress. He's the one holding all the cards there. Him and Cargill are like that.' She intertwined two fingers.

'How the hell am I supposed to do that?'

'I think you've maybe got a few ideas.'

'Maybe.' Cullen nodded as he took a sip of wine, not as sharp as he expected. 'I bumped into Bain earlier.'

'Jesus. Really?'

'Aye. He took great pains to remind me of my own mortality.'

'Charming.'

'Made me glad to have Crystal as a DI instead of him.'

'Is he still a DI?'

'Mm, not sure.' Cullen scowled. 'He was a bit cagey about it, shall we say.'

'Unbelievable. I heard he was getting demoted to DS.'

'What, seriously?'

'Aye.'

'In Glasgow, though, right?'

'No idea.' Sharon shrugged. 'It's one resource pool now, remember?'

'That's all I need. Competing with him for a DS gig.'

'It'll be tough. There's a lot of officers on the way back down these days.' Sharon nudged the cat away and leaned over to snuggle into Cullen. 'You need to prove to Methven you're capable of leading a team.'

'How?'

'Why not think about cutting back on the booze?'

'Are you saying I've got a problem?'

'Don't you think you've been drinking a lot recently?'

'Not really.' Cullen poured himself another glass of wine before topping Sharon's up. 'Come on, we're in Tenerife soon. The prospect of spending a week drinking with you is what's getting me through working tomorrow.'

'Scott, drinking isn't the answer.'

'I don't know what is then.'

She held his gaze for a few seconds before she looked away. 'This is about Becky, isn't it?'

Cullen stared across the room, eyes burning, gut lurching. He set the glass down on the table and rubbed his eyes. 'We shouldn't have named her. We really shouldn't.'

'We did it because you weren't talking about losing our baby.'

'I never wanted her in the first place.'

'I know, but we had her and now she's gone. You need to talk to me or your mum or Dr Byrne or whoever. Just talk to someone other than a pint glass.'

'Why?'

'Because you're drinking your career away. You and Buxton really aren't good for each other.'

'It's not that bad.'

'Scott, it might not be yet but it's getting that way, isn't it?'

'Maybe.'

'Just deal with it. Okay?'

Cullen nodded. 'I'll think about it.'

DAY 3

Christmas Day

Wednesday
25th December

14

'Your Christmas breakfast is waiting for you.' Sharon leaned against the door frame, wearing just her bedclothes — cotton shorts and a vest top.

Cullen blinked at the light as he propped himself up on his elbows, feeling the sweat ooze from his pores, booze seeping out. The heating was on high, the radiator at his head blasting out heat. Cooking smells hit his nostrils. 'Is that bacon?'

'Aye. Bacon roll with brown sauce.'

'Anyone ever tell you how much of a legend you are?'

'Fluffy does.'

Cullen laughed as he tossed the duvet to the side and staggered to his feet. 'Why are you up so early?'

'Just trying to get on with things. I've got a long day to fill with you at work.'

Cullen kissed her on the lips. 'Nothing to do with you not being able to sleep?'

'Maybe.' She tugged him by the hand through to the living area. On the table, two rolls sat on plates, steam wafting up from the mugs of tea. 'Ta-da!'

'Looks great.' Cullen sat down and tore into his, the bacon crisp and the butter melted from the heat. 'This is bloody good.'

Sharon sat opposite, squeezing tomato ketchup onto her roll. 'I went down to Crombie's at lunchtime yesterday to get some decent bacon.'

'Thanks, I appreciate it.' Cullen took a glug of tea, washing his breakfast down. 'Surprised the little big guy's not been ratting at it.'

'I got him a tin of special food.'

'For special cats?' Cullen spotted Fluffy hunched over his food bowl, purring as he violently chewed, a couple of splodges already dropped on the floor. 'Don't you want to get him a bow tie as well?'

'I thought of a little sailor outfit.'

'It'll need to be full-size one. He's a big boy.' Cullen finished and pushed the plate away. 'That was brilliant.'

'That's all the cooking I'm doing today. An organic chicken isn't going to be lovely once I've burnt it.'

'You'll be fine. I can just show up and do the tatties?'

'No.'

'Great.' Cullen took a deep breath, scowling at his empty plate. 'At least Crystal won't be in. I'll try and piss off early.'

'Come and open your presents.' Sharon got to her feet and padded over to the small inflatable Christmas tree in the corner.

Cullen took his mug and sat on the sofa, only just catching the parcel wrapped in purple paper. 'What's this?'

'Open it and you'll find out.'

He took a few seconds to slowly unwrap the paper, easing it open and keeping it intact. A Nintendo 3DS. Eh? 'What's this for?'

'Tom told me you used to play computer games at uni. It might stop your drinking a bit.'

'Bloody Tom...'

'Don't you like it?'

'No, it's good. Cheers. I'd been thinking of getting something like that.'

'I haven't got you any games but we could go to that shop up the road tomorrow?'

'Aye.' Cullen put it down and went over to kiss her. 'Just disappointed I can't get stuck into a Zelda game right now.'

'What's Zelda?'

'Never mind.'

'You've no time for games. You need to get to work soon.'

Cullen reached down to pick up her presents, heart thudding. 'Here you go.'

'Thanks.' She tore open the first one, chucked the wrapping on the floor. 'Oh, it's that perfume? Brilliant.' She opened the next with even more haste. 'And that necklace?'

'What can I say? I'm observant. I saw you looking at them in the shops just up the road.'

She tore open the last one, *The Wire* season two. 'Oh, thank God. Something decent to watch.'

'Hope you don't mind me watching it with you.'

'As if I could.' She leaned over and kissed him on the cheek. 'Thanks. I love them.'

'We didn't stop by a petrol station last night, so sorry for the lack of flowers.'

'I love them.' She kissed him on the forehead. 'You'd better get to work.'

'It's just Buxton in today.'

'But you told him to get there in twenty minutes time. You're the boss now.'

~

'TODAY WAS the first in ages I missed my old car.' Cullen slumped behind a desk in their office space, Caldwell's report stacked neatly in the corner. 'I usually love walking in but it's bloody freezing.'

'At least the streets are empty, mate.' Buxton tucked into a scone, smeared with butter and jam.

'Hardly. It was full of street cleaners dealing with last night's mess.'

'Until I moved up here, I thought mental drinking on Christmas Eve was just an English thing.'

'What, us 'sweaty socks' are all about tins of shortbread on Hogmanay?'

'Something like that.'

'Not any more. Hogmanay's shite these days, anyway. It's just loads of schemies and neds trying to get off with each other on Princes Street. My Gran used to tell me about how her and my

Grandad would wander round Dundee and go into random houses where there were parties on.'

'Seriously?'

'Aye. They called it first footing or some bollocks. Something about a lump of coal, as well.' Cullen took a sip of coffee. 'You'd get stabbed for doing that these days.'

Buxton chuckled before taking a bite. 'Barbara was doing her nut about how busy the station is.'

'I can imagine.' Cullen took another sip of the coffee. 'You didn't get to Argos, then?'

'Argos?' Buxton patted his hair, now flattened down and almost touching his eyes. 'No, didn't get the clippers. I'll be in there tomorrow first thing, Boxing Day sales or not.'

'What time did you leave last night?'

'Late.'

'Late enough to get off with a schemie?'

'Hardly. Ended up getting mashed with Wilkinson after you guys left. Don't feel too bad, mind.'

'The youth of today.' Cullen shook his head. 'Can't believe Methven forced all this on me. I'm such an idiot.'

'You love it, really.' Buxton crumpled his cup and tossed it towards the bin, just about getting it in. 'Sharon didn't seem too happy about you working today.'

'No, she wasn't.'

'Nightmare. Not sure how much we'll get done today, either.'

'I've got that report from Angela to check through. Can you type up the notes from yesterday?'

'Getting double time for doing that? Superb.'

'That's not all you're sodding doing, Constable.' Methven hung his coat up on the rack.

Cullen got to his feet. 'What are you doing here, sir?'

'I want to get a result on this today. You're both going to be busy.'

'Okay.' Cullen let out a deep breath. 'I thought you were putting me in charge?'

'I don't care about that. Come on, I want a briefing. Meeting room, now.'

∾

'AND I FINALLY SPOKE TO Donald Ingram last night.' Cullen shut his notebook. 'He's lived in Spain for the last two years.'

Methven nodded. 'Did he have anything to add?'

'Afraid not.'

'So it's out-of-date info?'

'Right.' Buxton sniffed. 'Doesn't mean he didn't have anything to do with McCoull's death, though, does it?'

'No.' Methven shut his eyes, lifting his head up. 'Simon, please add investigating him to your list of tasks.'

Buxton shook his head lightly as he scribbled a note. 'Will do, sir.'

'I want you two busting your sodding bollocks today, okay?' Methven shifted his gaze between them. 'None of this 'let's milk the OT and bugger off early', okay? We're here to do a job.'

Cullen rested on his elbows. 'Look, we've told you about the CCTV proving the alibi, which Simon's backed up with Young's phone records, and I'm going to follow up on the report DC Cald-well got us. What else is there?'

'Just get on with it. I haven't forgotten our discussion yesterday.' Methven grinned, dead eyes boring into Cullen. 'I've sat here and listened to your update and you've missed two key aspects.'

Rage burnt in the pit of Cullen's stomach. 'What?'

'First, there's the taxi Mr Walker spotted on McCoull's street. We're nowhere with that, are we?'

'You tell me, sir.' Cullen folded his arms. 'DS Rarity was looking into it.'

'Well, I'm sodding asking you two to investigate, okay?'

'Fine.' Cullen unfolded his notebook and made a note, under-scoring *taxi* twice. 'What was the other thing?'

'Mr McCoull was in a party of seven at the Living Room. You've interviewed three of them, leaving another three. Am I correct?'

'You are.' Cullen glanced at Buxton. 'Simon?'

'I gave the names to DS Rarity before she left last night.' Buxton switched his focus from Cullen to Methven. 'She said she was going to mobilise some of her team. Her words.'

'Very well. She's not in today so I'm telling you, Constable.' Methven gave a dismissive wave to Buxton. 'Off you go.'

Cullen got to his feet, relieved to be getting back to something resembling proper work.

'Not you, Cullen.'

Cullen sat, arms crossed, waiting for Buxton to leave the room. 'What is it, sir?'

'I need you to maintain focus, Constable.'

'I am.'

'This isn't a jolly. You're not in here to get rich at the taxpayers' expense.'

'I'm hardly going to get rich, sir. Twice nothing's nothing, right?'

'Don't give me that.'

'Why are you in today? You gave me this big spiel about showing I can lead and yet you're here, taking charge.'

'Yes, well, Superintendent Turnbull called me last night, just after I got home. He impressed on me how important it is to get a result. I'm taking it on myself to liaise with the press.' Methven held his gaze. 'I meant every word I said yesterday.'

'So did I, sir.' Cullen stared at the desk.

'And?'

'I'm thinking about it.' Cullen left the room and cleared Methven's line of sight, his heart racing. He took a moment to compose himself. Failed. He punched the wall just by the stairwell.

'Good news then?'

Cullen looked at the door, Buxton grinning at him. 'Can't believe that wanker. Micromanaging me yet again.'

'You're being a princess again, mate.'

'Am I? People keep saying that but I've had to deal with Bain, Irvine and Methven. It's a miracle I get anything done.'

'You're being such a diva, mate. Quit it.'

Cullen flared his nostrils. Was he? Really? Maybe... He nodded. 'Sod it, come on. We need to get somewhere with that taxi.'

15

'No, we're looking for any drop-offs to Woodhall Millbrae in Juniper Green between eight o'clock and nine on the twenty-third.' Cullen sat at his desk in their office space, phone to his ear, feet up.

'With you now.' The man on the other end of the phone yawned, taking a few seconds to complete it. 'Sorry, pal, our system's going slower than a bi— Sorry, it's going slow.'

'How slow?'

'I'll have to get back to you.'

Cullen let out a sigh. 'Okay. Can you call me on this number?'

'Will do, pal. Sorry about this.'

'Just be quick.' Cullen raised his pen over his notebook. 'What's your name?'

'Dodie.'

'Thanks, Dodie.' Cullen scribbled it down. He put his phone down on the desk and plugged in the power cable. He glanced over at Buxton, still on a call, before looking down his list. Second last of the taxi firms on his half, unable to put a cross against it. He picked up his phone and dialled the last one, the cable stretching to the limit of its reach.

'Southside Cars, Denise speaking.'

'Good morning, it's DC Scott Cullen from Police Scotland's Specialised Crime Division. I need to trace a taxi that dropped someone off in Woodhall Millbrae in Juniper Green on the twenty-third. Between eight and nine.'

'Oh, my sister stays out that way. It's lovely.' Furious tapping of keys. 'Just a second.'

Cullen looked across the deserted office — Buxton made eye contact, looking like he was just wrapping up his own call. He shrugged then made a gesture for a coffee.

Cullen shook his head as Denise came back on the line. 'Sorry, sir. Thanks for waiting. We've no cars dropping off on that street until after one o'clock in the morning yesterday.'

'Okay. Thanks for your time.' Cullen ended the call and dumped his phone on the desk. Marked an 'X' against Southside Cars.

'Sorry, mate, did you want a coffee?'

Cullen looked up. 'I thought you were asking if I wanted a pint.'

'Too early for that, mate.'

'True.' Cullen scored out Southside Cars from his list. 'That's me out of numbers. How are you getting on?'

'Same. Got one hit but the stupid twat was confused between Millbrae and Milton Road. Thank God he's not driving the motors.'

'True.' Cullen looked down his list, line by line. He jumped as his phone rang. Unknown number. 'Cullen.'

'Hi, pal, it's Dodie from Currie Cabs.'

'Have you got anything for me?'

'Aye. Got two drop offs after eight. One at eight thirty-nine and one at nine fifty.'

Cullen scribbled it in his notebook. 'Where was the eight thirty-nine picked up from?'

'Eh, George Street. Hailed on the street.'

'Do you know who hired the cab?'

'Sorry, pal. Cash transaction.'

'Would we be able to speak to the driver?'

～

DOUGIE JOHNSON SAT in the interview room in St Leonard's, leaning back on the cracked plastic of the chair and resting an

Adidas Samba on the shin of the other leg. 'Aye, buddy, I think I picked the boy up on George Street.'

Cullen stretched out his hands. 'You think?'

'Aye.' Johnson sniffed then swallowed. 'You going to keep being arsey here? I came in out of my own volition and you're acting like I did something.'

'Sorry, sir, that's not the case.' Cullen stared hard at the man, pink shirt peeking out of the navy Adidas tracksuit top, bookie's pen resting behind an ear. 'You say you picked up 'the boy'?'

'Aye.'

'There was only one person?'

'No, buddy. The boy hailed me, but there were two of them. Bloke and a bird. All over each other, I can tell you. Had to tilt my rearview to get a loo—' A cough. 'I mean, to avoid what was going on.'

Cullen scratched the back of his neck. This didn't make any sense. 'Tell us about the man who hailed the cab?'

'Big lad. Forties, I think. Looked like he played rugby. The bird he was with was mid-twenties maybe. Quite a fit lass.'

Cullen got out his phone and flicked to a photo of McCoull, beaming, at a rugby club event. 'Was this him?'

Johnson took hold of the phone and stared at it for a few seconds. 'Afraid not.'

Shite. 'This definitely wasn't the man you saw?'

'Aye, buddy. Definitely not him. He was a slaphead.' Johnson's eyes darted between Cullen and Buxton. 'I mean he was bald. Plus this guy's more a back than a prop forward.'

Cullen stared up at the ceiling. Not their man. 'Mr Johnson, we're investigating a murder. Any information you can provide could be extremely useful. Did you see anything unusual in that street when you dropped him off?'

'Not really. Nice part of town, I suppose. Go there quite a lot, given I work in Currie. Wouldn't buy a house there, mind, global warming will knacker it. The Water Of Leith will burst its banks and where would you be? No thanks, Charlie, no thanks.'

Cullen had half a mind to section the bugger. 'Were there any other cars on the road?'

'Not really.' Johnson screwed up his face, the stubble on his chin almost touching his eyelashes. 'There was another cab, mind.'

'You saw another taxi?'

'Aye. He flashed us on my way down the hill, just as he was coming up.'

'So he was there first?'

'Aye. Be about twenty to nine, I reckon.' Johnson reached down to tie a lace. 'I know the boy, though.'

~

CULLEN GOT out of the car and stormed off down Bath Street, stopping outside the taxi shop. Scowling, he stared back down the street, the cold air blasting from the beach to their right. The Chinese restaurant next door was already starting to fry up, the thick cooking smell spewing out of the vents high up on the shopfront.

The windows in the flats and houses revealed a mix of busy family occasions, empty rooms or — what he was missing at home — couples slumped in front of the TV, bottles already open. 'Not been back here in a while.'

'I'm sure someone will be organising an open-top bus tour to commemorate.'

'Cheeky bugger.' Cullen opened the door and entered the taxi office.

A fat man sat behind the counter. The only decoration was a plastic tree covered in a few strings of tinsel. He clicked his jaw and sucked his teeth. 'Can I help you, pal?'

'Police Scotland.' Cullen showed his warrant card. 'I'm glad you're open today.'

'Busiest day of the year for us, son. Except for New Year's Day, obviously.' He cackled with laughter. 'Keeps us away from our families, too. More of a blessing for them, I suppose.'

'I can imagine.'

'Anyway, how can I help? Take it you're not after a transfer to the airport, am I right?'

'Correct. We're looking to speak to one of your drivers, name of Billy Hogan.'

'Aye, sure thing.' The man got to his feet, stretching his shoulders back before thumbing behind him. 'Billy's just through the back there on his break.'

Cullen nodded at it. 'Mind if we head through?'

'Be my guest, son.'

Cullen pushed open the door behind him and entered the room. Two male telephone operators contended with the constant chirruping of incoming calls. The room stank of sweat, instant coffee and stale cigarette smoke. A waiting area lay off to the side of the office space, a skinny man with a moustache squinting at a golfing magazine, a mug of tea steaming in front of him.

Cullen walked up to him, standing over him. 'Billy Hogan?'

'Aye.' The thin man tossed the magazine on the coffee table in front of him. 'Who's asking?'

'DC Scott Cullen.' Cullen sat next to him, warrant card out. 'We understand you had a fare to Juniper Green at about eight fifteen on the night of the twenty-third?'

'I did, aye.' Billy coughed, his lungs rattling with the effort. 'That Woodhall Millbrae.'

'Where from?'

'George Street.'

Cullen rummaged in his pocket for his phone. 'Who was your passenger?'

'Boy in his forties, hailed the cab.'

Cullen swiped to a photo of Steven McCoull. 'Was this him?'

Billy took the photo and inspected it. 'Could be, aye. Boy wasn't smiling, though, I can tell you that.'

'The man's name is Steven McCoull. He died later that night.' Cullen pocketed his phone, watching Billy for a reaction. Nothing. 'Tell us about you picking him up.'

Billy shrugged. 'Like I said, I just picked the boy up on the street. George Street. Outside Tigerlily's.'

Cullen frowned. That was a few doors down from where he expected. 'Not from the Living Room?'

'No. Tigerlily's.'

'What time was this?'

'Just a sec.' Billy stabbed a finger at his phone, before swiping and prodding. 'Eight twelve p.m. according to our system.'

Cullen checked Buxton was making notes. 'Was he alone?'

'Nope.'

'Who was he with?'

'See, that's the thing. I didn't get a great look at the boy he was with.'

'Boy?'

'Aye. It was definitely a bloke, like.'

'An adult?'

'Aye.'

'Did you speak to either of them before they got in?'

'For the third time, the lad in your photo flagged us down from across the road. I had to pull across the street to get them. Asked for Juniper Green, Woodhall Millbrae. Nice bit there, down by the river and that. Boy'd clearly had a few ales, shall we say.'

'But you didn't speak to his companion?'

'No.' Billy shook his head. 'The boy he was with sat right behind us. This McCoull guy sat diagonal from him, so I got a good look at him.'

'But not who he was with?'

'Right, aye.'

'What *did* you see of him?'

'Just his back.'

'Not his head?'

'Nope. Had one of them parka jackets on. Couldn't see anything, I'm afraid.'

'Okay.' Cullen took a moment to think it through — McCoull had left the bar in a hurry and got picked up just minutes later with company. What happened in that time? 'Was the street busy?'

'Not bad. Usual. People milling about. Not like three a.m. busy, nothing like that.'

'Okay.' Cullen got to his feet, handing him a business card. 'Give me a call the second you recall anything about this man, okay?'

'Sure thing, son.'

～

'THAT WAS A COMPLETE WASTE OF TIME.' Buxton slumped at the desk, the floor around them completely empty. 'Total waste of time.'

'Not really.' Cullen hung his suit jacket on the back of his chair. 'We found out McCoull definitely met someone on George Street.'

'I suppose.' Buxton nodded. 'That CCTV still hasn't turned up yet.'

'Shite.' Cullen sat, hands clamping his legs. 'Can you chase them up?'

'I'll see what I can do. It's Christmas Day, remember.'

'You don't need to remind me. At least Crystal's not about.' Cullen picked up Caldwell's report and started leafing through it — it pertained to McCoull's financial arrangements. He glanced over at Buxton. 'Did you check on any crimes in McCoull's street?'

'Thought Angela was doing that?'

'Doesn't look like she got round to it.'

'Fine, boss.' Buxton jotted a note down. 'Another on the long list of stupid tasks for me to do.'

'Cheers.'

Buxton held his gaze for a few seconds before glancing away. 'You know you can talk about the drinking with me, right?'

Cullen sighed. Buxton was a good lad for drinking with but talking about anything other than football or the job? Sod it. 'Sharon reckons I should cut down.'

'And?'

'Don't know if I can face this without drinking.'

'There's a difference between cutting down and getting absolutely rat-arsed every time you go for just the one. It's never just the one, though, is it?'

'You can talk.'

'Lashing out there. Classy. It's true, mate.'

Cullen scowled at him. 'I'm not like that, am I?'

'Yeah, you are.'

'Shite.'

'Is this about the baby you guys lost?'

Cullen blinked. Grit in his eye. 'It might be.'

'You've never talked to anyone about it, have you?'

Cullen sighed. 'Who's there to talk to?'

'You've got a counsellor.'

'Yeah, I've not seen him for a while, though.'

'Maybe you should.'

'Do you honestly think I drink too much?'

'Maybe.'

'Bloody hell.' Cullen swallowed. Maybe there was something in it. 'So, do you think I should cut down?'

'Probably.'

'I'll think about it.'

'Busy, are we?' Methven popped his head around the door. 'Do either of you fancy a bacon roll?'

Cullen shook his head. 'I'm fine.'

Buxton nodded. 'Brown sauce, cheers.'

Methven left them to it, pacing off down the length of the office space, hand in his pocket.

Buxton grinned. 'See, he's not too bad.'

'Whatever.' Cullen switched his laptop on and logged onto the PNC, executing a check on McCoull. Nothing jumped out at him. Except for the latest entry. He nudged at Buxton. 'Have you seen this?'

Buxton wheeled over. 'What's this?'

'The PNC.'

'I was just in there myself. That's the burglary at McCoull's house in June, right?'

'You knew about it?'

'Just found out, mate. Don't go off the deep end, okay?'

'Have you done anything with it?'

'Just off the blower with the investigating officer.'

'What was taken?'

'That's the thing. Doesn't look like anything was missing. Just rearranged.'

'That's odd.'

'Tell me about it. What do you think it means?'

'No idea.' Cullen leaned back in his seat. Why rob a house and not take anything? He stared at the screen, the pixels shifting in and out of focus. The line above it looked odd. He tapped the screen. 'Action Fraud is that hotline for grassing people up, right?'

'Yeah. What's it mean?'

Cullen selected the row and accessed the full data view. 'Looks like there's an action pending by the National Fraud Intelligence Bureau.'

'That's City of London police, right?'

'Think so.' Cullen read through the text, the last update by *Det*

Insp Jeremy Atherton. 'Looks like McCoull was being investigated for tax 'irregularities'.'

'Shall we call him?'

'We can try.' Cullen locked the laptop and got to his feet. 'Come on, grab your coat.'

'What about my roll?'

16

'That DI Atherton's definitely away. Just got through to his guv'nor. Three weeks in Australia.' Buxton rang the bell and waited. 'But, of course, you reckon Young knows something.'

'If he doesn't, we're waiting till DI Atherton's back from the beach and barbecues.' Cullen looked around the street, the front windows of the houses lit up in the mid-morning gloom. A few kids cycled around, presumably on their main presents, while others used scooters or radio controlled cars. 'I used to love Christmas morning. Seeing what my mates got, playing with my own new gear.'

'I thought you were all Scrooge about Christmas.'

Cullen shrugged. 'Give me a Super Nintendo and I'm anyone's.'

'I was more of a Playstation kid.' Buxton smirked as the front door opened.

'Officers.' Young stood there, wearing the same apron as the previous day. 'What is it this time?'

'Need to ask you a few supplementary questions, sir.'

Young shook his head. 'Not today, I'm afraid.'

'It's important.'

'I'm sure it is. But it can wait. I'm just about to get the turkey in the oven then I have to drive to North Berwick to collect my in-laws.'

'We can do this down the station, if you'd prefer?'

'Very well.' Young flared his nostrils as he showed them inside, the house filled with the reek of the oven as it heated burnt-on grease. He led them into the study and sat, arms crossed, feet tapping. 'Well, what is it?'

Cullen took his time getting out his notebook. Let's throw a curve ball first. 'Mr Young, do you know who stands to inherit Mr McCoull's estate?'

'I'm not privy to that sort of information, I'm afraid.'

'Do you know who his lawyers are?'

'McLintock or something. Why?'

'Thanks.' Cullen sighed. Campbell McLintock was the last person he wanted to speak to. 'We understand you were being investigated by HMRC?'

'*We* weren't. It was just Steven.'

'Go on.'

'It was nothing. Really.'

'I'm not sure they'd agree with you. A DI in City of London police was investigating.'

Young steepled his fingers, flexing them in a quick rhythm. 'Listen, somebody got carried away about Steven putting his golf club membership through the company. It was a fair whack of cash, admittedly, but nothing too bad, you know?'

'Why would he do that in the first place?'

'Because otherwise you're paying it net.'

'How much are we talking about here?'

'It cost him about ten thousand pounds.'

Cullen noted it down. That's a good chunk of McCoull's income. 'So why not just pay it?'

'Because, if he didn't, he'd have been paying it out of his net receipts from the business. I'm not sure how mathematical you are.'

Cullen shrugged. 'Not very.'

'Fine.' Young leaned forward, rubbing his hands together. 'If Steven paid the ten grand out of his own pocket, he was effectively adding the tax onto it. Assume he's taxed at twenty-five per cent. That ten grand has another two and a half grand on it. Or, alternatively, if it's paid out of the business, it's effectively twenty per cent *lower*. It only costs him eight grand.'

'Not twenty-five per cent lower?'

'No.'

Cullen scribbled it in his pad. Need to check that out. 'How come?'

'Because he'd have to take the tax amount as well to get the same. I can write this up for you, if you wish.'

'It's okay, I believe you.'

'Additionally, the membership was offset against tax as a business expenses so it came off our liability for Corporation Tax. That's why he did it.'

'Did you do it as well?'

Young smiled. 'I don't play golf, I'm afraid.'

'How do you feel about the fact he's putting a big chunk of a personal expense through your company?'

'I was fine with it.'

'Why?'

'A number of our business leads came from the nineteenth hole, as it were. Chaps with a few grand sitting around who wanted it working for them rather than losing value.'

'So it was in your accounts as a golf club membership?'

'Well, not quite.' Young snorted. 'We managed it as 'Business Entertainment' and a few other expenses, I think. Our accountants were comfortable about that treatment. As were the Revenue for a few years until they got wind of what it was.'

'Any idea how HMRC found out?'

'No idea. Steven did ask them. An anonymous tip-off was about as specific as he got.' Young held up his hands. 'Happens all the time. And, believe you me, it's not in my best interests to get a business partner in the shit with the bloody tax man.'

'I can imagine. Who would want to get him into difficulty?'

'No idea.' Young sighed as he rubbed his forehead. 'Look, it's nothing like when Steven went bankrupt.'

A jolt went up Cullen's spine. 'Excuse me?'

'You must surely have heard?'

'Heard what?'

'Steven was bankrupt ten years ago. 2003, I believe.'

Cullen narrowed his eyes. 'No, we haven't heard about this.'

'I see.' Young looked away.

'Do you know what happened?'

'All I know is the business he owned at the time went to the wall. He was eventually discharged by Companies House and was allowed to become a company director again, hence us starting up JG Investments.' Young unfastened his apron and tugged it over his head. 'The receivers really went for him over it. HMRC was the main one. Inland Revenue as was.'

'So why did he play silly buggers with them this time round?'

'He honestly thought he wasn't doing anything wrong. I swear.'

'Was it just Mr McCoull involved in this business?'

'I think there was another man, but I don't know his name.'

'We'll need it.'

'Look, I'm sorry. This is before I moved here. I simply don't know. I've heard anecdotes after fifteen pints down the rugby club, that's it. Nothing concrete.'

'Who would know?'

'Donald Ingram might.'

'Really? Was he involved?'

'I can't remember. All I know about Donald is he just got fed up of whatever business he was in, sold up and moved to Spain.' Young got to his feet. 'Now, do you mind if I get back to watching my kids open their presents?'

'One last thing.' Cullen held up a finger. 'Do you know anything about a burglary at Mr McCoull's house in June?'

'Afraid not, no.'

~

'Look, officer, it's *Christmas Day*.'

Cullen swapped his mobile to the other ear, eyes scanning down the street as he leaned back in the car seat. 'I understand that, Mr Ingram, I just need to spe—'

'Look, I'm sorry, son, but I've got a busy day here. I've not got time for this.'

'Mr Ingram, as I've mentioned before, we're dealing with a murder. I'm really sorry to have to drag you away from the pool or wherever but there's something we need to discuss with you.'

Ingram paused for a few seconds. 'Right. What is it?'

'We understand Mr McCoull was declared bankrupt ten years ago.'

'That's correct. 2003.'

'Why didn't you disclose it to me last night?'

'Is it pertinent to your investigation?'

'It could be. Another witness just mentioned it to us.'

'Right. And?'

'He said you'd know about it.'

'Did he?' Ingram sighed. 'Okay. So what? Ten years ago, Steven was declared bankrupt. The business he had at the time went to the wall.'

'Do you know why?'

'Not really. I only know from chatting to Steven or stuff I've heard from others. I wasn't involved myself, of course. I was more into conveyancing. Property law.'

'We understand there was another party in the business.'

'That's correct. I think Steven's business partner was called Richard. I don't know his surname. Sorry.'

'Do you have a number for him?'

'Sorry, mate. I just knew he was called Richard. Do you mind if I go?'

'Fine. Give me a call if anything comes up.'

'Will do.'

The call ended.

Cullen looked across at Buxton, still on the phone himself. He stared up at the dark flat, lit up by the blue light of a TV.

His phone rang. Sharon. 'How's it going?'

Cullen sighed. 'Getting somewhere, I think.'

'Right. I'm not getting my roast chicken, am I?'

'I doubt it.'

'Shall I threaten you with my cooking?'

'The bacon roll was good this morning.'

'It's a bit harder doing a chicken.'

'That Delia Smith book flops open at the roast chicken recipe.'

'Mm.'

'Look, we'll sort something out.'

'Mum's been on the phone. We're welcome over there.'

'I'd rather just have a packet of crisps than hear your dad and your uncle Brian talk Hibs and Celtic.'

'At least you can talk that language.'

Buxton tapped his shoulder. 'Got something.'

Cullen glanced over at Buxton, the sunlight shining from behind and silhouetting him. 'Better go.'

'Right, please get home in time. Love you.'

'Will do. Love you, too.' Cullen pocketed his phone.

'Mwah, mwah, love you.' Buxton blew kisses into the air.

'Piss off.' Cullen scowled at him. 'And you want to listen to me talk seriously about stuff?'

'Offer still stands, mate.' Buxton stared straight ahead. He held up his own phone. 'That was Tommy Smith in the Phone Squad. He's pinned four calls on her and the GPS shows the phone stayed in the flat apart from a sojourn to Waitrose. His words not mine.'

'Right, I just spoke with Ingram.' Cullen nodded up at Evelyn McCoull's flat. 'I reckon your little cougar might know something.'

'Piss off.'

17

E velyn McCoull collapsed into her sofa, a glass of white wine in front of her, the TV paused halfway through a film with Sandra Bullock. 'Should I get my lawyer in here?'

Cullen nudged himself down on the armchair opposite, waiting for Buxton to do the same. 'This isn't related to the matter we discussed during your detention last night, Mrs McCoull.'

'What is it then?'

Cullen tried to drag his eyes away from the TV. 'We understand your husband was made bankrupt in 2003.'

A frown flickered onto her forehead. 'And what of it?'

'You didn't think to tell us?'

'It didn't seem relevant.'

Cullen sighed. 'Mrs McCoull, a lot of people lost money as a result of your ex-husband's actions. That's a lot of people we should be speaking to as potential suspects.'

'I'm sorry.'

'I seem to say this a lot, but I'd much rather exclude facts at a later date than not include them at the start.'

'I said I'm sorry.'

Cullen took a breath, just about calm. 'What happened to your husband after the bankruptcy?'

'Steven got a job on George Street at Standard Life Investments. Earned a decent amount and it kept his hand in. He saved up over that time. He used to talk about how obsessed with failure the British were. It's different in America. The whole thing just made him more determined than ever.'

'I assume his bankruptcy was discharged if he went on to own another company?'

'It was. It took ages, though.'

Cullen frowned as he recalled a previous case he'd worked with a bankruptcy. 'I thought it was usually just a year.'

'The receiver didn't like what he found.'

'Which was?'

'Well, the business wasn't doing so well and our house was secured against the company.'

'So they extended Steven's discharge period?'

'They did. They were trying to get the house sold and it took a long time. There were loads of new builds hitting the market and there was a wee scare about flooding in the street. Nobody wants a not-quite new build, do they? The bank wasn't exactly pleased with the contract we'd used to secure the business against it, either, but then their lawyers should have been more thorough first time, I suppose.'

'And you and Mr McCoull still lived in this house?'

'We did, yes. Steven managed to re-secure the mortgage once he'd got on his feet again. That allowed them to accelerate getting the discharge.'

'And you co-owned the property?'

'I did, yes. Once we'd unpicked the legalities, we managed to buy the house back by paying off the Revenue. Of course, when Steven and I divorced, he paid me.'

'And this shareholding in JG Investments?'

'Aye, well. That was part of the settlement.' Evelyn took a sip of white wine, leaving a red mark on the rim.

'Donald Ingram mentioned a Richard.'

'Richard Airth.' Evelyn nodded. 'He was Steven's business partner. He was going to sell his house to prop up the company.'

'Was going to?'

'There was a fire.' Evelyn sucked in breath. 'Richard's house burnt down. It wasn't suspicious, or so they said.' She leaned forward, tears welling in her eyes. 'Richard's family were in it, his wife and two children. They all died.'

'Where was the house?'

'It was on our street, two doors down. I think it's just been rebuilt.'

'This was ten years ago, though?'

'I think so.'

'So why did it take them so long to rebuild?'

'Richard disappeared. Nobody knew where he'd gone.'

Cullen raised his eyebrows. 'He just disappeared?'

'He did.'

'Was it reported to the police?'

'It was but nobody knew what happened. Nobody's seen him since. That was one of the problems with Steven's discharge, that Richard had just disappeared like that.'

'Why did he go?'

'I just don't think he could cope with the loss. Losing his wife and children like that...' Evelyn sniffed. 'When the business fell apart, Richard was having a very hard time. The failing business was all on his head. Steven was much more on the sales side, I think; going and speaking to people. Richard was managing their money. His mother was on a ventilator at the same time. He wasn't allowed to turn it off. His mother and his business died just like that.'

'So they thought Mr Airth committed suicide?'

'That was how they initially approached it, I think.' She looked away. 'They never found a body, though.'

'Is he still alive?'

'I think so.' Evelyn nodded her head. 'I get a Christmas card from him every year. It turns up on Christmas Eve. Hand-delivered. I've never caught him yet.'

'Did you get one this year?'

'Yes.'

'Would we be able to see it?'

'Of course.' Evelyn got up and wandered out of the room, Cullen clocking Buxton's eyes following her.

Buxton switched his focus to Cullen. 'What are you thinking here?'

'What do you mean?'

'I can see that glint in your eyes.'

'We need look into this.' Cullen recapped his pen. 'Feels like we're finally onto something.'

'She's still my favourite for it.'

Cullen smirked. 'I don't doubt she's your favourite.'

'What's that supposed to mean?'

'Nothing.'

Evelyn walked back into the room, holding some papers. 'Here, this is the only one I could find.' She fanned it out. 'I've got a couple of photos.'

'Thanks.' Cullen held up the photo so Buxton could see as well. Three men at a rugby function, bow ties let down, collars open. One of them was Steven McCoull, but the others looked like they could be brothers — large, round heads covered with beards and thick, curly hair. 'Who are these with your ex-husband?'

'That's Donald Ingram and Richard Airth on the right.'

Cullen scowled at the photo. Where did he recognise Airth from?

≈

'Constable.' Methven stood in the meeting room, jangling the keys in his pocket. 'Have you got a result yet?'

Cullen waited for Buxton to enter the room before shutting the door behind him. 'Not yet.'

'Well, what the sodding hell have you been doing?'

'We've just been speaking to Young and Evelyn McCoull. We might have something, sir.'

'Go on.'

'Couple of things. First, McCoull was being investigated by HMRC for tax fraud. Nothing major, just a ten grand golf club membership he'd been fiddling as expenses. It's a grey area, it might've been okay. I'm not an expert.'

'Still, ten grand sounds reasonably major.' Methven sucked his teeth. 'What was the other thing?'

'Turns out McCoull was declared bankrupt ten years ago.' Cullen tossed the photo on the table, tapping Airth's head. 'His partner in the business, a guy called Richard Airth, disappeared after a house fire killed his family.'

'And you think he could've killed McCoull?'

'It's possible.'

'Find him.'

'I've got a call out to the investigating officer, sir. Same guy did the fire and the disappearance.'

'Very well.' Methven glowered at Buxton. 'I got you that bacon roll but you weren't here.'

'Sorry, sir, we had a lead.'

'I don't like having to eat two rolls, Constable, especially when one was supposed to be a gift. And when it's covered in brown sauce.' Methven put his suit jacket on, pushing the meeting room chair back under the table. 'Keep me apprised of your progress. I'm off to the *Scotsman*. Got to sodding do this one-to-one while the media office are eating turkey in front of the Queen.'

Cullen watched him leave the room and march through the almost-empty office space. 'What a guy.'

Buxton creased his forehead. 'He's not gay, is he?'

'I said *guy*.'

'Right.' Buxton went back to typing on his laptop.

Cullen picked up the photo and stared at it. It still looked familiar. Who was it?

His phone rang. Unknown number. 'Hello?'

'Is that DS Scott Cullen?'

'It is. Who's this?'

'PC Johnny Stewart. I investigated the Richard Airth case back in the day.'

'Thanks for calling me back. Surprised you're working today.'

'Aye. I'm out in Wester Hailes now, sadly. Run off our bloody feet. I miss Colinton and Fairmilehead.'

'The reason I wanted to speak to you was Mr Airth's business partner, a Steven McCoull, was murdered the other night.'

'Christ.'

'I want to know if there was anything suspicious surrounding Mr Airth's disappearance.'

'The whole thing was suspicious, if you ask me.' Stewart exhaled down the line. 'We'd no idea what happened. He just fell off the map.'

'I understand there was a house fire?'

'Aye. His whole family was killed. We took that as the reason Airth scarpered.'

'Because of the trauma or because you suspected he caused it?'

'The trauma. He was in Glasgow at the time doing some business deal through there. We triple-checked the alibi. It was rock solid — no funny business like you get sometimes.'

'Did you speak to Steven McCoull as part of your investigation?'

'We did, aye. Nothing jumped out at us about him, I'm afraid. Well, other than the whole business thing.'

'What do you mean by that?'

'Ach, just the fact both houses were tied up in the business. We didn't really buy the fire being entirely innocent.'

'You said both houses were tied up?'

'Well, only McCoull's was secured against it. They were trying to do something with Airth's. Just looked suspicious. Business teetering on the brink. House fire. Insurance job written all over it.'

'Right. And was it?'

'Think the insurer eventually paid out, but the money went straight to the tax man.'

'Okay. Any idea what happened to Airth?'

'No, sorry. We searched high and low for him. Had a team of four looking for him at one point. Notices went all across the country and down south. Not a sausage.'

'Cheers.' Cullen ended the call and stared across the meeting room. He picked up the photo of Airth.

Where are you, Richard Airth?

He looked up at the ceiling tiles, focusing on a dark brown mark in the corner of one then glanced over at Buxton, fingers tapping the laptop keys. 'You got a second?'

Buxton didn't look up. 'I'm trying to finish typing this report up.'

'I want to run something by you.'

'Fire away.' Buxton shut the lid on the laptop.

'Let's start over again, okay? What do we know?'

Buxton folded his arms. 'First, McCoull was in the Living Room on the twenty-third. Bolted out of there. Got a taxi home.'

'Aye. Not alone, either.'

Buxton scratched his right eyebrow. 'According to that Gellatly geezer, McCoull was staring out the window for a while, most likely at his companion, the parka-wearing man.'

Cullen looked at the photo again, tapping it a few times. 'I'm thinking Richard Airth is our most likely suspect.'

'You think he's parka man?'

'Aye. He's disappeared after a house fire killed his family. McCoull dies in a fire. Fight fire with fire.'

'That's a bit of a stretch, mate.'

'I know. It's what I do best.' Cullen chucked the photo down on the desk. 'Did you get a chance to look at the CCTV?'

Buxton lifted the laptop's lid again. 'Think they're in here somewhere.'

'I take it that means you didn't look at it?'

'Mm.'

'Any idea where?'

'Sorry, I'm in the zone here, mate.'

'I'll believe that when I see it.' Cullen hauled himself to his feet and took in the heap of shit on the meeting room table, piles of papers and documents. Someone was going to have to tidy that lot up by the end of the day.

At the far side was a packet, brown parcel tape wrapped over it several times. He leaned over and inspected it — sent to DC Simon Buxton. He glanced at Buxton; the cheeky sod. He flipped it over, finding the address for the city council's CCTV unit stamped on the back. Sneaking a finger in a hole in the corner, he tore the tape off in a couple of goes. He popped the contents on top of a report. Three DVDs, all labelled with black marker.

'Come on, Simon, let's head downstairs.'

∿

'YEAH, sorry. Nothing I can do. I'll let you know when I'm leaving. Love you. Bye.' Cullen ended the call and dropped his phone on the table. 'Where are we?'

'This is the last of the discs. This bit here.' Buxton slowed the jog wheel right down. 'There.'

The camera was pointing west down George Street towards Charlotte Square. The grainy footage showed the front of the

Living Room, a few brave smokers leaning against its modern extension, laughing and joking amongst themselves in freeze frame. In the background, the street was busy with foot traffic. Cars occupied almost every parking bay. Someone was in the solitary phone box. Two teenage girls squared up to each other outside Tigerlily.

Buxton tapped the screen. 'Shame it doesn't show the inside of the ladies' toilets downstairs in there.'

'Piss off.'

Smirking, Buxton nudged the dial forward. 'Here we go.'

Steven McCoull burst out of the pub, the image frozen with his left leg in front of him, hands in pockets, looking back down George Street towards the camera but lower, at street level.

Cullen leaned forward. 'What's he doing?'

'He's spotted someone, maybe?' Buxton nudged it forward again, McCoull darting across the street in ultra-slow motion. He stopped by the phone box, arms crossed.

'Bollocks.' Cullen put his head up to the screen, almost touching the glass, each pixel distinguishable until it was just a white noise pattern. 'Who the hell is he speaking to?'

Buxton sped it up to normal speed.

McCoull kept on talking, occasionally refolding his arms or stabbing a finger at someone. He took a few steps forward, almost disappearing off the left-hand edge, his companion still off screen. He shook his head then nodded before waving towards the camera.

A taxi pulled into the kerb and McCoull leaned down to speak to the driver.

Cullen checked his notebook. 'This is Billy Hogan, right?'

Buxton nodded just as he freeze framed it. 'Unless he's lying to us.'

'Don't start.' Cullen managed to get the license number off the front of the cab. He flicked through his notebook; it matched Hogan's number. 'Looks like it is him. Keep going.'

'Sure thing, boss.' Buxton sniffed before playing the film again.

McCoull held the back door open then scowled for a few seconds before getting in himself. The taxi drove off, executing a tight U-turn across the motorcycle parking space in the middle of the road.

'Bloody hell.' Cullen slumped back in the chair. 'So we don't see who gets in with him?'

Buxton sniffed. 'Yeah, pain in the arse.'

Cullen picked up the other DVDs from the packet. 'And these were all from other vantage points along George Street?'

'Yeah.'

'You've checked?'

'Of course I did. When you were getting a bollocking off the other half. No dice, mate.'

'So what the hell are we going to do?'

'No idea.'

Cullen stared at the screen, the throng on George Street milling around, the girls from earlier now separated by two bouncers. Who was McCoull speaking to?

Cullen scratched his scalp, hair in desperate need of a cut, and frowned. What if...? 'Rewind it.'

'To when McCoull leaves the boozer?'

'Before. Like ten minutes before.'

'Sure.' Buxton pulled the dial all the way to the left.

The figures on the screen started dancing backwards, the girls getting back into their fight then breaking off and going their separate ways. The clock went back to eight o'clock.

On screen, Cullen staggered out of the front of Tigerlily, shouting and pointing at the bouncer. Sharon tugged his arm and dragged him along the street.

Cullen grabbed Buxton's wrist. 'Stop it there.'

Buxton paused it, a grin on his face. 'This what passes for a sex tape in the Cullen-McNeill household is it?'

'Very funny.' Cullen leaned forward; the phone box was empty. 'Put it back to just after he gets in the taxi.'

'Right.' Buxton pushed the dial to the right, the figures going through their motions again. 'Here.'

'The phone box is empty now.' Cullen tapped the screen. 'Go back.'

Buxton looped it back, the girls at the squaring-up stage again, Cullen himself a few steps down George Street, turning back the way to stab a finger in the air at the bouncer, Sharon shaking her head. 'You look absolutely destroyed, mate.'

'Don't I know it.' Cullen took a deep breath. He looked like an animal, the sort he'd expect to pick up on the average Saturday night for any number of violent crimes. 'Roll it forward a bit.'

Buxton nudged it to the right. 'That enough for you, big boy?'

'Aye.' Cullen leaned forward. The door to the phone box was still shut. 'Keep playing it.'

The Cullen on the screen jerked forward in big increments. Just after Cullen passed the phone box, the door opened and a figure went inside, leaving it open.

'Back a bit.' Once the footage rolled back, Cullen stabbed at the screen. 'There.'

Buxton laughed. 'Wish we could do that 'enhance that region' shit.'

'Remind me to tell you about Bain thinking we could actually do that one day.' Cullen held up the photo to the figure on the screen. 'Richard Airth, we've got you.'

Buxton scowled at him. 'Come again?'

'Phonebox Jimmy is Richard Airth.'

18

'I've seen him twice in the last two days.' Cullen pulled onto Queen Street, trying to remember if the Castle Street entrance was blocked up or not. 'How come when I want to find him I don't see him?'

Buxton sighed. 'This is a total waste of time, mate.'

'We might find him this way.'

'I doubt it.'

'Come on. We've got half the uniform on today out searching. He's got to be somewhere.'

'So you think he's killed McCoull?'

'He's top of the list, aye.' Cullen pulled onto George Street, hanging a left past Tigerlily and the Living Room, the Christmas lights hanging above their heads, glinting in the low winter sun. 'Come on, come on, come on. Where are you?'

'We've talked about this. There aren't many payphones left.'

'There.' Cullen pulled in at the side of the road by a call box, the one in the CCTV. It was occupied. 'Come on.'

They jogged down the street, he and Buxton surrounding the door. A yellow puddle trickled out of the bottom. He hauled it open.

The occupant tucked himself away, eyes almost rolling back in his head. 'Excuse me, pal, have you got the time?'

Not Phonebox Jimmy. Cullen left him standing before trotting back to the car. 'Where can he be?'

Buxton smirked as he got in. 'Not fancy busting that guy?'

'It's not worth it.'

'Phone boxes, sinks, it's all the same to you, isn't it?'

'Drop it, cougar boy.' Cullen pulled out and drove along the quiet street, the chains of lights coiling around the Dome's Greek pillars, and onto St Andrew Square, the gardens now a field of glowing toadstools. He turned left, rejoining Queen Street, the northern sky darkening. He checked the clock on the dashboard. 14.07. He turned right onto the street, back towards the station.

Buxton sighed. 'Scott, where you heading now?'

'I've no idea, to be honest. Leith? I've seen him at the foot of the Walk a couple of times.'

'Going to try the docks while we're down there?'

'Maybe.'

'Now you're getting desperate. It's all empty yuppy flats now, mate. They definitely don't have phone boxes.'

'We can't just sit around doing nothing.' Cullen passed through the traffic lights at the end of York Place, heading to the roundabout by John Lewis. What about Juniper Green? 'Wait a minute.'

Buxton rolled his eyes. 'Oh, here we go.'

'We saw Phonebox Jimmy up at Juniper Green yesterday morning.'

'Yeah, you're right.'

'Think he could've gone back to his old house?'

19

'Where are you?' Cullen tightened his grip on the phone.

PC Johnny Stewart paused. 'Sorry, we're about ten minutes away.'

'Please hurry.' Cullen pocketed his phone and got out first, leading down Woodhall Millbrae towards the rebuilt house. Lights burned in the windows of half of the street, the remainder lying dark and empty. The vague waft of barbecuing hit Cullen's nose.

Buxton refastened his leather gloves. 'This is a bit of a gamble, mate.'

'You first.' Cullen followed him down the path to the front door, looking up at the building, half a tiled roof, the remainder just sheeting flapping in the breeze. 'How can—'

A light flickered on and off in the living room.

Cullen got out his baton. 'There's somebody in there.'

'You think?'

'I saw a light.' Cullen inspected the front door, the wood covered in plastic sheeting. He tried the handle. It opened. 'Let's go.'

He entered the building, dark as the sun started setting, the rooms marked out by bare partition wood awaiting plasterboard. A set of stairs led up to the first floor, the wood uncarpeted. 'What do you think?'

'You're leading here.'

Cullen nodded and headed through the gap in the wall, a future door. He looked around, long shadows cast across the concrete floor.

'What's this?' Buxton darted off into the room, bending down to pick something up. 'There's a letter here.'

'Give me that.' Cullen snatched it off him and inspected it. Inland Revenue letterhead. Dated in May 2003 and heavily weathered. It informed Richard Airth of a pending investigation into JG Financial Services.

He flipped it over and read, the page covered in a looping scrawl:

To whom it may concern —

I am deeply sorry that you have found me like this.

The alternative would be to jump in front of a train, but it's Christmas Day and there are no trains. Besides, I've never been a fan of that sort of thing, disrupting people's days like that.

I suspect you're probably a police officer.

If not, I'm deeply sorry for you finding me like this.

If you are, I wish you'd been able to bring Mr McCoull to justice for what he did.

*My life has been **hell**.*

All that kept me going is watching Steven McCoull struggle.

All that kept me going these last few weeks was the thought of killing him.

He murdered my family.

They built this place up in the stead of my family home. I will add a fourth ghost to its young shell.

Have a very miserable Christmas.

Regards,

Richard Airth

'Shite.' Cullen handed the letter back to Buxton. 'He's killed himself.'

Buxton took the letter back. 'Okay, so where's the body?'

The front door slammed shut behind them.

Buxton shot off through the house. 'Not so dead, is he?'

Cullen followed, bursting out onto the darkening street. He looked around. No sign of Airth. 'Where's he gone?'

'Give me a second.' Buxton held up his Airwave. 'This is Simon Buxton for Johnny Stewart.'

'Receiving.' Stewart sounded out of breath.

'We've lost the suspect. Are you here yet?'

'Aye. Just got here. We've spotted him, son. He's heading to the Water of Leith walkway.'

Cullen let out a sigh. 'Thank Christ for that.'

Buxton grinned. 'Where?'

'Heading into Edinburgh.'

Buxton pocketed the Airwave and set off, heading back up the hill. 'This way.'

'You sure?'

'Trust me.' Buxton cut right past a block of flats then took another right. The Water of Leith lay in front of them, Buxton vaulting down a set of steps to the walkway before sprinting to the left.

Cullen followed him along the path, the metal guardrail between them and the river. He ran harder but Buxton was outstripping him as he crossed the shadow the City Bypass cast. He caught a glimpse of torchlight ahead.

'Got you!' Under a street light, Buxton tripped and stumbled, rolling forward on the concrete. 'You bastard!'

A figure came out of the gloom towards Cullen, wearing black clothes and a dark grey parka, eyes darting back towards Buxton.

Cullen slowed to a halt and waited. He swept forward with his forearm, catching the man beneath the throat and slamming him to the ground. He sucked in deep breaths. Almost vomited from the smell. 'Jesus Christ.'

He reached around for his handcuffs, slapping them on his quarry's wrists. 'Richard Airth, I'm arresting you for the murder of Steven McCoull.'

20

'For the record, the suspect has declined the offer of legal counsel.' Cullen leaned back, trying to push himself further from Airth and the rancid stench emanating from his body. 'Additionally, Mr Airth has been cleared by the duty doctor as being fit to be interviewed.' His eyes watered as he held up the sheet of paper found in the house, now bagged and tagged. 'Mr Airth, can you confirm this is your handwriting?'

Phonebox Jimmy — Airth — kept on as he'd done all along, staring at the tabletop, his mouth silently twitching. His hair was matted into a thick shell hanging down his back. His beard hid his face, though acne and scars were visible underneath. A bald patch ran from his left ear to his mouth, a purple scratch in the middle. His eyes flicked up to make brief contact with Cullen's and he gave a slight nod.

'For the record, the suspect has confirmed the note is his.' Cullen set the note down on the table and rubbed his hands together, feeling dirty in his presence. 'Mr Airth, this note confesses to murdering Steven McCoull. Did you kill him?'

Another nod.

'Mr Airth, can you please confirm you killed him?'

A heavy sigh. 'Aye.' Airth's voice was brittle and hoarse. The few remaining teeth inside his mouth were black stumps.

'Why did you do it?'

'Ruining his life was the only thing I had left to live for. He ruined mine.'

'What do you mean by that?'

'I mean he killed my wife and children.' Airth shut his eyes briefly.

Cullen held up the sheet of paper. 'How did you intend to ruin his life?'

'For starters, I told him his wife was having an affair with his neighbour.'

'How did you find out?'

'I've been watching the house for a few years now.' Airth twitched his mouth. 'Seeing what he was up to. Keeping an eye on the lizard. I saw his wife with that neighbour of his whenever Steven left the house.'

'So you sent him a note?'

'It's the honest thing to do.' A dark smile formed on Airth's face, eyes still locked on the tabletop.

'That wasn't it, though, was it?'

'No. I sent a note to the Inland Revenue about him repeating his old tricks.'

'You mean tax avoidance?'

'Aye. Mr McCoull should've shredded the documentation while he still had the chance.'

'So you broke into his house?'

'Just the once.'

'What did you take?'

'Copies of his accounts. Some receipts. Didn't have to look too hard.'

'Why did you do it?'

'To see what I could find. That's all.' Airth snorted. 'When I saw him the other night, drinking with his mates, I just couldn't take it any more.'

'What did you do?'

'I stood outside that pub. People walked past me, you know, as if I wasn't there. I'm kind of used to it. It took him a while but Steven noticed me.'

'And he left the pub to speak to you?'

'Aye. Tried to buy me. Can you believe it?'

'What do you mean by buy you?'

'He offered me a few grand to piss off.'

'So what did you do?'

'I said I just wanted to talk.' Airth flicked his gaze up briefly, focusing on Cullen before looking at the table again. 'We got a cab back to his house.'

'Where you killed him?'

Airth nodded. 'Aye.' He bared his teeth, his tongue pale and wilted. 'You might think me barbaric to pull a man's teeth and nails out.' He held up his hands and grinned wide. 'You'll notice I've got none of those left myself after what I had to do.'

'What do you mean?'

'I had to run away. I couldn't take it any more. The only choice I had was to take to the streets. If the banks couldn't find me, Steven couldn't get the money; if he couldn't get the money, he couldn't save the business. That animal got us into the shit.'

'You mean the business?'

'Aye. I was the one trying to get us out of the mess.'

'How?'

'Speaking to banks, trying to extend our overdraft. You name it, I tried it. Anything to get us out of the mess he got us into.'

'What mess is that?'

'He'd invested heavily in a property deal in Glasgow which never happened. We lost two hundred grand just like that.' Airth clicked his fingers. 'Our clients were hammering on the door asking for their money back. Steven was promising to repay them. He never could, of course.' He sighed. 'Of course, I didn't know he was trying something different.'

'You mean setting fire to your house?'

'Aye.'

'Why did he do that?'

'Because my house wasn't security against the business. His was.'

'I don't follow.'

'It was reflected in how the shares were divvied up. Him and Evelyn owned seventy percent of the company. They took seventy per cent of the profit.'

Cullen frowned. 'Why wasn't your house secured?'

'My wife wasn't keen on it. So we just put his in, working capital to get us started. Steven's idea — it saved him tax.'

'And he wanted to secure your property against the business?'

'He did. My wife was against it. Said I should just walk away from the whole thing.' Airth slammed a fist against the desk. 'My mother was dying at the time. I didn't have time for that shit.'

'So what happened?'

'Steven wanted to free up some cash, claw the money back into the business.' Airth almost snarled, his mouth wide open. 'So he burnt my house down. Once the insurer paid out, he could grab the money and put it in the business. But the house wasn't empty, was it? He killed my family.' He prodded his chest. 'He killed *me*.'

'Did he discuss his plan with you beforehand?'

'No way.'

'What about after?'

'Aye.' Airth smudged the tear on his cheek, a line now cut out of the dirt. 'He confessed, told me what happened. Said it was all a mistake. He was deadly sorry.'

'Why didn't you go to the police about it?'

'I had no evidence. I had nothing. There was nothing I could do. My house burnt down. I'd lost my wife, my boys. I had to get away and make that bastard pay.'

~

METHVEN FROWNED as he leant against the meeting room's glass wall. 'So how did you find him?'

'We knew he used to live in this house.' Cullen shrugged. 'We saw a light on inside, so we went in. He must have been on the stairs, waiting for us.'

'Well, I just spoke to James Anderson.' Methven jangled his keys. 'He's got some of his SOCOs going around the place. Looks like Mr Airth has been living here for a wee while. Must've been waiting for the workmen to head home every night to sneak in.'

Buxton let out a sigh. 'That's no life, is it?'

'No. It's not.'

Cullen slumped back in his seat, exhausted. 'So, is he going down for it?'

'You've got a confession, Constable, I'd say so.'

'Good.'

Methven rubbed the gauze on his cheek, the material now

encrusted with dirt. 'Mrs McCoull's another matter, however. Lying in her statement...'

'Glad you can get her with something, sir.'

'I'm not one to be malicious, but she's not getting away with what she's done.' Methven grinned. 'On the other hand, I just spoke to Campbell McLintock. It turns out Mrs McCoull wasn't due to inherit her husband's estate after all. The entirety was to be donated to the rugby club.'

'You're serious?'

'Yes. Campbell was his personal lawyer. Strictly hush-hush, but if there was something there, we could have prosecuted her.'

Buxton got to his feet. 'Do you mind if I get off home?'

'Sure thing, Constable. You can get on with the paperwork tomorrow.'

'I'm not in till Friday, sir.'

'Then Friday.' Methven smiled. 'That's a fantastic result today, gentlemen.'

'Cheers.' Cullen got to his feet. 'I'll be in tomorrow, sir.'

'Just a second.' Methven tugged at his sleeve. 'Simon, I'll see you on Friday.'

What now? Cullen shut his eyes as Buxton left the room, seemingly taking his time. 'What is it you wanted to say, sir?'

'Just that you've done well today, Constable.' Methven spoke with his eyes shut. 'All my efforts in getting a sodding press release out have been in vain as you've managed to catch the culprit. I'm impressed.'

'Thanks.'

'I know it was just yourself and ADC Buxton, but you've done a decent job of leading this investigation.'

'So you'll make me Acting DS again?'

Methven shook his head, laughing. 'I can't give you a compliment without you asking for a promotion, can I?'

Cullen folded his arms. 'I thought that's what we'd discussed yesterday?'

'Constable, I'm in no position to offer an Acting DS position to anyone.'

'So Bain's getting a DS gig here then?'

Methven shook his head. 'This again?'

'Deny it.'

'I wish I could.' Methven sat down again. 'Have you done any thinking based on our discussion yesterday?'

Cullen stared at the ceiling. 'I'm going to cut back on the drinking. Probably cut it out entirely.'

'That's a brave decision.'

'Thank you, sir.'

'However, I'll believe it when I see it.'

'Oh, you'll see it all right.'

~

'JESUS, SCOTT, YOU LOOK LIKE SHIT.' Sharon held open the flat door, the smell of roasting chicken wafting out.

'I feel like shit.' Cullen nodded as he sat on the sofa, dumping his phone on the coffee table. Fluffy ducked for cover. 'I could do with a drink but I think I'll let it pass for now.'

'You've thought about it then?' Sharon sat next to him.

'I have. I'm being an idiot. I've been an idiot. It's time to stop.'

'You're being brave.'

Cullen glanced over. 'That's what Methven said.'

'You told him?'

'Trying to get on his good side, right?'

'I suppose that's for the best.' Sharon sighed. 'I'll keep your glass in the bottle then?'

'Aye.' Cullen put his feet up on the coffee table. 'I saw CCTV footage of you and me leaving Tigerlily the other night. I didn't like what I saw.'

'Oh.' She reached over and pecked him on the cheek. 'I know it's not easy but you've made the right decision.'

'I hope so.'

'How was work then?'

'Got there in the end. We arrested Phonebox Jimmy for it.'

'You're kidding?'

'Wish I was.' Cullen shook his head. 'It's really sad what happened to him. He lost his family in a dodgy house fire and took to the streets.'

'Oh my God.'

'All the time I'd seen him and I'd been such an insensitive dick about it. I never knew.'

'Nobody did.'

'That's no excuse. Poor guy. He must've been totally destroyed by the end. He was going to kill himself. I feel guilty for catching him now.'

'It's okay. It's not your problem now. You've solved a case.'

He put his arm round her, pulling her close. 'I've missed you today.'

'Me too.'

'Thanks for cooking the chicken.'

'You're not getting off. You're taking over now. Try to cook the tatties like your mum does.'

'It'll help me take my mind off this.'

'I told Mum we weren't going out to East Linton.'

'Thank God. I just want to be miserable here with you.'

PART II

WINDCHILL

DAY 1

Hogmanay

Tuesday
31st December

21

'Cock-a-doodle-doo!'

Pauline opened her eyes and blinked a few times. Checked her clock radio — 8.00. She turned over, the bed springs groaning. 'Keith!'

'Cock-a-doodle-doo!'

'Keith! Shut that thing up!'

'Cock-a-doodle-doo!'

She hammered on the wall separating their rooms. Scrunched up her feet, trying to squeeze the ice blocks out.

'Cock-a-doodle-doo!'

'Keith!' She tugged the duvet tighter, the double bed otherwise empty, the room freezing and spinning — Jaegermeister and Red Bull formed the bulk of the acrid taste in her mouth. Aniseed. Chemicals. She swallowed bile down.

'Cock-a-doodle-doo!'

Enough. 'Keith, I'm coming through there! This isn't funny!'

'Cock-a-doodle-doo!'

She clambered out of bed. Woah. She slumped down, sitting on the edge for a few seconds, head thumping, the cold sucking up from the floor through her socks.

'Cock-a-doodle-doo!'

Reaching over, she flicked on the bedside light, the weak bulb barely illuminating half the room. Took a deep breath. Got to her feet, managing it this time.

'Cock-a-doodle-doo!'

She tramped across the floor, the door squeaking as she opened it. The dim morning light crept down the hall floor through the patterned glass of the bathroom door, bouncing off the pale laminate flooring.

'Cock-a-doodle-doo!'

Supporting herself against the wall, she paced over to Keith's room, across the hall from the kitchen.

'Cock-a-doodle-doo!'

'Keith, can you shut that bloody thing up!' She knocked on the door.

'Cock-a-doodle-doo!'

Resting against the stripped wood door surround, she sighed. 'Keith, I'm going to come in there and smash it against the bloody wall!'

'Cock-a-doodle-doo!'

She pushed the bare wood above the handle. The door creaked open. The light was on.

'Cock-a-doodle-doo!'

Frowning, she pushed the door till it was fully open and stormed in, heading for the bedside table. Slammed the base of her hand on the snooze button.

'Cock-a-doo—'

Finally.

The bed was empty. She felt the duvet — cold, unslept in. It stank, needed changing. She looked around the walls at his posters, cursing every footballer and golfer beaming back at her, arms raised and fists pumping the air. Cheeky sod had gone out and pulled, leaving his alarm clock on.

'Cock-a-doodle-doo!'

Scowling at the thing, she sat on the edge of the bed and picked it up. How did it turn off? She fiddled with the settings. There. 8.05.

The light on the other bedside table was on. Leaning across the bed, she reached over to switch it off. She lay there. Comfy. Might just sleep here for a bit.

A shoe, lying at the edge of the bed.

She got up on all fours before creeping across the bed and peeking over the edge.

Keith lay on the floor. Knife hanging from his stomach. The rug stained red. Looking up at her, eyes dead.

22

'It's bloody freezing.' Cullen wrapped his wool coat tight around him as he walked down Polwarth Gardens, the Victorian tenements glowing in the morning sunshine, stopping by the SOCO van. 'The wind chill factor must be infinite in Edinburgh. Takes a lovely sunny day like this and makes it feel like we're at absolute bloody zero.'

'You need to chill out, mate.' Buxton rubbed his hand over the stubble on his head as he looked at the uniform guarding the stairwell entrance. 'Pardon the expression. Don't want to blow a gasket before you go on holiday tomorrow.'

'Exactly. Crystal shouldn't have sent me on a new case. A day of paperwork would've been fine. Maybe a training course. And I need to get some new swimming trunks after work.'

Buxton play-wretched, poking fingers at his mouth. 'Christ, mate, I'm close to losing my breakfast.'

'Come on, let's get inside.' Grinning, Cullen headed over to the dark red door wedged between the two flats, the canopy of the corner shop next door fully extended, and signed them in. 'Is DI Methven inside?'

The uniform managing the crime scene nodded. 'Top floor flat. Causing the usual havoc.'

'Got to love him.' Cullen pushed open the tenement door, the maroon paint reflecting the sunshine. 'Come on, Simon.'

'Yes, boss.' Buxton let the door slam shut behind them. 'You're not even my boss.'

Cullen smirked at him. 'You act like I am, though.'

'Must be your natural air of authority.' Buxton chuckled as they trudged up the stone steps, the central balustrade laden with chained-up bicycles.

The whole stairwell reeked of second-hand cigarette smoke even at that early hour, like it was permeating the sandstone. The voices from the top of the stairwell boomed, the sound bouncing off the walls and multiplying, Methven's loudest of all.

'You're still cutting out the booze tomorrow?' Buxton was waiting on the second-floor landing.

'I've not had a drop since Christmas Eve.'

'That's mighty impressive for you.'

'Feels like a *very* long time so far.'

'It's not like you're an alcoholic, mate.'

'Yeah, I'm merely a piss artist.' Cullen climbed the last flight and stopped at the top, more out of breath than he should be. 'Good morning, sir.'

Methven swung round. Next to him stood Jimmy Deeley, the city's pathologist, who tugged up his SOCO mask and tiptoed inside.

'Good morning, Constables.' Methven folded his arms, the material of the suit crinkling. 'Glad you could finally join us.'

Cullen leaned back against the banister. 'What've we got?'

Methven frowned. 'You're heavily out of breath, Constable.'

'You're telling me.' Cullen gulped air down. Should've done more running in the last week. 'What's happened?'

Methven closed his eyes as he spoke. 'One Keith Lyle was found stabbed this morning.'

'Have you got an exact time of death?'

'Jimmy?' Methven turned round, finding Deeley was gone. 'Sodding hell, where's he gone?'

Buxton smirked. 'Think he's back inside, sir.'

'I can sodding see that.' Methven shook his head. 'Deeley thinks the boy's been there a good while. Maybe even since nine o'clock last night.'

'Christ.' Cullen took a deep breath, the endorphins from the climb kicking in. 'Mind if we see the body?'

'Be my guest.' Methven gestured to the uniform managing the inner locum. 'Get yourselves suited up and signed in.'

Cullen reached down to pick up a SOCO suit, putting his feet down each of the baggy trouser legs before pulling them up to his waist. 'Any idea who killed him?'

'None. It appears Mr Lyle was stabbed through his t-shirt.' Methven tapped a finger down the outside of the opposing wrist and hand in a chopping motion. 'There are what look like defensive cuts on his wrists and the edge of his hand.'

'So, someone's really gone at him?'

Methven nodded. 'Indeed.'

Cullen put his arms into the sleeves of the suit. 'Anything else?'

'Anderson and his SOCO army are still scouring the place. They've got the murder weapon and they're pretty confident they can get some prints off it.'

'That'll be a turn up for the books.' Cullen zipped up the suit and signed them into the crime scene. 'Ready when you are, sir.'

Methven did up his face mask and entered the flat. 'Come on.'

Cullen followed him down the corridor, rustling as he walked, the laminate floor not quite blending with the stripped skirting and doors. Flashes of light from a SOCO camera pulsed off the light blue walls, seeming to come out of the first door on the left. 'So what happened here then?'

'Mr Lyle's body was found by his flatmate.' Methven stood outside the door. 'A Pauline Quigley.'

Cullen peered inside the room, packed with similarly-suited figures as they dusted, photographed and catalogued. At the far side of the floor, partially obscured by the bed and two SOCOs, was a pair of legs clad in stonewashed denim, monster-feet slippers at the end.

Cullen stepped into the room to get a better view of Keith Lyle, lying on the window side. A short, stubby knife hung out of his plain T-shirt, a pool of blood staining the material and the Persian rug. 'That'll be the murder weapon then?'

Methven nodded. 'According to Deeley's initial observation. For what that's worth.'

A SOCO hovering over the body looked at them, a holdall open at his feet. 'You know I can hear you, Colin.'

Methven snorted, his mask constricting around his features.

'Sorry, Dr Deeley. Didn't mean anything by it. Have you got anything else yet?'

Deeley held up the left hand. 'Well, I think he's a southpaw.'

'How can you tell that?'

Deeley held up the pinkie and ring finger, marked with blue. 'There are ink stains on his left hand. Lefties get these, they smudge the page as they write. Looks like Mr Lyle here likes to write. A lot.'

'What sort of thing are you talking about? A ledger at work?'

Deeley shrugged, the shoulders of his suit crumpling. 'No idea. That's your remit, Colin. I give you the science, you do the art.'

Methven grumbled behind his mask as he looked around the room. He scowled at a SOCO by the desk near the window, over-looking the street. 'Mr Anderson, have your lot found any writing paper?'

'Maybe.' The gruff voice was James Anderson, one of the senior Scenes of Crime Officers. He held up an evidence bag containing a Pukka Pad, the lime green of the cover dulled by the container. 'Found this.'

Methven stepped across the clear areas and snatched it from him. 'What is it?'

'Not had a chance to look at it yet. We'll process it back at the lab.' Anderson grabbed it back. 'You can get it later, okay?'

Cullen looked around. The walls were covered with sporting posters — the Ryder Cup, Chelsea FC, Scotland's rugby team from the early nineties and a wall chart of the 2014 World Cup fixture list. 'Boy liked his sport.'

'Indeed.' Methven took a step back into the corridor to let Buxton get a better view.

Cullen got out of the way of a SOCO laden with evidence bags. 'So, what's the deal with this flatmate then? Were they a couple?'

'We don't believe so.'

'But it was just the two of them living here?'

'Yes.' Methven pointed at the bedside table nearest them — a plastic cockerel displaying the time on his chest, a matching one lay on the other side. 'Mr Lyle's alarm clock woke her up. She went to switch it off and found the body.'

'I take it you want us to interview this flatmate?'

'If you could.' Methven started off down the corridor. 'She's at a friend's flat just down the road.'

～

CULLEN KNOCKED on the flat door, two up from Keith Lyle's flat, and waited, his breathing even harder. 'He makes my blood boil.'

Buxton rolled his eyes. 'What is it this time?'

'Constable this, constable that. Wanker.'

'He doesn't mean anyth—'

The door opened and a young woman peered out, squinting into the gloom of the stairwell. 'Can I help?'

'Police. The door downstairs was open.' Cullen flashed his warrant card. 'We need to speak to Pauline Quigley?'

'Oh, okay. Come on in.' She opened the door and held out her hand. 'Beth Armstrong.'

Cullen shook her hand. 'DC Cullen and ADC Buxton.'

'She's in the kitchen.' Beth led them inside. The hall walls were covered with old film posters — *Taxi Driver*, *Breakfast At Tiffany's*, *Annie Hall*. Two mud-caked mountain bikes obscured a radiator. She entered the room on the right, a bright kitchen with a view of the tenements running west down the street. 'Pauline, it's the police for you.'

Pauline looked up, her eyes red. She sat forward, leaning her athletic figure across the kitchen table, tugging her dark hair into a long ponytail. Baggy grey tracksuit bottoms and an orange t-shirt. Her wide jawline betrayed Czech or Russian ancestry, with a deep scar just to the left of her mouth.

Beth patted Pauline on the arm. 'I'll give you some peace.' She left the room, leaving the door open to the hall.

Pauline's bright blue eyes tracked her friend's movement, staying on the hallway when she was out of view. 'How can I help?'

Cullen motioned for Buxton to take the only spare chair before looking around for any more. Bugger it. He leaned against the fake granite counter and got out his notebook, his gaze darting around the room. Dirty dishes in the sink, cheap electric cooker, ancient kettle, the metal sides of the toaster dimpled in a couple of places. 'We understand you found Keith Lyle's body?'

'That's right.'

'Tell us what happened this morning.'

Pauline let out a deep breath, hands shaking. 'I was woken up at about eight o'clock. Keith's got this cock-a-doodle-doo alarm clock.' A long sniff, deep breath. 'Two of them as I found out. He was always late for work so I made him get one. I knocked on his door, telling him to shut the thing up. The door just opened. I went in and switched it off.'

'That's when you saw him?

'Aye. Keith was just lying there.' She rubbed her left eye, the knuckle probing the socket. 'I just wanted to get back to sleep.' She clenched her jaw. 'Did Keith die last night?'

'We think so.'

'My God.' She put a hand to her face, almost slapping it. 'So he was just lying there all night?'

'It's likely.' Cullen nodded slowly. 'Were you here all last night?'

'Not all night, no. I was working till ten.'

'Did you get back late?'

'Late-ish. Went for a bit of a dance in that Club Tropicana on Lothian Road with a couple of the girls. Beth and Gill. Got back here at half midnight, maybe.'

Cullen noted it down. His stomach recoiled. Club Tropicana — shooters, cocktails, hen parties and the hits of the eighties. 'So you were only there for a couple of hours?'

'Aye. You know how it is. We were tired but we needed to let our hair down. Gill knows one of the bouncers so we got in for free. Had some shots, did some dancing then I came home when the other two started chatting to some rugby boys.'

'Were there any signs of disturbance when you got in?'

'No. None at all. I mean, our flat's never the tidiest.'

'I see.' Cullen made a note of it. 'So there were definitely no signs of forced entry, nothing like that?'

'No.'

'You didn't hear or see anyone when you got back to the flat last night?'

'No. Nothing.'

'Did you check on Mr Lyle when you arrived?'

'I'm not in the habit of going to his room at night.' She shook her head, looking away. 'Besides, I would've found his body then, wouldn't I?'

'So, when was the last time you saw Mr Lyle?'

'Yesterday morning. Breakfast time. I was just getting up, he was just leaving. He was on the early shift, I was on late.'

'So you work together?'

'Aye. At the Debonair pub, just off Lothian Road.'

'I know it.' Cullen noted it — a pretty rum boozer in a rough part of central Edinburgh. 'Would Mr Lyle have gone out after work?'

'Doubt it. He finished at the back of six. Would've just come straight back here. He's never one for lingering and he doesn't really go out much. It looked like Keith'd had a microwave meal for his dinner then some beers.'

'And it's just the two of you in the flat?'

Pauline wrapped her fingers around the coffee cup in front of her. 'It is, aye.'

'And you're just friends?'

'Aye.' Her eyes blazed at him, the blue surrounded by red threads. 'We've known each other for years. We were both looking for a flat at the same time.' She shrugged, moisture welling in her eyes. 'It made sense.'

Cullen looked her up and down before scribbling in his notebook. Probably more than flatmates.

Pauline stared past them, gazing out of the picture window behind. 'We were supposed to go to Princes Street tonight for the Hogmanay thing.'

'Just the two of you?'

She shook her head. 'There's a group of us going. Got the tickets through the pub.'

'We've just been to the crime scene. That's quite a nice flat you've got.'

Her eyes narrowed. 'Are you implying something?'

'Well, it looks pretty expensive and you both work in a pub.'

Pauline shrugged. 'Tips are good.'

'Is that it?'

'Aye.'

Cullen scribbled in the notebook again. *Flat ownership?* 'How old was Mr Lyle?'

'Twenty-five. Same age as me.'

Cullen stood up. 'Do you have any idea who'd want to kill him?'

Her eyes shot around the room before settling on Buxton as he wrote a swathe of notes. 'There's nobody I can think of.'

'Nobody from the bar?'

'None. The staff all loved Keith.'

'What about the customers?'

She shrugged. 'It's not the sort of place that has regulars, you know? It's for people out on the lash. Pre-club drinks. Burgers, steaks, nachos, shooters. Tourists wanting a fry-up in the morning.'

'Was Mr Lyle involved with anyone?'

Pauline glanced away. 'Not that he told me.'

Cullen held her gaze till she looked away. 'What family does he have?'

'He's an only child. His mum died about ten years ago. It hit him really hard. He was still at school. He was off for about a month.'

'So you knew each other from school?'

'Aye.' She nodded, eyes blinking back tears. 'We went to Firhill High together.'

'Nobody from school he fell out with?'

She shook her head. 'He was one of those kids who got on well with the geeks and with the hard kids. Never fell out with anyone, really.'

'What about Mr Lyle's father?'

'He still lives up Oxgangs way. Name's Bobby Lyle.'

'Got an address?'

'Aye. Swanston Park. Number twenty, I think.'

'Thanks.' Cullen frowned as he spotted something in his notebook. 'Did Mr Lyle keep a journal, do you know?'

Pauline nodded slowly. 'He did, aye. Kept a log of all the things he was thinking about.'

'What sort of thing?'

'No idea, really. Never let me see it. He talked about it, how he wanted to become this writer.' She sighed, eyes moist with tears. 'He'll not get that chance now.'

'That's probably all for now.' Cullen handed her a card. 'Give me a call if anything comes up, okay?'

~

CULLEN PULLED in outside Bobby Lyle's house, the bulky seventies building reminding him of streets in his hometown — rows of square boxes, disfigured by extensions over the years. 'Think she did it?'

'What, killed Lyle?' Buxton rubbed his scalp for a few seconds. 'Could've done, I suppose. We've only got her word that she found him. Forensics might be our friends for once.'

'You might be right. The motive's tricky. That said, I do think she was at it with him.'

'Seriously?'

'Aye.' Cullen got out his phone and dialled a number, listening as it rang through to voicemail. 'Boy and a girl alone in a flat like that? Of course they were at it.'

'You do know I live with a bird, right?'

Cullen frowned. 'Just the two of you?'

'Yeah.'

'Oh, Simon, sounds like there's something going on there. She's not in her forties, is she?'

'Piss off.' Buxton scowled out of the car window at the house. 'You got hold of Methven yet?'

'Still not answering his phone. I'll text him.' Cullen typed out a text. *Heading to Lyle's father's house. Nothing to report yet.* He pocketed his phone and got out, having to manually lock the pool car's doors. 'Doesn't look like anyone's here. You up for giving a death message?'

'Aye, sure thing.' Buxton led them up the drive. 'Just be thankful we're not knocking on doors on that street, mate.'

'True.' Cullen followed him up the paving, a silver Citroën parked in front of a garage at the top. In front, a small expanse of lawn surrounded by evergreen bushes, still heavy with leaves.

Buxton knocked on the door at the side of the house, before taking a step back. 'He better be in.'

'He'll be in.' Cullen pointed at the car. 'Unless he's gone for a paper or a jog or something.'

The door pulled open a crack, puffy eyes surrounded by a red face peering out. 'Can I help you?'

'Police.' Buxton held up his warrant card. 'DC Simon Buxton and DC Scott Cullen. Are you Robert Lyle?'

'I am. Folks call me Bobby.' Lyle opened the door to its full width. He folded his skinny arms, perching them on his swollen belly which stretched his polo shirt. He reached up to smooth down his hair, clinging to the last few strands, three or four clumps tugged across the middle of the red dome. 'What's this about?'

'We need to have a word with you, sir.'

'What about?'

'It's concerning your son, Keith.'

Lyle rolled his eyes and sighed. 'What now?'

'It would be preferable to do this inside, sir.'

'Aye?' Frowning, Lyle gestured inside the house. He led them through a dark hallway, pastel green walls and beige carpet. A faint smell of mould mixed with charred bacon and fat, the drone of an extractor fan in a room to their left.

Lyle stopped by the staircase. Behind him, a wide sheet of obscured glass showed blurred shapes in the living room, at least a couple of lights on. 'In here, then.'

'Thanks.' Buxton perched on a dark brown sofa, the green corduroy on the arms and headrest now worn black in places.

Cullen sat next to Buxton, getting his stationery out as he assessed whether Lyle had been briefed. Didn't look like it.

Lyle slumped in a cream reclining chair. He glanced at them, then down at his lap. 'Right. What can I help you with?'

Buxton shifted forward, his Adam's apple bobbing up and down. 'Mr Lyle, the body of your son, Keith, was found this morning.'

Lyle briefly closed his eyes before giving a slight nod of the head. 'Oh, Christ.'

'Did you know?'

'No, son.' Lyle stared at the ceiling, fingers digging into the chair's arms, bunching up the leather. 'Tell me what happened to my boy.'

'Keith's flatmate, Pauline, found his body just after eight o'clock this morning.'

'Does she know who did it?'

'She doesn't, no.' Buxton shifted his weight back a few inches.

'We're investigating Keith's death as a murder.' A glance in Cullen's direction. 'A Family Liaison Officer will be appointed to make sure you're kept up to speed on the investigation.'

'Right, right.' Lyle sank back into the chair, his polo shirt riding up at the front, eyes screwed shut, his whole body rocking. He reached over to a side table and tore off a couple of man-size tissues, dabbing his eyes before blowing his nose. He glared at Buxton. 'Who do you think killed him?'

Buxton ran his tongue over his lips, his forehead creased. 'We're currently looking to establish a credible list of suspects. We wondered if you might be able to help us.'

'Okay.' Lyle sat up in his chair, cleaning the fingernails of his left hand with the thumbnail on the right. 'My boy was a good lad, you know? Never said boo to a goose.'

'So there's no-one he might've had a disagreement with?'

'Nobody really springs to mind. Sorry.'

'We understand Keith worked at the Debonair bar.'

'Aye, that's right. Nice little pub, so it is.'

'Do you know of any arguments with staff or customers there?'

'Not the customers, no.'

Cullen frowned. 'But the staff?'

'Not really, no.'

'But you're aware of something?'

'I might be.' Lyle gave a deep sigh. 'I used to pop in there to visit him from time to time. Like I say, my boy got on well with everybody in there.'

'But?'

'Well, there's maybe something, I suppose.' Lyle stared at the gas fire for a few seconds, the beige brick surround charred in a few places. 'Like myself, the lad liked a wee flutter. Started with football but he soon got onto the horses. Before long, he'd got into that spread betting nonsense. A mug's game.'

Cullen noted it down. A great way to totally do yourself over financially. 'What sort of spread betting are we talking? I don't imagine it's currency markets or the price of copper?'

'No, son. Football. Number of corners, number of yellow cards, difference in score, that sort of thing.'

Cullen drew another leaf on his mind map. 'Where did he bet? Online?'

'Aye. Did a few sites, I think.' Lyle frowned. 'He said he'd stopped that, though. That said, I think he went to a bookies on Dalkeith Road instead.'

'Which one?'

'YouBet, I think it's called.'

Cullen added it to the map. Vaguely knew the place, just down the road from St Leonard's. 'Was Keith in any debt?'

'He was a bit, aye.'

'How much are we talking?'

'About a grand, last I heard.'

Cullen scribbled it down, underlining it a few times. 'But Keith kept on gambling?'

'Tried to win his way out, didn't he? I tried to tell the laddie, but he wouldn't listen to me.'

'So he could owe more?'

'It's possible, aye.'

'Who did he owe this money to?'

'Boy called Dean Vardy.'

23

Cullen parked in front of a Co-op Pharmacy on Mayfield Road, stuck in the pit of a valley, a block of shops on its own amongst the villas and mansions of the Southside. 'This the place?'

'Think so.' Buxton looked up from his notebook before waving across the street at what looked like some allotments. 'According to Google maps, that's it over there.'

A white building sat in the middle, *Southside Cars* scrawled on the side in purple, the phone number in orange beneath.

'Think I called that lot last week.' Cullen frowned. 'They used to sell Christmas trees when I was a student.'

'Still do, mate. My flatmate was on at getting one from here.'

'You didn't want to, I trust?'

'Damn right.' Buxton shook his head. 'An artificial one's much better than all that pine needle shit. Can get it out again next year, too.'

'You and this flatmate sounds serious.'

'Piss off. We're just mates.'

'I believe you. Come on.' Cullen got out and locked the car, waiting for the traffic to clear before jogging across the wide road.

The section beside the building was paved over, a couple of silver Škodas sitting on the drive, sunlight bouncing off the bonnets. The wind tore at the tall trees in the wild area behind, pushing them almost horizontal.

'Bloody hell.' Cullen shut his eyes to stop grit getting in. 'This bloody wind.'

'Got to love Edinburgh.' Buxton eased past the taxis before marching over to the office.

A pair of French doors almost filled the front, a matte black panel adjacent displayed the opening hours.

Buxton scanned his finger down the list. 'Supposed to be open today. New Year's Eve must be the busiest day of the year for taxi firms, right?' He opened the door, before heading up to the counter, warrant card out. 'Police.'

A burly man sat behind the desk playing with a giant Windows phone, tattoos crawling over his arms and neck. 'What's this about?'

'We're looking for Dean Vardy.'

'That's me.' Vardy sniffed, eyes tracking between them. 'What've I done now?'

Cullen looked around, the four fruit machines flashing through their attract sequence making the place feel more like a bookies than a taxi firm. Behind the desk was a set of doors leading out into the green wilderness beyond. 'Need to ask you a few questions about a Keith Lyle.'

Vardy set his mobile down on the desk. 'Aye, I know Keith.'

'Know him how?'

Vardy shrugged as he got to his feet, folding his arms, disco muscles pushing his t-shirt sleeves up. 'Works for me in the Debonair.'

'The bar?'

'Aye.'

'You own it?'

'I do.' Vardy switched his gaze between them. 'Listen, boys, what's this about?'

'Mr Lyle's body was found this morning.'

Vardy held Cullen's gaze for a few seconds. 'This on the level?'

'Aye.' Cullen nodded. 'You wouldn't know anything about it, would you?'

Vardy pushed himself back off the counter, propelling himself towards the doors at the back of the room. He fumbled with the lock then shot through, slamming the door behind him.

'Bloody hell!' Cullen scrabbled about, trying to find a latch in the counter. Failing.

'Go round the front!' Buxton vaulted over, following Vardy out.

Cullen complied, heading back the way they'd come. As he emerged into the daylight, he saw Vardy tugging the handle of the furthest away Škoda.

'Stop!' He raced towards him, catching him with a shoulder barge and sending him flying against the car.

'You prick!' Vardy was kneeling by the car, clutching his shoulder. He got to his feet, swinging with his good arm.

Cullen took a step back, the blow missing his head but catching his raised shoulder. He stumbled backwards, collapsing onto the bonnet of the other car.

Vardy sprinted onto the pavement lining the main road.

Cullen followed, his breath almost a distant memory. He sucked in a lungful. 'Get back here!'

Vardy weaved into the next unit, wild with weeds and puddles of mud, then running across a strip of cobbles and onto the patch of earth beyond.

'Stop!' Buxton jumped off the stone wall separating the lots, almost landing on Vardy.

Vardy lashed out with a leg, smacking Buxton in the middle of the chest and knocking him to the ground. 'Get away from me!' He raced on, tracing the line of the wall, before coming to a row of wooden sticks set out in a loose fence, just as Cullen gained on him.

Cullen snapped out his baton, holding it ready behind his head. 'Stop it, now!'

Vardy darted to the side, avoiding Cullen's swing. He kicked out at the posts, flattening a couple of them, before jumping into the scrubland beyond.

Cullen set off after him but he was no match for Vardy's speed.

Buxton soon caught up. 'Where's he gone?'

Cullen waved his baton in the direction of the rail tracks to their left. 'He went onto the line just there.'

Buxton set off down the hill. 'The mad bastard can't have, can he?'

'Oh, he can.'

Buxton propped himself against a birch by the side of the tracks. 'Do you know what line this is?'

'South suburban, I think.'

'Is it electric?'

'Don't think so.'

'Fine.' Buxton sprinted off, dust flying up from the ballast beneath the rails. 'Stop!'

Vardy was running across the tracks, making for residential gardens backing onto the railway.

Cullen heard the distant rumble of rolling stock. 'Shite, there's a train coming!'

As Buxton cleared the last of the four rails, he dived full length, catching Vardy with a rugby tackle, forearms locking around his knees.

Cullen ran across the tracks, eyes flicking between the two bodies rolling into the grass bank beyond and the oncoming goods train as it crawled round the bend.

Vardy lashed out, left hook connecting with Buxton's chin.

Cullen swung with his baton, smacking Vardy square on the back. He hit him again, clattering his head just as the goods trains trundled by, a long procession of shipping units covered in graffiti, the coach belching out diesel fumes.

Kneeling down, Cullen clicked the cuffs round Vardy's wrists.

≈

CULLEN RUBBED HIS SHOULDER, wincing as he touched the rapidly forming bruise, looking down the long corridor, the interview room still not yet occupied. 'You all right?'

'I'll live.' Buxton delicately stroked his nose, eyes closed, sucking in breath. 'Caught me good and proper, though. You?'

'I'll be fine. Nice few bruises for the beach.' Cullen smirked before narrowing his eyes at the interview room door. 'Why the hell was Vardy running?'

'Usually implies guilt.' Buxton stretched his shoulders back. 'Boy who owes him a wad of cash turns up dead, we confront him, he scarpers. Two plus two, mate.'

'Maybe.'

'What do you mean maybe?'

'I'm just not so sure. When we told him in that little cabin, it was like he didn't know Lyle was dead.'

Buxton leaned back against the door. 'You think he's *not* done Lyle in?'

'Maybe.' Cullen shrugged. 'Still, he'll get a fine for trespassing on the railway.'

'Yeah. I'll get him for clocking me one, too.'

Cullen looked up and down the corridor. 'Wonder where Methven's got to.'

'Post mortem?'

'Too soon, surely?'

'Just be glad he's not up your trouser leg, mate.'

'Yeah, there's that. I'm supposed to be his little Boy Scout at the moment. Don't want some other twat getting promoted.'

'Such a princess.'

'Will you qui—'

The fire doors next to them flew open, the desk sergeant accompanying a tall man in a pinstripe suit. 'That's him there.'

The suited man nodded. 'Thanks.' He smiled at Buxton. 'DC Cullen?'

Cullen offered a hand. 'That's me.'

'Neil Parker of Nelson and Parker.' He gripped the hand firmly, eyes taking them both in. 'I'm representing Dean Vardy.'

Cullen got a good look at Parker. He was a few inches taller than both of them, though with neither's bulk, his pinstriped suit and white shirt hanging off bony shoulders. 'I know the name of your firm from somewhere.'

Parker nodded. 'My partner, Michael Nelson, represented Evelyn McCoull.'

'That's where it is.' Cullen exhaled. Thank God that one's off our plates now. 'We're ready to start.'

'Do you mind if I have a minute with my client first?'

'We do, actually.' Cullen pushed open the door. 'He's lucky to get a lawyer after what he's just done.'

'I trust you're joking.' Parker barged past him, sharp elbows knocking into Cullen's arm. He sat alongside Vardy, now sporting a shiner, before taking great care to unpack a few items from a leather document pouch. 'I suggest we get down to formalities.'

Cullen sat opposite, leaning forward to speak into the recorder. 'Interview commenced at twelve thirty-six p.m. on Tuesday the thirty-first of December 2013. Present are myself, Detective Constable Scott Cullen, and Acting Detective Constable Simon Buxton. The suspect, Dean Vardy, is present, along with his lawyer, Neil Parker.'

He took a breath before continuing. 'Mr Vardy, for the record, can you please state your occupation?'

Vardy smirked. 'I'm a businessman.'

'And what's the nature of your business?'

'I'm an entrepreneur.'

'What kind of entrepreneur?'

'Got a few irons in a few fires.' Vardy shrugged. 'I run a taxi firm for starters. Southside Cars on Mayfield Road.'

'Which is where we apprehended you?'

'Which is where you *assaulted* me.'

'What other irons have you got?'

'I own a bookmakers on Dalkeith Road. Place called YouBet. Get a lot of coppers in there, I can tell you.'

'Anything else?'

'A pub. The Debonair. It's on Bread Street. In Edinburgh.'

Cullen ground his teeth. 'Do you own anything else?'

'Got a few flats.'

'Anything in Polwarth Gardens?'

'Maybe.'

Cullen made a few scribbles in his notebook. 'Now that's out of the way, can I just ask why you decided to run when we visited your premises?'

'I thought you'd try to fit me up.'

'What for?'

Vardy sat back, staring at the ceiling. 'For killing Keith Lyle.'

Cullen held his gaze. 'Well, did you kill him?'

Vardy broke the stare-out. 'No way did I kill him.'

Parker reached across to cover Vardy's clenched fist. 'My client has stressed the fact he didn't kill Mr Lyle. Please leave it at that.'

Cullen stared at him for a few seconds before switching his focus back to Vardy. 'How did you find out Mr Lyle was dead?'

'You told me when you arrived at my premises.'

'Not before?'

'Nope.'

'Please describe your relationship with Mr Lyle.'

'He's a good lad. Solid worker.'

'So, just an employer-employee relationship?'

'Of course.' Vardy sniffed. 'I trust him enough to share a flat with my bird.'

'Pauline Quigley's your girlfriend?' Cullen sighed as he closed his eyes. Methven would have his balls for missing that.

'She is, aye. They both work for me at the Debonair.'

'And they stay in one of your flats?'

'Maybe.'

Cullen flicked back a few pages, underlining his previous note on flat ownership. 'Must be very frustrating for you.'

'What must?'

'Your employee having sex with your girlfriend in a property you own.'

Vardy stabbed his finger at Cullen. 'They weren't having sex, pal. Okay?'

'That's a bit of an extreme reaction.'

'That's extreme bullshit from you.' Vardy ground his chair backwards as he got to his feet, gripping the tabletop. 'Complete bollocks!'

Cullen looked at Parker. 'Can you please get your client to sit down?'

Parker smiled at Vardy. 'Dean, if you'd please comply with the officer's instructions.'

Vardy sighed as he plonked himself down again. 'Aye, fine.'

'You're sure Mr Lyle and Ms Quigley weren't romantically involved?'

'Fucking right I'm sure. No danger were they at it.'

'What would you do if there was something going on?'

'I'd ditch the bitch.' Vardy shrugged. 'I'm a businessman. I've learnt when it's advisable to sever ties.'

'Do you mean murder her?'

'No I fucking don't.'

Parker held up a hand. 'Constable, please. You've asked enough. All you're succeeding in doing is angering my client. This is all after assaulting him for no good reason.'

'Running when we ask a few questions seems particularly

strange.' Cullen folded his arms. 'Besides, it seems like there's something in what I'm suggesting.'

'Unless you've got proof of a romantic entanglement then please desist from this line of questioning.'

'We'll come back to it later.' Cullen licked his lips. 'Do you manage the shifts at the pub?'

'Hardly. I pay a bar manager for that privilege.'

'And yet you were working at your taxi company today?'

'Usual girl called in sick. Night boy doesn't start till seven.'

'How close were you to Mr Lyle?'

'You've asked that.'

'I'm asking again.'

Vardy shrugged. 'What's that supposed to mean? How close were we? We didn't exactly go for cocktails in the Dome.'

'I meant, were you friends with him?'

'Like I told you, buster, Keith was an employee.'

'Do you let all of your employees get heavily into your debt?'

'What's that supposed to mean?'

'We understand Mr Lyle owed you a sum of money in relation to gambling.'

Vardy shot a glare at Cullen. 'Who told you that?'

Cullen smiled. 'You're not denying it?'

Vardy glanced over at Parker, who tilted his head to the side. He stared at Cullen, teeth bared. 'Aye, Keith was in debt to me.'

'How did this happen?'

'Keith was a bit of a silly boy up at my shop on Dalkeith Road. He put a few big bets on the football and the golf. The lad was chasing a debt. Got himself in the hole to the tune of a grand.'

'How did he get there in the first place?'

Vardy's tongue brushed across his teeth. 'Thought he'd sussed out a gap in the odds my lad was offering. Reckoned he could make a mint on the number of corners in certain football matches. Put a hefty bet on and he lost. Big style.'

'This was the grand he lost?'

'Aye.'

'How was he chasing it?'

'Bigger bets. Lost eight grand in one Sunday. I'll give you an example — silly bugger had a spread on a Chelsea match, reckoned they'd get beat by Southampton. Now, you or I, we'd put a straight bet on. Odds were like elevens or twelves — this was at Stamford Bridge, mind. Not Keith, though. Silly bugger put a spread on the margin of victory in Southampton's favour, a grand a goal. Ended up with a minus three swing. Three grand from one result.'

'And this is all legally binding?'

'Of course it is. I've got a boy up there does contracts as well as odds. Happy for you to speak to him, if you want.'

'We'll pass for now.' Cullen noted it down anyway. 'How did you feel about this magnitude of debt?'

'I wasn't best pleased, was I? I knew Keith didn't have that sort of dosh just sitting around in the flat.'

'So what did you do?'

'We came to an arrangement.'

'The sort of arrangement that involves concrete shoes and a trip off the Forth Road Bridge?'

Vardy smirked. 'I'm more of a Kingston Bridge kind of guy.'

Cullen rolled his eyes. 'Can I remind you of the magnitude of the investigation here?'

'Aye. Sorry.' Vardy cleared his nose, left finger covering a nostril. 'I let Keith pay the debt off slowly, you know? Took a small sum out of his pay packet every week, so long as he kept away from gambling.'

'Did you threaten Mr Lyle regarding the debt?'

'No way.'

Cullen frowned — complete bollocks. 'Mr Vardy, what were your movements last night between six p.m. and midnight?'

Vardy looked at Parker, his eyes contracting a few times before he faced Cullen again. 'I was out drinking.'

'Where?'

'I was in Teuchter's on William Street. That's in Edinburgh, Scotland, UK, Europe, Planet Earth, the fucking Solar System.'

'Very cute. Who were you with?'

'A good buddy of mine, Darren Keogh.' Vardy leaned over to the recorder. 'That's K-E-O-G-H, pronounced Kee-Oh.'

'Thanks.' Cullen flicked back a page and added it to his time-line. 'When did you arrive?'

'I think we met up about half six.'

'And before that?'

'I was in the shop on Mayfield Road till about five then I went down to the Debs. Had a burger with my girl, just before her shift started.'

'And what time did you finish up?'

Vardy grinned. 'No idea, mate. It was late. Closing time, probably.'

'Why didn't you go to your own pub?'

Vardy sniffed. 'I don't like to shit where I eat.'

'Okay, so what was the nature of the meeting?'

'Just two mates meeting for some beer. That isn't a crime, is it?'

'We'll see.' Cullen folded his arms. 'What did you do after?'

'I went home. That's Viewforth. Bruntsfield. Edinbu—'

'Okay, I get it.' Cullen rubbed the back of his neck. Walking distance from town, maybe ten minutes from Polwarth Gardens. 'And you just walked straight home, did you?'

'Well, I stopped for some chips. Can't remember where. Sorry.' Vardy grinned at his lawyer. 'Slipped my mind, Neil. I paid cash if that helps. Chips, cheese and coleslaw, I think. And a can of Dr Pepper.'

'We will check, you know.' Cullen leaned over to the recorder, eyes on his watch. 'Interview terminated at twelve thirty-nine.'

24

Cullen looked around Chesser House's reception area. Why had so many people waited until the last day of the year to do their business? Whatever that was. 'What do you think they do here?'

'No idea, mate.' Buxton stayed focused on his mobile.

'I've been here before. We met some guy out in the car park on Gorgie Road.'

'So why are we inside?'

'That was August, this is December.'

'Good point.' Buxton looked up. 'What's keeping him?'

'You think he's done a runner?'

'Maybe. Wouldn't be the first one today.'

'Bugger this.' Cullen stood and walked over to the reception desk, clicking his fingers to get the attention of the receptionist. 'How much longer's he going to be?'

'I've tried calling Mr Keogh a couple of times now.' The receptionist tossed her hair back, holding it in position. 'He said he's on his way.'

'Can you give him another call, please?'

'Okay. Take a seat.'

'Cheers.' Cullen went back to sit down next to Buxton, thinking about hitting something. 'You got hold of Methven yet?'

'Nope.'

'Right, I'll try again.' Cullen got out his phone and found Methven's contact entry.

'Sorry to keep you, officers.' A middle-aged man stood in front of them, smiling. Brown tank top, pink and navy striped shirt-sleeves underneath. Black trousers and brown brogues. Holding out his hand. 'Darren Keogh, please to meet you.'

'DC Scott Cullen.' Cullen got to his feet and shook the hand, Keogh's grip weak and clammy. This guy went drinking with Vardy? Looked fifteen to twenty years older. 'Thanks for seeing us, Mr Keogh.'

'Not a problem.' Keogh smiled at them, unsure who to concentrate on. 'I've managed to get a meeting room.'

Cullen waved a hand. 'After you.'

Keogh led them through a door, glancing at the receptionist, too focused on her magazine to care. He headed down a long corridor, glass windows on either side, an open-plan office at the end. He stopped halfway down and knocked on a door. No reaction. He nudged it open and cleared his throat. 'Excuse me. I've got this room booked.'

A fat, bald man in a suit stood and got straight in Keogh's face. 'No, you don't, pal. We've got it booked all afternoon.'

'Must be some mistake.' Keogh reached into his pocket for a sheet of paper, unfolding it and holding it out. 'I just printed this booking sheet off the system.'

The man took a look at it before sighing. 'Right.' He gave a waving motion with his arms. 'Come on, this boy thinks he's got it booked.'

Keogh's head twitched a couple of times. 'Thanks. Sorry to have to do this.'

Cullen raised his eyebrows at Buxton, who averted his gaze and coughed into his hand.

They followed Keogh inside, letting him sit at the far end, trapping him in the corner.

'Thanks for seeing us, Mr Keogh.' Cullen got out his notebook, writing a few notes to delay starting. 'We understand you were with Dean Vardy last night.'

'Dean Vardy?' Keogh creased his forehead. 'Dean?' Keogh coughed. 'Yes. Yes, of course I was.'

'Are you sure?'

'Yes. Sorry, been a bit busy today what with closing everything off before the holiday. Got a bit of a thick head, too. And I didn't expect the police to come visiting and—'

'So you were with Mr Vardy?'

Keogh took a deep breath. 'We were in Teuchter's on William Street.'

Cullen ground his teeth — an easy conviction was getting away. 'Between what times?'

'I got there about six but Dean didn't show up till half past, I think.'

'And when did you leave?'

'Last orders, I believe. I can't quite remember.'

'Half one? Ten?'

'Be nearer eleven, I think. Sorry.'

Cullen leaned back in the chair. 'If you don't mind me saying, you don't seem to be the sort to mix with Dean Vardy.'

Keogh shrugged. 'We're mates from back in the day, you know?'

'No. I don't. How old are you, Mr Keogh?'

'I'm forty-six.'

'And how old's Mr Vardy?'

'I don't know.'

'I'll tell you, shall I?' Cullen made a steeple with his fingers. 'He's twenty-eight. When did you used to hang out together?'

Keogh looked away. 'I don't remember.'

'You're eighteen years older than him, Mr Keogh. It's not like you were at school or university together.'

'Look, I used to go out with his auntie. Years ago. Lovely girl. I bumped into Dean a few years later and started going for a beer with him every couple of months, to catch up. He's a good lad.'

'And that's it?'

'It's the truth.'

'So, what you're saying is you're pretty much his uncle?'

'In a way, aye. I mean, me and his auntie didn't last very long, but Dean and I got on quite well.'

'Does the name Keith Lyle mean anything to you?'

'Doesn't ring any bells.'

'You're sure of that?'

'Of course I am. Never heard of him.'

Cullen took a long look at Keogh; lines around his eyes, hair streaked with grey, red blotches on his cheeks, beads of sweat dripping from his forehead. 'What did you do after you left?'

'Got the twenty-six bus home. I live in Corstorphine.'

'Did Mr Vardy mention what he was going to do?'

'He'd said something about chips.'

'I see.' Cullen got to his feet, business card in hand. 'Thanks for your time.'

~

CULLEN HADN'T EXPECTED a queue in the pub at the back of two. 'This is a load of bollocks.'

Buxton shrugged. 'It's New Year's Eve, mate.'

'Hogmanay.'

'Whatever. It gets busy early doors, doesn't it?' Buxton folded his arms as he leaned against the exposed stone wall splitting the two main areas. 'You can get your warrant card out and barge to the front, if you want?'

'I'll leave it for now.' Cullen held up his mobile and searched for Darren Keogh. Found his Schoolbook page at the top of the list. He clicked through — the page was mostly empty, like he barely used it. Keogh's profile photo was a few years old, his hair darker than now, his face the sort of confused scowl you'd see on a passport photo. Cullen selected it, saved it and showed his mobile to Buxton. 'Dodgy photo of the day.'

Buxton looked up from his own mobile and grinned. 'People in glass houses, mate.'

'Yeah, I need to change mine.' Cullen pocketed his phone and flicked through his notebook, trying to figure out where the case was going.

Vardy had to have killed Lyle, surely. The debt, running away from them, Lyle most probably sleeping with his girlfriend — it all added up.

Unlike the alibi. Keogh and Vardy just didn't seem like they belonged in the same city, let alone each other's company.

He took a step forward as a wiry man carried three pints in triangle formation away from the bar, and glanced at Buxton. 'Reckon the alibi's a lie?'

'I think so.' Buxton nodded. 'Chalk and cheese, them pair.'

'Agreed.' Cullen pocketed his notebook, retrieving his mobile. He searched through his missed calls — still nothing from Methven.

'What can I get you?'

'Police.' Cullen smiled at the barman as he produced his warrant card. 'DC Scott Cullen and ADC Simon Buxton.'

The barman's eyes darted between them. 'How can I help?'

Cullen rested his hands on the bar top, drinking in the smell of fresh beer and frying meat. 'What's your name?'

'Dave Weir.'

'Like the footballer?'

'Like it. He's David, I'm Dave.'

'Well, Mr Weir, we're validating an alibi for last night. Someone reckons they were drinking in here.'

'Oh aye?'

'Were you on?'

'Aye, I was. Till closing time. Just after eleven.'

'From what time?'

'Noon.'

'Do you know Dean Vardy?'

Weir shut his eyes for a few seconds, letting out a deep breath. He draped the bar towel on his shoulder. 'I know Dean, aye.'

'Did you see him here last night?'

'He was in.'

Cullen showed him the photo of Darren Keogh. 'Was he with this guy?'

Weir took a few seconds to examine the photo. 'Could be.'

'Could be or was?'

'Think it was him. Ninety percent sure, like.'

Cullen still didn't believe it. 'Okay. When did they arrive?'

'Be about seven. Maybe half six. Can't remember, really. That one on your phone was hovering about for a bit, though.' Weir leaned in close, resting on a beer tap. 'Look, pal, what's this about?'

'Mr Vardy's a suspect in a murder.'

'Jesus Christ.' The barman looked down at the bar top and started fiddling with a tub of wasabi peas. 'Who's he supposed to have killed?'

'You know a Keith Lyle?'

Weir shook his head without looking up. 'Sorry, mate.'

'Where were they sitting?'

Weir gestured behind them, directing Cullen's gaze into the seating area through the archway. 'They were through the back. On the sofas, you know? Dean and his mate were facing through here. I was just collecting glasses and dropping off pints for them.'

Cullen frowned. 'Didn't know you did table service?'

'We don't.'

'But you did for Mr Vardy?'

'Oh aye.'

'What were they drinking?'

'Brewdog Punk IPA. Same every round.'

Cullen noted it — Brewdog was an edgy brand Vardy would associate with, but Keogh? He pinned him as a Deuchars IPA kind of guy, weaker and more traditional. 'What time did they leave?'

'Closing time.'

'What, five past eleven?'

'Nearer quarter past.'

'No argy-bargy?'

'None.'

'Have you got CCTV in here?'

'Sorry, pal. We don't.'

'That the truth? I can check, you know.'

Weir made eye contact again. 'It's the truth.'

Cullen took a deep breath, looking around the busy pub, racking his brain for questions. 'Thanks for your time.' He handed the barman a card. 'Give me a call if anything comes up.'

Weir held it up. 'Will do.'

Cullen led Buxton out, walking down William Street to the pool car, pairs of shoppers pointing the windows of the boutiques, smokers laughing outside the other two pubs. 'This is getting worse.'

'Tell me about it.' Buxton tugged his coat tighter. 'Keogh and Vardy definitely being there blows him as a suspect, right?'

'Possibly.' Cullen opened his door and rested against it. 'There were three empty bottles in Lyle's kitchen, weren't there?'

'So? They could've gone back there for a nightcap. It's sort of on Vardy's way home.'

'Not on Keogh's.' Cullen glanced back at the pub, the wiry man from earlier lighting up a cigarette, shielding it from the wind, red ash flicking off the end. 'Neither Keogh nor Vardy gave us a precise time for when they left.'

'Weir did, though.'

'Quarter past eleven.' Cullen stared up at the low sun, the sky around it a frosted blue. 'Pauline Quigley reckons she got home about half past midnight, right?'

'Yeah.'

'Is that enough time to do it?'

'Go on the pretence of a nightcap, as I say. Drink the beer then slot him. Plenty of time, mate. Plenty of time.'

'What about the chips Vardy got?'

'Probably bollocks.'

'I think you're right.' Cullen weighed it up in his mind as he got in the car, the timeline crystalising.

Buxton got in and tugged his seat belt on. 'What's next then?'

Cullen held up his phone — nothing from Methven. 'In lieu of any guidance from a higher power, I'm thinking we should go and see Pauline again.'

~

CULLEN GOT out of the car on Polwarth Gardens and sighed. His phone rang. Methven. 'Afternoon, sir.'

'Christ, Constable, are you in a wind tunnel?'

'It's called Edinburgh, sir.'

Methven paused. 'Have you seen DS McNeill today?'

Crossing the street, Cullen frowned as he watched traffic hurtling through the roundabout system at the end. 'Not seen her all day, sir.'

'Very well. Let her know I'm looking for her.'

'If I see her.'

'Indeed. Where are you, Constable?'

'Just checking an alibi, sir.'

'Right, well, I've just been in with Superintendent Turnbull. Can you get yourselves back here promptly? I want to get my arms around this case.'

'Will do, sir. Be about half an hour.' Cullen ended the call, eyes locked on Buxton as he pocketed the phone. 'Sounds like Crystal's gone twelve rounds of bullshit chess with Turnbull.'

'What did he want?'

'Telling us to get back. He's reducing me to a messaging service as well.' Cullen looked up at the flats — a window of Beth Armstrong's open a crack. Two down, Pauline Quigley and Keith Lyle's flat still had curtains drawn, a lone uniformed officer guarding the doorway. Cullen looked at Buxton, finger ramming the intercom button. 'Any joy yet?'

'None.' Buxton hammered it again.

The intercom blasted static. Heavy breathing. 'Hello?'

Cullen frowned. Not Beth — Pauline.

Buxton leaned into the microphone. 'Ms Quigley, it's ADC Simon Buxton. We spoke this morning.'

'Aye, I remember.' A pause, five seconds or so. 'Come on up.'

The door sounded and Buxton pushed through. 'I'll race you.'

'Be my guest, especially if you want to deal with me having a heart attack halfway up.'

Buxton took two steps at a time, leaving Cullen to meander up the spiral stairs, blinking away the smell of burnt toast.

Pauline stood at the top, hands on hips. 'When do I get back into my own flat?'

'Nothing to do with us, I'm afraid.' Buxton shrugged as he stopped at the landing, waiting for Cullen. 'I'll chase them up when I get back to the station, if you want?'

'Please.' Pauline showed them inside, leading them back to the kitchen. 'Beth's gone out to get something to eat.'

Buxton sat across the kitchen table from her, leaving Cullen standing, struggling for breath. 'How are you managing?'

'How do you think? Shite.'

Cullen nodded. 'I understand this is hard. We can arrange for a Family Liaison Officer to—'

'Forget it. I don't need babysitting, all right?' She scowled, eyes narrowed until blue was the only colour. 'Have you lot found who killed Keith then?'

Cullen got out his notebook, breathing almost under control. 'Maybe.'

'What's that supposed to mean?'

'It means we need to ask you a few supplementary questions.'

'Be my guest.'

Cullen made a show of flicking through his notebook, his eyes skipping over the pages. He stopped at a page entirely unrelated to the case, slowly scanning down with his finger and stopping halfway. 'Do you know Dean Vardy?'

Pauline pulled her chin back, averting her gaze. 'Aye.'

'In what context?'

'We work for him at the Debs. Me and Keith.'

'Sure it's just that?'

Pauline tensed her eyebrows. 'Aye.'

'You don't rent your flat off him or anything?'

Pauline huffed. 'Aye, well, Dean owns our flat. We've been staying here about a year.'

Cullen flicked to a new page and noted it down — snared Vardy at last. 'You wouldn't happen to be romantically involved with Mr Vardy, would you?'

Her eyes shot daggers at him. 'Who told you that?'

Cullen shrugged. 'Mr Vardy himself.'

'Right.' Pauline fiddled with the scrunchie holding up her hair. 'Aye, Dean's my boyfriend. What of it?'

'Why didn't you mention him earlier?'

Pauline bit a fingernail. 'You didn't seem interested.'

'Oh, really? Why wouldn't we be interested in a guy Keith borrowed money from?'

She frowned. 'Borrowed money?'

'Ten grand.'

Pauline swallowed, her eyes shut. 'Shite.'

'Did you know about this?'

She shook her head, her eyebrows raised. 'No way.'

Cullen didn't know whether to believe her or not. 'Our understanding is this loan was to cover a gambling debt.'

'Keith liked to gamble. Football mainly.'

'We asked if you knew of anyone who'd want to harm Mr Lyle.' Cullen sucked in air through his teeth. 'Feels very much like something's being kept from us. Withholding information from a police investigation is pretty serious, you know, especially a murder inquiry like this.'

Pauline looked to Buxton for support, he remained focused on his notebook. She turned back to Cullen. 'Look, I swear I didn't know anything about Keith owing Dean money.'

'That's the truth?'

'It is, aye.'

'And you weren't sleeping with Mr Lyle?'

'No!'

'And Mr Vardy didn't suspect that you were?'

Pauline leaned back and let out a deep sigh. 'He didn't mention anything to me.'

'I'm finding this very hard to believe.' Cullen nodded at Buxton. 'What about you?'

'Seems to fit the facts.' Buxton shrugged. 'I believe Ms Quigley here.'

'Not sure I do.' Cullen shut his notebook and took a few steps forward, trying to intimidate her. 'When you got back to your flat last night, was it possible Mr Lyle had guests?'

'What do you mean, guests?'

'I mean having people in for a drink. We believe he might've gone to the pub after work last night.'

She shook her head. 'No. I told you. He was just coming straight back here, like he always does.'

'He didn't, say, meet up with Dean Vardy?'

She scowled, her nostrils flaring. 'They didn't have that sort of friendship.'

'Okay.' Cullen pocketed his notebook. 'That's all for now.'

25

Methven switched his attention to Buxton. 'What do you think, Constable? You've been very quiet.'

'I agree with Scott.' Buxton shrugged, light from the flickering strip light in the corridor bouncing off his shaved head. 'This Vardy geezer seems proper dodgy.'

'Why?'

'Well, he's got two possible motives we can think of to kill Lyle.'

'Which are?'

'First, we think Lyle was at it with his flatmate, Pauline Quigley.'

'Oh, good heavens. Okay, I can see that's a motive.' Methven focused on the whiteboard. 'Why would Vardy rent a flat he owns to his girlfriend and her old schoolmate, a young man?'

Buxton gnawed his bottom lip. 'No idea, sir.'

'Cullen?'

'Maybe Vardy reckoned Lyle wasn't a threat? They were old mates, deep into the friend zone.'

'So he just lets this man move in on his territory?'

'Seen it happen before.' Cullen shrugged.

Buxton snorted. 'Here's another thing, why would a guy who owns a taxi firm and a pub be out drinking with a guy who works for the city council?'

Methven shut his eyes and took a deep breath. 'Please explain.'

Buxton leaned back in his chair. 'Well, this Keogh boy's a bit square, if you know what I mean. You should see the geezer. He's *nothing* like Vardy. Tank top, almost fifty, like somebody's dad.'

'And Vardy's some sort of wide boy, I take it?'

'Yeah. Bulging biceps and pecs like a footballer, posh t-shirts, the whole shebang.' Buxton raised his mobile. 'I checked out this Keogh's record. Clean as a bell, sir. I just don't get why he's associating with a dodgy geezer like Vardy.'

'Have you checked Vardy out?'

'I did, yeah. He spent a year at a young offender's about ten years back.'

'What for?'

'Assault. Tore the other guy's ears off. Scott and I were lucky he didn't do the same to us when we apprehended him this morning.'

'So he's got previous?'

'Yeah. Nothing since, mind. Well, nothing bad enough to put him away, certainly. A rape got taken to trial. Couple of years ago, he got picked up with not quite enough dope to do him.'

Methven frowned. 'So why's he acquainted with this Keogh character?'

'Precisely.' Buxton pocketed his phone. 'Another thing, he clearly sees himself as some sort of godfather figure, right?'

'How do you mean, Constable?'

'Well, he's setting up this empire, isn't he? Typical criminal going legit — taxi firm, bookies, pub, flats.'

'But we don't know it's from dodgy money.'

'Right. It's got to be, though. Boy from that sort of background doesn't just get given a wad of cash to go starting businesses, does he?'

'I suppose not.'

Cullen joined Methven at the whiteboard. 'Plus, he's only twenty-eight and yet he's got three separate businesses.'

'You're suggesting the National Crime Agency might have something on him? SOCA, as was.'

'Worth a check, sir.' Cullen nodded. 'If we don't get him for this, I doubt it's the last time our paths will cross.'

'Quite.' Methven noted *NCA?* on the whiteboard before raising his eyebrows in Buxton's direction. 'What was the other motive, Constable?'

'As Scott said earlier, Lyle owed this Vardy geezer big style. Ten large.'

'You sound like an East End mobster, Constable!' Methven bellowed with laughter as he slapped Buxton's shoulder. He smiled at him for a few seconds. 'Those are two strong motives. I think he's probably our only viable suspect.'

'Only suspect full stop.' Buxton took a step back, eyes locked on Methven's hands. 'We've spoken to a few people and nobody can come up with anything else.'

'What about this flatmate, Pauline Quigley? Could she have done it?'

'Doesnt't have a motive, sir.'

'Well, we think Lyle was 'shagging' her, as you so eloquently put it earlier.' Methven rubbed his chin. 'Could he have threatened to tell Vardy about it?'

Cullen nodded. 'That's not a bad suggestion, sir.'

'I know.' Methven scribbled on the whiteboard — *Affair = motive?* — before wheeling round to face Cullen. 'I assume you pair went to speak to her again?'

'How did you guess?'

'I know you, Constable. Besides, you've been off the leash a long time. I'd be disappointed if you didn't chase after a few squirrels and rabbits.'

Cullen grinned. 'Aye, we spoke to her.'

'So? How did it go?'

'We just confirmed a few things.'

'Is it worth bringing her in for formal questioning?'

'Not sure what it would give us, sir.'

'Okay.' Methven noted her name down, adding *Suspect?* alongside.

'How are we getting on with the post mortem, sir?'

Methven glowered at Cullen. 'Sodding nowhere.'

'I thought that's where you'd been all day.'

'Sadly not. I've had meetings with Superintendent Turnbull on some other matters.'

'Which are?'

'Which are nothing to do with you, Constable.'

'When's the PM likely to happen?'

'Deeley's hopeful of finding time tomorrow.'

'Bloody hell.' Cullen rubbed at his neck. 'We're not getting a result today, are we?'

'No. With the holiday, the forensics will take even longer to process, I'm afraid.'

Cullen collapsed into a seat. 'Right.'

'Is there anything else we're missing?' Methven narrowed his eyes. 'What about CCTV or phone traces?'

'There's no CCTV in the bar.'

'There is on the streets. I assume at least one of Messrs Keogh and Vardy possessed a mobile phone?'

'Maybe.'

'Can I get you to check on that, Constable?'

'Fine.' Buxton rolled his eyes as he wrote it down.

'We've got a window of forty-five minutes where Vardy could've killed Lyle.' Cullen shrugged. 'Only problem is Vardy reckons he went to a chip shop on the way home.'

Methven hovered the pen over the whiteboard, waiting to write something down. 'Which one?'

'See, that's the thing.' Cullen rubbed his knuckles against the short stubble on his chin. 'He can't remember.'

'Sodding hell.' Methven rubbed at his eyebrows. 'Have you been to every single chip shop on Lothian Road yet?'

'Well, no.'

'Get someone up there!'

Buxton clenched his jaw. 'Sure thing, sir.'

'And I want CCTV of all likely routes home. And get onto the taxi firms, see if Mr Vardy was picked up in the vicinity of William Street.'

'Sure.' Buxton got to his feet and hurried out of the meeting room.

Methven watched him through the glass window as he trotted down the corridor. 'He's a rough diamond, isn't he?'

'I think he's good.'

'Well, you're doing a halfway decent job of polishing his rough edges off, Cullen.'

'Really?'

'I think so. We'll have to look at making his tenure permanent, assuming we can find the head count from somewhere.'

Cullen slumped back in a chair. 'This is going down the toilet, sir. I'm sorry.'

'Why do you say that?'

'Well, I'd hoped to close this off before going on holiday.'

'No need to beat yourself up. We've got a few leads. Once I get my full team back on Thursday, we'll hopefully make some inroads. I'm relatively philosophical about this.' Methven collapsed into a chair. 'We'll get there. You've done well getting to this sort of state so quickly.'

Cullen leaned forward in the chair, arms hugging his torso. 'I don't think we're anywhere, sir.'

'Well, it feels fairly healthy. I may shout and bawl a lot but I can recognise how well we're doing.'

'Cheers.'

Methven scratched the back of his head. 'Tell me your working hypothesis.'

Cullen thought it through for a few seconds. 'Vardy's got a window of opportunity between leaving the pub and Pauline Quigley returning to the flat.' He shrugged. 'Chips or no chips, Vardy gets a taxi, heads up there, gets inside, kills him, then heads home. It's not far — Polwarth Gardens to Viewforth is about five minutes' walk.'

'How do you explain the microwave ready meal and the empty beer bottles?'

'The bottles... Vardy and Keogh could've gone there for a nightcap with Lyle. The SOCOs might find something on them.'

'Or they might not.'

Cullen sniffed. 'The other thing is Pauline Quigley could be lying, sir. She might be complicit in this.'

'Feels like we're onto something here, Constable.' Methven got to his feet and paced back to the whiteboard. 'I'm not quite buying this Vardy's story.'

'Is there anything else can we do?'

'We've got a lot of investigation we can do. While you're on holiday.'

'Right.'

'You can go home now.'

'But it's half three.'

'Don't make me change my mind. You've been on nine days

straight, Constable. You've done a great job so far. You deserve your break.'

Cullen stood up. 'Thanks, sir.'

∼

'WHAT DID METHVEN WANT?' Cullen pushed open the door, stepping out into the lane at the back of the station, dark in the late afternoon winter gloom, the bitter cold hitting them.

'Methven?' Sharon pulled on her gloves.

'Aye, Crystal asked if I'd seen you.'

'Right.'

Cullen tucked his scarf into his jacket, the way he knew Sharon liked it, as he turned the corner onto MacDonald Road. 'Was it about Bain?'

She frowned as they started up Leith Walk. 'What makes you say that?'

'Well, he's been hanging around the last couple of weeks. And there are all those rumours as well.'

'Right.'

'That's all I get? Another 'right'?'

'I don't know anything about those rumours, Scott.'

Cullen pressed the button at the crossing for the side street. 'It's going to be a nightmare getting home, isn't it?'

'How do you mean?'

Cullen crossed the road, eyes on the long row of idling cars on Leith Walk. 'The street party. It's blocked off at Leith Street and North Bridge, I think.'

'Shit. It is.' Sharon quickened the pace as they headed up Leith Walk. 'What do you want to do about it?'

'Don't know.' Cullen smirked. 'Never got round to getting those budgie smugglers.'

'You could at least wait until Buxton's here before you make a joke like that.'

'Good one.' Cullen looked away. 'What time's the flight tomorrow?'

'Half six.' She glanced at him. 'Scott, tell me you've finished your packing.'

'That's the problem with you getting me that 3DS.'

'Scott, we're flying tomorrow morning!'

'I just need to get some budgie smugglers. That's it.'

'Can't you just wear those shorts you wore last year?'

'You don't like me in trunks?'

Sharon giggled. 'I don't like anyone in trunks.'

'Even Daniel Craig?'

'With that face? No way.' She walked past a hi-fi shop set back from the road. 'John Lewis will still be open.'

'Fine. Let's go there.'

She sighed. 'One more day then we'll be away from the pissing rain and the bloody wind, lying on the beach.'

'You're in a great mood.'

'Yeah, wonder why. I need a tan.' She stopped by Gayfield Square, the grass in the park sodden with rain. 'I had a meeting with Turnbull.'

'So did Crystal. What about?'

Sharon exhaled, her breath misting in the air. 'He's moving me to the Rape Unit in Bathgate.'

'Same grade?'

'It's an Acting DI gig.'

'Seriously?'

Sharon smiled. 'That's how he sold it to me. Good experience and everything.'

Cullen grinned. 'He'd have had me at Acting DI.'

'I told him I didn't want to go.'

'What?'

'He's forcing my hand, Scott. Apparently, I'm pissing Bill Lamb off.'

'Really?' Cullen frowned. 'Bill doesn't seem the type to be so petty.'

'That's what Jim told me.' She prodded a finger on the crossing. 'It was, like, 'I mean it, Sharon, this is your big break'.' She shook her head, looking around the busy street. 'Patronising git.'

Cullen nodded, but he didn't make eye contact with her. 'I don't think he really means you were pissing him off, though. Bill got the job you went for in March, remember?'

'Mm.'

'Are you going to take it?'

'I've got no choice.'

Cullen felt his mouth go dry. 'You're serious?'

Sharon shrugged. 'Aye. No option.'

'Congratulations.' Cullen wrapped his arms around her, kissing her on the forehead. 'This is brilliant.'

'Maybe.'

'There's no maybe. This is great for you.' Cullen felt a sting in his guts. 'Who's getting your job?'

'He didn't mention it.'

'Shite.' Cullen rubbed the back of his neck. 'You're sure it's not Bain?'

'No idea.'

'Well, Bain was really cagey when I asked him what he was doing here last week.'

'That's his way.'

'I suppose.' Cullen walked up the street, thinking it through. 'I don't want to work for that idiot again.'

'That's all rumour, remember?'

'Maybe.' He grabbed her hand, swinging it in the air. 'Moving on will be good for you, I think.'

'Seriously?' She was frowning.

'Of course. You've not been happy working for Lamb and I can't see you working for Methven or Davenport.'

Sharon smirked. 'It's made me think about having a baby.'

Cullen coughed and spluttered. 'Really?'

She reached across and held his hand. 'Relax, I'm joking.'

'Right.' He let out a deep breath, pain stabbing his guts. *Becky.* He held his eyes shut for a few seconds before wiping the tear away. 'Had me going for a bit there.'

'Sorry. I shouldn't have done that.' She closed her eyes. 'It was in bad taste.'

'It's okay.' Cullen rubbed the back of his hand against his cheek, trying to get all of the moisture away. 'It still hurts.'

Sharon put her arms around him. 'Come on, let's get your budgie smugglers.'

DAY 2

Thursday
8th January

(Eight days later)

26

'Sure you don't want to come up?' Cullen released his seat belt, letting it ride up, looking across the dark car park. 'For old time's sake?'

Sharon shook her head. 'At this rate, I'll not get any reading done before I meet my new DCI.'

'I'll miss you.'

'Me too. When do you think you'll be home tonight?'

'Early, I hope.' Cullen shrugged. 'Can't be arsed being in here till all hours first day back after holiday.'

'I'll believe it when I see it.'

He chuckled. 'I had a great time.'

'Aye, me too.' Her smile quickly lost its lustre. 'The holiday glow will be gone by lunchtime no doubt.'

'I know.' Cullen opened the door before leaning over to kiss her. 'Love you.' He got out and watched the orange Focus trundle across the underground car park, wishing he was still lying on a beach with his 3DS. He stabbed a reminder into his phone to head along Rose Street and get some more games.

'Morning, Constable.' Methven clapped his shoulder as he walked past.

Cullen pocketed his phone, grimacing as he caught up with the DI. 'Morning, sir.'

'I've actually sodding missed you.' Methven held out his hand. 'Good holiday?'

Cullen shook it. 'The best.'

Methven opened the door to the stairwell and stopped. 'Well, you'll be straight back into it today, that's for certain. I'm giving you DS McNeill's caseload.'

Cullen scowled. 'But I'm just a DC.'

'And you keep on insisting you're at Sergeant level. Prove it to me.' Methven checked his watch before he started up the stairs. 'Come on, we've got a catch-up briefing. DCI Cargill's instituted an eight o'clock meeting with the DIs every sodding morning, hence me needing an update first.'

'Great.' Cullen held the stair door open. 'Nothing big's happened, though, right?'

'Not really. I've lost DS Rarity to DI Lamb for the time being.' Methven paused outside the meeting room, looking Cullen up and down. 'Relax, I've got DC Jain as a replacement.'

Cullen followed him inside. Set up to do a DS role without the money. He nodded at Jain, wondering if the same carrot was being dangled. 'Morning all.'

Buxton sat at the head of the table, fiddling with his phone. 'Good day to you, sir.'

Angela Caldwell sat next to him, shifting uneasily on her seat, a pile of papers in front of her. She smirked. 'Nice tan.'

Cullen put a hand to his face. 'I'll be back to my usual shade of pink any time soon, don't worry.'

Methven clapped his hands together. 'Come on, let's get this over with.'

'Right.' Cullen sat down, reaching into his suit pocket for his notebook and pen. He caught a whiff from the material — he needed to get to the dry cleaners and swap it for the other one.

Methven stood by the whiteboard, not much more populated than just over a week ago. 'Let's recap the Keith Lyle case for DC Cullen's benefit, shall we?'

Cullen shrugged. 'Suits me.'

Methven pointed at *PM*. 'Deeley completed the post mortem last week.' He clicked his fingers at Angela. 'Pass Cullen a copy, would you?'

Angela tossed him a report up from the pile. 'Bit of bedtime reading for you, Scott.'

'I'll have no trouble sleeping now.' Cullen flicked through the report, before focusing on the executive summary at the front. 'So it's pretty much the same as we had last Tuesday morning?'

'Indeed. Angle of entry. Cuts through his jersey. Yadda yadda yadda. All point to murder. Deeley's able to prove the defensive cuts on the wrists were made by the knife in his abdomen.' Methven held up a photo of a ferocious knife, curved metal blade and smooth wooden handle, and pinned it to the board. 'The knife in question being a ShivWorks Disciple.'

Cullen pointed at the photo. 'That's not something you just pick up in B&Q, is it?'

'Quite.'

'Any prints on it?'

'Just the victim's.' Methven swallowed. 'Mr Anderson detected traces of nitrile on the shaft, which would indicate our killer used gloves.'

'So why are the victim's prints on it?'

'We believe he owned the weapon. Hoist by his own petard, if you will.' Methven held up a hand again. 'Okay, moving on. The SOCOs downstairs also obtained prints in the room for Mr Lyle along with those of Pauline Quigley and Dean Vardy.'

'So why would Vardy use gloves to kill him if his prints were there?'

'DC Jain and I spoke to him about this on Tuesday.' Methven tapped *Vardy* on the board. 'He admitted to owning the property and collects the rent in cash from a radiator in Mr Lyle's room. It's all done through the books, though.'

'And you believe him?'

'We're acknowledging it for the moment, shall we say.'

'What about the beer bottles?'

Methven tapped on *Lager*. 'All three were drunk by Lyle, according to the DNA in the saliva. Additionally, his blood toxicology showed what we'd expect for three bottles of beer given the time of death.'

Cullen nodded slowly, eyes narrowed. 'So Vardy got a cab round there before killing him, right?'

'And therein lies the rub.' Methven stabbed a finger at *Chip*

Shop. 'He did buy chips from a kebab shop near to the Debonair. Place called *D'Monte's*.'

'And you believe him?'

'You know how many takeaways there are on Lothian Road or just off it?' Buxton rolled his eyes. 'Thirty-eight. I know because I visited them all on New Year's Eve. Vardy went to the bloody last one.'

'What time?'

'Half past.'

Cullen totted it up in his head. 'Still fits the timeframe for him killing Lyle. Assuming Pauline Quigley's telling the truth.'

'Agreed, but there's one small problem.' Methven leaned across the table, his ID badge dangling from its lanyard. 'We can't find any taxi firm that picked him up.'

'So he walked?'

'It takes twenty minutes to walk from *D'Monte's* to Mr Lyle's flat.'

'How long to run?'

Methven snorted. 'We've had street teams out speaking to residents and shops on the likely routes — nobody was spotted running on the evening of the thirtieth. It's a busy area as you well know.'

Cullen glanced at Buxton. 'You were going to look into phones and CCTV, weren't you?'

Buxton nodded. 'Yeah. Cheers for that. Got nowhere with either. No CCTV cameras outside the kebab shop and Vardy conveniently left his mobile at the Debonair.'

'Did you check Pauline's statement?'

'In Club Tropicana? Yeah, I did. Chantal and I. It checked out.'

Methven sat on a chair. 'We don't currently believe Dean Vardy killed Keith Lyle.'

Cullen flicked back through his notebook. 'What about the NCA?'

Methven inhaled deeply. 'Mr Vardy's known to them. They've never been able to pin anything on him however, even going back to their SOCA days.'

'He's Al Capone, isn't he?' Cullen scratched at the back of his head. 'So, what? We're just dropping it?'

'That's correct.' Methven nodded, his eyes shut. 'I'm not prosecuting Mr Vardy yet because he has an alibi. We've already spoken to him again. The NCA aren't comfortable with us harassing him.'

'Even though he might've killed someone?'

'Correct.'

'I take it he's being prosecuted for trespassing on the railway?'

'Our colleagues in the British Transport Police are leading on the matter. You pair are in the clear for it, though expect a court appearance soon.'

'Cheers.' Cullen sighed. Need to get notebooks synchronised. 'Did you dig into how much debt he was in?'

Buxton nodded. 'Yeah. Just over ten grand. Spoke to the actuary at YouBet, the geezer who does all the odds and that. He showed me Lyle's account. Every bet was signed for.'

Cullen focused on the whiteboard. 'Okay, so what do we do next?'

Methven jangled his keys in his pocket. 'The Kenny Falconer case.'

'*Him?*'

'Indeed. Mr Falconer's selling knives again, illegally. This is one of the cases your better half was working on before she was sent out to West Lothian. They had an informant on his operation. A man called Andrew Smith.'

'So?'

'The trail's long since gone cold, Constable.' Methven stopped jangling. 'I want you to pick it up for me.'

27

C ullen let the seat belt ride up, looking west along Fountainbridge towards Fountain Park and the tenements beyond. 'Can't believe he's dumping Sharon's caseload on me.'

Buxton killed the engine. 'You keep bitching and moaning about how you're doing a DS job. He's calling your bluff, mate.'

'Didn't tell me the briefing timing had changed, either. I was just lucky Sharon was dropping me off early.' Cullen got out of the car, tall black hoardings blocking out the empty site of the old brewery to the left. He blinked away the early morning sun. Smith's address was a tenement just ahead, almost the only old building left on the strip. 'Used to be a sauna here, right?'

'Frequent it, did you?'

'Hardly.' Cullen smirked as they walked over, pausing to press the intercom. 'Had to do a raid on it once with Bain.'

'Which reminds me.' Buxton held up his mobile. 'Got a text from a mate in Glasgow MIT last week. He reckons Bain's heading back through here as a DS.'

Cullen felt his mouth go dry. 'Really?'

'Aye.' Buxton's tongue hovered between his open lips as he winked. 'Brilliant, eh?'

Oh for Christ's sake. Cullen loosened his shirt as sweat trickled down his back. 'If it's not a load of shit, I'll no doubt end up working for him again.'

'That'll bugger up any chances of me getting a full DC gig, won't it?'

Cullen held up his phone. 'Think I should call him and find out?'

'You want to put up with him going on about saving your life, be my guest.'

'Good point.' Cullen pressed the buzzer again. 'Anything else I've missed?'

'Well, Turnbull's been through in Glasgow and at Tulliallan a few times.'

'Bloody hell. What does that mean?'

'No idea. Getting his conkers toasted by the looks of things.'

Cullen sighed. Being shat on here — Methven dumping the extra caseload on him while the dangled carrot was swinging away.

Shielding his eyes from the low sun, he looked up at the flat, the top left of the block of nine apartments. There were no lights on inside, no stream of central heating exhaust, no signs of life at all. 'Where the hell is he?'

'Methven reckoned he's gone to ground, didn't he?'

'You've been here before, right?'

'Yeah. Came here with Chantal last Thursday.'

'Did you get in?'

'Nope.'

'I meant inside the house.'

'Piss off.'

'Right, come on.' Smirking, Cullen tried the stair door. It opened. 'I seem to have a magic touch.'

'You're like that Genesis song.'

'Wasn't that an invisible touch?'

'Whatever.' Buxton took out a pair of gloves, stretching them before slipping them on. 'You'd better get some gloves on to cover your magic touch if you're thinking what I'm thinking.'

Cullen laughed as they entered the building, pitch dark except for a light at the back giving an intermittent flicker. He started up the staircase, spotting a ceiling window at the top. The place stank of too much washing powder. 'It's like someone's shoved a whole packet of Persil in.'

'I know, it's totally rank, mate.'

Cullen stopped at Smith's stairwell, three doors leading off. On the right, a Post-It stuck to the door read *Flat 9 — A. Smith*. He rapped on the wood, the sound rattling down the staircase. He waited a few seconds then turned to Buxton. 'What do you think?'

'We've not got a warrant.'

'True.' Cullen knocked on the door in the middle. No answer. He tried the door on the left. Nothing.

A bolt released behind the middle door. It opened a crack, an eye surrounded by lined skin peering out. 'Hello?'

Cullen showed his warrant card. 'Police. We're looking for Andrew Smith.'

The door opened wider. An old lady checked them out, seventies at the youngest, five foot at most. She screwed up her eyes at the warrant card. 'Aye, I've not seen young Andrew for a wee while.'

'How long's a wee while?'

'Couple of weeks, maybe.'

'Do you know him well?'

'He looks after my cats when I'm away to my sister's. I water his plants when he's away.'

'Has he asked you to water them recently?'

'Not for a few months, no. When he went to Ibiza in September.'

Cullen glanced at Buxton, wondering if he was thinking the same thing — Smith had bolted.

'Why do you want to speak to young Andrew?'

'We need to ask a few questions about an important investigation. Do you have a key for the flat?'

'Just a second.' The door slammed shut.

Cullen glared at Buxton. 'Didn't think to try the neighbours the other day?'

'Of course we did, you cheeky sod.' Buxton shook his head. 'No response. Must be your natural charm and elegance.'

'Or my magic touch.' Cullen thumbed at the door. 'Thought she'd be more in your target age range.'

Buxton stared up at the ceiling. 'Christ's sake, mate. I put up with this Budgie shit from you for ages and now I've got to listen to this cougar shi—'

The door opened again. The woman held out a set of keys. 'Here you are, son. Drop them off when you're done.'

'Will do.'

The door slammed again.

Cullen sighed. 'Charming.' He headed to Smith's door, putting on a pair of gloves before twisting the key in the lock. 'Here goes.'

He pushed open the door and entered the flat. Red carpet, lime green walls, white woodwork. His nostrils twitched. 'Something doesn't smell good in here.'

'Agreed. I hope he's just left a pint of milk on the counter.' Buxton strolled down the hall. 'Mr Smith?' He waited a few seconds before trying the first door on the left. A bathroom. Empty.

The door opposite was slightly ajar. Cullen nudged it open with his foot. A bedroom — the bed messy, clothes heaped up in a pile on a chair. 'Looks clear.'

Buxton led down the hall, taking it slow, opening the final door — a living room cum kitchen. Laminate floor, IKEA sofa and chairs. Wooden kitchen units, dirty pots and pans.

The grey rug in the middle of the kitchen had a white trainer on it, obscured by the island.

Cullen leapt forward. A man lay on the floor, legs at crooked angles, hands cupped around the handle of the knife sticking from his guts. Blood caked on his tracksuit bottoms and t-shirt.

Cullen rested on the island. 'Shite.'

28

Cullen looked out of the window, the white SOCO suit creasing with the motion. Below, Methven got out of his Volvo SUV and looked up at the flat, making eye contact. He turned to Buxton. 'Here comes trouble.'

Buxton joined him at the window. 'Great.'

Cullen looked back across the room, the SOCOs already taking great care in their work.

Clad in a suit, Deeley stood over the body.

Andrew Smith lay on the linoleum, the pool of blood now congealed and dried in places. The knife jutting out of his stomach looked very similar to the picture Methven had stuck on the board. ShivWorks something or other.

Deeley shook his head and wandered over. 'Well, the boy's certainly dead.'

'Even I can see that.' Cullen grinned. 'When do you think?'

'Looks like he's been there a while. A week or so. Maybe longer. Won't know until I get the lad back to the lab.'

'I take it stabbing's the cause of death?'

'Most definitely.' Deeley looked around the room. 'Where's Colin?'

'Right here.' Methven stood in the doorway, eyes on the body, a SOCO suit already on, eyebrows revealing his identity. 'This does not look good.'

Cullen nodded. 'Agreed.'

'It's definitely Smith?'

'Aye.' Cullen pointed at the sideboard. 'We found his wallet. The face matches the driver's license, give or take a few pints of blood.'

'Cut the sodding humour, Constable.'

'Sorry.' Cullen led over. 'You see this?' He knelt down by the body and pointed to an envelope just to the side, pinned down by a numbered tag. 'It says *Ken Fa* and then cuts off.'

Methven stared at it. 'You mean he's trying to tell us who killed him?'

Cullen shrugged. 'Only logical explanation.'

'I trust you've got an APB out on him?'

'Aye.' Cullen let out a deep breath. 'I've dealt with Falconer a couple of times before. One thing about him is he's very good at keeping away from us. He almost stabbed my partner a couple of years ago, if you recall.'

'We need to bear that in mind.' Methven tugged a SOCO's sleeve. 'Mr Anderson, I need an update.'

'Morning, Colin.' Anderson slowly stood to his full height, stretching his back out. 'These suits are supposed to disguise us from you lot.'

'Cut the banter, please. I need an update right now.'

'Fair enough.' Anderson pointed at the body. 'Well, we've got the murder weapon. We'll check it for prints. Kenny Falconer's on file. Processed the little shit's prints a couple of times myself. Hope you're going to put him away this time.'

'We'll do our best.' Methven focused the eyebrows on Deeley. 'Have you had a look at him?'

'Aye, I have. Not much ambiguity.'

'What about time of death?'

'I was telling your laddies here, I've got no idea yet. More than a week, probably.'

'Sodding hell.' Methven folded his arms, his suit crinkling. 'How long's it going to take?'

'I'll get right on it once you let me breathe.'

'Very well.' Methven pointed at Cullen and Buxton then gestured towards the hallway. 'You pair, with me now.'

Cullen followed him out of the flat, glad no-one could see his scowl until he took the mask off. 'What is it, sir?'

Methven tugged his mask down. 'I don't like this one sodding bit.'

'Me neither.' Cullen undid the zip on the suit. 'What do you want us to do?'

'I don't like Smith turning up dead like this. This doesn't look good at all.'

'So...?'

'Find Falconer.'

'How?'

'I don't sodding know! Just make sure you do!'

∼

CULLEN LEANED against the car and swapped the phone to his other ear. There were so many police and related vehicles on the street that Fountainbridge was virtually closed off. 'Anyway, Methven's put me on the Kenny Falconer case.'

'Really? Thought that had gone cold.'

'It's just heated up a bit. We found your informant dead at his flat.'

'Andrew Smith? Oh, Jesus.'

'What was he doing for you?'

'Just giving us information.' Sharon sighed down the phone. 'He was working with Falconer. You know he had that knife shop on Leith Walk, right?'

'Aye, behind the Polish shop opposite the Chinese supermarket.'

'That's the one. Well, he's selling knives again from a bookshop in Gorgie.'

'Whereabouts?' Cullen flicked out his notebook and opened it against the roof of the car. He clicked his pen.

'Just by Tynecastle, I think. It's in the case file.'

'Okay.'

'According to him, you go in there and get a copy of a book. One called *Two-Way Split*, I think, can't remember who it's by. Take it up to the man at the till and you get to see the catalogue for the under-the-counter stuff. If you're a *very* good boy, you get to go through the back.'

'How dodgy is the stuff he's selling?'

'Not too bad. Nothing like his old shop. Standard American assault knives, that sort of thing.'

'And Smith told you all this?'

'Aye. We managed to shut down the knife operation, but we didn't get anything on Falconer, as per bloody usual. Didn't even find anything tying him to the place.'

'Perfect.' Scowling, Cullen tugged up the front of his hair. 'Is the shop still open?'

'I think so.'

'Okay, cheers for that. I'll give you a call later.'

'You haven't even asked how well it's going out here.'

'Shit. Didn't I?'

'No.'

'How is it going?'

'Fine. Just catch that wee shite for me.'

'Will do. Love you. Bye.' Cullen ended the call and dialled Angela Caldwell's number. Engaged. He pocketed his mobile and waved to Buxton, phone clamped to his ear.

'Hold on a second.' Buxton put his hand over the mouthpiece. 'What is it, mate?'

'You on with Caldwell?'

'Yeah, why?'

Cullen reached over and grabbed the mobile. 'Angela, it's Scott.'

'Great, what have I done now?'

'Nothing, I hope.' Cullen stared at the ground. 'Have you got the Falconer case file there?'

'It's around somewhere. Hang on.' Silence.

Buxton folded his arms and leaned against the car. 'What are you being such a rude twat for?'

'No worse than usual, right?' Cullen swapped ears. Still nothing. 'Might have a lead. Can you get Crystal?'

'Bloody hell.' Buxton marched off into the stairwell.

'Scott?'

'Yeah, I'm here.'

'Right, got the file. What is it?'

'Sharon said Kenny Falconer had a bookshop just by Tynecastle. Do you know where it is?'

'Yeah. Got it. *Boab's Books*. 132 Gorgie Road.'

CULLEN DRUMMED his fingers on the dashboard. He better not be getting away. 'Methven's definitely got a patrol out looking for him?'

'Yeah. Soon as we found the body, mate.' Buxton shook his head as he drove down Gorgie Road. 'You know how much of an annoying bugger you're being?'

'Sorry, I just don't like the fact we've no idea where Falconer is.'

'You're just back from holiday. Chill out, mate.'

'This is me chilling out.'

'Unreal.' Buxton pulled in on the red line on the other side of the road, stopping just by the tattoo parlour. 'We waiting for support?'

'He's probably not there, right?' Cullen shrugged. 'Come on.' He slammed the car door, just as a taxi behind them honked its horn. He held up his warrant card and waved him on. 'You got that 'On Official Police Business' sign out?'

'Yeah.' Buxton locked the car and jogged round to the front.

Cullen paused, checking out *Boab's Books*. The sign had red text on a black background, the square window displaying paperbacks and hardbacks — Scottish crime fiction in among some Booker-nominated titles. He squinted — a blackboard sat behind the novels at the back, yellow letters clicked into place.

This month's titles — Splosh!, Bumlove, 16+ and Girls&Boys.

'Shite.' Cullen rubbed both hands on his face. 'It's a porn shop.'

'Oh.' Buxton laughed. 'Brilliant.'

'Bugger it.' Cullen opened the door, heading inside the poky space. It was maybe five metres across, a wide table almost filling the space, buttressed by heaving bookshelves. Signs led through a corridor into the back of the shop, spotlights pointing at them, obscuring their view through a blanket of smoke. The harsh smell of incense sticks burning in an empty wine bottle.

Cullen checked out the shelves. What was the name of the book? *Two-Way Split*? He looked around — nothing on the table looked like it. Should've googled it. Sod it. He headed to the till, eyes screwed up to avoid the glare of the lights, the haze clearing as he made it to the counter.

The proprietor was sitting behind a wide table reading a book. Mid-fifties, beard, bald head, overweight, dressed in black. He beamed. 'First customers of the day!'

Cullen smiled. 'Hi, I'm looking for a book called *Two-Way Split*.'

The man swallowed. 'Any idea who it's by?'

'Sorry, I don't.'

He grinned and rubbed the side of his head. 'Might be better trying Waterstones or Amazon.'

Cullen rested his hands on the counter. 'I'm looking for Kenny.'

He frowned. 'Kenny?'

'Falconer.'

'I see.' He sniffed. 'I'm afraid Kenny's not here.'

'But he has worked here, right?'

'Are you police?'

'We are.'

'Then I'll need to see some credentials.'

Cullen nodded as he got out his warrant card. 'Here you go. DC Scott Cullen.' Thumb to the right. 'ADC Simon Buxton.'

'Look, pal, your colleagues visited us a few weeks ago and took all of Kenny's... paraphernalia.'

'Well, it's Mr Falconer we're interested in.'

'Ah.'

'Do you know where he is?'

'I've not seen him for a while.'

'Heard from him?'

The bookseller folded the paperback in front of him. Noam Chomsky, one of his linguistics works. 'Nope.'

'What about hearing from any mutual acquaintances?'

'Not quite.'

'What's that supposed to mean?'

'There are always rumours about Kenny.'

'And what are they?'

He zipped up his lips. 'Unless you're arresting me, I'm not saying anything.'

'Kenny's killed someone.'

The bookseller's eyes bulged. 'Excuse me?'

'Are you acquainted with an Andrew Smith?'

'Andrew? Andrew's dead?'

'We just found his body.' Cullen sniffed, letting his eyes wander over the back of the shop, stacks of magazines in mylar bags, girls with few clothes on, mouths hanging open or biting their lips. 'Fancy an accessory to murder charge?'

The bookseller stood up, hands in the air. 'Look, I've told you! I don't know where Kenny's gone.'

'Really?'

'I've absolutely no idea.'

'Can you think of any possibilities?'

'Well, there's one...'

29

'Up here!' Buxton leaned across the banister. 'Come on, you lazy wanker!'

Cullen jogged up the last few steps, feeling every second of his thirty-one years. 'Can't we just wait a bit?'

'He'll get away. You're really unfit, aren't you?'

'I usually rely on lifts out here.' Cullen stopped at the seventh flight and leaned against the scarred black railings, the air stale. Wester bloody Hailes. The large window across the stairwell looked out over the railway line to a sprawling golf course, the red roofs of Clovenstone in the distance. 'Falconer's not moved?'

'Nope.' Buxton shook his head. 'Still got two units outside in case this goes to shit.'

'You almost sound like a proper cop there.'

'Cheers, DI Cullen.'

'Piss off.'

'You caught your breath yet?'

'Just about enough, I think.' Cullen nodded before leading them through the fire doors into the long corridor, a waft of conflicting smells hitting him — cooking, smoking, heating. 'Which one is it?'

'Seven stroke ten.' Buxton looked along the corridor, Airwave clamped to his head. 'Just there on the right.'

Cullen got on the other side of the prison-standard steel security door. How the hell could they get past that? He leaned close to Buxton. 'Where are Methven and Chantal?'

'Still coming up the other stairwell, I think.'

Cullen clocked Methven jogging down the corridor, the fire door juddering shut behind him. 'There he is.' He held up his hands, forcing the DI back. He nodded at Buxton. 'Stay here.'

'Sure.'

Cullen met Methven fifteen strides away from the target flat.

Methven patted his shoulder. 'Good work, Constable.'

'We don't know if he's in there, sir.'

'All the same. You've made sure Falconer hasn't left, though?'

'Aye. Got two units downstairs watching the exits.'

Jain caught up with them. 'What's the drama?'

Cullen nodded at Buxton. 'There's a massive security door.'

'Ah.' Methven folded his arms, eyes shut. 'Any idea how we're getting in?'

Cullen shrugged. 'I'm thinking the old meter reader trick?'

'I like it. We've got a warrant, so go for it.' Methven waved at the door. 'On you go.'

Cullen led back down to the flat. He hammered against the steel, the din reverberating around the long corridor. 'Excuse me, pal, it's the gas man. Need to check your meter.'

'Aw, fuck's sake, man.'

Cullen carefully extended his baton — that was definitely Falconer.

A bolt slid back, followed by another, then a third. The door opened a crack.

Buxton barged in shoulder first, warrant card out. 'Kenny Falconer, you're under arrest!'

'Get to fuck!' Falconer ran back down the long hall, tugging a white door shut behind him at the far end.

'He's in there. You follow him.' Methven gripped the door surround. 'Buxton, wait here with me.'

Cullen led Jain down the corridor, matching Falconer's retreat, passing another door on the way.

Jain tried the door. 'It's locked.'

'Kick it down!'

Jain nodded before raising her leg and stamping forward, the sole of her boot connecting with the door handle, the plywood collapsing under the weight.

Cullen followed her in, eyes darting around the room. They were in a kitchen area, dishes and cutlery scattered across the granite worktop. The other half of the room was a lounge: TV, Xbox, laptop, settees, dining table.

A door at the far end lay open.

'Go back!' Cullen headed for the door.

In the hall, Falconer stood over Methven and Buxton, lying by the front door, prodding a baseball bat at them. He saw them and bolted through the door.

Cullen darted over, kneeling to check they were okay.

Buxton sat up, rubbing his skull. 'He got me.'

'Are you okay, sir?'

'I'll sodding live. Get after him!'

Jain shot past Cullen. He got up and followed her back out into the corridor.

A door slammed shut to the left.

Cullen called out to her, halfway down the corridor in the opposite direction. 'This way!'

She doubled back, overtaking him by the time they reached the stairs. 'Another Cullen arse-up, right?'

'Shut up.' Cullen leaned over the balustrade, the stairs descending around a square central gap, the noise of footsteps cannoning around the space. 'He's heading down.'

Jain took the steps two at a time.

Cullen tried to match it, worrying he'd go arse over tit. As he descended, he noticed Falconer across the gap, a flight further down the stairs.

Falconer spotted him, beady eyes narrowing as they focused. 'Think you can catch me, you pig scum?' He backed through a door, the level below Jain.

Cullen pointed. 'He's gone through that door!'

Jain swung round, almost stumbling. 'Got you!'

Cullen reached into his jacket pocket for his Airwave as he jogged down, calling Buxton's handset. 'He's heading along the corridor on the second floor!'

'Which way did you go outside the flat?'

'Left.'

'Good. We're heading to the right.'

'We're going back along the fourth floor. We'll meet you in the middle, okay?' Cullen pocketed the device as he stepped through the open door onto dark blue carpet tiles. The corridor was darker than upstairs, most of the windows to their left boarded up. Just ahead, a door opened and an Asian man walked out, face full of fury.

Cullen weaved to the left to avoid him, catching his jacket on the window surround and tearing the fabric.

Jain raced ahead, looking like she was losing Falconer as he barrelled through the door at the end.

Cullen tried to pick up the pace but couldn't, his breath almost torn from his lungs. He stepped into the stairwell, a mirror image of the other, footsteps cannoning from above and below. Shite — Buxton and Methven weren't going to catch Falconer.

He raced downwards, taking the steps two at a time — Falconer was almost at entrance level, baseball bat at his feet, Stanley knife in hand, doing a dance with Jain.

She glanced at Cullen then started to circle round, goading Falconer to follow her.

Cullen waited until Falconer's back was to the stairs then made his move, taking a few steps across the tiles before swinging with his baton and catching him above the wrist, the knife flying across the floor.

Falconer spun around to face Cullen, eyes blazing, just as Jain grabbed him in a choke hold.

Cullen got in Falconer's face. 'Kenneth Falconer, I'm arresting you for the murder of Andrew Smith.'

30

'Excellent work, Constables.' Methven beamed as he entered the meeting room.

'Cheers, sir.' Cullen slumped in the chair at the end. 'Didn't want the little bastard getting away.'

'He got me good and proper.' Methven scowled as he rubbed the scratch on his cheek before patting the fresh mark on his forehead and looking at Buxton. 'Are you okay?'

'I'm a bit of a baseball fan. Technically, he just bunted us.' Buxton held his hands up as if wielding a bat and made a gentle forward motion. 'That's when you let the ball hit off the bat.'

'I sodding know my baseball, Constable.' Methven glowered at him. 'Are we likely to get a lawsuit as a result of his arrest?'

'I don't think so.' Cullen rubbed the backs of his legs. 'He was trying to stab Chantal when I clobbered him.'

'Very well.' Methven leaned on the table at the end. 'Excellent work in finding the little toerag.'

'Has Deeley had a look at the body?'

'He has indeed.' Methven reached into his pocket for his own notebook. 'He confirmed stabbing as the cause of death, much as we suspected. Preliminary blood toxicology looks clean as well.'

'Did he get the time of death?'

'He did. Reckons Mr Smith has been dead a while. Given the

state of decay, he put it at any time between the thirtieth of December and the second of January.'

'We're going to be tying ourselves in knots covering that time frame, sir.'

'Agreed.' Methven held up a hand. 'The post mortem will narrow that down, of course. Deeley's fast-tracking it for this afternoon.'

'That's a relief.'

'Indeed.'

'Anything from the SOCOs?'

Methven grinned, nodding as he jangled the change in his pocket. 'Mr Anderson managed to pull Falconer's prints off the murder weapon.'

'That was quick.'

'Indeed. If you recall, it was the inadequacy of Mr Anderson's department that let Falconer off a year ago. He's as eager as us to catch him.'

'For once.'

'He's not my favourite colleague.'

The meeting room door clattered open and DC Jain walked through. 'That's Falconer's lawyer arrived now, sir. He's ready to speak to you.'

'Excellent.' Methven nodded at Cullen. 'Will you do the honours, Constable?'

'You want me and Buxton in there?'

'Yes, Constable. I do.' Methven raised his heavy eyebrows. 'I've got a post mortem to attend. And I'll need to brief Jim and Alison.'

'Good luck, by the way.' Jain smirked. 'Just wait till you see who's defending him.'

~

'AH, DC CULLEN.' Michael Nelson paced down the corridor, a stack of folders tucked in the armpit of his pinstripe suit, right hand outstretched. 'We meet again.'

Cullen frowned. 'You represented Evelyn McCoull, didn't you?'

'Still do.' Nelson glanced at Buxton before focusing on Cullen. 'I assume you're not comfortable with me having time alone with Mr Falconer?'

'Not until we've charged him.'

'I see.'

'Won't be long, I suspect.' Cullen held open the interview room door. 'After you.'

Nelson smiled before entering the room. He stood beside his client, dumping the files on the seat next to him. 'Good morning, Kenneth.'

Falconer rocked back in his chair, a snarl on his face. 'Nice to see you, Micky.'

'Michael, if you will. Thank you for the call.'

Falconer sniffed. He was late twenties, stick thin with a face full of freckles. While his ginger hair was shaved almost to the bone, a thin wave of red was still visible across his pockmarked skull. 'Just get us out of this place. Otherwise, I could shift my allegiances.'

Nelson stacked the files on the floor before taking off his suit jacket and draping it on the back of the chair. 'I'll remind you our association has thus far been mutually beneficial.'

Cullen sat down opposite and started the recorder. 'Interview commenced at ten twenty-nine on Thursday the eighth of January 2014. Present are myself, Detective Constable Scott Cullen, and Acting Detective Constable Simon Buxton. The suspect, Kenneth William Falconer, is also present along with his lawyer, Michael Nelson of Nelson and Parker.'

He raised his eyebrows for a moment as Nelson finished taking out his stationery, narrowing his eyes at Falconer. 'Mr Falconer, why did you stab Andrew Smith?'

Falconer leaned back, his snarl blending with a smile. 'No comment.'

'We've got evidence against you, you do realise that, right?'

'Makes no difference.'

'For the record, Mr Falconer, you've got a history of knife crime. In April of 2011, you stabbed a Wayne Dunbar and evaded arrest until you were eventually caught on Broughton Road.'

Falconer thumbed at Nelson. 'My brief here got me off. That case went to trial, as you well know, what with it being yourself who made a mess of it and everything.'

Cullen took a few seconds to calm down. 'Six months after that incident you allegedly murdered your friend's mother.'

'Aye, *allegedly*.'

'At best, you've been in the wrong place at the wrong time. You seem to associate with some fairly disreputable people.'

'Didn't go down for either of them, though, did I?'

'No. You had alibis in both cases.' Cullen ruffled some papers on the table. 'Very suspicious, especially given the weight of evidence against you.'

'They were valid alibis, pal.'

'Your fingerprints were on the knives in both cases.'

'Still, I wasn't there. Those boys stood up in court and cleared me. End of.' Falconer looked at his lawyer. 'Any danger you can stop this nonsense, Micky? I must be due some compensation for getting attacked by this lot.' He rolled up a sleeve of his jumper, a plaster sticking to a patch of ginger hair. 'See this? Burst into my mate's flat and pushed us down the stairs.'

Nelson cleared his throat, eyes drilling into Cullen. 'Constable, you're wasting my client's time here. Given I charge by the hour, it's costing him a sizeable sum. I trust you're leading somewhere?'

'I am.'

'Where?'

'You'll see.'

'No. Stop this interview now. You're clearly taking us on one of your infamous little meanders. In both previous cases you've referred to, my client was with two people, in his flat, at the times in question. If you recall — and I assume you do given you were in court on both occasions — all four witnesses testified. A jury of his peers exonerated my client.'

'And yet here we are.' Cullen waved around the room before settling on Falconer. 'He's done it again.'

'Done what again?'

'Become involved in a murder.'

Nelson pushed his glasses up his nose and dropped his fountain pen on the table, navy ink splattering across his notebook. 'I shall ask again, is this going somewhere?'

Cullen locked eyes with Falconer, heart pounding. 'Mr Falconer, we're looking into the death of one Andrew Smith at a flat in Fountainbridge. We've found your prints on the knife.'

'So?' Falconer rocked his chair forward, setting all four legs on the ground. 'I've sold a lot of knives over the years, haven't I?'

'We're not talking Japanese cooking knives here, are we?'

Falconer thumbed at Nelson. 'After legal advice relating to those close scrapes you referred to, I gave up any association with members of the criminal fraternity.'

Cullen recognised the lines Nelson had been feeding the little shit. 'With your record, Mr Falconer, I'm surprised you weren't a bit more careful to wipe them clean before selling them.'

'Can't trust anyone these days, eh? Someone could just have been careless with my knives.' Falconer smirked. 'Besides, it could be some sort of legacy deal. My shop on Leith Walk was open a good few years before you lot shut me down. I imagine there's still a lot of stock out there with my fingerprints on.'

Cullen checked the sheet in front of him. 'In that case, who did you sell the weapon in question — a ShivWorks Disciple — to?'

'Well, I can tell you I sold one to young Andy.'

'That'd be Andrew Smith?'

'Aye.'

'I thought you weren't selling any more?'

Falconer leaned forward. 'I sell to people for defence purposes only. Last I checked that knife was legal in this country.'

'And you've got this transaction logged somewhere?'

'Aye.'

'How much did he pay for it?'

'One-twenty.'

'One hundred and twenty pounds?'

'That's what I said, pal.'

'So you're suggesting Mr Smith stabbed himself with his own knife?'

'Must be, eh? Only thing I can think. Boy was quite an edgy punter, you know?'

Cullen glanced at his notebook. Mr Falconer, we need to ascertain your whereabouts for the period covering the thirtieth of December to the second of January.'

'The whole time?'

'Of course.'

'Are you serious?'

'Yes.'

Falconer laughed, staring up the way. 'Fuck off.'

Cullen looked over at Nelson. 'I suggest you ensure your client co-operates.'

Nelson bristled. He replaced the cap on his fountain pen before whispering in Falconer's ear.

Falconer shook his head for a few seconds before nodding. 'Where do you want me to start then, pal?'

'Let's just start with the thirtieth. The whole day.'

Falconer picked his teeth. 'If memory serves, I was at work from seven a.m. till seven p.m.'

'And where's that?'

'Tesco. Corstorphine.' Falconer smirked. 'I'm trying to make a clean break with my life, right?'

'Yet you're still selling knives?'

'Boy's got to have a hobby.'

'So, after work?'

'I went to the pub. Got the bus there. I've got one of them Ridacard things so you can check with Lothian buses if you want.'

'Who were you with?'

'None of your business.'

'Where were you?'

'None of your business.'

'What time did you leave?'

'Be about eleven. Back of, maybe.'

Nelson smiled, his head tilted to the side. 'Constable, my client's given you his movements. Please move on.'

'How did you get home?'

'Bus.'

Cullen fixed a glare on Falconer. 'What about the thirty-first?'

'Think I was at a house party in Armadale. Got there about ten in the a.m.'

'This is near Bathgate?'

'Aye. Got a few buddies out that way. Wayne and Emily Newall.'

'Got an address for them?'

'Aye. Drove Road. Number seventy.'

'Now what about the first of January?'

'I was still at the house party.'

'Really?'

'Aye. We like to let our hair down. 2013 was a hell of a year, you know?'

'You were there the whole day?'

'Aye.'

'What about the second?'

'Went to my pal's flat.'

'In Wester Hailes?'

'Aye. Been there ever since.'

'You're not lying low, are you?'

'I've been ill. Had a tickly cough for a few days now.'

'For over a week?'

'Aye.' Falconer sniffed. 'It happens, pal. I don't get enough nutrition in my diet, clearly.'

'So you've not been into work?'

'No. Called in sick.'

Cullen looked at Buxton, unsure what else they could do to progress. He reached over to terminate the recording.

≈

'So the upshot, sir, is he's got alibis for the whole period.' Cullen folded his arms and leaned back against the meeting room door. 'He's going to get away again, isn't he?'

'Maybe not.' Methven stared at the whiteboard in the middle of the far wall. 'Do you believe him?

'Of course not.'

Methven shifted his gaze to Buxton. 'Simon?'

'I don't believe him but I don't see what else we can do, sir.'

'He's still downstairs, correct?'

Cullen nodded. 'Aye.'

'So, unless we can get him to recant his statement, it looks like we'll have to release Falconer.'

'We've got another eight hours with him, twenty if we can get it extended.'

'I know that, Constable.' Methven tossed the whiteboard pen in the air and caught it. 'Is another twenty hours going to tear this alibi apart, though?'

'This is the third time we've almost had him, sir. Sharon's had him once. I've had him twice now. He's literally getting away with murder.'

'I know.' Methven scratched his eyebrows for a few seconds. 'Who's his lawyer?'

'Michael Nelson.'

'And he's been up to his games, correct?'

'Aye.'

'Well, we'll need to let Falconer go until we've got something more concrete.'

'Oh, come on.'

'Listen, Constable, do you have anything to charge him with?'

'Assaulting Simon and yourself with a baseball bat? Trying to stab Chantal? We can't just let him go.'

'I'll be the judge of that.'

'So?'

Methven glowered for a few seconds, chewing his cheek. 'In lieu of letting him go, what are your next steps?'

'We've got Falconer's prints on the knife used to kill Andrew Smith.'

'I know that, Constable, but we've got nothing proving Falconer killed him, have we?'

'Right. Fine. We'll get it.'

'I'm not sure how you're going to achieve that. This is a forensics case.'

'But, sir, if we ca—'

'You've got the rest of the day to pin it to him.' Methven jangled his change. 'He's been arrested. We've got time on our side for now.'

'I don't like the little shite one bit.'

'Nobody does, Constable.'

'What do you want us to do, sir?'

'What do you propose?'

Cullen frowned. 'Well, first, we should get out to Armadale and check out this story.'

'Go on.' Methven tapped his watch. 'Clock is ticking.'

31

C ullen pulled in at the end of Drove Road, the rolling hills of West Lothian lurking under a dark grey sky behind the houses. Getting out, he realised they were unprotected from the elements, the rain almost vertical as it cut along the street. 'Bugger this. I want to go back to Tenerife.'

'Cheer up, you bugger.' Buxton slammed his door. Cullen marched up the street, pushing his scarf over his mouth. 'I hate this town.'

'As much as you hate Methven?'

'Almost.' Cullen crossed the road before taking in the house, a two-storey construction in brown-harled concrete blocks and brick. Up an embankment, eight steps leading to the door, the front garden a balding patch of grass. The thud of a bass drum. His nostrils twitched at something sweet. 'Can you smell that?'

'What?'

'Hash, I think.'

Buxton raised his head. 'Proper hard-core skunk that.'

Cullen clenched his fists and marched up to the door. He hammered then stood back, waiting.

The music volume increased.

'Oh for Christ's sake.' Cullen rolled his eyes. He lifted up the letterbox and shouted. 'Here, Wayne, it's Kenny!' He stepped to the side and got out his warrant card.

Over the bass drum, he could make out the thumping of heavy feet down stairs. 'Just a minute, big man.' The door opened wide and an overweight man peered out, belly hanging out of a stained Kangol t-shirt, tatty tracksuit bottoms lower than hip level. A handmade cigarette hung from his left hand, smelling like cannabis. 'Get to fuck!'

Cullen stuck his foot in the door. 'Mr Newall, we need a word with you.'

'Like fuck! This is my house. I can play my music any level I like.'

'This isn't about your music. We need to ask you a few questions about Kenny Falconer.'

'Fucking having nothing to do with that thieving wee cunt.'

'Excuse me?'

'Nicked my MiniDisc player at New Year.'

What the hell? Cullen frowned. 'A *MiniDisc* player?'

'Aye. Cost me two hundred quid.'

'In 1998, maybe.' Cullen pocketed his warrant card, foot still in the doorway. 'We need to know if Mr Falconer was here on the thirty-first.'

'Aye, he was. Stayed till the first then choried my MD, man.'

'What was he doing here?'

'Usual.' Wayne pinched the end of his spliff and rested it on the shelf to his left. 'Drinking, smoking.'

'How did he seem?'

'Fucking usual, pal. Trying it on with any bird in a skirt or tight jeans. Looking to nick anything not chained down.'

'Didn't seem out of character at all?'

'No, pal. Boy's all over the place at the best of times.'

'Wayne! You're letting that draught in.' A woman appeared at the door, stunned eyes blinking at the daylight, dressing gown open to reveal most of a flabby breast, purple veins under white skin. She clocked them and tightened the robe. 'Who the fuck's that?'

'It's the police, Em. I'm helping them.'

'Have they got your MiniDisc player back? I really want to listen to that Sheryl Crow album.'

'No, hon, they've not.'

'Mrs Newall, was Kenny here over the New Year period?'

Wayne scowled at them. 'Do you not believe me?'

'We need the story backed up.' Cullen focused on Emily Newall. 'Was he here?'

'Aye. Tried it on with my pal, Dannii. Wee scumbag.'

'Thanks.' Cullen noted it down.

Emily stared at Cullen's notebook then her husband. She put a hand to her hip, the boob almost popping out again. 'You're a fucking idiot, Wayne Newall.'

Wayne patted her sleeve. 'Let me finish up here, sweetheart.'

'Fine.' She slammed the living room door shut behind her.

'Sorry about that.' Wayne sniffed before clearing his throat. 'Aye, where was I?'

'Kenny Falconer?'

'Wee cunt nicked my MiniDisc player.'

'Right.' Cullen smiled. Useless dickhead. 'Have you heard from him since?'

'Tried texting the wee fanny. Cunt's not replying, though, is he?'

'Have you tried calling him?'

'Aye. Like his phone's off.'

'But he was definitely here at the time?'

'Aye. Defo.' Wayne rummaged around in his nose. 'Do I need to file a report or something about the MD?'

'It might help if you want it back.'

'Fine. I'll get down there one of these days.'

'Thanks for your time.' Cullen led back to the car, glaring at the bolted door. 'MiniDisc player.'

'I know, right?' Buxton opened his door. 'What do you reckon?'

'I think we should speak to locals and find out if that pair are on the level.'

⁓

'OH FOR GOD'S SAKE, here we go again.' PC Duncan West put his head in his hands as he saw Cullen approach. 'Cowboy Cullen and his new squire. Got some fresh straw in for your chariot, my liege.'

'Charming as ever.' Cullen looked around the admin area of Bathgate station, the familiar smells and sounds hitting his brain

— Pot Noodle, stale farts, burps, keyboards clicking. 'You got a sec?'

West's gaze danced between Cullen and Buxton. 'What?'

'Just been to see Wayne and Emily Newall.'

'Drove Road, Armadale, right?'

'Aye.

'What of them?'

'Provided an alibi for a murder suspect and we need to know if it's dodgy or not. What's their story?'

'You got an hour or two?'

Cullen frowned. 'I'm not sure I follow.'

'Right, that place is a party flat.' West slumped back in his seat. 'We've got about fifteen in our patch, just boozing and whatever else until the wee small hours. All day, every day. Total nightmare. The council needs to get a handle on it and kick them all out.'

'And these two? Wayne and Emily?'

'Aye, they're among the worst. We get called out there twice a week. Usually there's a load of people boozed out of their heads. And worse.'

'Sounds like fun.'

'Aye, and you're saying they've given a murder suspect an alibi?'

'Aye.' Cullen tried to weigh it up — a dodgy alibi wouldn't be the worst thing they'd done. 'Could they be on the level?'

'Probably. They'll not want to stand up in court, if that's what you're getting at, but they're actually quite trustworthy.'

'How?'

'They might play gabba until the wee small hours of the morning, but they turn it off when we pitch up. Wayne's one of our DC's Covert Human Intelligence Sources.'

'You're kidding.'

'Wish I was.'

Cullen felt a hand on his shoulder.

'There you are.'

He turned around. Sharon. 'Hey.' He nodded at Buxton. 'Can you investigate with PC West here?'

Buxton nodded. 'Sure thing.'

West led Buxton off away from them, eyes locked on Sharon's behind. He looked up, scowling at Cullen.

Cullen patted Sharon on the back. 'Come on, then, DI McNeill.'

Sharon took him towards a meeting room, blinds drawn behind the glass. She slammed the door, making the walls shake.

'Woah, woah.' Cullen looked around the vacant room, the floor and table covered with case files, before looking back at Sharon. 'You okay?'

'Sit.'

'Yes, miss.' Cullen sat at the table. The walls were covered in photos and Post-It notes. 'Take it your first day isn't going well?'

'Don't get me started.' Sharon slumped in a chair, putting her head in her hands. 'This is a complete disaster.'

'In what way?'

'There's just too much reading to get through.' She patted the boxes. 'I've no idea what they've been doing, but they need a librarian more than a DI.'

'You'll get there.'

'Mm.' She raised an eyebrow as she let out a breath. 'I wish I was back on the beach.'

'Aye, me too. I've been pissing Budgie off about it all day.' Cullen leaned forward, elbows resting on the desk. 'Methven's given me your workload.'

'Seriously?'

'Aye. I'm not happy about it.'

'Well, it's all experience, isn't it?'

'Maybe. We caught Kenny.'

'You could've told me.'

'I'm telling you now. Sorry. Had a mental morning. He was staying with his mate in Wester Hailes. We got it out of that book-seller you told me about.'

'Always a weak link in the chain, isn't there?'

'Aye.'

'Do you think you'll get him?'

'I hope so. He's got an alibi for the whole time in question. That's the reason we're out here.'

'I see.' Her forehead creased. 'Sounds like he'll get off with it again.'

'Reckons his prints are on the knife because he sold Andrew Smith a ShivWorks Disciple.'

She nodded. 'That was in Smith's statement.'

'Not had the time to read through the paperwork yet.' Cullen cleared his throat. 'See when you raided the shop, did you get anything relating to the knife business?'

'Not that I recall. Why?'

'Well, Falconer reckons he's got a journal of transactions proving they were all above board.'

'It'd be a very useful thing to have.'

'Anyway, that knife was the murder weapon.'

'Which closes off the trail against Falconer. Smith was our only witness. Nobody to testify, no conviction.'

'Right. So, the only evidence you had was Smith's statement?'

'Correct.'

'So, now Smith's dead the case is dead.'

'Yup.'

'Shite.'

'Welcome to my world, lover boy.'

Cullen got to his feet. 'Right, I'll nail him for this stabbing.'

'You do that.' Sharon picked up a file and started flicking through it. 'When are you finishing tonight?'

'I'll hopefully get off early.'

'I've heard that before.' She tossed the file back on the desk. 'Do you mind if I book another holiday?'

∼

'SODDING, SODDING HELL.' Methven stood in the corridor outside the interview rooms. 'Why did they let Nelson leave?'

Cullen scowled at the closed door, Kenny Falconer safely under guard behind it. 'Sergeant Mullen should've known we'd be back in there with him sooner or later.'

'Nelson's obviously a busy man.' Buxton shrugged, eyes still on his mobile. 'Partner at a law firm and all that.'

'They're dodgy is what they are.'

'I resent that.' Nelson brushed past them, standing by the door, glasses halfway down his nose. 'Ours is a reputable firm, I'll have you know.'

Methven smiled at the lawyer. 'Please disregard those comments.'

'I shall do my best, sir.' Nelson prodded the door with his umbrella. 'Do you mind if I have a word with my client before we get started this time?'

'Be my guest.' Methven raised his hands. 'My officers have had a particularly fruitful morning out in West Lothian.'

'West Lothian? Interesting.' Nelson smiled. 'Thank you.' He hefted up his bulging briefcase and entered the room.

Buxton shook his head. 'Don't you just love him?'

Methven grimaced. 'Like a particularly despicable great aunt.'

Cullen took a step towards Methven. 'With all due respect, sir, what the hell are you playing at by letting him in there?'

Methven grinned. 'I'm afraid you've had a wild goose chase out west.'

Cullen scowled at him. 'I'm sorry?'

'While you were out there, I attended the post mortem. While it's yet to formally conclude, Deeley confirmed the time of death was sometime on the evening of the thirtieth of December.'

Cullen frowned. 'You're serious?'

'Do you know me to joke, Constable?'

'So you're saying the only alibi we need from him is the thirtieth?'

'Correct.' Methven nodded at the door. 'Nelson will be in there prepping a pack of lies for what Falconer was up to in Armadale.'

Cullen nodded. 'I'm with you now.'

'On you go. Let me know how it goes immediately.' Methven marched off down the corridor, hand reaching into his pocket.

Cullen watched him retreat. 'I don't know who's worse.'

'The lawyer, right?' Buxton grinned.

'I meant him or Bain, but you're probably right.' Cullen entered the interview room, sitting opposite Nelson.

The lawyer stopped whispering into Falconer's ear and started unpacking his briefcase. The stack of files he'd previously carried were now wedged into compartments, stretching the black leather.

Cullen started the recorder, staring at Falconer, leaning forward to speak into the microphone. 'Interview commenced at fourteen oh nine on Thursday the eighth of January 2014. Present are myself, Detective Constable Scott Cullen, and Acting Detective Constable Simon Buxton. Kenneth William Falconer is joined by his solicitor, Michael Nelson.'

He waited for Nelson to stop fidgeting with his pens. 'Mr Falconer, can you go through your whereabouts on the night of the thirtieth of December?'

Falconer rolled his eyes. 'This again?'

'Please.'

'I told you. I was in the pub.'

'Which one?'

'You must know it.' Falconer smirked. 'The pub.'

'We're going to need to be a bit more precise than that, I'm afraid.'

'Really?'

'We are.' Cullen nodded — games, games, games. 'It turns out Mr Smith was murdered on the thirtieth.'

Falconer swallowed. 'How do you know that?'

'We've got a man called James Deeley who works with us. He's the city's chief pathologist. He's had to look at the bodies of two of your previous victims, Kenny.'

'Shut it.'

'Did you say the thirtieth?' Nelson blinked a few times as his glasses slipped down his nose.

'Aye, that's when we understand Andrew Smith was stabbed by your client.'

'I see.' Nelson sifted through some paperwork.

'I didn't kill him!'

Cullen ran his tongue over his teeth, eyes boring into Falconer. 'Mr Nelson, your client needs to provide his whereabouts for the time in question.'

Nelson looked up from his paperwork and held his gaze for a few seconds. 'Very well.' He leaned over and whispered in Falconer's ear.

'Aye?' Falconer shrugged then focused on Cullen, his mouth twisting up into a smirk. 'We were in Teuchter's in town. Wee bar on William Street.'

Cullen frowned — Dean Vardy was there that night. 'Who were you with?'

'No comment.'

Cullen scowled. 'If you don't want to be marched into a custody cell just now, you'll tell me who you were with. Sitting in a pub on your own isn't much of an alibi.'

Falconer sniffed then glanced round at Nelson. He reached over and whispered in the lawyer's ear, getting a short response. 'Fine. Decent idea.' He nodded and focused on Cullen. 'I was there with a friend.'

'A friend?'

'Aye.'

'And who's your friend, Kenny?'

'My mate's called Darren Keogh.'

32

Cullen lurched away from the table — what the hell was going on? 'Did you say Darren Keogh?'

'Aye. Dazza's a good buddy of mine.'

'You're sure you were with him?'

'Positive.'

'On the thirtieth of December, you were in Teuchter's with Darren Keogh?'

'Aye.'

Cullen glared at him. 'Were you with anyone else?'

'Aye. There was this other boy there.'

'What did he look like?'

'Just a bloke. Nothing special.'

'How old was he?'

'I'm not good with punters' ages. Give me a bird and I can tell you right down to the month.' Falconer winked at him. 'It's all about the elbows.'

Cullen stared at him for a few seconds, his brain reeling. 'Did he have any distinguishing features?'

'Aye, he had a wooden leg and a hunchback.' Falconer shook his head. 'Of course he fucking didn't. He's just some bloke.'

'Any tattoos?'

'Not in the habit of checking out boys' tats, I'm afraid. Girls, aye. Of course.'

'Was he muscular or like you?'

'What are you saying, pal?'

'Did he have big arms, like he goes to the gym?'

'Might've done.'

'And you were with them for a few hours, right?'

'Aye. It'll be about four hours, all in. From about half seven till closing.'

'And you don't have any idea of this man's name?'

'No comment.'

Cullen gripped the edge of the table, the laminate cracking further. 'I'm finding this hard to believe.' He reached into his pocket for his phone, flicking through pages of holiday photos.

Nelson cleared his throat. 'Constable, I'd appreciate if you check the news when you get home.'

Cullen finally found one of Dean Vardy. He held the phone up, shooting a look at Nelson. 'Is this the man you were with?'

Falconer whispered into Nelson's ear, who whispered back, nodding. He cleared his throat. 'Aye, it was Dean.'

Cullen sighed. 'You're sure? This is an incredibly serious matter.'

'Aye, it was him. Sorry, it was a wee while ago, pal.'

'You were there for a long time. You must've drunk a lot of beer.'

'About eight pints of IPA, I reckon.'

'What brand?'

'Deuchars.'

'Deuchars?' Cullen frowned — this was making less sense. 'I thought you'd be a lager man, Kenny.'

'Why, cos I'm a scumbag?' Falconer winked again.

'Aye.'

'My old boy was into his real ale. Wouldn't let me drink anything else when I was growing up. I mean, when I was eighteen and went to the boozer with him.'

'So, you're in there for four hours and you had eight pints of Deuchars IPA.' Cullen tossed his head from side to side, eyes on the ceiling, to show the mental arithmetic going on. 'It's what, four quid a pint in there?'

'Thereabouts, aye.'

'So you spent thirty-two quid?'

'I didn't.'

'Why not?'

'Deano paid for it.'

'That's very generous of him. Paying for a guy he barely even knows to get hammered.'

'If you had a clue you'd know IPA's piss weak, man. It's a proper session ale.'

'All the same, that's a lot of cash to spend on a virtual stranger.'

'It's the truth, pal.' Falconer shrugged. 'He must be a kind-hearted soul.'

'This is what you're stating for the record, right?'

'Aye.'

'Very well.'

～

'YOU'RE NOT GOING to like this, sir.' Cullen pulled the meeting room door behind them — Angela sat alongside Methven, working on a laptop.

'What is it?' Methven shut his eyes, the lids flickering beneath his monstrous eyebrows.

'Simon, you tell him.'

Buxton cleared his throat. 'Falconer's given the same alibi as Dean Vardy. He's saying he was with Darren Keogh.'

'Sodding hell.' Methven closed his eyes fully. 'Sodding, sodding hell.' He reopened them, bloodshot whites encasing tiny pupils. 'Is this on the level?'

Cullen shrugged. 'We've got uniform picking Keogh up from his work just now.'

'Christ, Constable, you can't just do that!'

'Why not?'

'Because he's not done anything!'

'Keogh's lying to us, sir.'

'How?'

'He never told us Falconer was with him and Vardy.'

'But we know Vardy and Keogh were there, correct?'

Cullen folded his arms. 'Aye, well, according to the bar man in Teuchter's.'

'Right. So nobody's said there was a third man with them, correct?'

'Correct.'

'You did ask?'

Cullen shut his eyes. Shite. 'I don't think so.'

'Sodding buggery!' Methven shut his eyes, fingers rattling change and keys in his pocket. He took a deep breath and reopened them. 'Why not?'

'An oversight, sir.'

'So Kenny Falconer could very well have been with them?'

'No way, sir. No way can he have been drinking with them.'

'Why?'

Cullen looked around, reaching for some reason and coming up short. 'He just can't. This is too much of a coincidence.'

'We don't have to like the alibis we receive, Constable, but if there is one then we can't hold the suspect without cause.' Methven smoothed down his eyebrows.

'Nobody's actually confirmed Falconer was there. Keogh, Vardy, Weir. We need to speak to Keogh again.'

Methven nodded. 'Okay. Do it.'

Angela held up her hand. 'Once you two have stopped butting heads, I've just got off with Lothian Buses. Falconer did get a bus into town that night.'

'You're serious?' Cullen frowned. 'Where did he get off?'

'CCTV shows he got off near Haymarket, start of Shandwick place.'

Cullen thought it through. 'He could easily have walked to Fountainbridge from there and killed Andrew Smith.'

Angela shrugged. 'Or he could've gone to William Street like he says.'

Methven got up and inspected the whiteboard, shaking the pen between two fingers. 'Right, Cullen, go and speak to Keogh again.' He held out a finger. 'But go easy on him, okay?'

'Will do.' Cullen took his eyes off the dancing pen. 'What about the fact he's lying?'

'Find the holes in his story and tear it apart, okay? Then we'll discuss what to do with him. But not before. Am I making myself clear?'

'Aye, you are.' Cullen got up to leave. 'Are you going to release Kenny Falconer?'

'We'll keep him in for the time being.' Methven glanced at his wrist. 'We've got another seventeen hours or so.'

Cullen walked over to the door. 'Fine.'

'I know this is frustrating, Constable, but we need to do this by the book, okay?'

'Fine, sir. No cowboy antics from me this time.'

'That's what I like to hear.'

~

'I'LL SAY IT AGAIN, Mr Keogh, you're under no suspicion of any crime yet.' Cullen stared at the digital recorder at the side of the interview room table, its red light winking. 'The reason we're interviewing you is straightforward. We need to validate the statement you gave on the thirty-first of December in light of recent evidence.'

'Okay.' Keogh gave a flicker of a smile, a deep frown etched on his forehead. 'How can I help?'

'Can you confirm whether you were in Teuchter's bar on William Street on the night of the thirtieth?'

'We've been over this, haven't we?'

Cullen gestured at the recorder. 'Please, again for the record.'

Keogh scowled, eyes darting between Cullen and Buxton. 'As stated before, I was there that night, aye.'

'Who were you with?'

The frown deepened. 'I was with Dean Vardy.'

'Dean Vardy?'

'Aye.' Keogh blinked a few times. 'Look, shouldn't I have my lawyer in here?'

'Not unless you're lying to us.' Cullen sat back, hands clasped behind his head. 'Are you?'

'No, no it's the truth.'

'Good.' Cullen rocked forward in his chair, leaning on his right fist. 'So, let me get this straight. You were with Dean Vardy?'

'Aye.'

'And not with Kenny Falconer?'

'Oh, sorry. Yes. I was.'

Cullen sighed — what was he playing at? 'So you weren't with Dean Vardy?'

'No, I was.'

'So you were with both of them? Kenny Falconer and Dean Vardy?'

'Aye. They're good pals of mine.' Keogh swallowed, eyes locked on the table. 'Good mates.'

'We've reason to believe Mr Falconer was elsewhere at the time.'

'Oh?'

'Mr Falconer's our prime suspect in the murder of one Andrew Smith.'

'Kenneth was with me at the time.'

Cullen raised an eyebrow — Kenneth? 'He was with you all night?'

'Aye, well, till closing time. Back of eleven, I think.'

'Mr Keogh, can I just remind you that providing a false alibi is a serious offence?'

'I'm well aware of that.' Keogh wiped sweat from his brow. 'This is the truth.'

'If it's the truth, why are you sweating?'

'No reason.'

'People don't sweat for no reason, Mr Keogh.'

'It's hot in here.'

'It's the middle of January. It's not hot.'

'I'm not comfortable speaking to the police, that's all. That's why I want my lawyer.'

'Wouldn't be because you're lying about your whereabouts, would it?'

'Look, I swear I was with both of them.'

'Let's see how this sounds then, shall we?' Cullen smoothed down the margin of his notebook. 'On the thirtieth of December, two people were murdered. In both cases, alibis were given. In both cases, the alibi is they were drinking in Teuchter's with you.'

Keogh shrugged. 'Aye.'

'We spoke to you on the thirty-first about Mr Vardy.'

'Aye, I remember.'

Cullen slammed a fist against the table, pain jolting up his arm. 'When we spoke to you on Hogmanay, why didn't you tell us you were with Kenny Falconer as well?'

'You didn't ask.'

Cullen snarled, tempted to reach across the table and grab Keogh by the throat. 'How do they know each other?'

Keogh frowned. 'They don't.'

'Yet you were with both of them?'

'I'm mates with Dean and I'm mates with Kenneth.' Keogh shrugged. 'I'm the common link. It does happen.'

'So who was first?'

'Eh?'

'Did you arrive at Teuchter's first?'

'Aye. About half an hour before Dean.'

'I see. And when did Kenny turn up?'

'A bit later.'

Cullen shut his eyes. 'When?'

'I don't know. I'd had a few pints by then. That Brewdog stuff's pretty strong.'

'What was Mr Vardy drinking?'

'Same as me. He runs a pub, you know? Likes his beer.'

'Brewdog Punk IPA?'

'Aye.'

'And Kenny?'

'I can't remember what Kenneth was drinking.'

'Was it lager?'

'Can't remember.'

'Ale?'

'Maybe.'

'What kind?'

'I. Can't. Remember.'

'So you never went to the bar?'

'Dean knew the bar staff in there and we were getting table service. He just had to click his fingers and we got another round delivered.'

'Sounds delightful.'

Keogh scratched the back of his neck. 'If I recall correctly, I was just going to the toilet when Kenneth turned up.' He looked away, focusing on the far wall of the interview room.

Cullen leaned forward, arms on the table. 'You expect us to believe this, do you?'

'I do. It's the truth.' Keogh held up his hands. 'Look, can I get back to work?'

Cullen leaned forward. 'Interview terminated at fifteen eighteen.'

33

Cullen stormed into the meeting room, making his way to the whiteboard, Buxton following. He slammed the door behind them. 'Sir, Keogh just told us Kenny bloody Falconer *was* in Teuchter's with him and Vardy.'

'What?' Methven stood at the whiteboard, frowning. He huffed and looked over at Cullen, setting the pen down before digging his hand into his pocket, rummaging around for change. 'And what do you think of that?'

'I think it's a load of bollocks. There's no chance those three were there together.'

Methven marched over and put a hand on Cullen's shoulder. 'Constable, can I ask you to calm down?'

'Calm down?' Cullen pushed the hand away. 'I can't just calm down, sir. We're being fed a pack of lies by that wanker.'

'You're absolutely sure there was no-one with them?'

'Aye.' Cullen rubbed his neck. 'Well...'

'You do have the statement from the thirty-first to back this up, though, correct?'

Cullen looked away as he thumbed behind him. 'When Simon and I spoke to the bar manager on Hogmanay, we didn't ask who was with Vardy and Keogh.'

'So you're saying there could be independent confirmation of Falconer being with them?'

'I think that's what I'm trying to say, aye.'

Methven stood for a few seconds, lost in thought, hand jangling the keys. 'Let's get that checked out then. We need someone to go over the bar manager's story with him, preferably in a darkened room.'

'Sorry about this, sir.'

'It's fine. This sort of thing happens. Just try to minimise the number of times it occurs.'

DC Chantal Jain entered, carrying a tray laden with coffees. 'Sorry, Scott, I've not got you one.'

Cullen scowled at her. 'Cheers for that.'

Jain distributed the drinks, Angela smiling as she accepted hers, still rapt on her phone call. Buxton took a sip through the lid as Jain handed Methven a coffee.

'Thanks.' Methven took the lid off the coffee, eyes on the wall clock. 'Oh, sodding buggery, I'm late. Cullen, I'm leaving you in charge.' He dashed out of the room, coffee swilling over the cup.

'What a man.' Jain sat down, crossing her legs and fussing with her hair. 'So, what's the drama now, Scott?'

'We've just re-interviewed Darren Keogh. He reckons he was with both Kenny Falconer and Dean Vardy on the night in question.'

'Bloody hell.' Jain took a sip of coffee. 'And they were definitely there?'

'That's what we need to find out.'

'Take it you arsed up, then? I heard Crystal moaning. You didn't ask if there was anyone with them?'

'No.' Cullen tilted his head from side to side, eyes burning into Jain's coffee cup. 'We know for certain Vardy was there.'

'Aren't you a superstar?'

Buxton cleared his throat. 'I just got checks done on Keogh. As we thought, he's clean as a whistle.'

'Seriously?' Cullen shook his head. 'He's supposedly drinking buddies with a knife dealer and a guy who owns a bookies, a taxi company and a pub, and he's clean?'

'Nothing on him.' Buxton raised his hands. 'It's like he's from another walk of life from those two.'

Cullen folded his arms. 'It's because he is.'

'What do you mean by that?' Jain took a drink of coffee, peering over the rim of the cup.

'Well, for starters, Keogh's something like fifteen years older than the guys he was allegedly drinking with. Keogh reckons he's Vardy's uncle, sort of.'

'Sort of?' Jain was frowning.

'Used to go out with Vardy's aunt or some rubbish.' Cullen scowled before checking the whiteboard. 'Have we spoken to the aunt?'

Buxton kept his focus on his notebook.

Cullen cleared his throat. 'Simon?'

Buxton rubbed his neck as he looked up. 'Yeah, having a bit of bother there, ain't I?'

'How come?'

'Can't get hold of her. Got a name, though. Alison Vardy. I'll keep trying.'

'This doesn't feel right.' Cullen felt his stomach rumble from the smell of coffee. 'With the Lyle case, we were under the assumption Vardy got a cab up there to kill him.' He grabbed a pen and drew a line from six p.m. to midnight, marking the arrival and departure times. 'Even if he got chips at half past, Vardy's still got an hour before Pauline gets home. Plenty of time to kill Lyle.'

Jain scowled at the board. 'Assuming Ms Quigley's telling the truth.'

Buxton nodded. 'She's Vardy's girlfriend. She might be an accessory to murder.'

'Precisely.' Cullen added a note alongside *Pauline*. 'Have we got anything to suggest she's lying to support Vardy?'

'Nothing, really.' Buxton shrugged. 'Remember, our suspicions were in the opposite direction — that she was shagging Lyle.'

'Simon, come on... "Shagging"? Really?' Jain scowled at Buxton, making Angela giggle. She looked at Cullen again. 'What have you got on Falconer?'

'His fingerprints are on the knife that killed Andrew Smith.'

'That's it?'

'Aye. Why?'

'I'm wondering if Keogh's lying to protect Falconer. It's like he's added Falconer to the alibi. It's gone from two men in a pub to three.'

Jain tilted an eyebrow. 'Nothing to do with you pair not asking?'

'No.'

Jain scowled. 'So, what do you want us to do, *sir*?'

Cullen bristled — cheeky sod. 'Chantal, Angela, can you get back in with Keogh and go over his statement?'

'Will do, *sir*.'

'Cut that out. I'm just trying to provide some leadership here.'

'Sure thing, *boss*.' Jain scowled as she made a note. 'I was going to ask who died and put you in charge, but I don't even get the pleasure of going to Crystal's funeral.'

Cullen frowned at Angela. 'Once you've done that, can you get background checks done on everyone else?'

'Aye, will do.' Angela nodded as she patted her swollen belly.

Jain nodded at Buxton. 'What about you and your wee sidekick?'

'Buxton and I are going to find Vardy and get him in a room.'

34

'Bastard.' Buxton pulled the pool car up at the crossing, finger stabbing right across the street. 'It's over there, isn't it?'

'Corner of Viewforth and Montpelier.' Cullen nodded as he looked around, the street they were after stuck behind a wide railing. He waved up ahead. 'Pull in behind that bin.'

Buxton waited for the school kids to finish crossing before shooting off and parking on the single yellow. 'Can't believe there's a street in Edinburgh called Montpelier.'

'There's a nice bar just round the corner named after it.'

'Really?'

'It's a bit style bar for you, Simon.'

'Piss off. You're the one who always insists we drink in the Elm.'

'No, I don't.'

'Really? You're turning into Bain, mate.'

Cullen got out of the car and slammed the door. 'I'm *not* turning into Bain.'

'You are.'

'I'm not.'

'Are, are, are.' Buxton grinned as he locked the door, trying the handle. 'Just accept it, mate.'

'No danger.' Cullen crossed the side street then jogged over the main road at the crossing, before making his way between bollards and heading to Vardy's stairwell. 'Top floor, right?'

'Yes it is, Bain.'

'Piss. Off.'

Buxton smirked. 'Sorry, getting really angry about it isn't going to make me stop it now, is it?'

'Whatever.' Cullen held down the buzzer for a few seconds. No reply. He held it again, longer this time, eyes on the flat window. Curtains drawn, lights off. He took a step back. The others were all the same, apart from a flat on the first floor with lights on. He hit the buzzer. 'This better work.'

'Hello?' Woman's voice, elderly, Morningside accent.

'It's the police. We're looking for Dean Vardy.'

'Have you tried his buzzer, officer?'

'We have. There's no response.' Cullen stared at the flickering light of the intercom. 'Have you seen him?'

'I think I saw him leave early this morning.'

'In a car?'

'No, on foot.'

'What time was this?'

'Oh, it would've been about nine thirty.'

'Which way was he heading?'

'Up towards Bruntsfield Links.'

Cullen looked back the way, Bruntsfield Place almost visible in the gap at the end of the street. 'Okay, thanks for your help.'

'You are actually police, aren't you?'

'Do you want my warrant card number?'

'No, I can see you.'

Cullen looked up at the window. Nothing. The other one, an old lady waving down at them. 'The name's DC Scott Cullen if you're concerned.'

'Very well.' The curtains twitched and she was gone.

Cullen headed back to the car. 'Where the hell's Vardy?'

'I've no idea, mate.' Buxton zapped the car. 'So — pub, bookies or taxi company?'

'Bookies, I think.' Cullen shook his head. 'We seek him here, we seek him there but Dean Vardy's not anywhere.'

 ∼

CULLEN PUT his phone to his ear, dialling Vardy again. No answer. Voicemail. 'Where the hell is he?'

'Hopefully in there.' Buxton pulled in on double yellows outside the YouBet shop on Dalkeith Road, orange and purple paint gleaming in the sun, the front door on a corner with a leafy side street.

Buxton undid his seat belt and got out. 'Still not answering his phone?'

'Aye. Convenient.' Cullen slammed his door. 'You came up here last week?'

'We did, aye. Me and Chantal. Copies of their books relating to Lyle are in the case file. It all checked out, backed up by their bank statement.'

'Good.' Cullen pushed past two men in their forties leaning against the wall either side of the door and opened it, avoiding breathing too much of their smoke.

The interior shared the same colour scheme, the walls a matte orange, with the woodwork and floor in purple. An array of large TVs filled most of one wall, a ten-strong crowd of men watching a greyhound race, dogs tearing around a track to a wall of cheering and swearing.

Cullen went up to the counter, the tattooed brute behind the grille as intent on the screens as the punters. He got out his warrant card and waved it. 'We're looking for Mr Vardy.'

Tattoos sniffed before checking the screen again. A dragon crawled up his neck, red flames reaching one ear, balanced by a saltire behind the other. 'He's not been in the day, pal.'

'Are you expecting him?'

'He's not that hands on.'

'Have you heard from him?'

'I told you, he's not that hands on. If I hear from him, I know I'm in trouble. I don't hear from him, things are good.'

'Anyone in here know where he might be?'

Tattoos folded his arms, tight muscles flexing. 'No. If I was you, I'd head down to the taxis or the boozer. He's not here.'

Cullen took a final look around, the punters' attention diverted to fruit machines and form guides now the race was over — nobody queuing for winnings. 'Fine.'

'You could say thank you.'

Cullen ignored him, leaving the door open for Buxton. 'He was a lovely man.'

'Should see the woman who was on when Chantal and I visited last week. He'd not last two rounds with her.' Buxton unlocked the car and they got in. 'Where next?'

Cullen tugged on his seat belt. 'Taxi firm, I reckon.'

'Okay.' Buxton started the car and pulled out. He hammered the brakes as a Mini thundered round from Dalkeith Road, swerving to avoid them. 'Cheeky wanker.'

'Watch it. Don't want to end up writing off another car.'

Buxton waited for a gap in the traffic. 'Speaking of which, why haven't you replaced yours yet?'

'Apathy, to be honest.' Cullen got out his notebook and started searching through the entries — where was Vardy? 'I just can't be bothered with it. I should really get something new. It's a pain in the hoop not having the Golf any more.'

'Thing was a tank, mate.' Buxton finally joined the stream of traffic heading west.

'Better than walking everywhere.'

'I'm not sure.' Buxton smirked. 'I take it you owed money to the insurer after they wrote it off, right?'

'Aye, very funny.' Cullen rubbed his forehead as they hurtled down the street, the high walls of the rear of Blacket Place to the right, red tenements on the left, soon thinning out to Victorian mansions. 'Did you ever get round to looking through that journal we found in Lyle's room?'

'I did, yeah. We got another four of them from his room. Took an afternoon to get through the whole lot. Barrel of fun that was.'

'So?'

Buxton exhaled as he stopped at the crossroads, the long row of private hotels to their right leading into town. 'It was full of poetry, worse than that guy we found under the Royal Mile.'

Cullen nodded at the memory. 'Hopefully not as mental?'

'Well...'

'Oh, bloody hell. Why does every fragile wee flower have to write their thoughts down like that?'

'Looking for attention?'

'Maybe.' Cullen tapped his pen on the notebook. 'Was there anything about Dean Vardy?'

'I'm not the best to assess, but there was stuff about 'the devil in charge'.'

'Seriously?'

'Yeah.'

'What about Pauline?'

'Now you're talking.' Buxton got a green and drove over the road, passing houses neither of them would afford in a thousand years of work. 'The boy was clearly in love with her.'

'What did he say?'

'There were quite a few lines devoted to his 'Quine Pal'. Had to look quine up, mind. Means girl in bloody Aberdonian.' Buxton stopped at the end of the road, indicating left. 'Anyway, QP. You know, her initials reversed?'

'Right.' Cullen looked up at the church spire, partially obscured by empty branches, the clock face stuck at the wrong time. 'What was he saying about her?'

'Talk about running away if only she'd see it.'

'And the idiot was doing this in Vardy's flat?'

'Yeah. I know.'

Cullen scribbled in his notebook to check it out in further detail. 'Did you speak to her about it?'

'Only looked at it yesterday, mate. Last thing.' Buxton turned left, heading south. A Punto belched out dark fumes in front of them; he reached over to fix the circulation. 'This morning, we were out at some geezer's flat with a knife hanging out of his guts.'

'Fair enough.'

Buxton cut across the oncoming traffic to pull in beside South-side Cars, blocking the cycle lane. 'You want to speak to her again, don't you?'

'The thought has crossed my mind.' Cullen undid his seat belt before getting out of the car.

'Well, hopefully we can speak to Vardy this bloody week.' Buxton opened the black gates before storming inside the taxi firm.

A young woman sat behind the counter; navy trouser suit, white blouse, blonde hair hauled back from her scalp and the sort of dark tan that looked genuine. 'Can I get you a car, gentlemen?'

Cullen got out his warrant card. 'Police. We're looking for Dean Vardy.'

'Mr Vardy's not been in today, I'm afraid.' She patted her hair flat on the top of her head. 'He's not been in for a few days.'

Cullen exhaled through his nostrils. 'Do you know where he might be?'

'Have you tried YouBet?'

'We've just been there.'

'What about the Debonair?'

'Not yet.' Cullen tapped at the desk. 'What contact numbers do you have for him?'

'Just his mobile.' She held up a Post-It with an 079 number on it.

Cullen cross-checked it against his phone. 'Already got that.' He nodded at Buxton. 'Come on.'

Buxton held the front door open for Cullen. 'Think her or the geezer with tattoos is covering for him?'

'No doubt.' Cullen let the door slam shut behind him. 'We've got no evidence to say they are though. Where is he?'

'Pub?'

'Pub.'

~

'I'M GETTING REALLY FED up of this.' Cullen leaned forward on the dark oak bar in the Debonair, trying to determine if there were any staff actually working. 'Excuse me!'

He scowled at the optics in front of the large mirror, seeing his reflection — the mid-brown of the tan a few shades darker than the sunburnt pink he'd been all holiday.

Buxton looked up, thumbs still tapping his phone. 'So where could he be?'

Cullen stared at the beer pumps, part of his brain tempted to sample the fizz of the German, Dutch and Spanish lagers on display, another part glad he was cleaning out his liver. 'At home?'

'What about at Pauline's?'

'I'd hoped she was on today.' Cullen looked around at the brickwork, the vaulted ceiling harking back to a previous lifetime as a cellar. A few drinkers sat on their own at the far end of the wide room, across from the entrance. 'Doesn't look like anyone's working, though.'

'Can I help you?'

Cullen spun around.

A heavy-set man stood behind them, arms folded, dressed in black, the red Debonair logo embroidered on a pocket. He took a white bar towel from his shoulder and dried his hands. 'You look like police.'

'We are.' Cullen showed his warrant card. 'We want to speak to Dean Vardy.'

'Right you are, son.'

'Who are you?'

'Gareth Cuthbertson. I'm the bar manager here.'

'Has Mr Vardy been in today?'

'Nope.' Cuthbertson shifted his bulk over to the opposite end of the bar, resting on his hands just by the large, chrome coffee machine. 'Been a bit quiet, truth be told, but Deano's not been in the day.'

'Could he be at home?'

'Might be. Stays up Viewforth way. Just past Boroughmuir school, you know?'

Buxton held up his notebook. 'It's okay, sir, we've got his address.'

'Right.'

Cullen cleared his throat. 'Is Pauline Quigley on today?'

'She's not in till six, pal.' Cuthbertson checked his watch, chunky and metallic. 'It's just past four, buddy.'

'Fine. Keith Lyle used to work here, right?'

'Aye. That's true.' Cuthbertson folded his meaty arms again, resting his bottom against the bar. 'I spoke to some officers about him a week or so back.' He frowned at Buxton. 'Weren't you one of them?'

Buxton nodded. 'I was.'

'Damn shame what happened to Keithy. You lot not caught who did this?'

'No, we haven't.' Cullen folded his own arms. 'Keith was good friends with Pauline, wasn't he?'

Cuthbertson frowned. 'Aye.'

'How close were they?'

'They were flatmates, all right? That's it.'

'You're sure about that?'

'She was seeing Deano, pal.'

'Okay. One thing I'm struggling to understand is why Mr Vardy rents a flat to the pair of them?'

Cuthbertson shook out the bar towel and started inspecting it. 'Pauline wanted a place of her own a year back. She'd been staying with her folks and got fed up of it. Deano rented her that flat.'

'He didn't want her to move in with him?'

'None of my business, buddy.' Cuthbertson snorted. 'Deano was particular about who she shared with.'

'So Mr Vardy approved of Keith Lyle moving in?'

'He did, aye.'

'How close were Dean and Pauline?'

'They spent a fair bit of time together, you know? Dean does like to be on his own sometimes. Like that Madness song.'

A couple in their twenties entered the bar, nervously looking around as they approached.

Cuthbertson squeezed behind the bar, smiling at the new customers before glancing at Cullen. 'We done?'

35

'Yeah, Angela, I can wait.' Cullen held the phone to his head as they walked down Polwarth Gardens, the wind cutting through his suit jacket and overcoat — should've brought the scarf.

Buxton hammered the intercom button. 'You reckon she's still staying with Beth?'

'She's not in her flat, so probably.'

Buxton nodded at Cullen's phone. 'Angela got anything for you yet?'

'Off to check for me.' Cullen looked back down the dark street, across the roundabout and into Merchiston, the tenements switching to mansions, the yellow sodium streetlights to bright white. 'Do you reckon it's ten minutes' walk up to Viewforth from here?'

'Yeah, if that.' Buxton pressed the buzzer again. 'We can take a stroll up there after this if you fancy.'

'Driving's fine.'

'Lazy git.' Buxton chuckled. 'So, why do you want to speak to Pauline again?'

'Fifty per cent chance Vardy's up there, right?'

'Suppose. You hoping to catch them at it?'

'Piss off.' Cullen shook his head as he laughed.

The intercom crackled. 'Hello?'

Buxton leaned in. 'Ms Armstrong, it's the police. Is Pauline there?'

'Aye. She's in the shower just now.'

'All the same, can we come up?'

A pause. 'Okay.' The buzzer sounded.

Buxton pushed open the door and led up the stairs. 'What's she still doing here?'

'Would you let a friend stay where her flatmate's just been murdered?'

'Maybe not.'

Cullen followed, climbing slowly, phone still to his ear.

'Hey, Scott?' Angela sounded out of breath.

Cullen stopped on the second floor, watching Buxton head up. 'You got the journal?'

'Aye, just found it. I thought Simon was supposed to have gone through this?'

'He did. I wanted you to have another look.'

'Okay. So...?'

'Look for the initials QP or the phrase Quine Pal. Start at the back.'

'Okay.' Riffling of papers. 'Got it. Last entry is for the thirtieth.' Long pause. 'Bloody hell, this is some dark shit.'

'In what way?'

'It's all about blood and knives and dragons and tits.'

'About killing someone?'

'Aye. 'The Dark Lord' is the target.'

'That's got to be Vardy.' Cullen got out his notebook and wrote it down. 'What about earlier? Is it always this dark?'

'Okay. Middle of October...' Angela clicked her tongue. 'It's all sweetness and light. Stuff about escape with QP.'

'That's what Buxton said.'

'Right.' Pages flipped near the mic. 'The death stuff seems to start in December. Actually, the first.'

'What's the previous entry?'

'The thirtieth of November. Just says 'Tonight's the night'.'

Cullen leaned against the banister and swapped hands. 'So something happened then, right?'

'Right. St Andrew's Night.'

'The thirtieth? So it is.' Cullen stared at the green door opposite. What happened on the thirtieth? Something so bad it changed Keith Lyle's hope into despair, rage and anger, most likely at Dean Vardy. 'Did Vardy batter him?'

'Scott, he might've done. What's in this book is flowery gibberish. It's like all writing stuff, you know? Paragraphs of havering nonsense. One of them has 'like something' three times.'

'Like a simile?'

'Aye. It hurts my head to read it.'

'I feel your pain. I did a degree in English, remember?'

'You poor sod.' Angela snorted. 'Anything else you want?'

'No, that's cool. I'll see you back at the station.'

'I take it you've not found Vardy then?'

'No comment.' Cullen hung up the call and started up the stairs again. At the top, the flat door was open, a sliver of light creeping onto the red tiles. He entered. 'Hello?'

'Through here.' Beth's voice came from the kitchen.

Cullen went through, Buxton sitting opposite her, again leaving Cullen to stand. 'You said she's in the shower?'

'Aye. Sounds like she's just got out now.' Beth folded her arms. 'I was telling your colleague here — she's due into work this evening. I was going to give her a lift.'

Buxton smiled as he got out his notebook. 'While we're waiting, are you okay to answer some questions?'

'Sure.' Beth let her shoulders relax again.

'For starters, how has she been?'

Beth looked outside, dinner preparation activities going on in both bay windows opposite. 'Pauline's taken Keith's death pretty bad. I've been looking after her a bit. Driving her to work, listening, that sort of thing. I work at the Deb too, so I can be flexible when I go in.'

'She's still staying here, though?'

'She is.' Beth took a deep breath. 'My flatmate's in Ireland for a month, so it's kind of convenient.'

'Has Pauline talked about moving out?'

Beth nodded. 'It's on the cards. She asked Dean to see what other flats he's got available.'

'How many has he got?'

'I'm not sure.'

'So she's not going to move in with him, then?'

'Hardly.'

Buxton frowned. 'Why do you say that?'

'They've not got that sort of relationship yet, have they?' Beth bit her lip. 'Don't get me wrong, Dean comes round a lot and they go out together a fair amount, but he likes his own space. Always has.'

'Isn't there anyone else she can stay with? Parents, maybe?'

Beth shrugged. 'That's even less likely.'

'Was there anything going on between her and Keith?'

Beth scowled at Buxton. 'You're kidding, right? Keith and Pauline? No danger, son. Dean would go apeshit if he even got the whiff of any funny business going on. Besides, she was well out of Keith's league. Not to speak ill of the dead, of course.'

'Did Mr Lyle see it that way?'

Beth sniffed. 'Maybe not.'

The kitchen door snuck open and Pauline entered, wearing a dressing gown, her hair damp. She froze when she saw them. 'Oh.'

Cullen smiled at her. 'We wouldn't mind a word with you, if that's okay.'

Pauline nodded. 'Okay.' She squinted at the clock on the microwave. 'I've got to get off to my work soon. Beth's taking me.'

'We can give you a lift.'

'I'd rather not, if it's all the same.'

Beth got to her feet and padded over, patting Pauline on the arm. 'There's a chilli in the micro for you, Pauls. It just beeped before these two arrived.'

Pauline gave a slight smile. 'Cheers, babes.'

'I'll give you a lift, okay? I'll be in my room.' Beth left them to it, leaving the kitchen door wide open.

Cullen waited until the bedroom door clicked shut before starting. 'Ms Quigley, we need to speak to Dean Vardy.'

Pauline slumped down in the vacated seat, tugging at the long sleeve of her robe. 'He's not at the pub?'

'He's not, no.'

'Have you tried his flat?'

'We have. No answer.'

Pauline ran a hand through her hair. Looked like she'd lost weight over the last week or so, not that she was heavy to start with. Her cheeks had started to sink in and the skin beneath her eyes was dark and blotchy.

Cullen moved so he was between Pauline and the kitchen door, barring her exit. 'We wanted to ask you a few questions about your relationship with Mr Lyle.'

'We've been over and over this.' She looked at the table, bunching her fists up in the fabric of her dressing gown. 'There was nothing going on. I swear.'

'From your perspective?'

'Of course.'

'What about from Keith's?'

'Eh?'

'Did Keith think there might've been anything?'

'No!'

'Is that the truth?'

'Yes!'

Cullen returned to the cooker, leaning against it, the appliance stone cold. 'Did you know anything about Keith's journal?'

Pauline sat forward, pinching the bridge of her nose. 'I knew he was writing something.'

'Did he ever show you it?'

'No.'

'Okay. So, you'll know we found it in his room and took it into evidence.' Cullen waved over at Buxton. 'My colleague here has been through it, you know?'

Buxton smiled at her. 'It's quite interesting. It goes from being a very hopeful thing to suddenly full of despair. Seems to change around about St Andrew's Night.'

Pauline swallowed, her eyes blinking. 'Does it?'

'It does.' Cullen clenched his jaw. 'Pauline, what happened on St Andrew's Night?'

'Nothing.'

'You're sticking to that story, are you?'

'It's the truth!'

'Let's agree something, shall we?' Cullen knelt down in front of her. 'If you tell us the whole story, we'll consider dropping any charges regarding you not telling us. Deal?'

Pauline nodded as she shifted even further back in her seat, trying to push herself away. She stared up at the strip light on the ceiling. 'Keith tried it on with me on St Andrew's Night.'

Cullen got up and pointed a finger at her. 'This is the sort of thing I'd have appreciated knowing a week ago.'

Pauline shut her eyes. 'Look, I'm really sorry.'

Cullen nodded at Buxton. 'Cuff her.'

'No!' Pauline raised her hands. 'I swear I didn't mean anything by it!'

'I'm thinking we could do you with perverting the course of justice. What about you, Simon?'

'I'm thinking we could add in withholding evidence.'

'Agreed. That's probably enough for a custodial sentence.'

Pauline cowered back in the chair, pushing her body tight to the wall, the dressing gown riding up. 'Look, please! I didn't think! That's all!'

Cullen screwed up his face, tilting his head to the side. 'Really?'

'When I spoke to you, I'd just found Keith's body! I was upset!'

'I'm listening. St Andrew's Night.'

Pauline dusted herself off. 'Right, Keith tried it on with me that night after closing. We were alone in the bar.'

'The Debonair?'

'Aye. We had some drinks to celebrate – it was a good night. Keith set up a promo with a whisky chain. Dunpender or something, I can't remember. It was just me and him left. That's when he made a move on me.'

'What sort of thing?'

'He tried to kiss me.'

'Did you reciprocate?'

Pauline swallowed. 'Maybe.'

'You maybe reciprocated?'

'Okay, so I did. But it was just kissing. That's all. I swear. We got a taxi on Lothian Road and came back here, hands all over each other. I went to the toilet and had second thoughts. I told Keith it wasn't a good idea to take things any further. Things have been... strained since then.'

'I see.' Cullen nodded, looking around the kitchen, his mind whirring. 'So why didn't he make his move here at some other time?'

'I don't know, do I?' Pauline shrugged. 'We were both drunk at the bar. We don't really drink together here.'

'And Mr Vardy found out?' Cullen stood up, his knees creaking.

'Aye. He must've seen the CCTV from the pub.' Pauline stared out the kitchen window. 'Dean threatened to kill Keith.'

36

'So why the hell didn't you tell us?' Cullen turned around in a slow circle — she better have a really good reason.

Pauline chewed her cheek and tugged her gown tighter. 'Can I get dressed?'

'No, you can't.' Cullen got in front of her. 'This is serious, Pauline. You withheld information in a murder inquiry pertaining to a threat made to the victim.'

'And I'm really, really sorry.' Pauline buried her head in her hands, fingers clenching the sleeves of her gown. 'I don't know why I did it.'

'Nothing to do with covering up for Dean, is it?'

'How?'

Cullen folded his arms — take it slow here. 'Ms Quigley, I'll go through the facts as I see them.' He counted on his thumb. 'One, you're romantically involved with Mr Vardy.' Forefinger. 'Two, Mr Lyle — your flatmate — was found dead in this flat. Murdered. Only prints in that room are his, yours and Mr Dean Vardy.' Middle finger. 'Three, Mr Vardy has a gap in his alibi.' Ring finger. 'Finally, Mr Vardy has a reason to kill Mr Lyle.'

'I told you I'm sorry.'

'Did it just slip your mind?'

'No, I—'

'This should've been mentioned when we spoke to you last Tuesday. You know that, right?'

'I'm sorry. Yes, I—'

'You've withheld information before.'

'What?'

'The fact Mr Lyle owed a significant sum to Mr Vardy.'

'I swear I never knew it.'

'Really? What about Mr Vardy being your boyfriend?'

She looked away. 'Sorry.'

'Why did you do it?'

Pauline nibbled her lip for a few seconds before she flicked her damp hair over. 'Dean made me.'

'Really? You expect me to believe that?'

'I do.' Pauline swallowed and got to her feet. She opened her dressing gown on the right, left hand raising her small breast. Her ribs were black and blue. 'Dean batters the shit out of me.'

Cullen pursed his lips — this was getting worse. 'You can put yourself away.'

She sat down, shoulders hunched forward. 'So you believe me?'

'I'm wondering what else you're not telling us.'

'I swear it's the truth.'

Cullen sniffed — how do we deal with this? He nodded at Buxton. 'Simon, can you call Control and get a squad car out here, please?'

'Sure.' Buxton got up and walked to the hall, speaking into his Airwave.

Pauline looked up at him, her head almost on the table. 'Are you arresting me?'

'Not yet. We'll get you to make a statement covering everything relating to Dean Vardy — the information he's made you withhold, the beatings, how his mother didn't truly love him, whatever.'

'And if I don't?'

'Then I'll arrest you.'

She nodded. 'Okay. Fine.'

Cullen sat opposite her, the chair still warm. 'There's something else of course.'

'What?'

'We need to speak to Mr Vardy.'

'I told you. I don't know where he is.'

'Can you phone him and find out, please?'

She nodded. 'Okay.' She walked over to the counter, picking up a giant smartphone and fiddling with the screen. Placed it to her ear and stared at Cullen. 'Dean? Aye, it's Pauline. No, it's fine. Aye. Aye. I'm not sure I can do my shift tonight. Aye, Keith. Aye. Can I see you?' Eyes moved to the floor. 'Where are you? Aye, I'll come round. Be about fifteen minutes. Okay, love you too.' She ended the call, putting the phone back on the counter. 'He's at his flat.'

Buxton entered the room, clutching his Airwave. 'There's a car about two minutes away.'

Cullen nodded at Pauline. 'You can get dressed now.'

She picked up the phone and made for the door.

Cullen intercepted her. 'Leave the phone.'

~

'Thank you.' Cullen waited for the door to buzz before entering the stairwell and crossing the marble tiles.

'Think that old dear likes you.'

'She's just lonely.' Cullen looked up the spiral staircase, the lights flickering, before trotting up, two at a time. The flat on the right at the top had *D. Vardy* stencilled on the door. He rapped, making sure Buxton and he stood either side of the spy glass.

The door opened and Vardy peered out. 'That you, babes?'

Cullen flashed his warrant card. 'We need to ask you some que—'

Vardy slammed the door.

Buxton raised an eyebrow. 'Great plan, mate.'

'Mr Vardy! It's the police!'

An eye appeared at the spy glass. 'I've said all I'm saying to you lot!'

'We need to ask you some further questions.'

'You been in touch with my lawyer?'

Cullen frowned at Buxton, who shrugged. 'Aye, we have. He said to speak to you directly.'

'Well, this door's staying shut until I hear from him, okay?'

'We can get a warrant, you know?'

'Be my guest, pal.'

'Let us in!'

Silence.

Cullen glanced at Buxton. 'The cheeky bastard's just left us.'

'What are we going to do?'

'I've got an idea.' Cullen hammered the door. 'Mr Vardy, we understand why you killed Keith Lyle!'

The spyhole darkened again before the door opened a crack, a sliver of Vardy's face peering out. 'You fucking what?'

'You've got means and motive.'

'Fuck off, I haven't killed anyone.'

'You found out about Mr Lyle sleeping with Pauline, didn't you?'

'Now, wait a minute.' The door shot open and Vardy stormed out, hand reaching for Cullen's throat and slamming him against the wall tiles. 'You shut your fucking face!'

Cullen choked, his fingers trying to grip Vardy's hand, feet lashing out but missing.

Buxton lurched forward, tugging at Vardy's shoulders.

Vardy elbowed him in the stomach, Buxton collapsing to his knees and coughing. 'Nobody but me was riding Pauline! You hear me? Nobody!'

Cullen twisted his head from side to side, trying to wriggle free. The thumbs around his throat released.

Vardy pulled Cullen back by the collar, before smacking his head against the wall.

Cullen heard the crunch of the tiles as they cracked with the impact. His skull felt like someone had carved it open. 'Shite!'

Buxton snapped out his baton, one hand on his abdomen. 'Come here, you!'

Vardy dodged the blow from the baton, catching it on the downswing. He slugged Buxton square in the stomach, sending him down again.

Vardy grabbed Cullen by the chin, pushing his head back against the wall. 'Stop making shit up!'

'It's not made up.' Cullen got an inch of freedom and lashed out, knee crunching into Vardy's groin.

Vardy blocked the blow, both hands going to Cullen's throat, elbows pinning him back. 'You fucking pig scum! You can't do this shit to people!'

Cullen struggled to breathe, but managed to croak. 'Come down to the station with us.'

'Fuck off!' Vardy swiped out, taking Cullen's legs from under him. He collapsed into a heap and could only watch as Vardy put the boot in on Buxton. 'You fucking pair of fucking cunts!'

Cullen swept his leg round, catching Vardy below his right knee. He stumbled forward, smacking his face off the wooden banister, his head snapping back as he collapsed on top of a groaning Buxton.

Cullen reached into his pocket for his Airwave. 'This is DC Scott Cullen requesting backup.'

37

Methven lay his hands flat on the tabletop, looking across the interview room at Dean Vardy. 'Mr Vardy, you assaulted two of my officers just over an hour ago.'

Vardy switched his gaze to Cullen. 'This prick here was trying to get into my house. That's unlawful entry.'

Cullen took a deep breath, his throat still rasping from the encounter, the back of his head aching. 'We simply wanted to speak to you.'

'You were spreading a load of shite about my girlfriend.'

'We were, were we?'

'Aye, you were.' Vardy scowled at them. 'She'd never have let Keith Lyle anywhere near her.'

'Is that so?'

'Aye.'

'If that's the case, why did you threaten to kill him?'

'Watch your mouth, pal.'

'You're denying it?'

'Of course I am.'

'You knew Keith Lyle and Pauline Quigley had been intimate, didn't you?'

'No comment.'

'You saw it on the CCTV tapes.'

'No comment.'

'And you had a word with Mr Lyle about it, threatened to kill him.'

'No comment, pal.'

Cullen clenched his fists — getting nowhere with this approach. He leaned across the table. 'Can you detail your movements on the evening of the thirtieth of December, please?'

'This again?' Vardy rubbed the back of his neck, his right bicep bulging with the movement. 'I've told you a load of times. I was at the pub with Darren Keogh.'

'You're adamant?'

'Whatever that means.'

'You were definitely there?'

'I fucking was.'

Cullen folded his arms. 'Really?'

'Aye.' Vardy smirked at his lawyer, Neil Parker. 'We know he's checked this out, right, and yet he still asks. Why's that, Neil?'

Parker smiled at Cullen. 'You're wasting my client's time here. He's innocent and you're holding him for entirely spurious reasons.'

'He's a murder suspect.'

'He's an innocent man with an alibi.' Parker adjusted his tie. 'I suggest you let him go.'

Methven ran his tongue over his lips. 'Mr Vardy assaulted two of my officers.'

'So?' Parker gave a laugh. 'Your officers went in gangbusters on my client. You've been harassing him when he's given a perfectly credible alibi and one backed up by a number of sources, I believe.'

Methven snorted. 'We've got a missing hour in your client's statement where he could've killed Mr Lyle.'

'We've been over this.' Parker gave a final tug to the knot then let it go. 'Mr Vardy bought some chips. At the time of the initial interview, he couldn't remember where but we know you've sent out a squad of officers up there to find which chip shop it was. *D'Monte's* on Bread Street, correct?'

'That's correct, yes.'

'Thanks. It's been a great help to our case.'

Methven switched back to glaring at Vardy. 'What happened after you bought the chips, Mr Vardy?'

'I ate them.'

'Then?'

'I staggered home. I'd had a lot of booze.'

'You didn't pay a visit to Ms Quigley's flat?'

'No. She was working that night. Didn't want to force myself on her when she was tired, did I? I'm a gentleman.'

Cullen glared at Vardy — enough chicanery. 'Who else was in the pub with you and Mr Keogh that night?'

Vardy gave a chuckle. 'I can't remember. Sorry.'

'That's very convenient.' Cullen shook his head. 'Just the two of you, was it?'

'My client was under the influence that night, unfortunately.'

'Your client's going to get charged with murder.' Methven shut his eyes as he spoke. 'It'll be very difficult for him to manage his many businesses from a custody cell.'

Vardy sniffed. 'There was another boy with us.'

Cullen cracked his knuckles. 'Name, now.'

'Didn't really know the boy, right?'

Cullen grimaced — it was going to be Falconer, he just knew it. 'What was his name, Mr Vardy?'

'My client is unwilling to divu—'

'Like fuck I am. I want out of here, right fucking now.' Vardy shook his head at Parker.

'You're going nowhere.' Methven gripped the edge of the table. 'Except for a cell downstairs.'

Vardy stared at him for a few seconds before nodding at Cullen. 'The boy's name was Billy.'

Cullen frowned. 'Billy?'

'Aye. Dazza knows him. It was his mate.'

'It was definitely Billy?'

'Mr Vardy, I think you shou—'

Vardy prodded Parker in the chest. 'Listen, pal, I'm paying you for legal advice. I'm not asking you anything right now, okay? Just fucking sit there and look pretty.' He smiled at Cullen. 'Aye. The boy was definitely called Billy.'

Cullen frowned. 'Not Kenneth?'

'Kenneth?' Vardy screwed up his face. 'Eh?'

'Maybe Kenny?'

'No, it was Billy, as in short for William.'

'Inspector, please ensure your subordinate desists from this line of questioning.'

Vardy pointed at Parker. 'I said shut it, okay?'

Cullen waited till Vardy stared back at him. 'Do you know this Billy's surname?'

'Afraid not, pal. As I said, Dazza'll know. Why don't you check with him?'

Cullen wrote it down. 'Do you know a Kenny Falconer?'

'Mr Vardy, I mu—'

'Shut it.' Vardy's mouth twitched slightly. 'Aye. I know Kenny. We did some business transactions a while back.'

'You mean you bought knives off him?'

'No comment.'

'Was Mr Falconer with you in Teuchter's on the night of the thirtieth?'

'Just a second.' Parker whispered into Vardy's ear, the Custody and Security Officer out of earshot.

Cullen leaned over to Methven. 'What's he up to?'

'No idea.' Methven scowled across the table. 'That is some decidedly odd behaviour.'

Parker nodded then raised a bony finger and indicated for them to return. 'My client's ready.'

Methven folded his arms. 'Well?'

Vardy stared up at the ceiling. 'I've just remembered something.'

Methven gave a deep sigh. 'So what is it?'

Vardy lowered his eyes from the ceiling, locking onto Cullen. 'Kenny Falconer *was* with me and Dazza that night.'

Parker smiled, revealing perfect white teeth. 'For the record, he was with both Mr Keogh and Mr Falconer.'

Cullen frowned. 'And not with this 'Billy'?'

Vardy snorted, eyes flickering shut. 'Correct.'

'I'm not following you.'

'I was drunk.' Vardy laughed as he rolled his shoulders. 'It's an easy mistake to make. Brewdog make strong beer, you know?'

'Not really.' Cullen held his gaze. 'No matter how drunk I get, I'm usually still aware of who I'm with. Especially if someone's trying to pin a murder on me.' He looked away, rubbing his hands together. 'You've just changed your statement.'

'I remembered something.' Vardy thumbed at Parker. 'Something my brief reminded me I told him the next day.'

'But you knew Falconer and you were adamant he wasn't there.'

'Aye. I got confused.' Vardy sniffed. 'Thought he wasn't there cos I'd been out with the boy Falconer the night before. It was the same night, right?'

'And what about Billy?'

'I'm thinking of another night. Sorry.'

'So he wasn't there?'

'No. Just the three of us.'

'You expect us to believe this?'

'I'm trying to play fair with you boys. I don't want to lead you up the garden path or anything. Now can you let me go?'

Methven stood up. 'Very well.' He leaned over and spoke into the recorder, his voice wavering. 'Interview terminated at eighteen seventeen.'

38

'Purple sodding buggery.' Methven opened the meeting room door and entered, shaking it on its frame. 'Sodding, sodding hell.'

Chantal Jain looked up from her laptop. 'I take it that went well?'

'Give me a sodding minute.' Methven went over to the whiteboard, tearing off the marker's lid.

Jain pushed a coffee over the table. 'Here you go, Scott. Just got it for you. Sorry about earlier.'

Cullen picked up the cup. 'This isn't like you.' He took a sniff. 'Is there salt in it or something?'

'No it's clean. Simon guilted me into getting it.'

Buxton shrugged, his eyes still red raw from the fight. 'I'd never hear the end of it, would I?'

Methven turned from the board, arms folded, and scowled at Cullen. 'DC Cullen does like to go on a tad, doesn't he?'

'Cheers.' Cullen shook his head — charming bastard.

Buxton rubbed his left eye. 'So I take it the interview with Vardy didn't go very well?'

'It's still a closed door, Constable.' Methven put his hands in his pockets. 'Albeit a very strange one. Vardy said there was just one other person with them and it was definitely not Falconer.'

'Right? So?'

Methven frowned at the whiteboard. 'The strange thing is, after a word with his lawyer, he corrected the statement, insisting Falconer *was* with them.'

Buxton scowled. 'How can Vardy be sure it was Falconer?'

Methven scribbled on the whiteboard. 'They're acquainted of old, Constable. Sounds like Vardy bought a knife or knives from Falconer a few years ago.'

'Bloody hell.' Buxton stood up, hand delicately patting his stomach as he winced. 'Why did he change the story?'

'I don't know. What I do know is I don't like it.' Methven scribbled on the whiteboard — *Vardy, Falconer, Keogh.* This is a motley crew if ever I saw one.'

Cullen joined Methven at the whiteboard, tapping the section devoted to the pub visit. 'You need to add in Billy, sir.'

'Why?'

'Well, I don't like what Vardy just said there. One minute he's all 'Kenny wasn't with us' and swearing at Parker. Then his lawyer whispers sweet nothings in his ear and it's all, 'oh I might have made a mistake, officer'.' Cullen looked at Buxton and Jain. 'He changed his statement — he never met Billy that night. It was all a mistake. He thought he'd met Falconer the night before.'

Methven bounced the pen off his teeth, making a clicking noise. 'Agreed. Something's not right about it.'

Cullen slurped at his coffee. 'So what do you want us to do, sir?'

Methven focused on Cullen. 'Constable, what do you think of speaking to Keogh again?'

'I'd say he's in danger of lawyering up. Soon as he gets Parker, Nelson or any other lizard in there, he'll clam up.'

'Sodding hell.' Methven tapped his finger on the whiteboard. 'So, what do you suggest?'

'I think we need to speak to this bar manager again. Dave Weir.'

~

CULLEN LEANED against the stone wall. 'Not this again...'

While the seating area in Teuchter's had just a couple of

punters supping pints at separate tables — one going through the Herald, the other on his mobile — the bar had a six-deep queue.

'Hoy!' Jain tugged the black shirtsleeve of a passing man. 'Do you work here?'

'I do, aye.' Eyes on his sleeve, Jain still gripping.

'Police.' Warrant card out, Jain sniffed. 'We're looking for Dave Weir.'

'Sorry, love. His shift's finished.'

'Do you know where he is?'

'Think he was going out drinking.'

'On a Thursday?'

'Aye. Him and his flatmates are all off tomorrow. They all worked Hogmanay, so they were going out tonight. They arranged it months ago.'

'Do his flatmates work in pubs?'

'Aye. The Debonair, I believe.'

'All of them?'

'Aye, except Dave himself.'

'Did Mr Weir ever work there?'

'Aye. Before he was brought in here.'

'Do you have his number?'

'Aye. Give me a second, my mobile's just through the back.'

'An address would be helpful.'

'Right. I'll see what I can do.' He set off.

Jain grabbed his shirt at the back. 'What's your name?'

'John. John Owenson.'

'Thanks, John.' Chantal tilted her head at him. 'Were you working on the thirtieth of December?'

'Day off. Sorry.'

'Anyone on today who was?'

'Let me check.' Owenson pulled his shirt free and wandered off, finding a channel through the crowded bar area and going through a dark wood door to the side.

Jain ran her hands through her hair, pulling the knot tight at the back. 'Weir's out on the lash. We'll never find him.'

'He might've gone home. Shit, shower, shag, shave.'

'You sound more like Bain by the day.'

'Not you as well.'

'Ha, Buxton said you're getting sensitive to it.'

'Because it's total bollocks.'

'Mm, just wait till we're all working for him again.'

'Eh?'

'Just something I heard.' Jain checked her watch. 'It's just after six. That's early to be going out.'

'Eh? Tell me you've never been out this early?'

'On a proper night out? With my moustache? That's a good hour of trimming, Scott. And my arms. It's not easy being an Asian girl.'

Cullen shut his eyes. 'I don't want to hear this.'

Jain grinned, her eyes going to the top of her trousers. 'Don't get me started on my pubes.'

Cullen held up a hand. 'That's enough!'

Jain giggled then pointed back to the bar area. 'Here he comes.'

John Owenson handed a sheet of paper to Jain. 'Mobile number's on there.'

'Where does he stay?'

'Hart Street, just off Broughton Street. And I checked — no-one on tonight was working on the thirtieth. Sorry. Want me to get you their numbers?'

'Thanks. I'll leave it for now.' Jain made to walk off.

Cullen raised a finger. 'Just one more thing.' He smiled at Owenson. 'Would you be able to print us off a till receipt for the orders placed by Mr Dean Vardy on the night of the thirtieth of December?'

Owenson swallowed. 'Mr Vardy?'

'Is that going to be a problem?'

'No. That's fine.'

∾

CULLEN TOOK a step back onto the road on Hart Street, looking up at the top-floor flat then up and down the quiet street. He glanced at Jain. 'Call him again.'

'Your funeral.' Jain tapped the screen then put the phone to her ear. 'Still just ringing out.'

Cullen sighed. 'Dave Weir, where are you?'

Jain pocketed her phone. 'Why do you want to speak to him again?'

'Because someone's lying here. Kenny Falconer either was or wasn't in the bar. Weir will know either way.'

'You sound more like Bain every day.'

'I told you, stop it.'

Jain laughed, smug grin on her face. 'Right, so what are we going to do?'

'I've no idea.' Cullen reached over and pressed the buzzer to the next highest numbered flat. No response. He tried the one below.

'Hello?'

'It's the police. We need access to the stairwell.'

'What for?'

'We just need to speak to Dave Weir.'

'Oh, right. In you come.' The buzzer sounded and the door clicked open. 'Second flat on the first floor.'

Cullen opened the door, leading them inside. 'Jesus Christ, look at this place.'

Light from a chandelier bounced off cream walls, pastoral paintings of horses and cows. The staircase was carpeted, the balustrade the same colour as the walls, the wooden handrail varnished a deep brown.

'What's a barman doing in a flat like this?'

'I know.' Jain nodded, eyes full of wonder. 'This is just like where Budgie lives.'

Cullen frowned. 'You've been there?'

'Shite.'

Cullen laughed. 'Oh, ho ho!'

Jain prodded him in the chest. 'Keep that to yourself.'

'Don't know if I can.' Cullen skipped up the stairs, trying to put distance between them. He got out his warrant card as he reached the landing.

A table sat in the centre of the far wall, a mail pigeonhole resting behind a large bowl of potpourri. A man in his forties fiddled with the post, swapping some letters about. He smiled at their approach. 'Can I see some credentials?'

Cullen held up his warrant card. 'I'm DC Cullen. This is DC Jain.'

'Right, that all looks in order.' He held out a hand. 'James Court. How can I help?'

'You're a neighbour of Mr Weir, is that correct?'

'Aye.' Court pointed up the stairs. 'He shares a flat on the second floor.'

Cullen was bored with him already. 'How well do you know him?'

'Reasonably well. We've had some parties in the whole place. Makes it feel like a townhouse. I'm an architect and I was behind all of this.'

'I see. Do you have any idea where he is?'

'I heard them all trudging out earlier.'

'Them?'

'His flatmates.'

'How many of them are there?'

'Five, I think.'

'And Mr Weir was with them, correct?'

'He was, yes.'

'You actually saw him?'

'I did. I was just finishing off painting the walls downstairs. I finally got a tin of Farrow and Ball I'd been after since before Christmas. Needed another coat and I ran out.'

'Any idea where they were going?'

'Not at all. I much prefer a bottle of wine inside my four walls. Besides, I don't like to mingle too closely.'

Cullen waved a hand around. 'This seems a bit opulent for a bar manager.'

'It is but that's a shared flat he's in'

'Do you know who owns it?'

'I had some dealings with the factors when we got this place done up. Can't quite recall the name — Dean Bridge or something?'

Cullen noted it. 'Okay, thanks for your time, sir.'

Court smiled. 'No problem.'

Cullen handed him a card. 'Give me a call if anyone from that flat turns up, okay?'

'Will do.' Court pocketed the card and headed inside his flat.

Jain started down the stairs. 'I'm tempted to trek dog shite all over his lovely carpet.'

'Classy.'

'This is getting us nowhere. We need to speak to that Weir guy.'

'Agreed.'

'Okay, so what now?'

'I'm going to get back to the station. Can you try and find Weir?'

'How the hell am I supposed to do that?'

Cullen shrugged as he held open the street door. 'You're a DC, right? Use your skills.'

39

C ullen stared at the whiteboard then drew a ring around *Weir*. 'Have you heard from Chantal?'

'Nope.'

'Bollocks.' Cullen focused on *Falconer*. 'What have we got on Kenny Falconer's movements that night?'

'Nothing concrete.' Buxton flicked through his notebook before running his finger down a page. 'Other than his and Vardy's statements, we've got nothing confirming his presence in the pub. He might've been there or he might not. It's just their word for it.'

'But Vardy started off saying he wasn't there.'

'Hang on.' Buxton frowned. 'I'm getting myself confused here.'

'Okay. I'll go slowly for you.' Cullen rubbed out a corner of the whiteboard, writing *Keogh*. 'First, Keogh told us both Vardy and Falconer were with him.'

'Agreed.'

Cullen wrote *Falconer*. 'When we spoke to Falconer, after he finished messing us about, he said it was him, Keogh and Vardy.'

'Little wanker.'

Cullen wrote *Vardy*. 'Dean Vardy initially said Falconer wasn't there then he changed his mind and said he was.' He took a step back. 'So their statements match. Keogh, Vardy and Falconer.'

'Other than this twattery with Vardy's lawyer.' Buxton pointed at *Weir*. 'Weir told us Vardy was there, but he wasn't sure who with.'

'Correct.' Cullen screwed up his eyes. He scribbled on the whiteboard, linking *Vardy* and *Falconer*. 'Parker's at it, though, I swear.'

'In what way?'

'Just the way he grabbed Vardy and got him to change his story, insisting Falconer was there.'

Buxton frowned. 'What's that all about?'

'No idea.' Cullen looked over the whiteboard. 'Did you get anything on Vardy's aunt?'

Buxton nodded. 'Got a hold of her when you and Crystal were in with Vardy earlier.'

'So how cougarish is she?'

'Shut up, *Bain*. Christ's sake, mate.' Buxton snorted. 'I spoke to her on the phone.'

Cullen struggled to stop grinning. 'Did you confirm the story?'

'Not yet. Lives in Northern Ireland now. Somewhere in Antrim.' Buxton added three boxes to the board to cover it.

Cullen smirked. 'By the way, you never told me Chantal Jain went round to your flat?'

'Oh for fu—'

'Who's been at my sodding whiteboard?' Methven stormed into the room, hands flapping around as he looked up and down the white expanse. 'There's another six boxes on here!'

Buxton raised a hand. 'That was me, sir.'

'And what's the meaning of it?'

'Just adding the latest on the case.' Buxton shrugged. 'I did it in green so you'd see.'

Methven scowled at him. 'But *green* is for confirmed evidence, Constable!'

Buxton traced his pen all over the board. 'But everything's red or orange on here.'

'Precisely.' Methven narrowed his eyes. 'It's all sodding nonsense.'

Cullen put a hand to his chin. 'You were philosophical about it last week.'

'That was before DS McNeill's caseload got thrust at me.'

Methven snatched the pen from Buxton and started rewriting everything in red. 'Care to run me through the latest thinking?'

Cullen rubbed his chin. 'Well, Falconer and Vardy knew each other of old but neither were particularly forthcoming about them both being in Teuchter's that night.'

'Sodding hell.'

'We think they could just be playing us, sir.'

'In what way?'

'Well, if they were discussing a deal to buy and sell knives, for instance.'

'Sodding, sodding hell.'

'Aye, we were maybe lucky he didn't stab me or Simon.' Cullen shrugged. 'Everything goes back to Dave Weir, sir. If we confirm his statement, we're sorted.'

'Agreed.' Methven tapped on the board. 'Where are we with finding this barman?'

Cullen took a couple of steps away from the whiteboard. 'I've left DC Jain looking for him, sir. Not had an update.'

'I expect you to be on top of this, Constable.'

'Speak of the devil.' Buxton waved at the glass wall.

Jain entered the room, face like thunder. She slumped against the wall. 'Evening, gents.'

Methven scratched his forehead with the pen. 'Where have you been?'

'Looking for Weir. He's disappeared. Cullen and I went to his flat and spoke to a neighbour. Then I was up at Teuchter's again and about ten pubs.'

'And he's not there?'

'No. The neighbour reckons he left with his flatmates a couple of hours ago. I've been back to the bar to see if I could get any leads. Went to a few usual haunts of theirs.'

'Then where the sodding hell is he?'

'I've no idea.' She shrugged. 'I've got a search out for him.'

'You've been away a while. What else have you done?'

Jain kicked a heel back against the skirting. 'I spoke to the other bar staff who worked the thirtieth. Two of them. Neither saw Vardy or Keogh or Falconer. They were just pulling pints.'

'This is going nowhere.' Methven collapsed into a chair and

checked his watch. 'Right, clear off home, the lot of you. I expect you in at seven thirty tomorrow.'

～

CULLEN TRUDGED down the Royal Mile, past the rows of darkened tat shops and the World's End pub. He craned his neck round the corner, spotting Sharon's orange Focus parked in the residents' bay on Jeffrey Street. He took a deep breath as he walked past the two pubs at the end of the street, sorely tempted to go inside either.

Instead, he crossed at the lights and walked up the close.

'This is getting away early, is it?' Sharon was dumping a bag in the outside bin.

'Aye, sorry. Ended up getting wrapped up in Crystal's shite. Well, it's your shite we've been dealing with.' Cullen held open the door. 'What was in the bag?'

'Just had to empty Fluffy's litter tray again.' She started up the stairs. 'It's like he's not been to the toilet all holiday.'

'Poor wee bugger.'

'You've changed your tune.' Sharon smiled as they entered the flat. 'Last time I'm getting that cat sitter. She was rubbish. Never changed the litter once. My mum would be better.'

Cullen hung up his coat and scarf before slumping on the sofa in the living room. 'I miss my bloody car.'

'You've only had eight months to replace it.'

'I just can't be arsed with the hassle of getting a new one. And the parking's shite round here.'

'Thought you liked living here.'

'It's got its downsides, I suppose.'

Sharon sat next to him on the settee. 'I saw a nice new build in Bathgate on the way home. Checked it out when I got back. Three bedrooms for a hundred and fifty.'

'I'm not moving to Bathgate. End of.'

'Scott—'

'Seriously. Linlithgow at a push.'

'Right.'

'Don't be like that.'

'We need to get out of this place, Scott. I'm fed up with it.'

'Let me get my feet back under the table at work. I've not got time to think about this.'

'We've been talking about it all holiday. You'll just forget again, won't you?' She put a hand on her hip. 'More late nights, more Crystal, more moaning about your lack of promotion. We need to strike while the iron's hot.'

'Maybe.' Cullen looked around the poky flat, watching Fluffy making a nest out of a pile of dirty washing neither of them had bothered to shove in the machine. 'We got anything to drink?'

'Scott...'

DAY 3

Friday
9th January

'Morning, sir.' Cullen shut the meeting room door behind him. 'Sorry I'm late.'

Methven stood by the whiteboard, checking his watch in an exaggerated motion. 'Not by my watch.'

Cullen sat at the end of the table, between Buxton and Angela.

'Has anyone seen DC Jain this morning?' Methven folded his arms.

Angela shrugged. 'Not seen her, sir.'

Methven shifted round to the side of the whiteboard. 'Right. Let's get started. As you know, I've got to report our progress to DCI Cargill at eight o'clock.'

Cullen raised a hand. 'I'm not sure we're much further forward since last night are we, sir?'

'Correct. In which case, we've got very few options left. Dave Weir is the only person who can validate or repudiate the statements, but he's gone to ground.'

'Aye. That's true.'

Methven scowled at Cullen, his finger prodding *Billy*. 'This is where the case hinges, correct?'

'Agreed. We need to speak to Billy to see if Vardy was telling the truth to start with.'

Methven nodded. 'Angela, can I ask you to have a look for this Billy character?'

'Right.' Angela shook her head as she noted it down. 'Not sure where I'll get with just a first name but I'll try.'

'Is there anything else?' Methven looked around his small team. 'Anything at all?'

Cullen had lost track of who was where, in or out of custody. 'What's the custody situation?'

'We've still got Falconer in.'

'Thought we just had twenty hours with him?'

'I got an extension from DCI Cargill. I briefed his solicitor on it and he's comfortable with it.'

'Odd.'

'He'll use it against us at a later date, don't you worry.'

'I don't doubt it. I take it you let Vardy go?'

'No. He's up at St Leonard's. Even after he thought we'd let him go for his honesty. He's been charged with your assault yesterday. Not sure we'll get a solid conviction on that, but it's worth a shot.'

'What about Pauline?'

'We got her revised statement last night and let her go.'

'You're serious?'

'Not my decision, Constable.' Methven scowled at Angela. 'How are the background checks going?'

'Slowly.'

'Why's that?'

'I've got to cover a fair few people and there's a lot of stuff coming back. I'm looking into the financial records next, sir — just got their bank statements through. It'll be a while before I've assimilated it all.'

'Can't you hurry up?'

'Aye, I'll try.' Angela looked at a sheet of paper. 'I did get a check done on Dave Weir's flat, though?'

'And?'

'It's definitely owned by a company called Dean Bridge Developments. Only shareholder is one Dean Vardy.'

'Oh, sodding, sodding hell.' Methven shut his eyes briefly before glaring at Cullen. 'Did you know this?'

Cullen flicked though his notebook. 'I didn't know he owned that flat as well.'

'That would mean Weir's entire statement is a load of nonsense, wouldn't it?'

'Potentially. Not sure how much leverage Vardy could apply to a tenant, though.'

DC Jain opened the meeting room door and snuck in. 'Sorry I'm late, sir.'

Methven put his hands on his hips. 'Where the sodding hell have you been?'

Jain smirked. 'Downstairs.'

'Downstairs?' Methven was almost purple with rage.

'Aye. I've just put Dave Weir in an interview room.'

'You found him?'

'He found me.'

'How?'

'He called me first thing. That neighbour we spoke to went upstairs this morning before he went to work.' Jain grinned. 'Turns out he was in the Ghillie Dhu on Rutland Square all night. Pretty much the only pub in Edinburgh I didn't visit last night.'

'I see.'

'He's a bit worse for wear.'

'Is he able to be interviewed?'

'Duty doctor's just been in with him, sir. He's fine.'

'Sodding, sodding hell.' Methven circled *Weir/Teuchter's* in black pen. 'Our whole case is in danger of falling apart here and you're winding me up?'

'Sorry, sir. I wasn't winding you up, really.'

Cullen raised his hands. 'Calm down, we've got him.'

Methven stabbed a finger in Cullen's direction. 'You sodding get yourself down there and speak to him, okay?'

~

'Mr Weir, can you please go over your statement again.' Cullen leaned back in the chair, arms folded, fed up with the day already.

Weir sniffed as he wiped beads of sweat from his forehead, the stench of stale alcohol seeping out. 'Should I not have a lawyer in here?'

'You're not a suspect. You're a witness. We're just gathering intelligence.'

Weir nodded and cleared his throat. 'Right, this was a wee while ago, remember?'

'I do. I've had a very enjoyable holiday in that time.'

'Right. I've got a wee bit of a hangover so you'll have to bear with me.' Weir switched his gaze between Cullen and Jain. 'Okay, so that night, I was working in the bar. We were pretty busy, as I'm sure you can imagine.'

'I can.'

'As I told you last week or whenever it was, I was doing table service for them.'

'You never said there were three people at the table, though.'

'Right.'

'Were there?'

'Aye, there were. Why do you ask?'

'Well, we've got potentially conflicting statements.'

'Oh aye?'

'Tell us who you think was there, Mr Weir.'

'Darren Keogh and Dean Vardy, for definite. There was a third boy with them, drinking Deuchars IPA.'

Cullen picked up his phone and unlocked it before selecting a photo — Lyle. He showed it to Weir. 'Was it this guy?'

'You showed me him last time. It wasn't him.'

Cullen flicked to another photo — Falconer. 'What about him?'

'I don't know.'

Cullen dropped his phone to the table — this was playing into their hands. 'Have you ever seen this mysterious third person before?'

'Sort of. I didn't get a great look at the lad and he had a base-ball cap on, but I think I know his face from somewhere.'

'Okay.' Cullen locked eyes with him — why are you hiding things from us? 'Can you tell us who owns your flat?'

'My flat?'

'Yes, where you live?'

'It's rented.'

'I know that. Who owns it?'

'I don't know.'

Cullen looked at his copy of the information Angela had found. 'Looks very much like it's owned by Dean Vardy.'

Weir swallowed hard. 'Is it?'

'Very much so. Owned by a business called Dean Bridge Developments. Director and shareholder? One Dean Vardy.'

'Sure I shouldn't have a lawyer in here?'

'Not unless you've given us a false statement.'

'I swear I haven't. I'd no idea Dean owned the flat.' Weir tugged the collar of his polo shirt. 'All the money goes through one of my flatmates, Brian.'

'Does Brian work at the Debonair, perchance?'

'Aye.'

'As did you?'

'I did, aye.'

'But you fell out with Mr Vardy?'

Weir shook his head. 'That was before Dean owned the place outright.'

'But he was involved?'

'Aye. I could see the lay of the land. I didn't like the punter one bit so I got out of there.'

'Why?'

Weir shrugged. 'Seemed dodgy, like.'

'In what way?'

'Shifty. Just knew he was up to something.'

'Like what?'

'Nothing specific. Look, I've spent time inside, mate, okay?'

'We know.' Cullen checked the PNC print. 'Assault to Injury. Two counts. A hefty fine the first time, two-year stretch for the second.'

Weir looked away, one hand clamped to his neck. 'Great.'

'I'm not sure I follow your reasoning. Mr Vardy wasn't trying to get you to beat people up for him, was he?'

'Look, I don't want anything at all to do with punters like that. They're bad news.'

'You're on the level here?'

'Aye.' Weir shut his eyes. 'Look, I've not done anything dodgy, okay? I'm just trying to keep my head above water.'

'Fine. I'm not trying to implicate you here but you've got to start playing ball with us. Let's try again, shall we? How many people were there in the group?'

'Three.'

'Three. And who was amongst this number?'

'Darren Keogh and Dean Vardy. Like I told you before.'

'We believe the third person may've been called Billy.'

'Billy?' Weir clicked his fingers before pointing at Cullen. 'That's who it was.'

'You know who Billy is?'

'Aye. Billy Jones.'

41

'Let's recap where we've got to.' Methven gripped the edge of the whiteboard, his left hand jangling keys and change. 'We've got two murders and a suspect for each. Both suspects have means, motive and opportunity but also have alibis. The same alibi. Darren Keogh.'

Cullen nodded. 'Correct.'

'And now you're telling me we've got a conflicting witness statement?'

'We do. As I've been saying all along, sir, someone's lying. I don't take Dave Weir to be a liar.'

'But his flat's owned by Mr Vardy?'

'That's true but it was news to him. Says it's all done through his flatmate. Wasn't aware of Dean Vardy owning it.'

'News to him or convenient?'

'Not convenient, sir. He disagrees with him — he's backed up Vardy's initial statement — Billy Jones was with them.'

'Interesting.' Methven glared at him for a few seconds, the dark eyebrows almost covering his eyes. 'I don't like this one bit.'

'Nobody does, sir.' Cullen shrugged before sitting in a chair. 'It's called police work, right? It's shit, it's boring, it's frustrating. We'll get there, though.'

Jain tried to smile. 'So what do you want us to do, sir?'

'DC Jain, you and I are going to find this Billy Jones.' Methven shifted his gaze to Cullen and Buxton. 'Can you two speak to Mr Keogh again?'

'Will do, sir. Control were having him brought in.'

～

CULLEN GLANCED OVER THE TABLE, the recorder blinking, then back at Buxton. 'Mr Keogh, when we spoke to you yesterday, you told us you were with Mr Kenneth Falconer and Mr Dean Vardy on the evening of the thirtieth of December?'

Keogh swallowed. 'That's correct. Kenneth was with us.'

Cullen reached into a docket on the table in front of him, producing a long receipt. 'Here's a till roll of your drinks that night, time-stamped with each round.' He handed a photocopy to Keogh. 'You'll notice each round has two pints of Brewdog plus a Deuchars IPA. Three drinks. Three people.'

'There you go. My statement's been backed up.'

'Who was drinking what?'

'I was on the Brewdog. I think Kenneth was as well.'

'Oh, really? We've got him on the record saying his was the Deuchars.'

'Sorry. You're right. Dean would go for the craft beer over the real ale. Sorry. Kenneth was on the IPA, that's correct.'

Cullen frowned. 'Why do you keep calling him Kenneth? Everyone else calls him Kenny.'

'It's however I'm introduced to people.' Keogh licked his top lip, removing some of the sweat sheen. 'That's how I remember them.'

'So you're sticking to your story then?'

Keogh nodded. 'I am. There were three of us that night. Kenny, Dean and myself.'

'See, that's quite interesting.' Cullen flicked through his note-book, eyes locked on Keogh. 'Mr Vardy let something slip. He was adamant Mr Falconer wasn't with you. He said this person was called Billy.'

Keogh swallowed again before staring at the clock on the wall, his breath coming hard and fast. 'Billy?'

'Yes, Billy. Said you'd know his surname.'

'Well, I don't.'

'Wouldn't be Jones, would it?'

'I don't know.' Keogh shifted in his seat. 'You said he *was* adamant. I take it he changed the story?'

'He did.' Cullen smiled at Keogh. 'The thing is, Mr Vardy knows Mr Falconer. Quite well it turns out. They've done business together in the past. Seems odd not to recognise an old acquaintance.'

Keogh wiped sweat from his forehead. 'I've told you, we were with Kenneth.'

'You're one hundred per cent sure about that?'

'I am!' Keogh clenched his jaw, fingers massaging his temples. 'You said Dean told you he was mistaken. I'm backing that up. Kenneth was with us. Please drop it.'

'Even in the light of a conflicting statement?'

'Excuse me?'

'We have another statement placing Billy Jones with you, not Kenny Falconer.'

'I want a lawyer in here.'

~

'He's lying his arse off, sir.' Cullen slammed the glass door behind him, causing the wall to vibrate.

Methven looked up from a pile of paperwork. 'I presume the interview with Mr Keogh didn't go to plan?'

'Aye.' Cullen scowled. 'Lying bastard's lawyering up right now. That's all we're getting out of him.'

'He's sticking to his story, guv.' Buxton went over to the whiteboard. 'Can I scrawl *Darren Keogh is a lying bastard* all over this?'

Methven scowled. 'I presume you've got evidence to support that statement?'

'It's the truth, though, right?'

'The truth is he's lying?'

'Yeah, something like that.'

'He's got to be lying.' Cullen perched on the edge of the desk, the hard wooden edge digging into the back of his leg. 'Weir reckons Billy Jones was there, not Kenny Falconer. Why would he lie about it?'

'Mr Vardy owns his flat?'

'Like I said earlier, sir, Weir disagrees with Vardy's statement.'

'Well, what do you propose to do, Constable?'

'We could kick the shit out of Keogh until he confesses?'

Methven nodded. 'I've thought of doing that a few times. Not going to stand up in court, I'm afraid.'

'More's the pity.' Cullen stood up and focused on the whiteboard. 'Did Angela get anywhere finding him?'

'I've not had a chance to catch her sin— Ah.' Methven flared his nostrils before his gaze switched to the door. 'DC Caldwell, I hope you've got some good news for us regarding Mr Jones.'

Angela nudged the door shut behind her before waddling over to a seat at the far end of the table. 'Who's Mr Jones?'

'Billy's surname's Jones. I texted you.'

Angela pointed at a mobile next to a pile of papers on the table. 'Sorry, my phone's been in here.'

'So what have you been doing?'

'What you asked, sir — background checks on Lyle, Keogh, Falconer and Vardy.'

'Anything?'

'Maybe.' Angela held up a wad of paper. 'I've found recurring payments from both of Vardy and Falconer's bank accounts for a grand each.'

'Who to?'

'Needs a bit more digging, sir. I thought you'd be pleased.'

'I am. Can you start looking for Billy Jones, please?'

'Will do.'

Methven focused on Cullen. 'Constable, can I ask you to investigate these transactions for me?'

Cullen rubbed his face — hardly DS duties. 'Sure.'

～

CULLEN SAT AT HIS DESK, trying to tune out the noise from the office around him. He stared at the transactions, the numbers blurring before his eyes.

Sergeant duties did not equal checking bank statements.

Start again.

Cullen put the stacks of paper in front of him — Vardy on the left, Falconer on the right. He marked each of the interesting transactions with an asterisk — the narrative for each transaction read 'D/D WINDCHILL LTD' — the money coming out on the second of each month and both paying exactly one thousand pounds a month.

Were the payments made to the same account? He checked the account number field — they matched.

What the hell was Windchill? He googled it — a few air conditioning companies down south called Windchill Factor or derivatives of it. Nothing that looked like it would accept a grand a month from two dodgy Edinburgh criminals.

Look elsewhere.

He reached for the pile of paper at the back of his desk — Keogh's transactions — and flicked through until he found the most recent page.

Bingo — payment for two grand every month on the twentieth. 'BAC WINDCHILL LTD'.

BAC meant a payment in.

He checked Keogh's balance — just over thirty-six quid overdrawn. Naughty boy. Flicking through the records, Cullen noticed the payments had been made for a couple of years at least. He picked up his phone and dialled. 'Angela? It's Scott. Can you get me prints of the older transactions?'

'I'm not sure. I'll see what I can do.'

'Cheers.'

He picked up the final set of paper, Lyle's transactions. Nothing involved Windchill. No transactions above one hundred quid, except for cash withdrawals which would tally with his rent, the cash in hand deal with Vardy.

So Lyle was clear. What next?

He got to his feet and made for the stairwell, taking the steps two at a time, thinking as he climbed.

Focus — Falconer and Vardy paid a grand a month to a company Keogh received two from. Could only mean one thing.

He stormed across the Forensic Investigation floor, the curtains drawn and the place receiving the bulk of the exhaust from the canteen across the stairwell. He rapped on a desk at the back.

'Oh, it's you.' Charlie Kidd slumped back in his chair, one hand tossing his ponytail, the other rubbing the freshly shaved hair round the sides.

Cullen perched on the edge of his desk. 'That's no way to greet an old buddy.'

'Aye, right. Always get my arse battered after I help you.'

'Charming.' Cullen dumped the pages on the only empty space, between an empty Peperami Hot and a half-full bottle of Lucozade Sport. 'You've been working with DC Caldwell on this, right?'

Kidd picked up the sheets and checked them before nodding. 'Aye. Just got the extracts for her, mind. Chasing a paper trail beneath you these days?'

'Wish it was.' Cullen pointed to one of his asterisks. 'Can you dig into these transactions for me?'

'Can you not do it?'

'We don't have the access downstairs. It's your job, unfortunately.'

'Right.' Kidd switched a few windows on his screen, bringing up a black and white page. He hovered the mouse over a line. 'This one here, right?'

'Aye.'

Kidd clicked and it filled with data. 'Looks like the account belongs to a limited company called Windchill.'

'That's what the transaction said, right?' Cullen drummed his fingers on the desk. 'What sort of business is that?'

'Not sure. Let me check.' Kidd selected a chunk of text and pasted it into another window. The cursor changed to a fish growing legs, turning into a lizard then reverting.

Cullen tapped the screen. 'I like that.'

'Good, eh? Don't tell anyone, I'll get pelters for it.'

'Your secret's safe with me.'

Kidd switched to another data view, this time in classic Windows grey. He selected a row, turning the text white and the background blue. 'This might help you.'

'What is it?'

'It's the company ID number. You could give Companies House a call.'

'I could?'

Kidd raised his hands. 'Aye, that's my bit done.'

'Seriously? What about getting me a list of people who've received money from them? Or paid them?'

'Well... Okay. Fine.'

∼

'CHEERS, CHARLIE.' Cullen ended the call as he pushed into the meeting room.

Methven was jabbing hard at the whiteboard. 'Where the sodding hell is Billy Jones?'

Cullen shut the door behind him, Caldwell and Buxton looking up. 'You not found him yet?'

'No, Constable, we haven't.'

'Well, I think I have.' Cullen held up a sheet of paper.

Methven snatched it from him. 'What the sodding hell is this?'

'That is a list of all the payments received by Windchill, the company Vardy and Falconer have been paying. That's over a hundred and fifty payments received every month.' Cullen handed him another sheet, taken with as much aggression. 'This is the twenty who are paid. Darren Keogh is on there, as is Billy Jones.'

'Who are Windchill when they're at home?'

'I don't know, sir. Companies House aren't returning my calls yet. I can get onto them after this. Think we've got a liaison in the City of London police.'

'You say that like I might want you to get onto something else.'

Cullen handed him another sheet of paper. 'Kidd did manage to find a registered address for the company. It's the same address as Nelson and Parker.'

Methven grabbed the sheet. 'What, Dean Vardy's lawyer?'

'And Falconer's, remember. Among others. We checked — Windchill's company address is the same unit.'

'So it's them?'

'Well, we don't know yet. That's why we need to speak to Companies House.'

Methven scowled at Angela. 'DC Caldwell, can you work with Charlie Kidd on this?'

'Will do, sir.'

Methven cleared the bottom left corner of the whiteboard. 'Tell me about this business.'

'Well, they've received payments from two suspects in our case and paid the idiot who's provided an alibi to both of them.'

'This is looking sodding dodgy.'

'Damn right. What are you thinking?'

'I'm thinking if they've half a brain cell between them they'll have shredded everything.' Methven shook his head at the whiteboard as he scribbled. 'Get out there, Constable. Bring the pair of them in here. Let's see what they've got to say for themselves.'

'We'll need support.'

'Get some officers from the West End. I'll get a warrant arranged.'

42

Cullen pulled in on Torphichen Street, just around the corner from the West End police station. He looked across the road at Nelson and Parker's office, the gleaming tower block incongruous with the rest of central Edinburgh. 'Cheeky buggers have been doing it right under our noses.'

Buxton opened his door and got out, the street crowded with pedestrians in business suits, snuggling under thick winter jackets and carrying briefcases. 'What exactly have they been doing, though?'

'Good point. I'm not sure.' Cullen locked the pool car and set off across the street, stopping outside the office block and leaning against a street light to wait for support. His phone rang — Caldwell.

'Hey, Scott. Just got an inch forward with Companies House.'

'Go on.'

'Michael Nelson and Neil Parker are both listed as directors of Windchill.'

'You're kidding?'

'Nope.'

'Tell Crystal.'

'Told him a few minutes ago. You've not been answering your phone.'

'I've been driving.'

'Okay. Look, I'd better go.'

'Cheers.' Cullen hung up and checked his mobile — there was a text from Methven. *Approved; West End officers have it.* 'Looks like Crystal's somehow got the search warrant approved.'

'How the hell has he swung that?'

Cullen tapped his nose. 'Not what you know, Simon.'

'Ha, yeah.' Buxton looked up and down the street. 'Shall we?'

'We're waiting on back-up, remember. I don't want anyone slipping through here.'

'Acting like the big boy now, aren't you?'

'Maybe I've just had too many idiots run from me over the years.' Cullen clocked a team of uniform trotting up the lane from the station.

'Here we go.' Buxton started off.

Cullen waved at the oncoming officers, one of them lugging the Enforcer battering ram. 'As much as I think he's a wanker, Methven's pulled out all the stops here.'

Buxton nodded. 'Getting access to the Torphichen Place big key isn't bad, is it?'

'I love that name.' Cullen smirked. 'Just hope we don't have to use it.' He looked around the squad of six officers, not recognising any. Cleared his throat. 'Okay, I want two of you to cover the front door and the rest to accompany us inside. Two take the downstairs, covering the lifts, stairs and rear exits. The other two accompany myself and ADC Buxton up. Okay?'

General agreement. One of them handed Cullen a print of the search warrant.

'Good. Come on.' Cullen jogged to the building, accidentally pushing the revolving door and having to wait till it unjammed. He entered a large atrium area leading into the bowels of the building, filled with people in meetings or drinking coffee while talking on phones. The space was artfully lit, just some coloured lights at the sides giving illumination while relying heavily on daylight. The place stank of harsh cleaning chemicals but there was no sign of cleaning staff.

Cullen headed to the rear, a set of six glass-fronted lifts climbing to the heavens. A wide desk sat in front, a security guard sitting in a chair staring into space. Dark grey uniform, logo of a local security firm; looked very much like ex-services, though a good few years ago.

Cullen got his warrant card out and coughed. 'Excuse me?'

The guard jolted forward, eyes wide. 'Can I help you, son?'

'We need access to unit four.'

'Okay.' He peered at Cullen's ID. 'That's Nelson and Parker, right?'

'It is, aye.'

The guard leaned over the desk, reaching for a phone. 'I'll just call up.'

'I'd rather you didn't.'

'I see.'

'Is there anyone in?'

'Think so.'

'How many?'

'Just a sec.' The guard looked down at a screen. 'Got thirty-seven employees. Oh hang on — looks like only two of them have swiped in this morning.'

'What about either Michael Nelson or Neil Parker?'

'Aye, that's them.' The guard pressed a button opening the security gate. 'Third floor, on the left.'

'Cheers.' Cullen walked toward the lifts, gesturing for one of the uniformed officers to stay, another to mark the stairs and the other pair to follow. He waited for the Enforcer to be dumped in the lift before hammering the 3 button and waiting for the doors. 'Let's see if they're answering.'

'You'll be glad not to have to take the stairs, right?'

'Aye. I really need to get back in shape.' As the two uniforms laughed, Cullen looked out of the window. The lift cleared the top of the townhouses opposite, the giant wheel on Princes Street Gardens becoming visible through the glass.

The lift shuddered to a halt, waiting a few seconds before its doors opened into the bright corridor.

'Finally.' Cullen got out first, squinting in the half-light at the Nelson and Parker logo and an arrow pointing left. He trotted down the hallway to the dark wooden entrance. He tried the handle. 'It's bloody locked.'

Buxton glanced back at the two uniforms lugging the Enforcer. 'Want to use the big key?'

'Might have to.' Cullen hammered on the door. 'Got a delivery here for Mr Parker!'

Buxton leaned in close. 'What are you playing at?'

Cullen stepped off to the side. 'We need to get their computers. If they think it's the police, they'll set them on fire or something.'

'Hello?' A voice called out from behind the door. 'We're not expecting anything.'

'Not my problem, pal. I need you to sign for a package!'

A key turned and the door opened. Neil Parker stuck his head through.

Cullen flashed up his warrant card in one hand, the search warrant in the other. 'Mr Parker, we have a warrant to search these premises.'

'Shite.' Parker tried to push the door shut.

Cullen led with his shoulder, taking a few seconds to prise it out of Parker's grip. He gave another push, the door flying open and knocking the lawyer over.

'Mike! It's the police!'

Cullen glanced at Buxton as he stepped over Parker. 'Cuff him!'

Buxton slapped a handcuff around each of Parker's wrists. 'Got you!'

'You can't do this!'

'Mr Parker, we've a warrant to obtain any and all documentation pertaining to Windchill.'

'I've no idea what you're talking about.'

Cullen stared at the uniformed officers. 'One of you stay with him, the other come with me.' He marched off, heading for the open door behind the vacant reception desk.

He entered a wide corridor, eyes blinking in the strong light. The rooms leading off were in darkness, two offices at the far end were lit up. 'Come on.'

Buxton followed him down the corridor, snapping out his baton. 'These geezers are definitely up to something dodgy.'

'Tell me about it.' Cullen crept up and looked in the first office. Empty. He held up a hand to halt the other two and sneaked a view into the second. Nelson sat at a desk, fingers hammering on a laptop.

'Here we go.' Cullen shot off, pushing into the office, warrant card out. 'Mr Nelson?'

Nelson got to his feet and threw the laptop at Cullen, colliding with his left arm.

Cullen clutched it, pain searing his muscles.

Buxton swiped with the baton, hitting Nelson across the throat. He pushed him to the ground, kneeling behind him, locking him in a wrestling hold.

Cullen staggered to his feet, clocking the fact a shredder was churning paper. He dived over and tugged the power cable from the wall.

'Give us a hand over here!'

Cullen looked over at Buxton. 'What?'

'I need your cuffs! I used mine on the other guy!'

43

Cullen leaned across the interview room table. 'For the record, Mr Michael Nelson has decided to represent himself.' He raised an eyebrow. 'Please confirm that is correct.'

Nelson sniffed. 'That's correct, yes.'

'Mr Nelson, we wish to speak to you regarding two murder cases, namely those of Andrew Smith and Keith Lyle. Under suspicion of murdering Mr Smith is one Kenneth Falconer. Under suspicion for the death of Keith Lyle is Dean Vardy. In both instances, the same alibi was given — Darren Keogh.' He pushed a sheet of paper across the table. 'This page shows transactions were paid by both Mr Falconer and Mr Vardy to a company called Windchill.'

'And?'

'Curiously enough, Mr Keogh receives payments from the same company.'

Nelson smiled, his eyes narrowing. 'So?'

'Mr Nelson, this company shares premises with Nelson and Parker, your business.'

'And?'

'You represented Mr Vardy as a defence lawyer.'

Nelson leaned forward, resting his forearms on the table. 'This is a lot of conjecture on your part, Constable. You've raided my place of work and impounded business-sensitive IT equipment.'

'This IT equipment would, of course, include an item you threw, would it not?'

'It might.' Nelson glanced away. 'This is a charade.'

'This is a formal police interview, Mr Nelson. I'd appreciate if you'd treat it as such.'

Nelson pushed his glasses up his nose. 'Please continue then.'

'Why were you and Mr Parker the only people in this morning?'

'The rest were at clients or in court. Possibly on leave, either sick or planned.'

'Thirty-five people were conveniently out of the office?'

Nelson blinked slowly before nodding. 'That's what I said, yes.'

'What's your connection to Mr Keogh?'

'We've done property conveyancing for him, I believe. That's all.'

'Your firm represents Mr Kenneth Falconer as well, does it not?'

'Never heard of him. Must be one of Neil's clients.'

'What can you tell me about this Windchill company?'

'No comment.'

'Would that be because you're listed as a company director?'

Nelson sat back, folding his arms and keeping his gaze locked on the clock to his right. 'No comment.'

'Mr Nelson, what's the purpose of Windchill?'

'No comment.'

'See, we've managed to get access to the records pertaining to that business. You're aware what an industrial classification is, yes?'

Nelson nodded. 'I am, yes. We've set up a number of businesses for clients over the years.'

'See this company is listed under code 80100. Do you know what that stands for?'

'Enlighten me.'

'It means 'private security activities'.'

'So?'

'So, why does a law firm have a sister company doing private security activities?'

'No comment.'

'Mr Nelson, what are you playing at with that company?'

'Nothing.'

'You're not using it to buy and sell alibis?'

Nelson blinked furiously. 'Excuse me?'

'This business isn't there to sell alibis to criminals, is it?'

Nelson laughed. 'Of course not.'

'You've changed your response from 'no comment', I note.'

'Please treat that as a 'no comment'.'

'Mr Nelson, what does this company do?'

'No. Comment.'

44

'I gather congratulations are in order.' Campbell McLintock beamed as he marched down the corridor to the interview room.

Leaning against the wall, Cullen frowned. 'Excuse me?'

'Your other half received a promotion, did she not?'

'Aye, she did.' Cullen rolled his eyes — how the hell did McLintock find out? He thumbed at the door. 'Mr Keogh's waiting for you inside.'

'Ah yes, of course.' McLintock opened the door. 'In that case, I shall join him.'

'That's fine.' Cullen put his foot in the door to stop it swinging shut and waited outside, checking his watch and scanning the corridor in both directions. Where was Methven?

Inside, McLintock took off his dark purple suit jacket and draped it on the back of a chair, revealing his lime green shirt, before taking out an array of stationery. He smiled at Keogh as he sat, locking eyes with Cullen before he tapped his gold wristwatch.

Cullen typed a text to Sharon. *How the hell does McLintock know about your promotion?*

'Are you ready, Constable?'

Cullen looked up. Methven. He stood up. 'Just about, sir.'

'Apologies — I had to brief DCI Cargill on our progress.'

Methven rested against the doorframe. 'How did it go with Nelson?'

'No comment.'

'To be expected. Any ideas what they're up to?'

'Like I said earlier, I think they're buying and selling alibis.'

'I'm of a similar mind. I've instructed DC Caldwell to dig out all cases represented by Nelson and Parker over the last few years.'

'Good idea.' Cullen shook his head. 'Keogh's lawyer is here now. Campbell McLintock.'

'Ah.'

'Or we could speak to Parker, if you'd prefer. Heads or tails?'

'If heads is Keogh then let's go with that.'

'Not Parker?'

'I'm not entirely convinced he'll give us anything Nelson hasn't, i.e. sod all.' Methven scowled. 'I fully expect he'll be playing the same game as his partner.'

'You're probably right.'

'There the pair of you are.' Angela tottered down the corridor, one hand underneath her belly, the other clutching some papers. 'Christ, it wasn't this bad with Jamie.'

'I'm surprised you're even showing given how tall you are.' Methven bellowed with laughter at his own joke.

'I do seem to give birth to absolute monsters.' Angela handed them a sheet of paper. 'Anyway, Charlie Kidd's been doing some digging into the laptop Nelson chucked at Cullen. The stuff he was working on wasn't encrypted. Everything else had been.'

'And all the paperwork was shredded?'

'Aye. Not sure you want me to stick it back together?'

Methven shook his head. 'We'll leave that for when we're really desperate.'

'Hopefully after I'm on maternity leave, sir.'

Cullen looked down the page, nothing more than a list of names and numbers plus a few other fields. He recognised Keogh, Falconer and Vardy on there. Jones, too. 'So what's this?'

'Not entirely sure but we think it's a client list. Looks like Nelson was working on some sort of year-end accounts.'

Cullen shook his head. 'Does it give us anything?'

'Only another forty-six people to speak to.' Angela shrugged.

'So we've no real idea what this company does?'

'Other than 'private security activities'? No, nothing.'

'Vague as hell.' Cullen leaned against the wall. 'Cheers for doing that.'

'No problem.'

Methven gripped Cullen's shoulder. 'Come on, let's see what Mr Keogh has to say.'

'Aye.' Cullen smiled at Angela then entered the room, still clutching the sheet. He started the recorder while Methven sat. 'Interview commenced at ten twenty-nine on Friday the ninth of January 2014. Present are myself, Detective Constable Scott Cullen, and Detective Inspector Colin Methven. Darren Keogh is accompanied by his solicitor, Campbell McLintock.' He rubbed his hands together. 'Mr Keogh, what can you tell us about Windchill Limited?'

Keogh looked at his lawyer for a few seconds, getting nothing in return. 'I've no idea what you're on about.'

'Are you seriously telling me you've got no idea?'

'Absolutely none.'

'Even though Windchill was paying you two grand a month?'

'Aye.' Keogh swallowed.

'If someone paid me two grand a month, I'd wonder what it was for. The city council will be interested in this, especially as you're not reporting it.' Cullen clicked his tongue. 'See, if it was me, I'd have done some digging, maybe put the money in a savings account until whoever's it is came calling, looking for their cash. Not you, though.'

'Eh?'

'You've been spending it, haven't you?'

Keogh looked away. 'Might have been.'

'No, you have. Your account is in overdraft, Mr Keogh. None of the *twenty-seven* payments you've received so far have been put away for a rainy day, have they?'

'I don't know anything about the money, I swear.'

Cullen gave a mock grimace. 'See, here's the other thing. Mr Vardy and Mr Falconer each paid money *to* this company. That's very interesting, especially when you consider who's giving them both alibis.'

'I told you, I don't know—'

'Cut the crap, will you?' Cullen stabbed a finger at the sheet of paper. 'You're providing alibis sold by Windchill, aren't you?'

Keogh looked again at his lawyer.

McLintock focused on Cullen, before pointing at the recorder.

Cullen leaned over. 'Interview paused at ten thirty-four.' He sat back. 'What?'

'Constable, my client might know something. What would be on offer?'

'Depends on what your client has.'

McLintock tapped his fountain pen on the desk. 'Let's just say you're warm with your suspicion.'

Cullen twisted round, arm resting on the chair back. 'DI Methven, what do you reckon?'

He rubbed his chin. 'If Mr Keogh was prepared to go on the record and testify in open court, I suppose we might be able to consider immunity from prosecution for providing a false alibi.'

'That's what I thought.' Cullen lightly shook his head. 'What do you think, sir?'

'If Mr Keogh can prove there's some sort of criminal conspiracy at play here, then we could potentially be able to swing something.'

'Okay.' Cullen shrugged then nodded at McLintock. 'Shall we?'

'After we've seen the offer formally presented.'

Methven wagged his finger. 'We're calling the shots here, Campbell. Info first, then the offer.'

The lawyer whispered in Keogh's ear. He looked up at the ceiling for a few seconds, scratching his ear. 'Aye, okay.'

McLintock nodded slowly. 'Get the tape rolling, Constable.'

Cullen leaned forward again, starting the machine blinking again. 'Interview recommenced at ten thirty-seven. Mr Keogh, please explain your relationship with Windchill.'

'Okay.' Keogh swallowed as he leaned forward, resting his weight on his elbows, fingers kneading his forehead. 'They pay me two grand a month for providing what they call alibi services.'

'What does that mean?'

Keogh clenched his jaw. 'If a client gets caught doing something, I get called in by Neil or Mike. They send me a message on my phone telling me what to say if the police come.'

'Jesus.' Cullen glared at Keogh. 'How many times have you done this before?'

Keogh looked away. 'Once, two years ago.'

Cullen flared his nostrils. 'How did you get into this?'

'I was at school with Neil Parker.'

Cullen felt sweat dripping from his armpits. 'Were you with Kenny Falconer on the thirtieth?'

Keogh looked away. 'No, I wasn't.'

'And Dean Vardy?'

'I was, aye.'

'You're changing your story?'

Keogh sniffed. 'I am.'

'But you're still saying Vardy was with you?'

'Aye. Dean was with me.'

'Why are you sticking to that line?'

'Because it's the truth. Dean and I were in the pub.'

45

'This is a load of nonsense.' Cullen got to his feet and wandered round to Parker's side of the desk, standing over him. 'We've got one of your alibi providers on record blowing your operation wide open.'

Parker smiled. 'You've got nothing.'

'We've got your computers and files. It might take some time but we'll get evidence to back it all up.'

'You won't.' Parker stood up, a good few inches taller than Cullen. 'This will fall apart in court. It's one man's statement against ours.'

'We've got financial transactions.'

'Relating to what, though?'

'Providing false alibis.'

'Really? Each transaction lists that as the reason for payment, do they?'

Cullen took a step forward. 'Mr Parker, you've been paying Darren Keogh two thousand pounds a month for over two years.'

'Mr Keogh's an old school friend of Neil's. Got himself into a bit of financial difficulty with a property venture a few years back. We were just helping him out.'

'Through Windchill?'

'It's a charitable organisation for homeless people, hence the name. Mr Vardy and Mr Falconer both made donations to the fund.'

'And they're reputable businessmen?'

'Please don't besmirch the reputation of our clients.'

'Why weren't they paying this retainer to Nelson and Parker?'

'Because it's not a retainer. It's a charitable donation. Messrs Vardy and Falconer could, if they wish, have deducted the amount from their own tax liability.'

Cullen frowned. 'But it's registered as a limited company. Why's it not registered with the Charities Commission?'

'That level of transparency isn't particularly useful to the sort of business we want to run.' Parker grinned as he sat again, looking up at Cullen. 'We'd much rather give the money to needy cases such as Mr Keogh than waste it on bureaucracy.'

'But you've been taking profits from the company?'

'Another of the benefits of being a limited company.' Parker shrugged, eyes shifting to the scarred tabletop. 'We've paid corporation tax on those earnings. It's all above board.'

'Why's it registered as a private security business then?'

Parker sniffed. 'An admin oversight, I suspect.'

Cullen stepped back, eyes trying to communicate his defeat to Methven.

'Interview paused at eleven oh six.' Methven got to his feet before pointing at Parker. 'We'll be back shortly, Mr Parker.' He nodded at the PCSO.

Cullen held the door open for Methven, waiting for it to close before speaking. 'We're screwed, right?'

'*He* certainly thinks so.' Methven nodded at the door. 'We've got very little actual evidence, Constable. He'll try and push that client list DC Caldwell found as a donors list.'

'It's dodgy.'

'Tell me about it.' Cullen watched Parker roll up his sleeves, a smirk on his face. 'He's just playing us here.'

'What do you propose, Constable?'

'I suggest I go through the specifics of what we've got, get him on the record denying it, if nothing else.'

'That's probably the only option we've got. You lead.' Methven opened the door, sitting down across from Parker and leaning across the table. 'Interview re-commenced at eleven oh eight.'

Cullen sat down, arms folded, keeping his eyes on Parker. 'Can I explain my thinking?'

Parker leaned back, beaming out a smile. 'I'll be delighted to listen.'

'You're selling alibis to people.'

'Interesting. Go on.'

'Basically, you provide an alibi if one of your clients gets caught by the police. You match the criminals up with one of your alibi sellers, like Mr Keogh.'

Parker scratched at his neck. 'Continue.'

'You make sure the mates are people like Darren Keogh, reputable people with steady jobs. Pay them a retainer from the money you get from your clients. Mike Nelson and yourself cream the profits off the top.'

'Fascinating. How would they know what alibi to use?'

'Because you're their solicitors. Nelson and Parker represents both Vardy and Falconer. I'm guessing you'll only give them the alibi if it's a serious crime.'

'And why would that be?'

Cullen snorted. 'Because we've got very few sheriffs and judges. They'd recognise Darren Keogh if he was providing alibis for wee Johnny stealing biscuits from a corner shop in Prestonpans.'

'Right.'

'You provide the alibi to the clients in the interview. Just like you did when you got Dean Vardy to change his story.'

'How did I manage that?'

'Vardy had just spent ten minutes denying he knew anything about Kenny Falconer, kept shutting you up. One wee whisper in his ear and he's changed his tune.'

'That was a correction he made himself.'

'Oh aye? I'm struggling with one bit of your system. How did Kenny and Dean both have the same alibi?'

'That's just how it happened, I'm afraid.'

'Nothing to do with you not having enough people like Mr Keogh and too many like Kenny and Dean?'

Parker shrugged. 'I'm not sure how they came to be in the same place at the same time but they were.'

'But they weren't.' Cullen prodded the table a few times. 'Vardy and Keogh were there with a William Jones.'

'Mr Vardy told you Billy wasn't there. Mr Falconer was.'

'Mr Vardy told us he was there until you changed his story. I'd like to point out that Mr Keogh has just confirmed Falconer wasn't there.'

'It'll be interesting if this gets anywhere near court, won't it?' Parker grinned. 'You've just given me your case.'

46

Methven shook his head as they entered the meeting room. 'What a pair of bloody idiots Nelson and Parker are.'

Cullen raised his eyebrows. 'We're the ones who look like idiots, sir.'

'Agreed. They've got away with this ever since that sodding Cadder case made us have those leeches in interviews. They've been doing this a long time, right under our noses.'

'Another way to look at it is we've got forty guilty people we can finally put away.'

'Not so sure.' Angela scowled as she held up a page of hand-scrawled text. 'While you two have been in there with Keogh and Parker, I had a look through some of the cases. I've scanned through twelve so far, all murders that went to trial. At least two of the alibis seem to have cleared people. Spoke to the SIO on one of them, reckons the guy was innocent.'

Methven perched on the edge of a desk. 'What else?'

Angela pushed a sheet of paper over. 'One of the cases I checked, the alibi was provided by one William Jones.'

Methven's eyes bulged. 'Are you serious?'

She nodded. 'Aye.'

'Wait.' Cullen looked through the stacks of paperwork on the meeting room table, eventually finding the page he was after. He handed it to Methven. 'Here. Jones is one of the guys receiving money from Windchill.'

'Sodding hell.' He looked at Angela. 'And we still haven't found him yet?'

'No, sir.' Angela sat opposite the whiteboard. 'There was a phone number on the list of alibi providers. I passed it to Control but I haven't heard anything.'

'Get onto it.' Methven scowled at her. 'Where's ADC Buxton?'

'No idea, sir. I think he said he was chasing up some leads.'

'So, Cullen, you're telling me Mr Jones may be another of these clowns providing false alibis?'

'Maybe.'

'Sodding, sodding hell.' Methven jangled his keys in his pockets for a few seconds before uncapping a pen and turning to the whiteboard. 'So where do you think this leaves us?'

Cullen tapped at *No Alibi* on the whiteboard for a few seconds before looking around the otherwise empty meeting room. 'I think we can get a conviction for Falconer.'

'How?'

'He's not got an alibi, sir. Keogh said he wasn't there.'

'We've sodding been here before with Mr Falconer.' Methven shook his head. 'I'll believe it when I see it.'

'Without the alibi, he's got nothing, whereas we've got his prints on the knife used to kill Andrew Smith.'

'That's circumstantial, Constable.'

'Falconer's got a motive to kill Smith. He was ratting on him about the shop in Gorgie.'

Methven focused on the board. 'I think you've got something there.'

'How do you want to progress it?'

'Write everything up, Constable. This is going to be a lengthy paper trail, I'm afraid.'

Cullen tightened his grip on the edge of the board — bloody months of tedious grind. He watched Buxton enter the room, mobile to his ear, avoiding eye contact. 'So what about Vardy then?'

'Now that's a different beast entirely.' Methven stroked his chin for a few seconds. 'Keogh's refused to play ball on that one. He still insists he was with Dean Vardy. Have we had that backed up by this dodgy barman?'

'Aye. Reckons they were both there.'

'Remind me, what's the connection between them?'

Cullen frowned. 'Keogh used to go out with Vardy's aunt.'

'That sounds like a cock and bull story.'

Cullen scowled at Buxton. 'Simon, did you speak to Alison Vardy?'

'I did, yeah.' Buxton spun his phone on the table. 'Just been on with the Police Service of Northern Ireland. Turns out she's legit.'

'So what did she say?'

'She backed up their story. She used to go out with Darren Keogh. Apparently young Dean's a bit of a tearaway. Real black sheep of the family.'

'And Vardy kept in touch with him?'

'Yeah, that's what she reckoned. Good mates.'

'Why?'

'She had no idea, mate. Didn't get it herself.'

'Nothing at all?'

'Well, she said it could possibly be something to do with Keogh's connections.'

Methven scowled. 'But Keogh doesn't have any connections?'

'He was at school with Neil Parker.'

Methven stabbed a finger in the air. 'Constable, it was Michael Nelson he was sodding at school with.'

'Right, yeah. Get those two confused.' Buxton shrugged. 'Anyway, she reckons they were influential in young Dean's rise.'

Methven pinched his nose. 'Sodding hell.'

Cullen focused on the whiteboard. 'So, Dean Vardy's alibi looks like it could be sound?'

Methven nodded. 'Come on, Constable, let's get in there with him. He should have a proper lawyer by now.'

∿

'WHAT DO YOU SODDING MEAN?' Methven got in the face of the PCSO. 'Where is Mr Vardy's lawyer?'

Cullen took a step back, pretending to use his mobile but

secretly enjoying the scrap. He texted Buxton. *Crystal going for it with the fat PCSO.*

'He's not turned up yet.' The PCSO rubbed his neck. 'Vardy's made the call and he's on his way.'

'Who?'

'Boy called Reynolds, I think.'

'Alistair Reynolds?'

'Aye, him.'

'Sodding hell.' Methven took a step back. 'We were told his lawyer had arrived. How has this happened?'

'You know how it is, sir. We're absolutely rammed here, St Leonard's are full up and don't get me started on the West End.' The PCSO snorted. 'Your case is taking up half the cells here.'

'But we've only got Falconer and Vardy in.'

'Aye, plus those two lawyers.' He held up four fingers. 'Makes four.'

'Okay. That's hardly turning this into Bethlehem on Christmas Eve.'

The PCSO counted out on his thumb. 'Plus William Jones.'

'What?'

'Turned up about an hour ago. Been hogging interview room four for the last hour. DI Lamb's bee—'

'Sodding hell.' Methven rubbed his forehead. 'Who brought him in?'

'Some uniform boy from Gayfield Square, sir.'

'Get out of my bloody sight.'

Cullen watched the PCSO trundle off then looked up at Methven, his face a dark purple. 'Shall we speak to him, sir?'

Methven pointed at the interview room door as he got his phone out and started prodding the screen. 'I'll just be a second.'

Cullen opened the door, the stale smell of sweat hitting him. His eyes started to water. 'Sorry about the delay.'

Billy Jones stood at the side of the room, his gut lurking out of the bottom of his red long-sleeved t-shirt, saggy jeans in need of a wash a few months ago. His red face was twisted into a gurn, cheeks twitching as he smiled. 'It's okay.'

Cullen frowned as he sat. 'No, it's not okay. Leaving a witness alone in an interview room for this long isn't acceptable.'

'I'm a witness?'

Cullen hovered his hand over the digital recorder then glanced back at Methven, still fuming in the corridor. 'What exactly have you been told?'

'Nothing. Just got to answer some questions.'

'I see.'

'Is Michael here?'

'Michael?'

'Aye, Michael Nelson.' Jones rubbed his hand through his thinning hair, clumps sticking up. 'He's my lawyer.'

'You don't need a lawyer.' Cullen opened his notebook and checked it through. Another glance at Methven, looking like he was close to wrapping up the phone call. 'We'll get round to the questions once my colleague arrives.'

'What's this about?'

'The evening of the thirtieth of December.'

'Oh.'

'What's that supposed to mean?'

'Nothing.'

'Right.' Methven slammed the door shut behind him then collapsed into the chair. 'Mr Jones?'

'Correct. Billy Jones.'

'Let's get started.' Methven reached over and started the recorder. 'We don't need this on the record, do we?'

Jones shook his head. 'Not unless you're thinking I've done something. In which case I'd like a lawyer.'

'Let's just see how we go.' Cullen cracked his knuckles. 'Mr Jones, we need to ask you some questions pertaining to your whereabouts on the thirtieth of December.'

'That's a while ago now.' Jones chewed the knuckle of his right hand ring finger. 'I was out drinking, I think.'

'You think?'

'Aye, well I was.'

'Who were you drinking with?'

'Erm, a friend of mine. Darren Keogh.'

Cullen felt his heart thud. 'Just the two of you?'

'There was another chap with us.' Jones switched to the middle knuckle. 'I can't remember his name, sorry.'

'For the purposes of the tape, I'm presenting a photograph tagged P-09C.' Methven showed him Kenny Falconer. 'Is this one of the men you were with?'

Jones took a long look at it. Shook his head. 'No, this isn't him.'

'Definitely?'

'Aye. Definitely.'

'What about this?' Methven showed another, this time of Dean Vardy. 'I'm showing photograph P-08D.'

Jones lifted it up, shaking the photo backwards and forwards. He handed it back. 'This isn't him.'

'Seriously?'

'Aye.' Jones frowned. Grabbed the photo back. 'No, hang on.' He squinted at it, eyes disappearing behind their lids. 'Dean something, right?'

'Dean Vardy.'

'Dean Vardy... Oh. Yes, it was him. Dean was the man with Darren.' Jones flipped the photo over and returned it, then clicked his fingers a few times. 'He bought us drinks all night. Knew the barman. Or had something on him, at least.'

'Definitely?'

'Aye, absolutely. Got a load of pints out of him.'

'Was Mr Vardy well acquainted with Mr Keogh?'

'Aye, I think so. Something about Dean's auntie, I think.'

'Thanks.' Methven smiled and got out his mobile, stabbed the screen a few times. 'That appears to be correct.' He looked up. 'On the other hand, we've done some digging into your background.'

Jones ground his teeth, his jaw pulsing with the effort. 'Oh?'

'We couldn't find you and we needed to speak to you. It's due process, I can assure you. However, I'd like to draw your attention to the fact you received the princely sum of two thousand pounds a month from a business known as Windchill.'

Jones swallowed. 'That was an administration error.'

'Was it? They paid you this for fifteen months.'

'I contacted them and asked them to stop.'

'Oh?'

'It's the truth.'

'Sounds very much like a lie to me. What about the payment of twenty thousand pounds in April of this year?'

'I think they attempted to get a refund from me and accidentally put more cash in my bank account.'

'Sounds like rot to me.' Methven flicked to the right on his phone. 'What can you tell us about a William Abercrombie?'

'Excuse me?'

'Looks like you gave Mr Abercrombie an alibi for murder in 2012.'

Jones put his head in his hands, his breath slow and heavy. 'I need a lawyer in here.'

'Why do you need a lawyer?'

'I just do.'

'Mr Jones, have you done something illegal?'

'No comment.'

'You're not being recorded here, that won't wash.'

'Right.'

'Mr Jones, does that money relate to you giving William Abercrombie a false alibi?'

'I know William, we used to go to schoo—'

Methven smacked the table. 'Mr Jones, this is utter poppycock. You provided a false alibi for Mr Abercrombie.'

'I didn't.'

'The parents of his victim have gone through hell for the last two years.'

'I'm not saying anything.'

Cullen shook his head. 'Did you provide a false alibi for Mr Vardy?'

'Excuse me?'

'You and Mr Keogh in Teuchter's with Dean Vardy.'

'What of it?'

'You weren't there, were you?'

'No, I was. That's the absolute truth.' Jones reached into his pocket for his mobile. He unlocked it and flicked through some screens. He held it up. 'Here.'

Cullen took the phone. A selfie — Jones, Keogh to the left and Vardy to the right, holding up pints of beer. The distinctive mirror in Teuchter's. Time stamped at ten thirty on the thirtieth of December. Dave Weir stood behind them, scowling as he stacked up three empty pint glasses.

∾

'MR VARDY, QUIT IT.' Methven sat back in his chair, tapping his fingers on the interview room table. 'You still had a small window of opportunity to visit Mr Lyle's residence and kill him.'

'I didn't do it!' Vardy shook his head, turned to the side and focused on his lawyer. 'Tell him.'

Alistair Reynolds cleared his throat. 'I'm sorry, Inspector, but my client maintains his innocence.'

'If we look at that evening's timeline, we know your activities up to the point of visiting a takeaway on Bread Street.'

Vardy smirked. 'Aye, knew you'd get there in the end, pal.'

'We've nothing after that.' Methven grinned. 'We know for a fact Keith Lyle was murdered sometime between eleven and twelve that night.'

'So?'

'Pauline Quigley found the body in the morning. Are we to doubt her statement?'

A frown crept onto Vardy's forehead. 'Why would you do that?'

'Well, it's apparent she's complicit in Mr Lyle's murder.'

'Keep telling yourself that, mate.'

'Isn't she?'

'You've got nothing, have you? Sweet Fanny Adams.'

'We've got your prints in the room.'

'How about on the knife, though?'

'It'd save us all a lot of time if you just confessed, Mr Vardy.'

'It isn't even a murder.'

'Excuse me?'

'I said, it isn't murder. Keith topped himself.'

Cullen felt his mouth go dry — this was bollocks. Wasn't it? 'He committed suicide?'

'Aye. The little fanny tried it on with my bird. I told him what's what. Good little worker and everything but I'm not having him thinking he can do that.'

'Which is why you killed him, right?'

'No. He killed himself. Like I just told you.'

'Why do you expect us to believe that?'

'Because it's the truth, maybe?'

'Is it now.' Cullen folded his arms. 'What evidence is there?'

'Pauline's got his suicide note.'

47

Cullen held up his phone. 'That was Buxton. They've just picked her up from her flat. Should be here soon.'

'Excellent.' Methven scowled as he paced around Deeley's office, the place rammed with papers, files and assorted medical equipment. 'Well, of course it's not bloody excellent. I don't like being lied to.'

'No. You get used to it, though, right?'

'Knock, knock.'

Cullen spun round.

'Sorry I'm late, gents.' Deeley stood grinning at them, dressed for the elements in his overcoat and scarf. 'Had another gruesome crime scene to attend to and Kathryn's on another bloody course.'

Methven glowered. 'We've been here for over half an hour.'

'Aye, sorry about that. Guess young Gerry didn't think I'd be so long.' Deeley shut the door, hanging up his coat and scarf before sitting behind his desk, almost completely covered with paperwork. 'Guess who I bumped into on the way over from the car park?'

'I don't sodding care.' Methven was jangling the keys hard.

'Come on, Colin. Guess!'

'No sodding idea.'

'Your predecessor. Brian Bain.' Deeley shook his head. 'Thought he was dead.'

'If he was dead, you'd have done the autopsy.'

'Good point, well made.'

Cullen clenched his jaw. 'His name keeps popping up.'

'Indeed. Wonder what the hell he's doing through here? He was as cagey as ever. Reckoned he's going to be based in Edinburgh again.' Deeley shrugged before getting out his ancient Nokia. 'Got your voicemail, Colin.'

'And?'

'Well, I shall need to have another wee look at Mr Lyle.'

Methven scowled. 'Thought you'd ruled out suicide.'

Deeley exhaled slowly. 'We had.'

'Even though there was only one set of prints on the murder weapon?'

'That's the sort of puzzle I usually leave to you chaps.' Deeley smirked. 'Unless it's a time traveller we're dealing with?'

Methven tutted. 'Keep to the facts.'

'Sorry.' Deeley cleared his throat. 'The fact there's only a single set of prints on the knife made me think the killer wore gloves. That's more James Anderson's department, though. Usually to assess suicide, we check for things like whether they were stabbed through their clothes, defensive marks on wrists, you know the drill.'

Methven nodded. 'I do.'

'And on your side, you'd be looking for financial and medical reasons. Debt, terminal illness and so on. You found none of these, am I correct?'

'Right.'

'Well, come on through. Let's have another look at him.' Deeley got up and led them through the double doors at the opposite end of the room, heading into the mortuary. He took a left into another room, stacked high with refrigeration units. He ran his finger along the edges of the doors and found the relevant one. 'Here we go.' He pulled it out — Keith Lyle's white face looked up at them, eyes shut.

'Let's go through my thinking concerning this being a murder, shall we?' He pointed at a deep wound on Lyle's stomach, a clean cut into his flesh. 'This is what killed him, okay? I checked the angle of entry — it was a nice clean blade, no serrations, so I've got a pretty good understanding of what happened. The blow just went in his abdomen here and cut the aorta there.' He lifted up a flap of skin. 'Nice and clean, like I say. Would've killed him in minutes at the most.'

'And why do you think it's not suicide?'

Deeley held out a scalpel, thrusting the blade towards his guts but stopping just short. 'The injury sustained is a perfect match with this knife. A ShivWorks Disciple, right?'

Methven nodded. 'Correct.'

'As I've told you a few times now, the stabbing was through clothes. It's rare for a suicide to do that.' Deeley widened his eyes. 'Add in the defensive cuts and we've got a likely murder.'

'Could he have stabbed himself?'

Deeley stared at the body for a seconds. 'It's possible, aye. The angle of entry would support that.'

'What else is there?'

'The big thing was the lack of a suicide note.' Deeley folded his arms. 'Remember that poor bugger on Christmas Day? Didn't even manage to kill himself, but he'd left a note. Most suicides do.'

Methven shut his eyes. 'Is there anything to suggest Lyle took his own life?'

'Like what?'

'You're the expert.'

Deeley stared up at the lights for a few seconds, lips twitching, then focused on Cullen. 'While you were drinking yourself silly in Tenerife, young Skywalker, I spent a good few days looking into what killed young Master Lyle here. Not himself was my conclusion.'

'But Anderson only found his prints on the knife?'

'It happens.' Deeley shook his head. 'The injuries sustained weren't consistent with suicide.'

'Explain.'

'I look for hesitation wounds. This is where the victim has tried to kill himself — a knife entering your body bloody hurts. If you do it yourself, no matter how determined you are, you'll flinch.'

'So it's completely impossible?'

'Well, I'm not saying no. I'm saying I just don't think it's at all likely based on the evidence.' Deeley let his arms fall to his sides. 'Now, if you'll let me get back to doing some proper work?'

48

'Pauline, you should have a lawyer.' Cullen sat back in the interview room chair. 'I'm serious.'

Pauline patted the digital recorder, the red light blinking away on the table. 'This thing's recording, right?'

'Aye.'

'Well, just get on with it.' She folded her arms. 'I don't need a bloody lawyer.'

'Fine.' Cullen sat back in the chair. 'Can you please detail your movements on the morning of the thirty-first of December.'

'I've told you a few times over.'

'And every time you've given us a different story. When did you find Mr Lyle?'

'That morning.'

'You're absolutely sure about that?'

Pauline nodded. 'Aye.'

'Not the previous night?'

'No.' She folded her arms again. 'I got back about half midnight.'

'See, we believed Mr Vardy killed him.'

'Based on what I said?'

'Yep. It certainly added up. All the facts. He had an alibi up to half eleven — just enough time to get to your flat.'

'You said you *believed* Dean killed him. What's the but here?'

Cullen looked away. 'We have a statement suggesting Mr Lyle killed himself.'

'Who from?'

'I'm not at liberty to divulge that, I'm afraid. Usually people who take their own lives tend to want everyone to know why. It might be to do with a physical illness or a mental one. It could be financial. Or it could be to do with a girl or a boy.'

Pauline blinked a few times but didn't speak.

'The trouble is, Mr Lyle didn't leave a note so we're struggling with that. Hence thinking it's most likely murder.'

Pauline inspected her fingernails before chewing her knuckle.

Cullen rubbed his hands together. 'At least, we weren't given a note.'

Pauline rubbed at her eyes. 'He left one.'

Cullen frowned. 'How do you know?'

'When I found him. I just sat there with him for a few minutes. Then I spotted his note on his desk, looked like it had been torn out of his journal.'

'Okay, now we're getting somewhere.' Cullen glanced over at Buxton. 'Do you still have it?'

She nodded. 'It's in my drawer at home.'

'What did it say?'

'I told you how Dean threatened to kill Keith, right?'

'You did.'

'The note was full of that. It was... It was quite hard to read.'

'I'll ask again, what did it say?'

Pauline wiped her cheek. 'It blamed Dean. For threatening Keith. All that sort of thing, you know?'

'He killed himself because Dean threatened him?'

'And because of the debt. Dean was adding interest to it every day.'

'How much?'

'Like those adverts on the telly, the APR was in four figures.'

'I see. And Keith couldn't cope with this?'

'That's right.' Pauline shook her head, her eyes red raw. 'If I had my time over again, I'd have gone out with Keith over Dean any day. I just can't believe what's happened.'

'I understand.' Cullen sat back in the chair. 'Why did you keep the note from us?'

'I thought you might think Dean killed him. That's the only way I can get away from him without him killing me.'

'That's why you've been so vague with us?'

Pauline nodded. 'I knew he left the pub at closing time. I know the barman there. Dave Weir. He used to work with us at the Deb. He reckons Dean was there to intimidate him. He texted me a few times during the night, he was really freaking out.'

'So you were framing Mr Vardy?'

'I'm sorry.'

Cullen got to his feet, gesturing at Buxton. 'Can you please accompany my colleague here to retrieve the note?'

49

Methven leaned against the wall outside the interview room and checked his watch. 'Where the sodding hell is he?'

'Reynolds knows we want to get back in with Falconer, sir. Typical delaying tactics.' Cullen thumbed at the shut door. 'Falconer's fucked.'

'Eloquent as ever, Constable.' Methven gave a quick shake of the head then stood up tall and dusted himself down.

Alistair Reynolds made his way down the corridor, his suit jacket soaked through and a mangled umbrella in his hand, most of the spokes disconnected from the material. He stopped outside the interview room and nodded recognition at Cullen and Methven. 'The wind in this city never ceases to amaze me.'

'Indeed.' Methven placed his hand on the door. 'Can we have a brief chat before we commence discussions?'

'Another of the Nelson and Parker mop-up cases coming my way. Why, DI Methven, this feels like an honour.'

'The pleasure's mine, believe me.' Methven took a step away from the door. 'We've reason to believe Mr Falconer's alibi is false.'

Reynolds dumped his briefcase on the floor. 'Oh?'

'The person providing the alibi has now changed his statement to say Falconer wasn't there.'

Reynolds closed his eyes. 'Well, let's just see what he has to say, shall we?'

Cullen sat down next to Methven and started the recorder, eyes boring into Falconer. 'Interview commenced at fourteen twenty-nine on Friday the ninth of January 2014. Present are myself, Detective Constable Scott Cullen, and Detective Inspector Colin Methven. Also present are the suspect, Kenneth William Falconer, and his lawyer, Alistair Reynolds.'

He folded his arms, still staring at Falconer. 'Mr Falconer, you've still not submitted your ledger to a police station to go into evidence.'

'Keeps slipping my mind that, sorry.'

'It's the only proof you've got of the knife being sold to Mr Smith, you do know that?'

'Aye. Can we just get on with this?'

'Very well. Mr Falconer, when we were in here the other day, I asked you why you stabbed Andrew Smith.'

'I didn't.'

'See, we think you did.'

'You can think what you like, pal. It's a free country after all.'

'Mr Falconer, Darren Keogh has changed his statement. He's taking back the alibi he provided.'

'That's complete bullshit, pal.'

'Kenneth, you're not listening to us.' Methven rested his elbows on the interview room table. 'Mr Keogh has admitted he provided a false alibi regarding your whereabouts on the night in question.'

Falconer glanced over at Reynolds, the lawyer doodling on a pad of paper. 'But I was *there*.'

'Were you really?'

'I was.'

'You like to drink in the pubs on William Street, do you? Mixing with the bankers and the lawyers?'

Falconer pushed himself up. 'What are you saying, like?'

'You don't strike me as the type to drink on that street. It's full of boutiques and expensive pubs.'

'Where do you think I drink?'

'Lothian Road, maybe? The Debonair?'

'Not going in that place again, I tell you.'

'Is that because of the owner?'

'Maybe.'

'Mr Falconer, where were you on the night of the thirtieth of December between leaving work and heading out to Armadale on the thirty-first?'

'I told you, I was drinking in Teuchter's with Darren Keogh.'

'You weren't.'

'I fucking was!'

'Mr Falconer, Darren Keogh has recanted his alibi.'

'Fucking waste of money that is.'

'Excuse me?'

Falconer rolled his eyes. 'Nothing.'

'Kenny, that was recorded. You said it was a waste of money. What was a waste of money?'

'Nothing.'

'Really? It wouldn't be the alibi you paid for, would it?'

'No comment.'

'Nelson and Parker? Windchill?'

'No comment.'

Methven grinned. 'You've no proof as to where you were that night, have you?'

Falconer looked again at his solicitor, getting neither recognition or response. 'No comment.'

Reynolds leaned over and whispered in Falconer's ear.

Falconer shook his head. 'No fucking danger!'

Reynolds shrugged. 'So be it.'

'Mr Falconer, do you wish to alter your statement?' Methven arched an eyebrow.

'No. No fucking comment.'

Methven steepled his fingers. 'Mr Falconer, we're offering you an opportunity here. We know you paid a thousand pounds a month to a limited company called Windchill. We know they set you up with an alibi that doesn't hold water.'

'Aye, fuck it. Over twenty grand I gave those wankers. And I get nothing in return.'

Reynolds covered his eyes with his hands.

50

'Well done.' Methven put the lid back on the pen. 'I'm inviting you all to the pub once we've finished tonight.'

'Thanks, sir.' Cullen leaned against the meeting room window, nodding slowly. 'It's not been easy but we've got there.'

'I think you should all be proud of yourselves.' Methven reached into a Tesco carrier bag, producing a bottle of Likely Laddie, a cheap brand of whisky, and plonking it on the table. 'Most of us will be driving, but I wondered if you might like a drink while you're typing up reports. Chantal?'

'Not whisky.'

'Angela? Oh, of course.'

Cullen raised a hand. 'I'm off the booze for now.'

'Of course, of course.' Methven smiled.

Jain grinned. 'I'm sure Buxton'll help you out when he gets back with that suicide note.'

'Indeed.' Methven put the bottle back in the bag and beamed. 'Have you heard from him?'

Cullen patted his mobile, sitting in front of him. 'He's got the note. Reckons it looks like Lyle wrote it. Same handwriting, same smudging.'

'That's a relief. I was beginning to wonder whether Ms Quigley was spinning us a line.'

Cullen nodded. 'I think she's telling the truth for once, sir.'

'Had to be a first time. Anyway, I was on the phone to the NCA as I went across the road. They believe they can use Ms Quigley's testimony to mount some sort of operation on Mr Vardy's loan sharking business.'

'Excellent.' Angela grimaced. 'Do you mind if I get off home, sir? I'm aching all over.'

'No problem, Angela. You've done a stellar job.'

'Thanks, sir.' Angela got to her feet and waddled off. 'See you all tomorrow.'

Methven chuckled as he watched her walk down the corridor outside the meeting room. He shoved his hands in his pockets and looked at Cullen and Jain. 'What do you think of Nelson and Parker, eh? What a pair of plonkers.'

'Going through all those cases is going to be a nightmare sir.'

'It will but this is a big thing. Not a bad effort for such a small team. Not bad at all.' Methven shook his head. 'I can't believe they were so bloody stupid.'

'It's the arrogance of it more than anything.' Jain shrugged. 'They did well hiding it for so long.'

'Indeed they did.'

Cullen slumped on a chair. 'I hate coincidences.'

'How do you mean?' Methven was scowling.

'We've only caught them because two clients decided to kill on the same night.'

Methven brushed his eyebrows. 'We'd have caught them eventually.'

Cullen stretched out and yawned. 'True.'

'Besides, you heard what Nelson said — they don't have enough alibis to go around. This was bound to happen sooner or later. They were adding clients at a rate of knots but the alibi providers were still somewhat scarce.'

'You're right.' Cullen frowned, staring out of the window. 'Bloody hell, is that Bain?'

Jain squinted through the glass. 'It is. What's he doing here?'

Methven cleared his throat. 'I sincerely hope the sodding rumours aren't true.'

Cullen flushed red. 'What rumours would those be?'

'Him coming back through here under my command.' Methven scowled. 'That would be a complete nightmare for all concerned. Would be just my rotten luck, as well.'

Cullen watched Bain, loitering in the open-plan office space beyond, now deserted. 'What the hell is he doing?'

'Waiting for someone by the looks of things.' Methven jangled his keys.

There was a knock, a hairy hand waving through the frosted glass. Detective Superintendent Jim Turnbull put his head around the door, eyes bouncing between the three officers in the room. 'Can I have a word in private?'

'Certainly, sir.' Methven got to his feet, beaming at him.

'Not you, Colin.' Turnbull stared at Cullen. 'With DC Cullen.'

'Of course.' Methven waited until Turnbull was in the room before leaving, taking Jain with him.

Cullen sat at the end of the table, his eyes peering at Bain through the glass. Shite — reporting into Bain again. 'Sir.'

Turnbull sat next to him. 'How was your holiday, Scott?'

'A distant memory, sir.'

'As they all are after a couple of days back.' Turnbull smoothed down his tie. 'How's Sharon doing out west?'

'Fine.' Cullen's mouth had gone dry. His heart was thudding at a Dutch trance tempo. 'Think she'll enjoy it, sir.'

'Oh, aye, of course.' Turnbull fiddled with the tie pin. 'There's something I need to brief you on.'

Cullen closed his eyes for a second. 'Okay...'

'I see you've already got some idea what this is about.'

Cullen nodded, staring at the wall above the superior officer's head. 'I've got some idea.'

'Which is?'

'That I'm reporting to DI Bain again.'

Turnbull smiled. 'Interesting how the jungle drums in this place work, isn't it?'

'That's one way of putting it, sir.' Cullen sighed. 'So it's true then?'

'Over the last week or so, I've been contesting a bit of a war of attrition with my superiors regarding Brian Bain.'

Cullen was losing patience with the delaying tactics. 'Okay.'

'When we arranged that Acting DI post for Sharon, DCS Soutar ordered me to give the ensuing DS position to Bain, following his return from long-term illness.'

'So I'm right then?'

Turnbull reached over and play punched Cullen's shoulder. 'Believe me, the last thing I want is to have him back here, pissing in the shallow end.' He peered through the glass at Bain. 'I've managed to do a little charm offensive of my own. Acting DS Damian McCrea of the Glasgow South MIT has been demoted to DC again.'

'Eh?' Cullen frowned. 'I thought he was a full DS?'

'No. A lot of officers are very keen to pretend they're something they're not.' Turnbull grinned. 'That's one of the things I like about you, Cullen. You're honest. I mean, I know you have your more colourful moments, of course, but you're straight down the middle. You don't pretend you're something you're not. It'll hold you back getting to a DI position, obviously, but it's something we all admire about you.'

Cullen felt a vein throbbing in his temple. A DI position? 'I'm not sure what you mean?'

'I mean we like officers who appreciate their position in the hierarchy. Over the last couple of years, you've certainly demonstrated that. Colin informs me you've stopped drinking?'

'That's correct, yes.'

'Why's that?'

'I want to focus on my career, sir.'

'I see.' Turnbull's smile quickly turned to a frown. 'DI Bain's through here because Superintendent Graham is skiing in France. I've been asked to break the news to Brian of his demotion to DS. I'm keeping him waiting on purpose.'

'Should you be telling me this?'

'I can trust you.'

'He told Jimmy Deeley he's going to be working here again.'

'That remains to be seen.' Turnbull made a steeple with his fingers. 'Scott, we're making you a DS.'

Cullen swallowed, his pulse hammering. 'Acting?'

'No. Full Detective Sergeant.'

'Seriously?'

'Aye. You've got Colin to thank.'

'Excuse me?'

'It was DI Methven who pushed for your promotion.' Turnbull held out his hand, his thumb kinked over like he was going for a Mason's grip. 'Congratulations, Detective Sergeant Scott Cullen.'

SCOTT CULLEN WILL RETURN IN

"COWBOYS AND INDIANS"

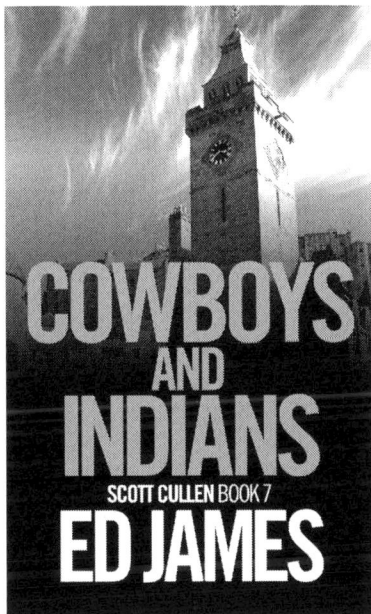

Out now!

If you enjoyed this book, please consider leaving a review on Amazon.

The seventh book in the series, COWBOYS AND INDIANS, is out now — keep reading to the end of this book for a sneak preview. You can buy a copy at Amazon.

If you would like to be kept up to date with new releases from Ed James, please fill out a contact form.

AFTERWORD

There. That's it done.

First, sincere thanks to the hundreds who pre-ordered this book - this has been my day job since January so being in profit before it's out is a seriously good thing. I hope it doesn't disappoint. I'm nothing without you guys.

Thanks this time go to Kitty for the cover, the alpha reading and the harsh criticism, and to Rhona for alpha reading, structural editing, copy editing and proofing.

Been a bit of a tricky bugger this book - it started out as a wee stopgap short story, then I remembered about another idea I had kicking around somewhere, something I'd seeded in GHOST and DEVIL but then got waylaid with other stuff. Then it grew into a novella length thing, with the second part split between Cullen and Sharon's point of view. That didn't work (I'll send out one of the Sharon scenes in the next newsletter; email me if you're at all interested in it). Then it went through a structural edit and the second story was a bit undercooked. Then the first one paled in comparison. Those fixed, the connections between the two stories grew and I knew where I wanted all the pieces on the board for the next book, COWBOYS & INDIANS.

So. It's not been easy to write but I'm pleased with it and where it's got Cullen to. It's let me do some stuff with my writing style I've never done before and it's let me do some stupid stuff too (apologies if you were offended by the sink incident...).

2014 has been a mental year for me, Cullen-wise. While I've only written two new novels, I've severely edited the first four (DYED took a monster kicking, losing 28,000 words it didn't need) and Cullen has been infecting my brain a bit too much. Got to love the guy.

2015 will most likely have two more Cullen novels; I'll get round to starting COWBOYS & INDIANS in a couple of months. Might even do a wee short story or two, you never know.

But there will be lots of other stuff. My newsletter (link below) is the best place to keep on top of this stuff.

One final note, if you could find time to leave a review where you bought this, I'd really appreciate it - a critical mass of reviews is a huge benefit to indie authors like myself.

-- Ed James
East Lothian, October 2014

ABOUT THE AUTHOR

Ed James is the author of the bestselling DI Simon Fenchurch novels, Seattle-based FBI thrillers starring Max Carter, and the self-published Detective Scott Cullen series and its Craig Hunter spin-off books.

During his time in IT project management, Ed spent every moment he could writing and has now traded in his weekly commute to London in order to write full-time. He lives in the Scottish Borders with far too many rescued animals.

If you would like to be kept up to date with new releases from Ed James, please contact a contact form.

Connect with Ed online:

Amazon Author page

Website

OTHER BOOKS BY ED JAMES

SCOTT CULLEN MYSTERIES SERIES

1. GHOST IN THE MACHINE
2. DEVIL IN THE DETAIL
3. FIRE IN THE BLOOD
4. STAB IN THE DARK
5. COPS & ROBBERS
6. LIARS & THIEVES
7. COWBOYS & INDIANS
8. HEROES & VILLAINS

CULLEN & BAIN NOVELLAS

1. CITY OF THE DEAD (Coming March 2020)

CRAIG HUNTER SERIES

1. MISSING
2. HUNTED
3. THE BLACK ISLE

DS VICKY DODDS

1. TOOTH & CLAW

DI SIMON FENCHURCH SERIES

1. THE HOPE THAT KILLS
2. WORTH KILLING FOR
3. WHAT DOESN'T KILL YOU
4. IN FOR THE KILL
5. KILL WITH KINDNESS
6. KILL THE MESSENGER

MAX CARTER SERIES

1. TELL ME LIES

SUPERNATURE SERIES

1. BAD BLOOD
2. COLD BLOOD

COWBOYS AND INDIANS

EXCERPT

PROLOGUE

Detective Sergeant Scott Cullen barged through the crowd at the bar, clutching a metal tray. Six tumblers rattled as he carried them, each containing sparkling amber and a shot glass filled with black liquid. A bleary-eyed man in a tight shirt nudged into him, spilling some. Cullen glared at him and walked on, dumping the drinks on the high table. 'Here we go. Jägerbombs all round.'

Acting DI Sharon McNeill grabbed one and kissed Cullen on the lips, her familiar taste mixing with Red Bull. She tugged her purple top, showing off her bare arms, almost stick thin. Her ponytail smoothed out the worry lines on her forehead. Could get away without wearing a bra these days. She raised the glass, her gaze wandering around the busy club. 'Cheers.'

Four other hands snatched a drink.

Cullen raised the last one in the air. 'One, two, three!' He necked it, the shot glass chinking off his teeth, the contents blending with the Red Bull, and slammed it on the table. 'First!' He wiped the dribble on his chin.

Sharon finished hers next and winked at him. She leaned over to peck him on the cheek. 'Cheers, Scott.'

Cullen leaned in close. 'You think he's here?'

'Not sure yet.' She peered around the bar again, nudging her empty tumbler across the table. 'That's a great idea, by the way.'

'What, Coke instead of Jägermeister?'

'Thank Budgie for me.' She nodded back to the bar, the queue three deep, an array of tenners in the air. 'Hope our guy's not working with the bar staff.'

'You've interviewed them, what's your take?'

'I think they're as worried as we are.' She raised her eyebrows at a man near them, grinding away at the edge of the dance floor. 'What about him?'

Tall and lithe, maybe late twenties. Fists pumping the air in time with the beat. Skinny jeans, patterned shirt open to the waist, a thin line of hair tracing down his flat stomach. His sculpted beard would take more effort every morning than Cullen spent in a month.

Cullen rubbed his chin and sniffed. 'More likely he's a potential victim. He's out of his tree.'

'Drink or drugs?'

'Maybe both.'

The man spun around, moving away from them, stomping his feet in time to the song's heavy thud. He stopped by a pair of men — rich students, judging by their jeans and jumpers. Both tall and athletic-looking. He worked one of them away from the other, like a lion separating a gazelle from the herd. Got in the guy's face, shouting the song's lyrics at him. He grabbed his hand and led him across the dance floor. Stopped at the bar and raised a finger at the barman.

'Nice queue jumping.' Sharon leaned in to Cullen, her perfume cloying. 'This is looking possible. Do you think he's being helped?'

'Let's see.' Cullen watched their target take two shot glasses and lead his prey towards a booth, his hand passing across the top of a glass. What the hell was that? 'Shite, he's put something in one of them.'

Sharon spun round to her team — two men and two women. 'Think we've got a suspect. You know the drill.' She marched across the crowded club.

Cullen followed her. The first pair of officers headed to the front door, the other towards the toilets.

The men reclined next to each other on a red banquette, the fake leather frayed in a few places. The older one slapped a hand on his prey's thigh and raised his glass, glowing in the UV light.

'DI Sharon McNeill.' She held up her warrant card. 'Police Scotland Sexual Assault Unit. I'm detaining you under—'

Liquid splashed across her face.

Cullen reached into the back of his jeans and snapped out his baton.

The older man leapt towards him. His skull thudded into Cullen's forehead. He tumbled backwards, slipping on the floor and collapsing on the sticky tiles.

He made it up onto all fours, blood spurting down his face, covering his mouth.

Black trainers darted away from him through the crowd.

The younger man cowered in the booth. 'What happened?'

'You had a narrow escape.' Cullen got to his feet and pointed at the glass, rubbing his bleeding nose. 'Don't drink that.' He jogged through the gap in the crowd as it parted further, nostrils stinging.

DC McKeown hunched over by the bar, hands over his groin, eyes screwed up.

Cullen shook his shoulder. 'Did he get you?'

'What do you think?'

'Where did he go?'

'Out the front. Rhona's gone after him.'

Cullen shot off towards the front door, passing the cloakroom. The other two officers overtook him and barged past the gorillas on the door. He climbed up the steps into the warm night air and stopped on the pavement, getting out his Airwave. 'Control, this is DS Cullen. Requesting immediate support outside the Liquid Lounge on George Street.'

'*Receiving. DS Lorimer and DC Lindsay are in pursuit of a suspect down Frederick Street, heading towards the New Town.*'

'On my way.' Cullen wove between crowds of staggering drinkers and confused tourists and slid round the corner. He wiped his bloody nose.

The two who'd outflanked him in the club were chasing a man down the hill, footsteps and shouts echoing off the grand buildings.

Cullen squinted at their target. Definitely him. 'Control, suspect's now on Queen Street.'

'Received. Alpha fifteen are attending an incident on Great King Street. Want me to redirect them to support you?'

'Affirmative.'

'Acknowledged.'

Cullen sprinted across Queen Street, his outstretched warrant card stopping the long queue of evening traffic. He powered on down the hill, passing the darkness of Queen Street Gardens on his right. No sign of his quarry or the other officers. 'Control, need an update.'

'Suspect has entered Jamaica Street.'

Shite. Cullen bolted past Howe Street's Georgian town houses and swung a left into a side road. Boxy sixties concrete lit up in sodium yellow. Footsteps clattered from the right. He curved round the bend to a row of stone mews houses.

One of Sharon's male officers lay on the ground, blood bubbling from his mouth. 'Fucker got me.'

'Support's on its way.' Cullen raised his baton and jogged on.

His target punched out, cracking a fist into Rhona's face. She tumbled backwards, her head crunching against the pavement.

Cullen wheeled round to him, baton poised just as a uniformed officer stormed round the corner. He swung out, thwacking the backs of the suspect's knees.

The man fell forward, hands slapping against the cobbles. 'You bastard!'

Cullen stuck a knee in his back and applied his cuffs. 'What's your name?'

The man from the club twisted his head round, as if he was sucking it into his neck. 'No comment.'

Cullen nodded at the uniform. 'Thanks for the help, Si.'

'Let me help in future, mate.' PC Simon Buxton unclipped his stab-proof vest and let it hang open. 'This weighs a ton.' He ran a hand through his full beard, then across his shaved head, the dark stubble ending in a line with the tops of his ears. His forehead creased. 'You know you're bleeding, right?'

Cullen put a hand to his nose. Wet. Warm. 'Christ.'

'This your guy?'

'I think so.' Cullen hauled the suspect to his feet, grip tight on the cuffs. 'Let's read him his rights down the station.'

⁓

THE SEVENTH SCOTT CULLEN BOOK, COWBOYS AND INDIANS, is out now. You can get a copy at Amazon.

If you would like to be kept up to date with new releases from Ed James, please fill out a contact form.

Printed in Great Britain
by Amazon